Tagged:

A War Child Remembers

by

Anne Harper

AUTHOR'S NOTE

Finland fought three wars between 1939 and 1945; the Winter War, the Continuation War and the Lapland War. During these years Finland was the only European country bordering the Soviet Union that was never occupied or annexed and the only country to fight against both the Allies and the Axis under the same military leadership. It was the only country siding with Nazi Germany, in which Jews were never in danger of persecution. It was also the only co-belligerent of Germany to maintain its democracy and independence, and the only country fighting Communist Russia in which Communism never gained a foothold after the wars.

Over 70,000 Finnish children were evacuated out of the country. Approximately 15,000 of them never returned.

Most of the rest of this story is fictional.

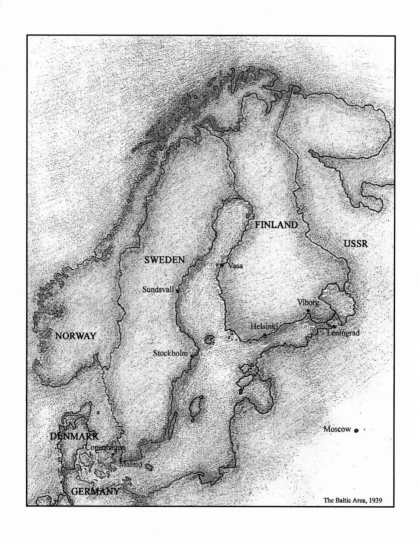

NORWAY

SWEDEN

FINLAND

USSR

DENMARK

GERMANY

Vasa

Sundsvall

Stockholm

Helsinki

Viborg

Leningrad

Copenhagen

Malmö

Moscow

The Baltic Area, 1939

Tagged: A War Child Remembers

BOOK 1

FINLAND

Summer 1939.

Strawberries. Enormous, juicy, red strawberries. That's my last happy childhood memory from Karelia. My last moment of true innocence.

The day is warm and sunny. It's summer and I turn seven today. I don't remember the strawberries being this big on any other birthday. My little sister and I are sitting in the strawberry patch behind our house, with red juice running down our chins. Little Sister is almost three years old, she's very shy, and follows me everywhere. We were supposed to pick strawberries for my cake, but got distracted and started eating the berries instead. Little Sister's new white dress is covered with strawberry juice. Mother gave me strict instructions to keep her clean, and I think I may have failed. We're having too much fun to care. The berries are delicious. Just listening to Little Sister's giggle when she bites into another berry will be worth the scolding for ruining her dress. Not that Mother will scold either of us. She believes in reasoning and guilt. Not corporal punishment. I know the look she's going to give me and the slow shake of her head, and then she'll have Nanny wash us up and change our clothes. So, I'm not worried, as I suck on another strawberry.

We live in Karelia, Southeastern Finland. Father moved here from Vasa when he joined the Army base at Huuhanmäki. He met Mother and they got married. Then my brother Johan was born, then me the next year, then my brother Carl, and finally, Little Sister. And soon Mother will have another baby, we're told. Little Sister does have a real name, but for some reason she's always referred to as 'Little Sister'. Just like that. Like it's one word. 'Littlesister'. Nobody knows why. Father calls her his little angel, as her hair is so blonde it's almost white, and so curly that it hurts her to have it brushed. Her eyes are pale blue; so pale that they almost look transparent, whereas mine and my brothers' are intense blue, like Father's. Muori, our grandmother, said that by the time she was born, our parents had run out of pigment. I'm curious to see what color eyes the new baby will have. Calling Little Sister 'angel' or 'princess' and dressing her in frilly girly things with lace and bows is our parents' way to make her think she's a girl. She's really a tomboy, as could be expected of someone who grew up with three older brothers and a dog. She can whistle almost as well as me, climb any tree almost as fast as Carl and she's the best of the four of us at skipping stones. Johan claims that that's just because she closest to the water. By that I think he means that she's short.

As we're sitting among the strawberries, Little Sister is wearing a big white bow on the side of her head, holding her curls in place. She looks like a little cherub. In fact, our Uncle Johannes, who's an artist, sketched her as a model for one of his church paintings. We're going to see that painting later today. Going to church is an interesting experience. Little Sister sleeps; I study the art, Johan is devout, and Mother is trying to pin Carl to the pew.

We live next to our grandparents, Ukki and Muori, and they gave Father and Mother a piece of land as a wedding gift. Although Ukki and Muori are our next-door-neighbors, it's a very long hike to their house. Father built our house himself. It's big. It's got two stories and two wings. We each have our own rooms. There's a large kitchen, a dining room, a drawing room, and a formal entertaining room into which children aren't allowed, unless specifically invited. We're there all the time. When Father was still home we used to gather in there and he would play the violin for us. He's really good at it. Never took one lesson, or so he claims. Nanny lives in a small room at the end of our corridor; the kitchen staff shares a room off the kitchen. And Renki lives in the loft above the stables. Just recently I found out that Renki isn't his name at all, it's his title. He's the foreman of our field hands. It did seem odd that there'd be a man called Renki on every farm, but I just thought it was a popular name.

Mother's roses have never looked as good as they do this summer. The flowers are nearly as big as my head, and the colors are rich and clear and intense. Everyone in our village envies Mother's roses, and this year I finally understand why.

Father was hoping to become a farmer, but the call came from the Army that the troops need training, so Father will stay with the Army. For a while, anyway. We haven't seen him in a long time. Johan has already been told that he's to inherit our farm, so he's learning the trade. I don't think he cares much about farming, but he understands his calling and as the loyal first-born son, he's stepped up to his role. Carl, on the other hand, who's only six and already almost as tall as me, loves helping out on the farm. He sits in Renki's lap, driving the tractor, and he tries to pitch hay and milk the cows. If Johan is the pensive, analytical one, Little Sister is the quiet, shy one, and I'm the artistic one, then Carl is the wild rambunctious one. He's always in motion. Which makes him always hungry.

Yes, I'm artistic. It sounds like bragging, but it isn't really. It's a statement of fact. I have a talent, and I love to use it. Watching my peers draw stick figures while I draw portraits or caricatures of them drawing stick figures, I know this is something I'm good at. Maybe I can't tie my shoelaces properly, or write a thank-you note without help, or milk a cow, but I can draw.

My favorite adult in the world is my Uncle Johannes, Mother's younger brother. He's everyone's favorite person. Mother loves him so much that she named her first son after him. He attends the Art Academy in Viborg and will one day become a famous artist. He's very talented, and has taught me lots already. For my birthday I hope I can get some of his old paints. One day I hope to be a famous artist just like him.

I have a dog, Tor. He's a shepherd mix, possibly border collie. Father says he's got some terrier in him as well, because he likes to chase rodents. Well, not chase so much, as just run with them. He's never actually caught one yet, and I don't think he'd know what to do with one if he did. He just showed up from the forest one day when I was three and he was a puppy, and made himself at home. Both Mother and Father were against us having a dog at first, but then one day, when Father saw him instinctively taking to herding, he decided to keep him. Tor works twice a day during the summer. After the morning milking, he herds the cows out of the barn and into the pasture. And then he herds them from the pasture into the barn for the evening milking. The cows have done this daily for years and you could probably set your watch by them, but Tor has found his calling and it'd be cruel to deny him this pleasure. The cows quietly tolerate him. The spring calves, on the other hand, do pose an actual challenge.

We named the dog Tor, because he's always pounding like thunder. Even as a puppy. He's very big, boisterous and full of energy, and doesn't understand what walking is. Uncle Johannes says he's 'fifty kilos of uncontrollable muscle'.

As I'm sitting in the strawberry patch on my seventh birthday I see Tor running up the hill toward our house. He's wet, and I know he's been swimming. There's a little pond in the forest behind our house, where we like to go swimming on warm summer days. On clear days we can see all the way to Lake Ladoga, but it's too cold and too far away for a quick swim. Tor pounds up to us and licks our faces. Little Sister is giggling uncontrollably as he knocks her over and shakes himself dry all over both of us. Then he makes himself comfortable next to me. He circles around a few times and I think he's about to plop down, when suddenly he starts growling and turns toward Lake Ladoga in the distance. Out of nowhere, I hear the roar of airplane engines. I can't see anything, but recognize the sound. Father told us that they've gotten new fighter planes at the base. As we live so close to the base, we can sometimes hear them in the distance. This time the noise is different, somehow. It sounds much, much stronger and is becoming increasingly louder. The noise is coming toward us.

Little Sister starts clapping her hands. "Me!" she laughs and stretches her hands in the air.

'Me' is her favorite word. It means everything. This time I think it means that she wants to go flying.

The planes suddenly become visible over the tree line. Tor is barking now and charges at them. They are terrifyingly low. Instinctively I grab Little Sister's hand and start running. I look over my shoulder and see three planes in formation. They're low, and continue to descend. Little Sister can't run as fast as I need her to, so I pick her up. I'm trying to make it into the forest, in an angle away from their flight line. The noise is so loud now; the ground seems to be shaking. I know they're right on top of us, so I throw myself onto the ground, covering Little Sister with my body, just as the planes pass us, lifting up dirt from the ground around us. Tor is barking in the distance and keeps following the planes.

I'm confused and scared. As quickly as they appeared, they're flying away from us, making a turn to the east. They don't look like the planes as Father described them. They look brand-new and I don't recognize the emblem on the tail. They appear and disappear so quickly that I can't make an accurate mental image of them.

"Paul!" I hear Carl's voice calling my name. He's running toward us from the barn. "Those weren't ours! Wanna go after them?"

Tor comes running back to us, and Carl and I get on our bicycles and start pedaling after the planes. We can't get far, because Mother gets in our way. I'm even more scared now. The look on her face doesn't bode well. Her eyes are scared, and she's breathing heavily. She ushers us into the house, and we gather in the drawing room and turn on the radio.

Suddenly I'm not worried about a scolding anymore. Suddenly our soiled clothes are unimportant. Suddenly my seventh birthday has taken an unplanned turn.

> Not trusting Stalin to honor the 1932 Non-Aggression Pact, Finland erected a number of forts during the summer of 1939 all along its main line of defense, the Finnish-Soviet border on the Karelian Isthmus, later to be known as the Mannerheim Line, designed by Carl Gustaf Emil Mannerheim. It was designed to be an extensive web of fortifications across the Isthmus. Unfortunately the line was never fully completed.
> The threat of a Soviet invasion was imminent, and one not easily ignored. The border regions

```
felt the enemy's show of strength as early as the
summer of 1939, although no shots were fired, no
bombs were dropped and no war was declared.
Finland was determined to defend itself, and
the full field Army of some hundred thousand men
was mobilized and sent eastwards into position
along the Soviet border during the late summer
and early fall of 1939.
The Finnish Army troops were probably the best
trained in winter warfare in Europe and were
excellent marksmen.
```

Harvest break 1939.

It's harvest time, so school's out for a week. I hate school. Last year was bad enough, because our teacher was giving me a hard time about my reading. She says I pronounce things in Swedish, not Karelian. When I told Father about this, he just laughed, and told me to be proud of my heritage. We're Swedish Finns. He also said that Teacher was probably just jealous, because I speak two languages fluently, and she's stuck with the old Karelian twang. This year, Teacher has decided to introduce us to what she calls 'history' and 'world events'. Mainly this consists of criticizing Russia. This is odd, as she has a very Russian name, but acts more Karelian than us real Karelians. To make school nearly intolerable, Teacher has us stand up and recite multiplication tables. This irks me to no avail. What could I possibly gain from this?

Father is still not home, so I unload my frustration on Uncle Johannes, who's back from the academy to help with the harvesting. Usually we wouldn't need his help, but this year many of our regular hired help have joined Father in the Army.

We're sitting at the dining room table, just finishing breakfast.

"Multiplication tables are stupid and useless and a waste of time and I'll never, ever, ever need to use them in real life," I whine to him.

Uncle Johannes looks at me quietly for a moment. Then he reaches for a sugar roll, and tosses it at my brother.

"Carl, you're doing Paul's chores today," he says, grabs his sketch pad and a wad of pencils and cocks his head toward the door. Carl has already disappeared toward the fields, always easily convinced by food and always ready to help with the farm. "Come with me, Paul."

It's early fall, and the air outside is crisp, but sunny. Uncle Johannes beckons me to take a seat next to him on the lawn. We're facing the house.

"Draw your house," he says. "No details, just basic outlines."

I start drawing. We've had art lessons like this on numerous occasions in the past, but this time he just lets me draw, without interrupting or correcting me. Is this a test, or am I just doing really well? His silence worries me a little. When I'm done, I sign my name in the corner, and hand over the drawing. Uncle Johannes takes my pencil from me, and uses it to point.

"See here, Paul? Now look at the house itself. Do you think this beam is strong enough the way you drew it, to carry the weight of the roof? And here," he points at a window. "If this plank is at an angle, instead of a straight line, the entire wall under the windows would cave in."

Looking at my drawing, which I had been pleased with enough to sign, I'm confused. I look at the house, and my drawing looks nothing like it. I take the drawing back, tear it up and start again afresh. I wonder if this art lesson has anything to do with my frustration over multiplication tables or just a way to get my mind off them. Mother often jokingly claims that Uncle Johannes lives inside his own head, and I think this might be proof of it. I wonder if he's slightly mad, and if that's why I like him so much.

We sit quietly on the lawn for a while, and I'm really concentrating on getting it right this time.

"How many windows in your house, Paul?" Uncle Johannes says unexpectedly.

The question takes me by surprise.

"On this side of the house?" I count them. "Eight upstairs, eight downstairs and four on each wing."

Uncle Johannes has been lying on his side, but now sits up, and grabs the pad again. "So, let's pretend that the wings are a floor by themselves, how many floors would that make?"

"Three," I wonder where he's going with this.

"If you have three floors and eight windows on each floor, how many windows do you have?"

"That's easy - twenty-four on this side of the house!"

"And if you need new windowpanes for four of the windows, how many will you have to order?"

"Three panes per window and four windows make twelve."

"And if this beam you drew can support one tonne, but your roof weighs three tonnes, how many of these beams will you need?"

"Three."

"And the way you drew the wall, if you have ten planks on that wall and it caves in under each window on that floor, how many planks need to be replaced?"

"Ten planks per window, eight windows ... Eighty planks!"

"And how many bushels of apples did you pick yesterday?"

I'm trying to think. I actually didn't count them. "Probably five, maybe six."

"Let's say five, with a hundred apples in each bushel. How many apples total?"

"Five hundred." That's a lot of apples! Good for me! No wonder I was so tired this morning.

"And if we sold them, you'd get five markkas per bushel. How many markkas does that make?"

"Five bushels at five markkas each makes twenty-five markkas."

"And that's how you use multiplication in real life," he says and hands me my drawing back.

It all starts making sense to me now. It's so simple! "But why doesn't Teacher explain it this way?"

"Who's your teacher?"

"Veera Borikoff."

"That old crow is still alive? I thought she was old when *I* had her," Uncle Johannes laughs. "Look, don't let her get to you. You're a smart kid; you just need to learn from life, not school. Now, see that bird?" There is a male wagtail in the birdbath. Uncle Johannes covers my eyes with his hand. "Still see it?" he asks.

"Of course not, your hand's on my face!"

"I mean, can you *picture* it inside your head?"

Oddly, I still have an image of the bird sitting on the birdbath, although I only saw it there for a second.

"Draw it, without looking at it," Uncle Johannes says, removing his hand from my face. "Everything in life is math," he continues, as he guides my hand. "Although that bird weighs probably only a few grams, it needs bigger claws than that, or else..."

"Or else it'll fall on its beak into the water," I fill in. I get it now. "And both wings need to be exactly the same length or else it would only be able to fly in circles!" The bird flies to a nearby rose bush, and dries its beak. "And the weight of the bird made that twig bend!"

That's it - I've learned more sitting on the lawn with my uncle this morning, than all semester repeating multiplication tables out loud with the rest of my class.

We spend the rest of the day drawing different angles of the house, until every square centimeter of Uncle Johannes' sketch pad is full. On both sides. I've made a very important, life-altering decision.

"Uncle Johannes, I don't think I need to go back to school. Can I come live with you, and learn from life?"

He laughs again, and pats my back. "And have your mother hunt me down and kill me? Not a tempting offer, boy. No, unfortunately you do have to finish school. But judging by the state of the world right now, I have an odd feeling that you may just learn from life a little sooner than any of us might wish." He gets a strange look in his eyes, and I know I shouldn't pry and ask him what he means.

"What do you mean?" I ask. I can't help myself.

He heaves a deep sigh and looks into the horizon. "Just keep your eyes and ears open," he says, just as the dinner bell rings.

I've never seen him like this. Serious and introverted. We start walking toward the house, and I try to get him to tell me what has him so worried, but he won't. It's almost as if he doesn't even hear me.

> During the fall of 1939 Estonia, Lithuania and Latvia, Finland's neighbors south of the bay, were forced to agree to Soviet military bases within their borders.
> In October the Soviet Union issued the following demands to Finland:
> * Finland will lease the Hangö peninsula for the next thirty years to be used as a Russian Naval base.
> * The Soviet Navy will have the right to use Lappvik near Hangö as a berth.
> * Finland will cede islands in the Bay of Finland, among them the fortressed Björkö.
> * The Finnish-Soviet border on the Karelian Isthmus will be moved farther west.
> * The Mannerheim Line will be demolished.
> * Finland will cede the Åland Islands in the Baltic.
> * Finland will cede part of the Salla area, as well as the Kalastajansaarento peninsula in the Barents Sea.
> Mainly out of loyalty to her Scandinavian neighbors, Finland refused these demands, and prepared to face the consequences.

Winter 1939.

We're sitting at the dining room table, when Tor starts growling. Mother, passing the potatoes, suddenly freezes, and looks out the window.

"Now, who would be foolish enough to be skiing on a night like this?" she says, and we all follow her glance.

I can barely make out a figure crossing the field in the moonlight. It's freezing outside. My nose, fingers and toes have barely thawed from having collected firewood earlier this evening. The figure keeps approaching. Mother goes to the front door. Johan and Carl are quick to follow.

"Me!" Little Sister cries and stretches her arms toward me.

I pick her up and follow the others. Uncle Johannes is standing in the foyer, red-faced and panting. It strikes me how much older he looks than he did when I last saw him. This morning. Maybe it's because he has icicles on his eye-brows.

He puts both hands on Mother's shoulders. "They're coming," he says.

All color vanishes from Mother's face and she nearly collapses.

"Who's coming?" I whisper.

Mother swallows hard and ushers us to bed. Carl is protesting that he's still hungry. But then again, he always is. Although we each have our own rooms, on cold nights we all sleep in Johan's room. It has a big ceramic wood-burning oven. It also sits directly above the kitchen, and we boys press our ears to the floorboards hoping to find out who's coming. We can hear the radio being turned on. Father must have built this house too well, because I can't hear anything of interest. I tip-toe to the door, and open it. I can only hear murmurs and the monotone voice of Tanner, the foreign minister, whom I've become accustomed to hearing lately. Maybe because he's always on. I can extract words like Stalin, Red Army, evacuation, assault. I know Stalin is not to be trusted, but I can't recall why.

Johan and Carl quickly grow bored and go to bed. Little Sister has already fallen asleep. I can hear the familiar voices of some of our servants. They all sound anxious and alarmed. I can hear Tor pounding up the stairs, but have no time to react, before he wedges his body in the gap of the door, and slams it into my forehead. He licks my face, and nuzzles next to me on the floor, ready to go to sleep. Obviously Tanner on the radio doesn't bother him one bit. I feel sleepy, and sensing Tor's rhythmic breathing doesn't help.

I wake up to Tor's whining. I know something must be terribly wrong because the only other time he whines is when Little Sister pulls his tail. Mother's voice reaches me. She's rocking me gently.

"Paul? I need you to be a big boy now," she says, and suddenly I'm frightened. Mother walks over to the bed Johan and Carl are sharing, and wakes them up, too. "Boys, I need you to wake up and get dressed in every piece of clothing you can. Paul, dress Little Sister. Johan will help Carl."

"I can do it myself," Carl announces sleepily.

Mother gives a weak attempt of a smile; everyone knows he can't button his shirt, or put his boots on their right feet. Actually, he can, but he's always in too much of a hurry to do it right.

She tousles his hair. "I know you can, son, but tonight we must be very quick and very quiet. Johan, Paul? I need you to gather up the blankets from the beds, and make them into bundles and pack the clothes you can't wear into them. You can take one small toy each. Just one," she says and gets up to leave.

Horses are neighing in the courtyard and muffled voices sound downstairs. One of the voices is Father's.

"Father is home?" I excitedly ask Mother.

She sighs deeply, and her eyes are red-rimmed. Obviously she's fighting back tears. I just want to rush to her and squeeze her tight, but she says she needs me to be a big boy, and I don't think big boys do that. I'm trying to read her face but can't. Her face is closed. Inanimate. Impassive.

"Father has come to help us pack," she says.

"Where are we going?" I ask, but I really don't want to know. My entire world is here. It's dark and cold outside, and I just want to curl back to sleep. The hell with Tanner.

Tor is getting more anxious. He nuzzles his head under Mother's hand, hoping to be petted. Absent-mindedly, she strokes his ears. I don't think she knows what she's doing. Suddenly she jerks, and puts a hand on her ballooned belly. The baby must be kicking.

"Please be careful with Little Sister's ear, but be quick," she says and leaves the room.

I do as I'm told. Little Sister is tired and fussy and I sing to her to calm her down. Mother told us to be quiet, and the last thing she needs is for Little Sister to start wailing. She has an ear infection. Her second one this winter and it's not even December yet. I think she's in constant pain and cries a lot in her sleep. Actually, she cries a lot even when she's awake. Dressing her in every piece of clothing she owns, she thinks this is a game. She's giggling as she can't move her arms and legs for all the padding. I can't find her hat, and think it may be downstairs, so I put my fur one on her head. It covers most of her face, but at least she'll be warm. I tie a scarf around the hat to keep it in place.

Glancing over my shoulder I can see Johan packing his bible and Carl's tin soldiers into a bundle. Little Sister is clutching her stuffed toy puppy, as always. I reach for my piggy bank, and crash it on the floor. My siblings jerk at the noise.

"Ssshhh! Mother told us to be quiet!" Johan hisses.

I collect my money and stuff it into my pocket. I don't know where we're going, or why, but surely money can't hurt.

Johan collects the other three piggy banks, stuffs them into a pillowcase and smashes it against the oven. No noise. He starts collecting all the money.

"Hey! That's not all yours!" Carl complains.

Johan ignores him, collects the money and stuffs it into my coat pocket.

"Some of it is yours, some of it is mine and some of it is Little Sister's," he explains.

"How come Paul gets it all, then?"

"Because I trust him to keep it safe for us."

Once we're done dressing and packing all our clothes, we make an attempt to descend the stairs. It's nearly impossible with the layers and layers of clothing. Adding to that, Tor keeps herding us. Always the analytical mind, Johan tosses the bundles down the stairs and the dog sets off after them. Little Sister keeps giggling. I'm hot under my several layers of clothing, and I try to pick her up to carry her down the stairs. Without a word, Father meets us halfway down, picks up Little Sister and Carl and carries them down. He is so official looking in his white Army uniform, but his face is carved of stone.

Something suddenly hits me. We're leaving this house. This can't be good. I run to the drawing room and see that Father's violin is still hanging on the wall. Quickly I grab it, and the bow, and in the semi-darkness I start looking for the case. I don't know where it might be, as the violin is always hanging on the wall. If we're all allowed to bring just one toy, I'd rather bring Father's violin than any toy in the world. Tor pounds over to help me. I don't think he knows what he's looking for, but his nose follows my hands everywhere. Finally I locate it in the compartment under the grandfather clock. I quickly pack the violin in its case and rush to the excitement outside. As I open the front door, the cold night air hits me like a tonne of bricks. The night air is so cold that my nose and eyes start running. The tears freeze on my cheeks.

In the courtyard are two sleighs, fully harnessed and getting loaded with our belongings. I see Mother crying with Ukki and Muori. As I move closer I can hear him say "I have faith in my Maker. No bombs will ever fall on me."

Bombs? My heart is racing so fast, I have to put a hand on my chest to keep it in inside. There has been talk of war. I've heard the adults talk about it, and I've heard it on the radio. But it's taking place far, far away, and with Father's base just next door, surely…

A pair of strong arms whisks me up on the second sleigh. Little Sister is already settled between Johan and Carl, on top of bundles of clothing. I can see the first sleigh full of barrels of food and odd bundles. Driving it is Renki, and driving the other sleigh is Uncle Johannes. Mother climbs in next to him. She's carrying her fur cape under her arm. It looks oddly boxy, and I assume she's hiding something inside it. Possibly her jewelry box.

I turn around and face Father. I'm scared. It is very, very cold, and I don't understand what's going on. Why doesn't Father climb in the sleigh with us?

"Goodbye, children," he says. "Be brave, take care of Mother and look out for each other." He turns around quickly and walks toward the house.

I try to coax Tor to jump into the sleigh with me.

"He stays here," Mother says sternly, but gently.

I can't hold back the tears anymore. "Noooo!" I wail, and the vise around my chest tightens.

"He won't fit, and we can't feed him."

"He can have my food, and we need him to keep Little Sister warm! Please, Mother!"

I'm interrupted by the barn doors slamming open. There's a rifle shot from inside the barn, and all our cows start running out. Tor sets off after them.

"Tor, come back!" I yell, but my throat is dry and it's too cold to talk.

The sleighs take off. Tor herds the cows into single-file behind us.

"How come we can take the cows, but not Tor?" I ask Mother.

"We're not taking the cows," she says. "We just don't want the Reds to have them, either," she adds under her breath.

I'm searching my brain to see if I know who the reds are, but I don't think I do. My mind is more focused on getting my dog back. I try to whistle for him, but my lips are dry and cracked.

Our roads are icy, and the horses are running now. I look back to see if Father is trying to catch up with us. All I can see in the moonlight is the outline of Tor making a frantic leap into the forest. My chest is heavy and tight. I clutch Father's violin. A string snaps. Then another. It's as if the violin wants to tell me something. Part of me knows the strings snapped because it's so cold. But another part of me is now crying because I've broken the last thing I'll have to remember Father by.

"Don't look back," I hear Uncle Johannes say to Mother.

I can't keep my eyes from the last place I saw Tor. The air is cracking like a bonfire and I smell a vague scent of smoke. As the sleigh plows down our road, I see the flames. Our house is on fire.

Breathing is cumbersome, because it's so cold. And I'm crying. I look at my siblings in the sleigh, and see the reflection of the fire on their faces. They all look terrified, although I think Little Sister is too young to fully comprehend what's going on. Even I don't. I know I should do something to make them - us - not look, but I cannot help staring at the blaze. Johan starts reciting the Lord's Prayer quietly to himself. I feel like jumping out of the sleigh, running back to the house to make sure Father and Tor are alright. I know there are wolves in the forest, and I fear Tor won't understand how to keep clear of them. I think this is the reason we're going so fast, that the wolves won't catch us. But then again, with all these cows roaming freely about, why would the wolves want to eat us? Because a child is easier prey than a cow? I'm even more scared now.

I haven't realized until now that I'm bareheaded and my ears are freezing. I wrap my scarf around my head. Little Sister and Carl are falling asleep in the rhythmic motion of the sleigh. Johan is still reciting the Lord's Prayer. I know I should stop crying, but I can't. I can't see our house anymore, but know it's still ablaze, for the sky in the horizon is glowing yellow and mauve, and in the moonlight I can see a heavy plume of smoke.

I'm tired. I rest my head on the jolting back railing of the sleigh. Maybe this is a nightmare, and I'll wake up warm and safe in my own bed.

"Tor," Little Sister's voice wakes me up. She's pointing at the trail we've left behind us.

I jerk my head up so fast, that the skin on my cheek is torn off. My tears must've frozen to the sleigh. A dark shadow follows us. It's Tor trying to catch up. I turn to look at Mother. Her back is turned to us, and she is resting her head on Uncle Johannes' shoulder. I hope she's sleeping. I stand up, trying to find firm support under my feet, but can't. Tor is gaining on us. He's covered in icicles, and I can see his breath in the moonlight. His tongue is hanging off one side of his mouth. I urge him on. I know he can make it onto the sleigh, I've seen him do it a million times before. Although never with the sleigh in motion.

"You can do it, boy," I encourage him. "Come on!"

Tor makes a leap, and bounces off the sleigh. He rolls over on the side of the road, gets up and starts running toward us again. The horses are neighing. They must be freezing, too. If possible, it's even colder now than it was when we left our house. I lean my entire upper body over the railing of the sleigh.

"Come on, boy! Up!"

He makes another attempt at the sleigh. This time his front paws meet my hands, and I haul him toward me. His hind legs are frantically seeking support on the back of the sleigh. I lean my entire weight backward, and pull him toward me. He's climbing now, and I fall backward, with him on top of me. Tor is safely in the sleigh with us! He starts licking my face, and his icy tail whips at the inside walls of the sleigh. He's just as happy to see me as I'm to see him. I don't know how far we've traveled, or where we are, but suddenly I feel less worried. I curl up with my arms around my dog on top of the bundles of clothing at the back of the sleigh and fall asleep, his breath keeping my face warm.

> In the coldest winter in nearly a century, on November 30th, 1939, four Soviet armies, totaling nearly half a million troops and two thousand

tanks, began advancing across the eastern border of Finland. Josef Stalin, in an unprovoked,
all-out assault, unleashed his Red Army, and
thus erupted the Winter War.
After the Finnish Civil War, which ended in
1918, Finland had all but neglected its military. The Finnish troops consisted mainly of
light infantry and home guard units, no anti-
tank weaponry, and only a few dozen opera-
tional fighter aircraft.
Earlier the same year the Molotov-Ribbentrop
Pact had been concluded by Stalin and Hitler,
dividing most of still-unoccupied Europe as areas of interest between the two powers, giving
Finland to Stalin. During the fall of 1939, when
Finland refused to meet the Soviet's unreason-
able territorial demands, Stalin mobilized his
armies. Their objective was to reach Helsinki
in less than two weeks and occupy the entire
country by the end of 1939.

We've been traveling for what seems like forever. It's now almost daylight. I'm tired and cold and sore all over. Along the sides of the road I can see carcasses of frozen, dead farm animals. I wonder how far our herd made it. There are also bundles, bags and barrels, thrown or fallen off sleighs. Every now and again we see people walking, or on skis. We aren't the only ones moving. If Mother is awake, she makes Uncle Johannes stop and offer them a ride. So far, everyone has declined. Mother is so strong; I cannot help but admire her. I remember the last time she was this big, Little Sister wasn't far from being born. I just hope the new baby won't come until we get to wherever we're going.

I look over at Little Sister. She's sleeping. In the scarce morning light I can see that part of her face is streaked in a dark criss-cross pattern. It's light enough for me to realize that she's got blood on her face. Her head is resting against Johan's shoulder, who's also still sleeping, and carefully I crawl over to them to see where the blood is coming from. It has frozen on her face. Johan wakes up, startled. Motioning to him to stay quiet, I point to Little Sister's face, and we examine him. He's not the one bleeding. Tor comes over and licks Little Sister's face. She wakes up with a jolt, tastes the blood, which has trickled into her mouth, and starts wailing.

Mother turns around. "What now?" she says, frowning.

Uncle Johannes stops the sleigh and Mother collects Little Sister in her arms. She looks at her face, lifts the scarf, holding my hat in place, and we can see that her ear is bleeding. I gasp. That has to hurt.

"Who has a knife?" Mother says.

Silly question - we all do. I'm afraid to give her mine, for fear of what she'll need it for. Is she going to cut Little Sister's ear off? Uncle Johannes carries his knife in his boot, and hands it to his sister. Mother plunges the knife into one of the bundles, tears into a sheet, and bandages Little Sister's ear with the strip. Her hands move effortlessly, like she's done this all her life. While she's bandaging Little Sister, she calmly talks to her, trying to get her to stop crying. Silently she rearranges her head gear, bundles Little Sister closer to her, and climbs back into her seat.

"Let's go," she tells Uncle Johannes.

We're moving again. Little Sister cries herself to sleep in Mother's arms. My heart goes out to her.

"You're bleeding, too," Johan says, pointing to my cheek.

Very carefully I touch it. It feels lumpy and sore, and if I look down, I can actually see a brownish bump under my eye.

I can see Mother and Uncle Johannes talking, but I can't hear what they're saying. I don't know where we are, but the terrain looks very much like home, and as it's only just past dawn, I don't think we could be far. Thinking about Father, I'm trying to be brave. I'm so cold and scared and hurting all over, but like the string of Father's violin pinging in my mind, I'm brought back to reality. That reality is that we're running away from something. For us to leave so hurriedly and not stop moving, even when Father's little angel is bleeding from her ear, this can't be good. My thoughts automatically return to the wolves.

Johan and I are playing the staring game, when I notice that we're slowing down. Johan is winning, but I think only because he has his back turned to the wind, and my face is into the wind, making it twice as hard for me not to blink. The sun is high, but it is still crucially cold. Tor hangs his head over the sleigh railing and starts sniffing. Little Sister's wailing has subsided to a soft sob. Carl has been telling us that he's hungry since he woke up, but now we're ignoring him.

Mother turns around to face us. "Boys, we're going to use the bathroom here," she says. "We're getting close to a town, and we'll see if we can't find a doctor there."

The sleigh stops and I look around. We're still in what seems like a deserted road in the forest. Actually, not so deserted, because there are sleigh tracks, making it easier for our horses, but even though I scan every direction I cannot see any evidence of civilization. Not so much as an outhouse. Now, we boys can go in the forest, we've done that often enough. But Mother?

"Now's not the time to be prudish," Mother continues, as if reading my mind. She gets off her seat. "Quickly and quietly, please, boys."

As I scamper back from the forest, Mother gives us each a piece of bread. I share mine with Tor, who swallows it whole.

Mother examines my cheek. "Does it hurt?" she asks.

I shake my head. She takes my chin into her hand, smiles, and kisses my forehead, like she's done a million times before. Little angel kisses. Oddly, this familiar gesture makes a knot form in my throat. She takes out her handkerchief, rubs her tongue over it quickly and dabs it over my cheek. I try not to wince, but she senses my discomfort anyway. It *does* hurt. She kisses the bruise.

"That's my big boy," she says.

The knot in my throat is choking me. Right now I don't want to be a big boy. I don't know where we are or why we're moving. I don't know where Father is or why he didn't go with us. And I still don't know who's coming.

"Mother? Where are we going?" I finally ask.

She heaves a deep sigh, and her voice is breaking. "As far west as we possibly can," she says in earnest.

"Why?"

Her eyes are so sad. "No more talking. Let's get moving."

I grab her sleeve, holding her back, if only for a second longer. "I didn't bring a toy, Mother," I say.

She looks like someone has abruptly awakened her from a deep sleep. She looks at me, but I don't think she can see me. Tor is nudging his head under her hand. She cuts each of us another piece of bread.

"So, can I please keep Tor?"

Mother makes another futile attempt at smiling, as she watches me share my bread with my dog. "I think you'd better, son, as it seems that he'd follow you around the world."

"And back!"

Mother tightens the scarf around my neck, and wraps it around my face, leaving only my eyes visible. She cuts another piece of bread for Carl, and then Uncle Johannes helps us back into the sleigh. Absent-mindedly, Mother's hand rubs her belly.

"Is the baby coming?" I ask Uncle Johannes.

"Dear Lord, I hope not!" he exclaims.

"Then why do we need a doctor?"

Rolling his eyes, he shakes his head. "Little Sister's ear," is all he says, before he climbs back into the driver's seat and we're moving again.

Seems like we're not the only ones leaving in a hurry this morning. We pass many scorched houses along the way, but it's obvious even to me that we're the only living beings around. Uncle Johannes slows the horses down to a trot, and he and Mother converse. I can't make out every word they're saying, but judging by the pitch of their voices they are arguing. Sounds like Uncle Johannes wants to avoid the bigger cities, but Mother demands that we see a doctor.

After a few more kilometers of cantering, with the horses' mouths foaming, us bouncing around in the back, fighting off pangs of hunger and thoughts of frozen appendages and motion sickness, Tor starts barking uncontrollably. It takes all my strength to restrain him, to keep him from jumping off the sleigh. Uncle Johannes abruptly stops the sleigh.

"What's the matter now?" Mother says, voice irritated.

Uncle Johannes puts a hand to her mouth. "Listen!" he says.

He lets off a sharp whistle, and signals to Renki to stop his sleigh. We're all as still as we possibly can be. I don't dare breathe. Tor is growling now. He's anxious. I try to make my hands wrap around his muzzle. I can't bend them. My fingers are too stiff from the cold. He looks at me and cocks his head, the way he does when he's confused. I have no explanation to offer him. The sleigh jerks, and Uncle Johannes makes a mad dash to move it off the road and into the forest. The horses are neighing, obviously not liking the prospect of wading through meter-deep snow with a full load. Uncle Johannes gets out of the sleigh, and starts pulling the horses behind him.

We're at the edge of the forest, when I hear them. Fighter planes. Coming toward us fast. I turn my head toward the sound, and I can see them in the distance. They're closer than they sound, and flying in line with the road we're traveling on.

I turn to Carl and Johan. "Run!"

With Tor leading the way, we scramble out of the sleigh and start running for cover in the forest. The snow is up to my armpits, and with several layers of clothing, running is ridiculously impossible. There's a crust on the snow, and I throw myself down on my stomach and glide into the forest. Mother is carrying Little Sister, and clambers into the sanctity of the trees, just as the planes pass us. We're crouching together on the edge of the forest, wide-eyed and panting.

The first bomb drops in the distance. Simultaneously we all jerk and draw for breath. Seconds later, the ground shakes under our feet. Little Sister starts sobbing. The tremors go up the trees surrounding us, and they drop their heavy load of snow, covering us. Still, we dare not move. Johan starts praying, mumbling words incoherently. I can hear my heart thumping in my ears. Tor is whining.

Quickly we lose track of how many bombs fall. We're all nearly paralyzed by fear. We were supposed to be in that town. If we hadn't stopped for a bathroom break, we'd be there now. The pieces of the puzzle finally fall together in my head. Silently I curse that I've been so dense. We're running away from war. Part of me wishes I hadn't found out. I was better off scared and not knowing than scared and knowing.

> Molotov renounced the Soviet-Finland Non-Aggression Treaty signed in 1932. Soviet aircraft bombed 16 Finnish localities during the course of the first day of the Winter War.
> Finland's President Kyösti Kallio relinquished his authority as Commander-in-Chief of the Armed Forces to Marshal Mannerheim and declared the country to be in a state of war. Marshal Mannerheim issued his first Order of the Day: 'We shall fight to protect our homes, our religion and our country.'

It's deadly quiet all around us. We don't talk. We're out of tears. We hardly dare to breathe. The bombing has stopped, but still we dare not move. Even Tor and the horses are still and silent. Everyone's eyes are enormous. Our ears are perked for any sound other than our stomachs grumbling. I'm trying to imagine what could possibly be going through Mother's head right now. If she's scared, she's hiding it well.

We never hear the planes return. Maybe they took another way back, or maybe they went to bomb some other place. I want to ask Uncle Johannes his opinion, but don't want to be the one breaking the silence.

"I think it's safe," Uncle Johannes finally says. "Let's go."

After having spent all night and most of the day racing at high speed, we're now moving surprisingly slowly. We're scouting every direction, especially the sky. If someone had told me this in a story or I had read it in a book or seen it in a movie, I would've found it exciting. But living it - I've never been more terrified in my life. Smoke is rising in the horizon in front of us, and I know that's the town that just got bombed. The town we were supposed to be in.

At the edge of town we get off the sleigh.

"You know where to go?" Renki asks Mother.

She nods. "Tend to the horses and offer help to anyone who needs it, including food and transportation. We'll be back as soon as we can," she says, and starts walking into town with Uncle Johannes. She's still clutching Little Sister in her arms.

"Paul!" Little Sister screams, and reaches for me.

Mother nods me along. I command Tor to stay, and join Mother and Uncle Johannes.

Everything seems to be smoking. There's a huge pit in the middle of the street. The buildings lining the street are windowless, and gape at us like skulls. We make our way through rubble and smoldering pieces of wood. There's a child, younger than Little Sister, screaming in the middle of the street. Not calling out for anyone, just screaming. That's the only sound we hear. Otherwise it's eerily quiet. People are scurrying about. Out of nowhere a woman comes up, and scoops the child in her arms. They start running in the direction from which we came. I want to call out after her. They're running in the wrong direction! That's where the planes came from.

We find the hospital. One part of it was hit, leaving a gaping void. The overhead lights are flickering, and the heating must be out. Doctors and nurses in white coats are running around yelling out orders to each other. If the town was empty and quiet, it's probably because everyone is here. We go to what once may have been a reception area, but is now as busy as a town square on market day.

Silently Mother hands Little Sister to me. We sit down on a pile of rubble. Along the intact wall opposite us is a bench, crowded with people, in various stages of bleeding. There's a chorus of moaning. Little Sister clutches my neck so tightly that she nearly suffocates me.

Mother walks up to a man. He's holding something to his head. Mother removes it. He's bleeding profusely. She starts bandaging him with her scarf and the rags he'd been pressing to his head, while talking to him in the soothing voice she uses when she's cleaning up our scrapes and scratches. She does that to the next person as well. He's bleeding from his arm and leg. Mother finds a piece of wood and makes a splint, when a nurse walks up to her.

"You don't work here," the nurse says.

"I do now," Mother replies, without looking up.

"Are you medically trained?"

"I'm the mother of four; I have two fully functioning hands and enough wit to know that you need help." She's still not looking up. "The sooner we're done with the injuries from the bombing, the sooner someone can have a look at my little girl," Mother continues, while finishing up the splint. "Johannes, make yourself useful. Go find something to fashion into a crutch."

"God bless you, miss," the man with the broken arm and leg says.

The nurse harrumphs and leaves.

"I want to help, too," I offer.

Mother looks at me over her shoulder and smiles wearily. Her hands never stop working.

"Run back to the sleighs," she says. "Collect all our bed sheets and start tearing them into bandages."

I'm on a mission. I run through town so fast I break into a sweat under my many layers of clothing. I can't bend my knees, and my arms flail helplessly at my sides, but I'm moving. This is the warmest I've been since we left. On any other day, seeing a seven year-old Michelin Man racing through town would've been a humorous sight, but now, nobody looks at me twice.

When I reach the sleighs, I can see that Renki must've had the same idea as Mother, because Carl and Johan are already tearing up our bed linens. There are about half a dozen men and an old truck by our sleighs. An unfamiliar odor hits my face. It smells so bad I have to take a step back.

"What's that smell?" I ask Carl.

Carl reaches a hand to my cheek and starts picking at my crusty blood. I swat his hand away. Johan nods his head toward the gathering of men. I turn to look.

"Don't look!" Johan hisses and grabs my sleeve. "It's really disgusting."

Too late. On the back of the truck I see the sooty outlines of a man. His face reminds me of a picture Teacher once showed us of an Egyptian mummy. My stomach turns, and I cover my mouth. Burning flesh. That was the smell I sensed. Renki and the other men are rubbing snow on him.

"Is he dead?" I whisper.

"He will be soon if we don't get him to a hospital," Renki says. "That's about all I can do for him."

The burned man moans. "Hurts…" he says. That's what it sounds like, anyway.

I don't understand war. I mean, I understand that this is war, but wars are meant to be fought between two armies, or Indians and cowboys. There's not a feather or a Stetson hat among us.

Out of nowhere, Renki's hand reaches toward my face with a piece of torn sheet and some snow. He's rubbing my scar. I cringe.

"I'm alright," I swat his hand away.

The snowy sheet has blood on it. My cheek is bleeding again.

"It doesn't hurt, if people would just quit picking at it," I try to be polite, but the words come out rather rude. After all, Renki was just trying to help.

"You can't get to the hospital in that truck," one of the men says. "Main Street got hit." He waves his arm along the street with the crater in it. His hand is bandaged with my pillowcase.

"I can take Birch Street to Oak and cut through Fir and then to Runeberg," a second man says.

"No, the best way is to take Main to Birch, bypass Oak, cut through the Square…" a third man argues.

Renki shakes his head and leaves. Where's he going? Is he going to just leave us as well? Now I wish I hadn't been so rude to him.

"The Square got hit as well, but Birch Street to Oak, right on Fir and then up Runeberg," the second man insists.

"Will you stop it with Runeberg? No one can get through Runeberg this time of day!" a fourth man offers his opinion.

"What do you mean 'this time of day'? Have you seen any other traffic?"

I've lost count of who says what.

A sharp whistle silences them. Tor's head perks up. Renki joins the squabbling men. He's carrying two boards.

"Toss me your belts," he hollers at the men.

Silently they do as they're told. The burnt man is still moaning. At least he's still alive, and didn't die listening to that stupid argument. Renki fastens the two boards together.

"Help me lift him," he tells the men around the truck.

Very carefully they move the burnt man from the back of the truck onto the boards.

"Follow the boy!" Renki says. He gives me a bundle of sheets, and sends me back to the hospital, with four grown men in tow, carrying the stretcher with the burnt man on it between them.

It's nearly dark again. When we get back to the hospital, I can't find Mother or Uncle Johannes or Little Sister anywhere. The place has emptied some, but the nurses are still running about chaotically. They give the burnt man priority and I start looking for Mother. Surely she didn't leave already? I would've passed her on my way back. She wouldn't leave me. Would she? She left her parents, her husband, her home and very nearly Tor... I'm so tired that I'm getting more angry than sad. I hand my bundle of sheets to the nearest doctor, who gratefully accepts them, and scurries along.

Then I hear it. In the far distance. A sound so familiar that it could come from inside me. I start running toward it. I should be sad or mad or both, but I'm elated. The sound gets louder. I look into an examination room.

"I -hic- want Pau -hic- aul!" Little Sister is wailing.

She's sitting in Mother's lap, while a doctor is bandaging her ear. Her face is streaked with tears, and from the way she's hiccupping, I can tell that she's been crying a long time.

As I walk up to her I hear the doctor say "She'll be sleepy. Try to keep her warm, and change that bandage only if there's pus present. Find medical assistance at your destination."

"Paul..." Little Sister whispers and reaches an arm to me. Her eyelids are droopy, and with her other arm she's holding her little stuffed toy puppy up to her face. Puppy is drenched in tears and snot.

"Will it affect her hearing?" Mother asks, as the doctor helps her off the table.

"Possibly. And most likely her equilibrium, too. Not that you would, but she shouldn't be allowed to swim in cold waters for a while," he says. He scans her from head to toe. "How far?" he asks, his gaze on her belly.

"Twenty-eight," Mother answers.

Twenty-eight what? We've traveled twenty-eight kilometers? That's not far. We've only got twenty-eight more to go? That's not so bad either.

"You will take it easy, now, won't you? When was the last time you ate?" the doctor asks, and lifts Mother's eyelids.

Then he puts two fingers to her wrist. Mother doesn't answer. He digs through her layers of clothing, and puts a stethoscope to her belly.

"At the next opportunity, get off that sleigh and on a train."

Then he turns to me, and lifts my chin up. He turns to his desk, and wets a cotton ball.

"This may sting, son," he says and swabs my cheek.

It does sting, and it brings tears to my eyes. It had stopped hurting already! Why does everyone have to keep messing with it?

"You may have a bump there for a while," the doctor says as he bandages my cheek. "It'll look somewhat like a birthmark, but if you don't pick at it, it should heal nicely."

Is he kidding? I'm the only one yet who *hasn't* picked at it! I have no intention to pick at it!

"Thank you, sir," I say, between gritted teeth. "Mother, can we go now?"

On our way out of the hospital, we pass the man with the broken arm and leg. Uncle Johannes is with him.

"You're heaven-sent," the man whispers to Mother and clutches her hand. "How can I ever thank you?"

Mother pats the back of his good hand. "Don't give up," she smiles. "Never give up."

From his pocket, he pulls out what looks like a piece of felt. He gives it a shake, and it flops into an interesting looking hat. It's like a cowboy hat, only it's flat on one side. He plops it on my head.

"Stay warm and strong," he says, when we leave.

I wave at him until I can no longer see him.

I hate this time of year. Father says I should be careful with words such as hate, but here I think it's appropriate. It's always dark. And cold. You never know what time of day it is. It's depressing. It's pitch black when you go to school and it's pitch black by the time you get out. Daylight hours are spent in school. I hate that. Of course, right now, I think I'd rather be in school than here. I'd rather be anywhere but here. And I don't even know where 'here' is. I've completely lost track of time. Have we been traveling for days, or did we just leave this morning? I don't know. Renki and Uncle Johannes haven't stopped. I doubt that this continuous running is good for the horses. I can't recall the last time we took a bathroom break. But then again, we haven't stopped to eat, so that's a moot point. After we left the town with the hospital, Mother moved a barrel of frozen apples and a loaf of bread from Renki's sleigh into ours, and we've been helping ourselves. Maybe I do need a bathroom break. The more I try not to think about it, the more I actually do think about it.

We've stopped caring about our eyes and noses running. Everything just freezes to our face anyway. Our eyebrows and lashes are covered with icicles. We've wrapped our scarves around our faces, and they have icicles on them as well. I do like my new hat, though. As soon as we returned to the sleighs from the hospital, Carl wanted to try it on, but I wouldn't let him. If I did, I'd never see it again. The hat has a string around the brim, which I tied around my chin. The crown is slightly pointed and is split in four, rather than two, like in a regular gentlemen's hat. My four fingers fit nicely over the crown, and I can lift the hat that way, which I do. A lot. It's quite warm, actually. Renki calls it a Baden-Powell. I don't know what that means, but I intend to ask him just as soon as we stop moving. If ever we do. I wonder where the man at the hospital had gotten it from. I don't know if it's less cold now, or the hat makes such a difference, but I feel less uncomfortable. Also, we finally discovered that it's more comfortable, and warm, to sink into the bundles, rather than try to keep our balance on top of them.

At one point I rather enjoyed watching the stars, making up stories for Little Sister about them, and re-naming them. I only know the Big Dipper and Orion's Belt, so the rest of them got names depending on my imagination at the time. But now the sky is cloudy, so I don't even have that to occupy my mind. My cheek is throbbing again, and I'm bored. My body is aching from being still for so long. I just want shed all these layers of clothing and run. Just jump up and down and not stop until I have stitches in my side and I spit blood. This must be driving Carl crazy!

We haven't heard another plane since that first day. But then again, we've been traveling on what seem the most remote roads in the history of man's ability to build roads. I don't know where we're going, and frankly, have stopped caring. It's obvious that either Mother or Uncle Johannes or Renki or all three knows, because the direction hasn't changed once. That much I could tell from when the stars were still visible. Except for the times when we found ourselves on the shore of a lake, and Mother wanted to cut straight across them, and they got into this huge argument about staying out of visible areas, such as lakes and fields. How many lakes could we have crossed? Dozens. Hundreds, possibly. Wonder how much time we could've saved by doing that? I wish I had paid more attention to the size of the moon when we left, so I could tell how long we've been gone. I know it shone brightly, but that's about it. There were more pressing matters at hand at the time, than to look at the moon.

I'm trying not to think about Father, about where he is and what he's doing right now. I wonder if he survived the house burning up. Who burned our house, anyway? And why? Is that where the war started? Why didn't our grandparents go with us? Have bombs dropped on our town, too? I wonder if my friends from school are also sitting in sleighs somewhere, wondering what's going on. And what happened to all our help? Did they make it out in time? And why is everyone too proud to accept a ride when it's being offered? Mother probably has some answers, but I know that now isn't the time to ask. In fact, very little has been said since we left the hospital. I don't know if Mother has slept at all. We kids doze off every now and then. Little Sister slept really well and for a long time after we left the hospital, and hasn't whined once when she's awake. The doctor must've given her something.

We're slowing down. I look up from the sleigh. It seems as though we're approaching civilization again. I can see farm houses, and barns and fields. They're intact, not bombed or burned down. This is a nice change of scenery to the endless forests we've been traveling through. Uncle Johannes drives us through a pair of old, wrought iron gates, that are hanging open. At the end of the drive sits a mid-sized, two-story, dark house, with several outbuildings. In the faint, cloud-covered moonlight, Mother climbs down from her seat, waddles to the door and knocks. Uncle Johannes helps us out of the sleigh. Finally! Solid ground! My muscles and joints ache, and it takes me a while to get used to moving on my own accord again, after having been still for so long.

Tor takes off immediately, and makes a round around the house. I quite need to go, too. Uncle Johannes lines us up behind Mother, the way we're always lined up, with Johan and me on the flanks and Carl and Little Sister in between. Carl is yawning, and rubbing his eyes.

"Where are we?" he asks, looking around. "I'm hungry."

Mother knocks again. Someone lights something upstairs, because we can see a faint stream of light moving about. The door is opened carefully. An older woman, with her hair in rollers, clutching a heavy fur coat around her, and holding a small lantern stares at us. Then her gaze falls on Mother.

"You made it!" she exhales in Swedish, opens the door wider and throws herself around Mother, giving her a fierce hug.

"What's all this devilish noise?" A grumpy old man in long johns appears at the door. He also speaks Swedish.

His face looks odd in the dark. I rub the sleep out of my eyes. He doesn't have any teeth!

"Oh, be quiet, old man!" the woman shushes the toothless man. "Put your teeth in, and come help us!" She turns back to us. "Come in, come in. Let's get you out of the cold. You must be tired and hungry. Look how much you've grown!"

We don't dare move. Yes, we're tired and hungry, but who is this woman? Obviously she knows us. She looks vaguely familiar, but I can't place her. Who do we know that speaks Swedish, apart from Father? And if we're in a Swedish-speaking part of the country, we must've been traveling for days. It certainly feels like we have.

Mother turns to us. She's pale and breathing heavily. Her voice is barely audible.

"Children, please bow and curtsy for your paternal grandparents," she breathes in Finnish, and collapses into Uncle Johannes' arms.

January 1940.

We're in Österbotten. I vaguely remember meeting Father's parents for the first and only time three years ago back home in Karelia, when they came for Little Sister's christening. Mummo is a darling, generous, fun person, who doted on us, whereas Farfar found fault in everything. It was too hot, us kids were too loud, Tor was a nuisance, our house was too big, we had too much staff, there was too much food, there wasn't enough food, Mother's gooseberry wine was too tart, the apple cider wasn't strong enough, we were too snobbish to have moonshine, the trip was too long and uncomfortable... Well, *that* I actually agree with. It seems like whatever we did, we did it wrong and finally we simply avoided him. I remember him as being mean and grumpy, and now we're living in his house.

Uncle Johannes and Renki returned to Karelia to join the fight, the same night we arrived at Farfar's house. And I didn't even get to say goodbye. All of December is spent gathering and sending care packages to our brave soldiers. There's a post office in this little town, and with aching hearts and hoping faces, we rush there every day, sometimes several times per day. We have yet to receive anything. There's also a small penny store in town, which sells hard candy. Ten pieces for a penny. I draw a little sketch of the six of us (Mother, us three boys, Little Sister and Tor), and wrap some licorice inside it. I hope Father will like it. I miss him. I write a letter telling him that I fixed the strings on his violin, and hung it on the wall of Farfar's drawing room, and how dearly I hope for him to come back to us soon, so we can all sit around and listen to him play it again. No answer yet. Then I write another letter, telling him how much we've all grown, the adventures of the trip from Karelia to Österbotten, how good we've been, doing our chores without grumbling, and how his little angel is learning how to make snow angels. Still no answer. I fear he may be dead, but don't have the courage to ask Mother.

> The Ministry of Supply urged evacuees to adapt to their new circumstances and attempt to support themselves, if possible, and to work for their hosts who were providing them with shelter. Meaning - Karelian evacuees were not to expect government assistance. Prime Minister Risto Ryti earmarked 100,000 markkas for the families of the fallen and wounded in the 1940 budget. President Kallio had been struck by illness, so the presidential duties and state leadership had fallen on Ryti and Mannerheim. On the home front, civilians were urged to correspond with their loved ones at the front, encouraging them and keeping up the morale. Officially, civilians were told very little of how the war proceeded. In late December 1939 the numbering of some of the Finnish Army divisions was changed in an attempt to confuse Soviet intelligence, making postal delivery difficult.

Today, we have to go to school again. I'm really not looking forward to this. I thought, since there's a war going on and all, that school would be out. Mother is still weak, but makes a splendid effort of dressing us up in the best clothes we brought with us. Our boots are spit-shined, we were scrubbed raw in the sauna last night, and our hair is slicked back. I pull my new hat down low over my head.

Mother walks us to school and introduces us to our new teacher. She insists we call her 'Fröken' and no name. It sounds odd. Fröken looks at my scar and asks Mother if I'm trouble. Mother responds that I'm a curious child. Of course I'm curious - how else am I ever going to find anything out? Nobody ever tells me anything. We're going to attend a Swedish school. It's so small that Johan and I are in the same classroom, although we're one year apart.

The first thing Fröken does is to have Johan's class sit and read quietly, while my class is to stand up and recite multiplication tables! I can't believe it! We just moved clear across to the other corner of the country and we're doing the same thing in Swedish. As I'm in the middle of six times six is thirty-six, something hits my neck. I swat at it, thinking it's a bug. There's quiet snickering from Johan's side of the classroom. We finish the six tables and continue with seven, when something hits the side of my face. It lands on my shoulder. It's a chewed-up, wet ball of paper. I look around. All the girls are sitting with their heads down, reading, whereas all the boys are looking at me, with stupid grins on their faces. All except one, Johan, who's busy reading. My eyes narrow in on one particular boy. He's hiding something in his hand. It looks like a rolled-up piece of paper. A straw. The boy is the biggest one in the room, taller even than Johan, with sandy-blond hair and piercing slate-blue eyes. He's so tall, that I think he may have been held back a year. He sticks out his tongue at me. I retaliate. He loads the straw, takes aim, and shoots another spit-ball at me. I duck, and it hits the girl standing next to me. She screams out in disgust. Fröken beckons me to the front of the class. She tells me to hold up my fingers. I do as I'm told. She slaps them, hard, with a ruler, right across the tips of my fingers. The shock hits me before the hurt does. My eyes are stinging.

"Why'd you do that?" I ask, baffled.

"You may do things differently in Karelia, but in my class there'll be no horsing around."

The spit-balls keep flying the next hour as well, but I decide to ignore them. In our old school back home we didn't have note pads; we had slates, so I'm thrilled to have my own paper and pencil. I start sketching. When I first met Fröken, I thought that she was quite attractive, but after she slapped me across my fingernails, she turned hideous. In my drawing, she has a long, crooked witch's nose, with hairy warts all over her face. Her hair is stringy and black and stands straight up in every direction.

"What's this?" a voice says, and the note pad is yanked from my desk.

Fröken. She summons me to the front of the class again, and raises the ruler again. Instinctively, I hide my fingers behind my back. She grabs my wrist, squeezes my hand around so tightly, that it feels like my skin is going to peel off. And then she slaps me. Right across the tips of my fingers, and sends me to stand in the corner.

"What purpose will that serve?" I ask.

There's no logic to her demand. Never did I think that I'd admit this, but I miss Veera Borikoff, my teacher in Karelia. She may be an old crow, but she's a saint compared to Fröken. I stand in the corner until we're dismissed for the day. Fröken hands me a note to give to Mother.

We grab our boots, hats and overcoats as quickly as we can, and storm out of the classroom. I intend to run all the way back to Farfar's and ask Mother if I can go back home. Or go to the front with Father and Uncle Johannes and Renki.

It's dark as we enter the schoolyard. Somehow, if possible, it feels darker here than home. Neither the yard, nor the streets are lit, although they have lampposts.

"Itä-Karjalainen, kävelee kuin nainen!*" someone sing-songs behind us, just as we're about to leave the schoolyard.

I turn around, and I see the tall boy from Johan's class, whose name I gather from Fröken is Harri, along with four other boys, pointing and laughing.

"Let's just keep walking," Johan whispers to me from the side of his mouth. He grabs me by my coat sleeve, and tries to pull me along.

"Do I really walk like a woman?" I ask Johan.

"No, and you're not East Karelian, either," he says, and we start walking faster.

Harri and his gang are hurling snowballs at us.

"Harri's a bully, but apparently his father's the Mayor, so we should probably be nice to him," Johan continues, ducking just in time to escape a snowball hitting him in the head.

"So what? That doesn't make him any better than us," I try to argue, as a snowball hits my shoulder. I so badly want to make a snowball myself, and start throwing back at them.

"No, it doesn't, but..."

"Hey, fellas! What's the reason 'refuge' sounds so much like 'refuse'?" Harri shouts after us. "You are! Someone should take this garbage back to Karelia! You stink!"

They're only a few steps behind us. My blood is starting to boil; I'm gritting my teeth, trying hard to keep my mouth shut. I pull my hat down lower over my eyes. I don't want to see them, hear them or acknowledge them. We keep walking. They keep following us.

"Hey, Karelian! Why are you pulling your hat down? To hide your third eye? Three-eyes! Why are you wearing a ladies' hat, anyway? Are you a girl? That looks like something my mother would wear to church!"

"Well, your mother must have pretty good taste then," I retaliate. I'm not accustomed to this type of dialogue. "Except when she kept *you*!"

"Oooh! A come-back from three-eyes! Why are you running away? Are you afraid to stand up and fight like a man? Is that why you left Karelia? Left the fighting to real men? Cowards! Chickens!" Harri is making the sound of a chicken, and flapping his arms like wings.

I've had enough. Tearing out of Johan's grip, I leave him standing, holding

---

* Author's note: 'Itä-Karjalainen, kävelee kuin nainen.' = 'East Karelian, walks like a woman.' A popular Finnish children's teasing song. Can be used with most words ending in -lainen.

28

my overcoat. I ram into Harri, and we land in a pile of snow, fists and knees flying. The other four boys fly over us. I punch everything that I can reach. Johan joins the fight. It's five against two. Our odds are only slightly better than Finland's against Russia. A fist flies across my face from out of nowhere. My eyes feel like they're going to explode out of their sockets, and then my vision goes black for a while. With pain shooting inside my head, I swing my arms everywhere. My head is buried in snow. Suddenly Harri is yanked backwards. I try to make my eyes focus. Carl and Tor have appeared and are joining the fight. Where did they come from? Did they smell a fight and follow their noses like both of them do with food?

"Who the devil are you?" Harri asks.

For the first time since he was born I'm grateful for Carl's size. He's nearly as tall as I am, although there's eleven months between us. Silently I pray that he won't let anyone know that he's my little brother. It would be beyond embarrassing to be rescued by your *little* brother and your dog. Thankfully Carl doesn't bother with introductions, he just keeps fighting.

Tor is barking and growling at everyone, sinking his teeth into the leg of the boy who's hitting me. We're dirty and wet, and our clothes are torn. Johan has a split lip, and I can feel blood running from my eyebrow. But we keep fighting. It's about pride now. And our odds have improved. Other kids from our school have gathered in a circle around us. They're egging us on. Seems like Harri isn't very popular. From the corner of my good eye I can see that two other boys, whose dialect I recognized as Karelian, have joined the fight. One of them has Harri pinned down in the snow. Harri is panting, and flailing helplessly, while trying to spit in his face. The girl sitting next to me in class, also Karelian, undoes the belt of her book bag and starts slashing the backs of Harri's gang with it. I think we might be winning! Before I have time to finish that thought, I'm yanked backwards, and thrown to the ground. I scrape my knee in the process, tearing my pants on the frozen, salty gravel.

I look up. Fröken is already writing another note. Does she bring that note pad with her everywhere? She probably sleeps with it. Everyone stops fighting. Harri is whimpering.

"Harri Holgerson, go home," Fröken says, handing me the note.

I start to open it. She slaps my hand. We're both wearing gloves, so it doesn't hurt.

"For your mother's eyes only," she hisses, and a little saliva hits me in the face.

Luckily my eye is starting to swell shut, or else her spit would've hit me in the eyeball.

"What are you doing here?" I ask Carl, as we're approaching Farfar's house.

We leave the schoolyard only moments behind Harri, and walk behind him almost all the way to Farfar's house. As it turns out, the Mayor's house is only about half a kilometer from Farfar's. None of us speaks a word, until we pass it.

"I found out that the ocean isn't that far away, and there's a boat stranded on the beach and I wanted to see if you fellas wanted to help me set it loose!" Carl responds excitedly.

My heart skips a beat. A boat! I could sail away from here. Away from multiplication tables and bullying Mayor's sons. I could take the boat and return home. Maybe even go to the front and find Father and help him fight the war. My country needs me! That'd shut Harri right up! Karelians aren't afraid of anything, least of all standing up to oppression.

"Why aren't you in school?" the ever-logical Johan asks.

"Mother says there's no class for my age, so I have to wait until fall to start first grade again. So, what do you say about the boat?"

After walking in silence for a while, Johan says "We'd better go Sunday after church. It's too dark right now."

> In December 1939 The League of Nations expelled the Soviet Union and urged its remaining member nations to give Finland all possible humanitarian and material assistance. Hjalmar Procopé, Finland's Ambassador in Washington, conveyed to the United States Government a request for a sixty million dollar loan to Finland. President Franklin D. Roosevelt said the USA could extend a non-military loan as this would not compromise neutrality, noting that Finland was the only country that in the crisis years of the 1930's continued to pay her World War I debts in full. Further, at a press conference he said that any American who enlisted in and swore allegiance to the Army of a foreign country at war would thereby lose his American citizenship. However, he emphasized that there had been no official declaration of war, the United States did not consider Finland to be a country at war, and American volunteers in Finland would therefore retain their citizenship. The first American volunteers, around one hundred officers, pilots, mechanics and soldiers, arrived in Finland on January 7th, 1940.
> The surge of foreign aid to Finland was as surprising - albeit ineffective - as the

official condemnation of Russia's assault. The first country to respond to the League of Nations' call was Argentina, sending fifty tonnes of grain and sixty sacks of coffee. Many others quickly followed. Norwegian schoolchildren started a collection of backpacks, sending twenty-five thousand bags, filled with food and clothing as well as six trainloads of apples. South African winemakers sent wine and brandy. An anonymous Danish businessman donated fifty trucks, and in the United States, the 'one dollar collection' raised one million dollars for the Finnish War Fund. A similar drive in Sweden collected nearly fifteen million kronor, as well as four ambulances and two Fokker reconnaissance planes. Nobel laureates Selma Lagerlöf, Albert Szent-Györgyi and F. E. Sillanpää donated their medals. Confectioner Karl Fazer later bought Sillanpää's medal for 100,000 markkas, to be paid to the War Fund, and returned the medal to the author. What Finland needed most desperately was troops and military supplies.

On January 24th, 1940, Finland's Minister of Social Affairs, K. A. Fagerholm, arrived in Stockholm to discuss the details of the evacuation of Finnish children. By then, hundreds of children had already been sent away in anticipation of the possibility of a Soviet victory and Stalin's national extermination programs.

All I think about the entire week is the boat. I find an old map and trace my escape. There's a direct sea route from here to home, and I intend to take it.

Harri continues to bully me all week. I try to ignore him, and for the most part I'm successful, but at the end of each school day, my patience runs out, and we're in a fight in the schoolyard. And I get a note. By Friday, I decide to focus my energy on the boat instead, and basically let him beat me up. Oddly, I again, am the one receiving a note.

I hate this school. I hate my teacher, I hate Harri and I hate being away from home. And I almost hate Father for telling me not to hate.

Carl has been uncharacteristically secretive about the boat, but after a few bribes, consisting mainly of hard candies, he tells me that 'the shore is only a quick ski trip away', and that 'the boat sits right there'.

By Saturday night I have gathered all the things I need for my trip home. In my old backpack I've packed what little money I have left, a loaf of bread, my knife, some pencils and paper and the old map. I also find a book of matches in

Farfar's sauna, and take those as well. Because, you just never know. The hard part will be how to not let my siblings know what I'm up to. I haven't quite figured out yet how I'm going to just set sail on the boat, and leave them behind. Tor is going with me, of course. He's been aware of my plan all along. But what about Mother? Should I tell her? Maybe I'll send her a postcard when I find Father. That way she'll know that we're both alright.

Sunday church service is painfully slow, and I feel guilty for not giving our Maker my full attention. We're praying for peace and for the safe return of our soldiers. We're praying for wisdom and strength in these trying times. Or so the priest says. I know he's referring to the war, but my personal trying times will end just as soon as he lets me go.

When church finally lets out, we rush to Farfar's house to change clothes and get into the skis we've borrowed from our cousins next door. Little Sister is adamant about going with us to see the boat. I know she's only going to slow us down, because she's only three and never did quite learn how to ski. Johan has a brilliant idea of tying Father's old sled to Tor and letting him pull her.

The weather is turning nasty. It was sleeting this morning, and now it's freezing with a cold, skin-piercing wind. Johan points out that we have to wax our skis or else we'll break our necks skiing on this icy crust of snow. This frustrates me. I just want to go already. So what, if it's slippery? At least we'd be moving.

None of us has ever waxed skis before, and our cousins are reluctant to help, just pointing out that there should be a jar of tar in the barn. Somewhere. Hauling our skis into the barn, we take one wall each, searching for it.

Little Sister finds several cans, and picks each of them up, saying "Found it!"

Not helpful, because she didn't. My frustration is growing. When we finally locate it, and pry the top open with our knives, the tar is a congealed, grungy mass. Carl suggests that we melt it, so we set off building a fire. Johan, who's really starting to irritate me now, points out that we shouldn't build a fire inside the barn, because with all the hay and stuff, we might set it on fire.

"Well, what do you suggest we do then?" I spit out. I'm anxious to get going, and everything is delaying my departure to go and find Father. "It's too wet and windy to do it outside. We'll never build a fire in this weather."

"What about the crawl space?" he suggests.

The front of Farfar's house is built on support pillars, and has a crawl space underneath that's just high enough for Johan, who's the tallest, to stand up straight. It's shielded from the wind on one side by the bedrock the house was built on.

Quickly we gather our skis, along with armfuls of hay from the barn and set out for the crawl space. I really don't want to tell anyone that I have matches, but I also don't have time to wait for someone else to go and find any. Dusk is already starting to set in.

We build a pyramid of the hay, put the jar of tar on top of it, and I produce the matches. I light the hay, which flames up immediately. Light crackling noises emanate from the jar of tar, and before we know it, the jar explodes into the ceiling. The flames lick the molten tar, spreading quickly. Before anyone of us has a chance to react, the flames are snaking along the side of the house. We start stomping the fire. Carl runs out and back in with an armful of wet snow. We toss it onto the ceiling. Finally the fire is out, but the side of the house is black.

I flip Johan over the head. "Great idea, dummy! Look what we did!"

He flips me back. "That's fresh soot. Get some snow and start scrubbing it off!"

"Are we in trouble?" Little Sister asks, and grabs my hand.

Looking into her angelic face, with her eyes wide open with fear, and her lower lip starting to tremble, my selfishness drapes me like a wet cloth. How can I run away and leave her? I can't. Little Sister depends on me. I can't abandon her to face the terrors of this new life alone. And what's worse; I'd be breaking my word to Father. I could never live with myself after that.

"Not today," I tell her.

Another week passes before we can get away to go see the boat, but finally, after church, with our borrowed skis tarred and strapped to our boots, we're on our way. Little Sister's ear is bothering her again, so it's just us four boys. Johan, me, Carl and Tor. It's a cold, but clear, sunny day, and the ocean turns out not to be as far away as we thought. Carl was right; it's only a short ski trip away. However, what Carl called a 'boat' turns out to be an enormous barge. It's badly rusted and surrounded by ice. It's sitting slightly lopsided a little less than a hundred meters from the shore, and looks as though it ran aground and has been left to rust. That thing has been there a while. From its bow, there's a thick iron chain going straight down through the ice. We're guessing it's the anchor.

We leave our skis and poles on the ice, and start climbing up the anchor chain. We're pirates, taking over a victim's vessel. We take turns being the pirate captain, sailing off into the high seas. Tor is running around in circles on the ice. There's no way we can get him on board, and he's anxious.

In the bow sits an enormous crank wheel, to which the chain is attached. Carl suggests that we try to turn the wheel, and lift the anchor. We do. It doesn't budge. We put all our strength into trying to turn it, but it refuses to move.

"Maybe we could hack a hole in the ice, and release it," Johan suggest.

We climb down the anchor chain, and start hacking at the ice with our ski poles and knives.

The sun is setting; we're exhausted and have only managed to chip the ice surrounding the anchor. So much for taking the barge to fight the war. We decide to come back when the ice has melted.

Winter 1940.

It's Sunday morning and we don't have to go to church, because Mother isn't feeling well. Mummo and Aunt Martta, who lives next door, have been with her all morning. Farfar took the car and went off somewhere. Carl and Johan went skiing with our cousins, Aunt Martta's thirteen and fifteen year-old sons, and I'm reading to Little Sister when Mummo comes rushing in. She's excited and flustered and tells me that Mother just broke something, and that I have to go in to town to find the doctor. If I can't find the doctor, to bring a midwife. In great detail Mummo explains to me where the doctor's house is, as she's helping me get dressed. She could've saved herself the trouble of explaining by simply telling me that the doctor's office is in the yellow house with white trim behind the penny store.

It's really cold outside, and I'm running as fast as I can. The cold air burns my throat, and by the time I get to the doctor's house, my eyes are watering and the tears are frozen on my cheeks.

There's a note on the door: 'Gone to the front. Heikkilä's Martti will tend to my patients. Old Andersson's Aini is a trained nurse. Pray for peace and the safe return of our men.'

Martti Heikkilä and Aini Andersson are both just names to me. The clerk at the penny store is the source of all gossip in this town, and the only store that's open on Sundays, so I ask him.

"What you need them for?" he says.

"Mother broke something."

"Did she cut herself? Is she bleeding? Did she break a bone?"

I hate to admit that I don't know. I never asked. "She's been in bed all morning, and then Mummo said that she broke something and she needs a doctor. Or a midwife."

"Well, why didn't you say so in the first place?"

Suddenly he's all action. He makes a few calls, and sends out his son to old Aini's house, that doesn't have a phone. Then he asks me to tend the store, while he runs across the street to the little café. Now I'm worried. Is Mother going to be alright? The store clerk returns, with a tall, stout woman in tow. He closes the store and offers to drive us back to Farfar's house.

"Is Mother going to be alright?" I ask.

"Oh, yes," old Aini says. "She's had four. There's nothing to number five."

The new baby was born that evening.

A few weeks later I'm not in school, because Mother is still weak and can't handle both the new baby, Carl and Little Sister by herself. The baby still doesn't have a name; everyone just calls her the new baby. We'll wait for Mother to feel better, to let her make the decision. Johan and I take turns going to school. I love not having to go to school and deal with Harri and his pack of bullies. I don't think our teacher notices or cares that I'm not there. Lately, there haven't been the same children in attendance two days in a row. In fact, most of the other Karelian kids haven't been to school for a good two weeks now. Someone told me that city kids don't have to go to school, because the schools are used to house refugees. This thought both frightens and excites me at the same time. On the one hand, I'd love not to have to go to school. At all. But on the other, I'm a refugee myself. I'd hate to *live* in a school.

Mother hasn't been out of bed since the new baby was born. Mummo is working at the local telephone operators' and Farfar... well, I'm not exactly sure what he does, but he disappears in the mornings after breakfast and doesn't return until supper. So, today, I'm making sure that Little Sister and new baby are not bothering Mother. As usual, Carl is out skiing.

There's a sharp knock on the front door. Tor hasn't left Mother's bed since the new baby was born, but now I hear him pounding down the stairs and before I know it, he's growling right beside me. As I open the door, the cold wind whips my face. I only open the door a crack. Tor starts barking, and I'm straining to keep him still.

The two women standing on the front steps ask to speak to Mother. Ordinarily I would lie, and tell them Mother's not here, but something about how these women are smiling isn't right. Their neck muscles are straining. Part of me thinks maybe it's the chilly wind, but another part of me knows they're masking something. They're fake. They have that 'kids are meant to be seen, not heard, and although we're here to talk to your parents about *you*, we don't want to waste time on you' - look about them, that adults so often do. I hate when adults treat children as if they were ignorant.

I ask them to take a seat in the drawing-room, and close the door behind them. I leave Tor to watch them.

When I tap on Mother's door I hear a faint "Come in, son."

As I enter, she's trying to prop herself up on the pillows. Her beautiful face is so hollow-looking, her hair has lost its shine and her eyes are blank, but she smiles at me and waves me over. I tell her about the two women.

"Why didn't you tell them I'm too ill to receive callers?" Mother asks. She doesn't scold me; she just prompts me to know better.

"They have a secret," I say in earnest.

Mother looks at me quizzically. "A secret? Is it a good one?" she asks.

"I don't think so," I say, and I hope she won't ask me to explain how I know this, I just do.

"What does Tor think of them?"

"He doesn't trust them."

"Very well, son," Mother says, and ruffles my hair. "Go make us some coffee. Not the good kind. And tell the ladies I'll be right down."

I can see that it takes all the willpower she can muster to make her body move. I hope she's not going to be like this for the rest of her life. Although she's still as sweet as strawberries, watching her ache makes me ache. Also, I miss sitting in her lap, listening to her read to us, hug us, and kiss us. Mother has the most comfortable lap in the world. Until she got big with the new baby, all four of us could fit in her lap at the same time.

I'm just pouring very weak coffee, made of ground pine-bark and dried, ground dandelion leaves and who knows what else, into cups, when I hear Mother's voice from two rooms away.

"Absolutely not! You must be insane to even suggest something this absurd!" she says, her voice high-pitched and agitated.

I quickly place the coffeepot on a tray on the kitchen table and peek into the drawing room. Mummo told me to keep Mother from getting anxious or excited and I failed. She's anxious *and* excited. I can see her red-faced, gesticulating wildly and pacing.

"You'll kindly leave this house," she says to the women callers.

I open the door. "Mother?"

One of the ladies walks toward me, and ushers me out. "Leave us be, young man," she says.

I try to make eye-contact with Mother, but she's sitting on the settee, with her face buried in her hands. Tor's head is in her lap, and he's whining. He very rarely whines, so I know this conversation hasn't gone well. The lady closes the door in my face. I press my ear to it, ready to burst through if need be.

"It's not safe anymore," a voice says.

"The war will be over any day now," Mother's desperate voice argues.

"That's wishful thinking, dear, and we're happy to hear that you haven't completely lost all hope. However, you wouldn't want to be the only Karelian family with children still here, would you? What would the others think of you? There's a movement in Sweden…"

"Oh, I know all about your little movement in Sweden," Mother interrupts. "A group of bored housewives making 'Finland's cause ours'. Don't make me laugh. If Finland's cause truly was theirs, they'd send troops."

I miss part of the conversation, because Little Sister has woken up the new baby, by climbing into her crib. They're both making odd noises. I go to check on them, and they're just smiling at each other, then at me. Little Sister makes the crib swing and the new baby is making more odd little noises. I know I should feed her, since she's awake, but since she's not crying, I decide it can wait, and return to eavesdropping.

"...Karelian children," a voice is saying as I again press my ear against the door.

"I will ask you again, not to refer to Karelians as if we're third-class citizens," Mother snaps, in her 'behave or I'll reason with you' - voice.

There's a long silence.

"We have several carefully selected foster families, all with excellent values, who will make sure that they are safe, warm, clothed, fed and educated," the other voice eventually breaks the silence.

"What about loved?" Mother's voice sounds deflated now.

Silence.

"Where ...?" Mother finally asks.

"Denmark."

"*Denmark?!* That far away and next to a war? Out of the fire and into the wolves' den? Never! You just try to force me! They aren't going anywhere! Do you hear me? Never! And what will happen if the German Army crosses the Danish border? Where will you send them then? Poland?" Mother is getting excited again and her voice rises an octave and several decibels. At least. "And you dare to portray yourselves as 'saving the children'. This is ludicrous!"

The other ladies are becoming harder to hear, because they in turn have lowered their voices.

"Hundreds, maybe thousands, have already left. If we arrange for you to speak to one of the parents, will you co-operate?"

Who can they be talking about? Us? Moving to Denmark? But why? And why is Mother so opposed to moving? We've already moved. But surely this time we'd move with Father? Do they really hate Karelians that much that they're now sending people to their houses to make them move to Denmark? We're not bad people!

"Do you have children?" Mother asks. Another silence. "Then you have no right to ask me what you're asking of me! You might just as well tear my heart out right now with a dull knife!"

"It wouldn't be long, only until it's safe to return."

"Which of course, you understand, we cannot predict at this time."

"Think about it - we're trying to help you. You're a single mother with five mouths to feed. Your husband's at the front or with his Maker and by the looks of you …"

"Get out! Now! As long as there's even a drop of blood in my veins and a breath of air in my lungs, you will not get away with this without a fight!"

The door bursts open, and I have barely time to step out of the way. Mother is literally pushing the other women out. Maybe she is stronger than she looks. I help her. I even accidentally step on one of their toes on purpose. Tor is also helping by herding them toward the front door. We're nearly in the vestibule, when one of the women turns to Mother.

"Don't make this any more difficult for yourself than it needs to be, dear. They're only children, for heaven's sake!" she says.

Mother and I gasp simultaneously. She did *not* just say that? What a witch! Without another word, Mother slams the front door in their faces, and bolts it tightly. She's breathing heavily and I hope she won't faint.

"Call Mummo, and tell her to come immediately," she says.

> Following a Swedish initiative, in an effort
> to practice charity during a war the country
> wasn't directly involved in, numerous Finnish
> children were evacuated to safety from the rav-
> ages of war to the neighboring countries. Child
> evacuation was initially met with resistance,
> but as the threat of Soviet occupation seemed a
> looming possibility, many mothers finally caved
> in - mainly to pressures from society.
> Sweden had previously offered refuge, but was
> not prepared for such an exodus as the children
> later proved to be. The first surge of evacuees
> left when the Finns had reasons to fear a human-
> itarian catastrophe following the expected So-
> viet occupation. As early as December 8th, 1939,
> the Finnish Consulate in Gothenburg announced
> that nearly five hundred Swedish families had
> offered to take in Finnish refugee children,
> and by January 2nd, 1940, another ten thousand
> Swedish homes were available to help.

The next week or so is a blur of events. All of a sudden, Mother's energy has returned. The very next day after Mother's argument with the women callers, we're told that we aren't to go back to school. Instead, we end up spending lots of time with Aunt Martta. Every time we come back to Farfar's, we walk into a heated conversation between Mother and our grandparents or Mother and some strangers. As soon as she spots any of us, she clams up and either sends us outside or asks the other party to kindly leave. Often, we hear her crying, and words like 'genocide' and 'occupation' send her into convulsions.

Then, finally, one morning, about two weeks after the first visit by the pruny ladies, the oddest thing happens. Farfar takes the four of us out to town in his car. This is very exciting for us, although we don't know the occasion for such a treat, but we really don't care, either. First we go and get our hair cut by a professional barber. Then we go to the clothing store, and Farfar charges several entire outfits for each of us, including overcoats, hats, boots and gloves. And, to end the day, we go and have our picture taken. This has been the best day since we left Karelia. Maybe Farfar isn't all that bad, after all.

When we return to the house, there are four identical, brand new little leather suitcases in the hall. Farfar tells us to pack the new clothes into the suitcases, along with one toy each. Here's where I start getting worried. I so easily recall the last time I was asked to pack in a hurry, and to only bring along one toy. What's going on? There's an odd feeling in the pit of my stomach.

Mother enters the hall, and invites us to the drawing-room. The table is set with strawberry juice and butter rolls. Carl starts devouring immediately. The uneasiness takes hold of my chest, and it's becoming hard to breathe.

Mother takes a seat opposite us. "Children," she starts in a quivering voice. Her eyes are red-rimmed, like she's done nothing but cry for days. "You're all going on a little trip."

All four of us stare at her blankly.

"Just us?" Johan asks. "Alone? By ourselves?"

"Just you."

We all erupt in a cacophony of questions.

"…why just us?…"

"…where are we going?…"

"…why?…"

"…why can't you go with us?…"

"…we haven't done anything bad!…"

"…don't you love us anymore?…"

Mother turns to Farfar and Mummo, who are standing in the doorway. They're both avoiding eye contact with us.

"I can't do this," she whispers. Her shoulders slump and her bottom lip starts to quiver.

"Be strong," Mummo whispers back.

Mother takes several deep breaths and then finally turns back to us.

"Children," she starts again. "Farfar will take you to the train tomorrow. You'll be going to Denmark for a while, where it's safe and there's no war." She looks expectantly at our dumb-found faces. "Do you understand where Father is?"

We all nod. "He's killing the Red Army," Carl says proudly.

"Very good, son," Mother encourages. "Unfortunately, it seems that the Red Army is threatening to move in and take our country, and if that should happen, I don't want them to have you, too." She turns to Mummo again. "I'm not making any sense," she sighs.

"It's like, when we left home, and we let the cows go, right?" I ask.

A hint of a glimmer returns to Mother's eye. "Exactly!" she laughs weakly.

"But the cows died on the side of the road," I continue, regretting the words as soon as they leave my lips.

Mother looks deflated again, and the glimmer in her eye is gone. Forever, I fear.

"Son, you'll be traveling by train. And boat. You'll be safe and warm the whole time, and you'll come back just as soon as the war is over."

"Promise?" Little Sister asks.

Mother averts her eyes to her hands, clutching a handkerchief. She doesn't answer.

"Promise?" Little Sister repeats. Her voice is quivering now.

I put an arm around her shoulders. I'm willing Mother to make this promise, but she just sits there, staring at her hands. I notice how violently her hands are trembling.

"Is the new baby going too?" Johan asks.

"No, the baby is staying," Mother whispers.

"Why does she get to stay and we have to go?" Carl argues. "That's not fair!"

"Don't be difficult!" Farfar snaps from the doorway, and yanks Carl by his arm. "Go pack your suitcase and then get in the sauna. I've spent a lot of money on you today, and I expect you to behave, be quiet and grateful," he says as he drags Carl out of the drawing room.

"Can I take Tor?" I ask, although I know the answer. My eyes are starting to well up.

The realization of the situation is hitting me. Not only do I have to leave Mother, not knowing whether Father is alive or not, but now I have to leave my dog, my best friend, too?

Mother shakes her head quietly. "You'll make new friends, Paul. And you'll go to school. And you'll send me letters every day, and pretty drawings of all the exciting new things that you're doing. You'll have to be brave little soldiers, and represent your family and your country with honor and pride. Different place - same rules."

Pride. It always boils down to pride. If we weren't so proud we probably wouldn't be in the war to begin with. Life would be so much easier if we weren't so proud. And stubborn.

Johan interrupts my thoughts. "Will we be together in Denmark?"

Mother takes a quick breath, and I can see a new fear cross her face. Either she didn't expect this question, or she never thought of it herself.

"You big boys make sure that you do," she says, referring to our pride.

Mummo quickly crosses the room to us. "Come along now, children," she says, and her voice sounds cheery, but oddly strained. "I want to see all your nice new things."

As she closes the door to the drawing room behind us, I catch a glimpse of Mother collapsing on the table in a heap of gut-wrenching sobs. Had I known that this would be my last image of her, I'd have rushed back and done anything in my power to make her stop crying.

> The Finnish troops were rapidly running out of supplies, no foreign aid appeared available except through volunteers, and a Soviet occupation seemed inevitable. The motti warfare had been tremendously successful, however, and the Finnish troops captured more materiel as booty from the enemy than the country had received in the form of aid from any friendly power.
>
> The motti tactic was a double envelopment maneuver, using the ability of ski troops to quickly travel over rough terrain and the forests to surround a larger enemy, mechanized and therefore restricted to easy terrain and roads. The heavily outnumbered Finnish troops were thus able to cut off and immobilize segments of the Soviet Army, despite the Soviets' numerical superiority. The smaller pockets of enemies could then be dealt with individually by concentrating forces against them. If the encircled Soviet unit was too powerful, the motti was besieged until it ran out of ammunition, fuel and food to the point of elimination or surrender. At one particular motti, the Finnish troops captured thirty-two assault tanks, forty trucks, six field kitchens and the instruments of a military band, further fuelling the rumor of Stalin's proposed victory parade through Helsinki before the end of 1939. The Soviet unit had only managed to advance less than fifty kilometers across the border.

> The Red Army newspaper Krasnaya Zvezda acknowl-
> edged in its January 20th, 1940 issue the slow
> progress of the Soviet troops and demanded that
> the Red Army be taught how to ski.
> Sweden faced harsh criticism both from its own
> press and foreign dignitaries for not offering
> Finland assistance in the form of both arma-
> ments and troops. Sweden stood firmly behind
> its neutrality policy. The British and French
> press believed Sweden would come to regret this
> decision. The outnumbered Finnish troops were
> alone, fighting enemy tanks with infantry, and
> without anti-tank guns. From loyalty to Sweden,
> Finland had stood steadfast against the Soviet
> demand to cede parts of Bothnia. Now Sweden
> wasn't returning that loyalty. The Swedish Prime
> Minister's negative reply to Finland's request
> for assistance was received with satisfaction
> in Moscow. The Soviet leadership believed that
> Finland's fate was finally sealed, and Molotov
> announced through the Swedish Foreign Minister
> that the Soviet Union was 'in principle will-
> ing to discuss peace'. The Finns were forced to
> retreat.

It's cold. And dark. I'm tired, hungry and confused. And a little sick to my stomach. We spent last night at Aunt Martta's house, and left before dawn this morning. I haven't said goodbye to Mother or Tor, and now we're sitting in a train
station with dozens of other children. None of whom we know. I'm trying to
make sense of this situation, but can't. I understand there's a war. I understand
that Mother wants us to be safe. Logically, it almost makes sense to me. But then
I start thinking about it. How has the war really affected us? Apart from our house
burning, and not really having seen Father in months, and hearing bombs in the
distance once while on the evacuation sleigh - not much. We're told stories about
starving children in countries of war, but we always seem to have food. And shelter, once we got off the sleigh. I just cannot understand why we're being shipped
away. How can Mother do this? Why is she sending us away? Doesn't she know I
promised Father I'd look after her? And then the guilt drapes me like a heavy, wet,
wool blanket. Was it something I did? Or didn't do? Could I have prevented this?
I rack my brain, and my thoughts take me back to the day that changed Mother's
behavior. The day I let the two pruny-faced ladies in the house while she was still
ill. Is this all my fault?

Farfar doesn't say much. He woke us up this morning, loaded us in his car,
and told us to behave and be quiet. We're sitting on a hard, wooden bench in a

freezing train station, uncertain of what's about to happen next. We huddle close together, to keep each other warm. Johan and me on the flanks and Carl and Little Sister in the middle. Little Sister keeps nodding off, and I'm happy for her. She's probably the most comfortable of us all. She's clutching her stuffed toy puppy and is sucking her thumb. I don't know when she started doing that again, but I'm not going to stop her. I look around the station. I don't think I've ever been around this many quiet children at once. Except in church. Those who aren't crying look like they're about to start. Or they look confused, like I imagine I do. I wonder if all these other children are going to Denmark, too.

A sudden realization hits me. I don't know where to go! I mean, I know we're going to Denmark, but then what? It's not like going to church or going to Aunt Martta's or going to the penny store. Denmark is an entire country! I'm racking my brain on how much I know about Denmark. I know it's a bunch of islands south of Sweden, and they speak a language that's close to Swedish and... oh, yeah - they have a king. Uncle Johannes was right; I should've paid more attention in school. I'm seriously worried now. What are we supposed to do once we get there? And what are we supposed to do about money? My thoughts automatically return to the dead cows on the side of the road as we evacuated Karelia. I'm even more scared now.

A lady dressed in a grey wool suit beckons Farfar over, just as I'm about to ask him what we're supposed to do once we get to Denmark. There's some shuffling of papers going on, and the woman's brows keep going up and down. After a lot of pointing and scribbling, she comes over to us, and ties a string around each of our necks. From the string hangs a tag with our names and addresses printed on them. We're tagged. Last night, Aunt Martta, with her immaculate handwriting, printed our names and addresses on the tags of our new suitcases. I feel like a piece of luggage, as I read my tag. I'm less than a piece of luggage; I'm numbered. In the corner of my tag I've been given a number. Like a prisoner.

Carl pokes an elbow in my side. "Want to be Carl for a day?" he whispers. He pulls off his tag and reaches for mine.

We both giggle quietly, as we exchange identities.

The lady in grey appears from nowhere, and snags the tags back. She speaks directly to Farfar, ignoring us, as if we were inanimate objects.

"Explain to your hooligans, that these tags are *never* to leave their necks! They will be quiet and grateful," she says.

Farfar stares us down, and we slump back in our seats, with our own names around our necks.

More paper-shuffling ensues and eventually all the children at the station are tagged. I'm trying to keep my mind from wandering and pull out a pencil and paper from my suitcase. We are allowed to bring one toy with us, and that's what I brought. Directly opposite me is a little girl, who's been leaning her head on the shoulder of what I would imagine is her older brother. Her hat is askew, and partially covers her face, and one of her stockings has sausaged around her ankle. I sketch her before anyone can straighten her out. The grey lady's brow still keeps going up and down, and I sketch her as well. When her brows go up, her ears follow, and when her brows are down, her jowls drop even further. Oddly, in profile she looks like an ostrich, but in portrait, she reminds me of a bulldog.

I miss Tor. I wonder how Mother will explain to him that I'm gone. I hope this separation won't be as heart-breaking for him as it already is for me. Thinking of Tor makes a lump form in my throat, and I drop my gaze quickly, so no one can see I'm about to cry. My eyes fall upon our new suitcases, lined up on the floor in front of us like soldiers. Shoulder to shoulder, patiently waiting to be picked up and taken away. Unable to protest. Unable to move. Unable to speak their minds. Helpless, brand new, spit-shine polished and tagged.

> The very first Finnish children to be evacuated left from Åbo for Stockholm by sea on December 15th, 1939. The initial emphasis was to evacuate the children who lived in the cities, as they risked becoming victims of air raids. These evacuated children were commonly referred to as 'War Children'.
>
> On January 30th, 1940, Finland received the main points of the Soviet Union's peace terms. The central question was the Soviet demand for bases on the Gulf of Finland. The Finnish response was a resolute 'No'. The fighting continued.
>
> In a broadcast speech to the public, Winston Churchill urged the British Government to send troops to Finland: 'All Scandinavia dwells brooding under Nazi and Bolshevik threats. Only Finland - superb, nay, sublime in the jaws of peril - shows what free men can do. […] They have exposed, for all the world to see, the military incapacity of the Red Army and of the Red Air Force.'
>
> The Allies pledged to send twenty thousand troops to Finland on March 12th, 1940.

We're sitting on a train that's taking us across the border into Sweden. This much I've learned from an older boy, who's sitting behind me. The train is full of children, all with tags around their necks. There's a woman in each car, who keeps telling us to be quiet and grateful. Other than that she doesn't speak much. I don't know whether it's day or night, because the windows have been painted black, so you can't see out. Once, I tried to open the window to peek out, but it was nailed shut. It's dark inside the train as well. There was an air-raid siren wailing shortly after we left, and the lights were turned off and haven't been turned on since.

Finally, the train slows down, and eventually comes to a complete halt. The woman in our compartment tells us to gather our belongings and form a single line. We're being ushered outside. It's bitter cold, but the sun is out. We're at the station in Haparanda. Or so I gather from the sign on the station building. Little Sister clutches her hand in mine, as we walk toward the station.

Inside, we're made to strip to our underwear and stand and wait. The train empties, and the station building quickly fills up. It's eerie quiet. No one dares say a word. At the far end I can see a small table and chairs behind a small screen. A man in a white lab coat sits by the table. I take him to be a doctor. One by one we file to the table. A nurse runs a tight-toothed comb through our hair. She's not being gentle. She makes Little Sister cry, because her curls are so tight, and the nurse can't run the comb through them without yanking her scalp. Three teeth break in Little Sister's curls. Behind the screen, the doctor puts a freezing stethoscope to our chest and back and asks us to breathe in and out and cough. Then he looks into our mouths. No one ever explains what all this is for. I overhear one of the nurses talking to the doctor about the scar on my cheek. I guess she assumes that I don't understand Swedish.

"It's a birthmark," I lie.

I don't know why, but I'm embarrassed by the memory of tears freezing on my skin. Big boys aren't supposed to cry, after all.

The last nurse goes through our suitcases. There's a wooden crate at her feet, and it's already half full of stuffed toys. She pries Little Sister's puppy from her fingers and tosses it into the crate. Little Sister starts wailing. Her cries echo through the station building, which is now starting to empty again, as those who've already been examined are escorted back onto the train by their chaperones.

We're told to get dressed again, collect our belongings, and wait for our chaperone. I can't make Little Sister stop crying. The doctor and the nurses seem unfazed. They all seem bored and hating their jobs. They've probably handled thousands of children, and wish they were doing something more worthwhile instead. There are no smiles among the lot of them. Very few words are spoken, mainly, I think, because they don't think we understand Swedish, which, I suppose most of the other kids here don't. Mechanically and wordlessly they go through each one of us. Hair, lungs, luggage. Stamp on the paper. Sit and wait. Next.

"I want puppy!" Little Sister screams.

I try to hug her and rock her back and forth, and even sing to her, but nothing seems to be working. Huge tears roll down her cheeks, and wet her collar. She's hiccupping now. I hug her tighter.

"It'll be alright," I whisper into her hair, not believing it myself.

How dare they? We've already lost our home, our parents, and quite possibly our country and identities as well, but now they're taking away a stuffed toy from a little girl. I hand Little Sister over to Johan, and turn to Carl.

"I'm going to get puppy back," I whisper from the corner of my mouth.

"How?" he whispers back.

"I don't know. Can you create a diversion?"

Carl looks around. "Normally I could, but nothing seems to bother these people."

"Try real hard," I say and start walking toward the screen. "Wait for my signal."

I pretend to casually be loitering about the screen. I can see puppy in the crate. It's just beyond my reach, because the nurse's chair is in the way. Now or never. I nod to Carl. He starts making heaving noises. The doctor looks up at him. Carl gets up from his chair, presses his arms to his sides, and throws up right in front of the screen. The doctor, the nurses, and some chaperones all rush to him.

I grab puppy, and swiftly slip him under my overcoat. Nobody sees me. I pretend to be big-brotherly and worried, as I look at Carl, being surrounded by adults. I nod to him again.

"All better now!" he says and we take our seats once more.

We return to the train, and we're moving again. I give puppy back to Little Sister, and she hugs and kisses him, and tucks him under her arm. She gives me one of her cherub-smiles, and I know I would've made Mother proud. She leans her head into my lap, and soon the motion of the train lulls her to sleep.

I turn to Carl. "How'd you do it? How'd you make yourself sick?"

He stifles a giggle. "I swallowed my tag string, and then yanked it right out again!"

> The majority of War Children were transported on trains with blacked-out windows through the border station between Tornio, Finland and Haparanda, Sweden. At the border crossing, the children were examined for lice and tuberculosis. If a child was found to be ill, he would be quarantined in Sweden. Sick children would not be sent back to their parents, nor

would they be eligible for foster care until
they were well. Although rare, tuberculosis
did appear among Finnish War Children and was
extremely contagious. Pneumonia and whooping
cough were more common.

Carl and Little Sister are sleeping. Johan is reading his bible in the dim light. I'm a bit bored, so I pull out my sketch pad and pencils. I start drawing everyone around me.

"That's really good," a voice behind me says. "Where did you learn to do that?"

I turn around, and see a young woman looking over my shoulder. She's probably Uncle Johannes' age and speaks with a Karelian accent. She's wearing grey slacks and a grey pull-over. Why does everyone have to wear grey all the time? On her arm she's wearing a white armband with a red cross. Her dark hair is cropped short, leaving small, almost sharp curls around her face and neck. Her eyes are intense blue, like Mother's. She has an angular look about her, with the most piercing cheekbones and twinkling eyes I've ever seen.

"Are you hungry?" she says, and now I see that she's carrying a basket of sandwiches and apples.

My stomach answers in my place. I'm ravenous. I grab four sandwiches and four apples.

"I guess that answers that," she laughs.

"For all of us," I explain. "They'll be hungry when they wake up."

"Well, aren't you a good big brother,..." she says, and reads my tag, "...Paul. I'm Natalia."

She takes a seat next to me. The apples smell really good, and I bite into mine. They're overripe and haven't been properly stored, but right now a rock would taste good. Natalia pours milk from a canteen and hands it to me. I haven't had milk since we left Karelia. I'd forgotten how good it tastes, and I drain the cup in two big gulps.

"What happened here?" she asks, pointing at my scar.

She has an air of confidence, rare for a lady her age. Maybe it's because she's wearing trousers. I don't think I've ever seen a lady wearing trousers before. Somehow I feel that I can trust her not to make fun of me, so I tell her what really happened. How I got my scar.

"That must've hurt!" she says.

I shrug. "It did, but not anymore."

"So where are you headed?" she asks and refills the cup.

I hand it to Johan. I really feel like waking up Little Sister and Carl, too, so they could have some milk, but I think I'd better not. If they can sleep, I'm going to let them. I'd welcome sleep myself. I bite into the sandwich. It's got a thick blob of butter and a slice of ham. It's delicious.

"Denmark," I say between bites. "You?"

"I'm not a War Child, if that's what you're asking. Too old, thank heavens. No, I just travel back and forth on this train, helping out where I can."

"What's a War Child?"

She laughs, and pokes a finger in my shoulder. "You are, silly!"

"What?!"

Natalia looks serious. "You don't know? How much did your mother tell you, before putting you on this train?"

"That we're going to Denmark, where we'll be safe, and we'll be back when the war is over."

"Why?"

"I'm not sure. Genocide?"

"That's a big word for a little man. Where'd you learn it?"

"Heard someone say it. I don't know what it means, though, only that Mother got really upset."

"Okay, here's how I understand it; the Soviet Army is in all likelihood going to win this war. When … I mean, *if* they do, there's a fear that Stalin will slaughter… um, kill all Finns, so to avoid certain death, the Finnish kids are being sent away. That makes you a War Child."

Her brutal honesty is shocking. "But… does that mean that Stalin will kill those who didn't leave?"

"Probably."

Mother is dead. So are new baby and Tor. Most likely Father, too. And Uncle Johannes and Ukki and Muori and all my cousins…

"But, hey! Try not to worry, okay?" Natalia says lightly. "I just heard that Norway is offering to take mothers and children, and anyway, we're in peace talks, so the war should be over any day now. Either way."

"Move along, Natalia," our car's grey chaperone urges my new friend.

Natalia winks at me. "Keep drawing, Paul. You're really talented."

I don't want her to leave. She's the first adult who's been honest with me and I want her to tell me more about the war, and what's going to happen. Maybe she'll know what we're supposed to do when we get to Denmark. Also, she's the first person whom I've seen smile or laugh in a really, really long time. It's a welcome break from all the crying, grumpy, grey people.

"Will you come see me again?" I ask anxiously, as she's starting to leave.

"You can come with me, if you like," she says. "Help me hand out sandwiches."

I want to so badly. "I can't. We're not supposed to separate."

"Good little soldier. Make your mama proud. I'll see you before the next stop." And she's gone.

Good to her word, Natalia shows up by my side when the train is pulling to a stop. Almost everyone is sleeping, and definitely Little Sister, Carl and now even Johan, so I go to the door, trying to catch a glimpse of where we are. The doors are opened from the outside, and I can see that it's pitch black. But not as cold as it has been. The cool air smells salty. I'm stretching my neck to see the station, when a hand comes up from nowhere.

"Get back on the train, and stay there," a man's voice says. He's brusque, but not as grumpy as the doctor at the border, and he speaks Swedish with a twang, but I understand him nonetheless.

I turn to Natalia. "Why have we stopped?" I'm hoping we won't have to be examined again, and in my mind I'm already getting ready to steal back Little Sister's puppy if needed.

"Some of you are getting off here," Natalia says.

The man with the voice boards the train, and shoves us backward. He moves into our car and converses with our chaperone. All but eight of us are awakened, and told to get off the train.

"Not us?"

"Not you. You're going to Denmark, and we're still in Sweden."

Craning my neck I try to peek into the station, to see what's awaiting my fellow travelers, so as better to prepare myself for what's in store for me in Denmark. A line of sleepy children, clutching their luggage, makes its way from the train to the station.

"What happens next?" I ask Natalia.

"Well, now the foster families are going to come and pick up their War Child."

"What foster families?"

She looks at me oddly. "You really weren't told anything at all, were you?" she says. "You'll live with a Danish family, and go to school in their town, and eat with them, and maybe, if they have children of their own, you'll make friends with them. Look, it's just like being at home, only it's a different family. And a different country. And a different language, I suppose, but still the same. And you don't have to worry about the war. I know it's asking a lot of you, trying to grow up pretty much overnight, but I say - be a kid! Look at this as an adventure, that's what I do."

"But you said you're not a War Child." Already I'm not liking those words.

"No, but I'm an evacuee nonetheless. And still really just a kid."

"Where are your parents?"

"Father died at the front... Mother died of childbirth when we evacuated Karelia." She shudders at the memory.

"I'm sorry."

"Thank you."

"Don't you have any other siblings?"

"I did."

"Where are they?"

"My brother is at the front and the little ones are with our Maker and the Baby Jesus."

"What happened?"

She pauses for a moment, and looks me over carefully. "I don't want to frighten you, so remember that this doesn't happen to every War Child. But being Karelian orphans, we didn't have a choice but send them away. They just left a few weeks ago, back when you still went to Sweden by boat. The boat sank." A dark shadow crosses her face.

I marvel at this girl's positive outlook. I can't imagine where she gets the strength to get up in the morning, much less smile. I couldn't imagine my life without my family.

"I'm sorry," I say again.

"Hey! I'm still here! I'm still young. This war isn't going to lick me. I'm having the time of my life."

"Riding back and forth on a train? Making sandwiches for War Children?" Yes, I definitely do *not* like those words. But the conversation I eavesdropped on a few weeks ago between Mother and those two pruny ladies finally makes sense to me.

"Got to meet you, didn't I?" she winks.

The last of the children have left the train, the doors are closed, and we're moving again.

> The peace talks continued. Foreign Minister Tanner received a communication from the Soviet leaders, by way of Stockholm, containing a precise statement of the Soviet Union's terms for peace. The terms were distressing, and utterly unacceptable to Finland. Adding to the shock was Sweden's blatant refusal to allow Allied troops, which were scheduled to appear in a matter of weeks, to pass through Sweden en route to

Finland. The Finnish public was kept in the dark
about the details of the peace talks.
Foreign volunteers continued to arrive. Finnish immigrants in the United States and Canada
returned home, and many other volunteers traveled to Finland to join its forces: hundreds of
Finnish expatriates, nearly ten thousand Scan-
dinavians, one thousand Estonians, and over
two hundred volunteers of other nationalities
made it to Finland before the war was over.
On January 31st, 1940, a ship carrying four hundred civilians to Sweden, mainly War Children,
was sunk by Soviet submarines. In the icy waters
of Bothnia, there were no survivors.

On numerous occasions the train slows down, but doesn't stop, and I can't tell why, because I can't see out. This continues for days. Finally, we stop at a station, more children are unloaded, we leave most of the cars behind, and ours is filled up with children from the others. And then we're moving again. We stop and go. It's really frustrating not to be able to see outside. I don't know what time of day it is, what day it is, or where we are, and I'm becoming more and more claustrophobic. As I'm trying to picture the map of Scandinavia in my mind, I find it hard to believe that we're not there yet.

I'm awakened by something burning my ankle. I look around in the pitch black train car, and make out the outlines of Little Sister sleeping with her head on my foot. Her ear is burning hot against my cold skin. She's pulled my sock down and my trouser leg up, and where her ear isn't touching, my skin is freezing. I don't dare move, but try to feel around to see if she's bleeding again. Luckily she isn't. I get cramped all over and am very uncomfortable, but when I move she whines softly in her sleep, so I lie perfectly still, and let her cool off her bad ear. She's really been a trooper about her ear, which I'm sure still bothers her. Sometimes she whines in her sleep, and when I ask her how she's doing she just says "I'm a big boy!" which, of course, she isn't. I pray that she'll feel better in the morning, as the steady chugging of the train lulls me back to sleep.

Natalia often comes to sit with me, and tells me stories. Her voice is soothing and she has a vivid imagination. She produces the smallest little flashlight I've ever seen, and by its light I illustrate her stories. Paper is hard to come by, so I fill one page, front and back, the same page I started on at the station in Vasa, sign it and give it to her. She says she'll cherish it forever. I think I love her.

At some point I must've fallen asleep again, because I wake up to Natalia gently shaking my arm.

"Wake up, Paul," she says. Her voice reminds me of Mother's. "We have to get off the train now."

The train has stopped. I sit up with a jerk. My heart is pounding. I feel a mixture of anxiety and anticipation growing in my chest.

"Where are we?" I look around, and everyone is being awakened, and in a mass of yawning and stretching, they start getting dressed and gathering their things. Carl is asking about breakfast.

"Come outside," Natalia whispers. "Quick!"

We're allowed to do that? I jump into my boots, grab my hat and overcoat and follow her. I can't believe I'm getting off the train! I get to see the sky. I can stretch without inadvertently kicking someone in the face. And I can breathe fresh air. This makes me just want to run, run, run until my legs fall off, and scream at nothing and everything. I feel as free and wild as the spring calves and I can't wait to see where we are.

Oddly, we're not at a station. The train has stopped on the banks of what looks like a wide river. The air is cool and fresh in the first faint rays of the rising sun. It's not nearly as cold as it has been all winter, and the air has a wonderful mixed scent of salt and thawing dirt. Of course, after days of stuffy air in a small train compartment, any air would smell sweet. I take several deep breaths, until I get a little dizzy.

Natalia turns me around and points across the water. "That's Denmark," she says.

I look at where she's pointing. In the dim morning light I can see a point stretching out in the water, and the outlines of buildings far, far away across the water in the horizon.

"How will we get there?" I ask her.

She points at a dock just below us. There sits an old iron boat. Suddenly I'm scared. I remember the old barge stuck on the beach by Farfar's house. Although, seeing how close we are to land on either side, running aground here might not be that big a deal. Now I'm excited again.

"I've got to tell the others!" I say eagerly, and turn to run back to the train.

Natalia grabs my hand. "Paul, wait," she says. "I want to give you something." She pulls out a piece of paper from her trouser pocket. "This is the address where they know how to reach me. Will you promise me you'll write?"

"You're not coming with us?"

"No. The train will turn around here, and I'll be going with it. I spoke to your Danish chaperone, and asked that she do whatever she can to keep the four of you together. I'm sorry I can't promise you anything, and I doubt the outcome of that. I don't speak Danish too well yet."

"I don't speak it at all!"

"But you speak Swedish, right? Well, it's pretty much the same thing. Just speak like you have a hot potato under your tongue, and you'll do fine. Some words are totally different, and really confusing, but you'll get the hang of it soon enough. Promise you'll write?"

I throw my arms around her waist and hug her tight. Leaving Natalia is like severing the last tie I have of home, and I just want to hold on to that sense of familiarity a bit longer.

She crouches down in front of me and takes my face in her hands. "You're about to embark on a great adventure, Paul. Make the most of it."

We're separated by a mass of bodies and with an aching heart I wonder if I'll ever see her again.

We're sitting at another train station. There are easily a hundred of us, all with our names around our necks, clutching each other, wide-eyed and silent. The boat ride across the strait was uneventful, although Carl found it fascinating, how the boat could plow its way through ice. He wants to engineer something similar for the barge back by Farfar's house. I can't imagine how, but for once, he's not thinking about his stomach.

Across the station is a group of adults milling around, trying not to stare at us, but all of them, without exception, casting glimpses at us from the corners of their eyes. I'm trying to overhear what they're murmuring about, but not only are they too quiet, and too far away, but Natalia was right about the hot potato under the tongue.

Suddenly an affluent-looking younger couple breaks away from the crowd and starts walking directly toward us. They both have fake smiles plastered on their faces. They walk up to Little Sister, and read her tag. The lady picks Little Sister up in her arms, while the man picks up her suitcase. They turn, and start walking away.

"Paul!" Little Sister screams, and reaches her arms to me. Her voice echoes through the stone station building.

Johan, Carl and I jump up as if we're on fire. I grab Little Sister, pulling her away from the lady, Johan tugs at her suitcase and Carl kicks the man in the shins. The lady won't let go, and I find myself in an odd tug-of-war.

"Let go of my sister!" I yell at her in Swedish. All thoughts of hot potatoes under my tongue are gone.

She won't let go. Little Sister is screaming. I sink my teeth into the lady's hand. She squeals and lets go. I cuddle Little Sister in my arms, and back up to the bench. My brothers join me. The three of us build a protective barrier with our bodies around Little Sister. No one would dare penetrate our fort. Even if it kills me, I will not let them take my sister.

The young couple seems flustered and confused. He's grimacing and limping. She's rubbing the back of her hand. I can see that I hadn't drawn blood, for which, frankly, I'm sorry. I wish Tor were here.

What appears to be a chaperone is summoned. She pushes Carl and Johan aside, and yanks Little Sister from my arms. The three of us are scrambling to fight again.

"These are her foster parents," the chaperone says in very poor Swedish. "Don't be difficult, or no one will pick you," she continues between clenched teeth.

But we're supposed to be together! We keep hammering our fists into the man's back. We're kicking and biting anything within reach. Two more chaperones appear. They hand Little Sister over to the lady again, and the couple starts walking out of the station carrying my little sister with them. Huge tears roll down her cheeks, and the last thing I see, before the doors close behind them, is her outstretched hand. I run after her. We must stay together! I promised Mother I would make sure we are!

Someone grabs my coat and whisks me around. "Sit down, and be quiet," the new chaperone hisses, as she shoves me back in my seat. "You should be grateful you're given this opportunity. Don't spoil it."

Hanging my head I sit down.

Everyone tells us to be grateful. I've started loathing that word. How can I be grateful? What do I possibly have to be grateful for? I'm in a foreign country, away from my own mother and my dog, and now my siblings and I are being separated. That's nothing to be grateful for.

One by one all the children at the station are picked, and among tears and screams are led away by their new foster families. A clear pattern is established. The little girls go first. Then the smallest boys. Then the rest of the girls. Except one. She's been picking her nose ever since we arrived. Well, not picking, really, more like excavating. Her straw-colored braids have come undone. Although, I can't blame her for that. After the hair check in Haparanda there was no one onboard, except Natalia and some older sisters, who could re-do the girls' hair. And we've all slept since.

Two huge men with black fingernails break away from the crowd, and scan our little group. One of them has a swollen upper lip, and brown juice running down his teeth. Even though they're clear across the station, talking to our Danish chaperone, the stench of manure wafts over to us. I know I'm not supposed to wear my hat indoors, but now I pull it down so low over my head, that it nearly covers all of my face. I wish I had been allowed to bring my Baden-Powell hat. It would've covered my face entirely. I don't want to be picked by these men. I wish I were invisible. One of them picks the biggest boy in the room, and the other one takes Johan. Stoically, Johan gets up, looks at Carl and me, nods and walks out. As always, he has accepted his fate. Carl jumps up, and starts hammering the brown juice man with his fists. Sighing, I get up, take Carl by the hand, and lead him back to the bench.

"Come on," I say and sit down.

"What's the matter with you? Are you just going to give up without a fight?"

"What's the point?" I sigh.

A red-faced man, with a huge girth and red hair starts walking toward us. He has a friendly smile and a twinkle in his eye. He is followed by a short, round woman with braids around the crown of her head, and with the same genuine smile.

"They're going to pick you," I say to Carl.

"How do you know?"

"Because you're the youngest one left."

I've never seen Carl cry. Out of the four of us, he's always been the tough one. He runs the fastest, yells the loudest and spits the farthest. He's a real boy. To my utter astonishment, when the red-faced man reaches for Carl's tag, he throws his arms around me, burrows his face in my neck and starts making odd high-pitched sounds.

"I don't want to go!" he sobs. "Don't let them take me!"

The round couple sits on the bench next to Carl, and the lady starts talking to him quietly in Danish. She smells of cinnamon and hops. Odd mixture, but very comforting. Finally, she takes Carl by the hand, and they walk out. Carl is still sobbing. His eyes never leave mine and he's waving. I wave back, fighting the lump in my throat.

I'm the last one from our family left at the station. All my siblings are gone. I don't know where. So much for us staying together. I've disappointed Mother. My eyes feel like they're about to pop out of their sockets, I'm fighting my tears so hard. Instead of tears, my nose starts running.

I look around the station. There are only six of us left, including the nose-picking girl. A new thought enters my mind. She hasn't been picked, because of her nasty habit, so I mustn't have been picked because I'm ugly. Nobody likes the look of my scar. Everyone wants chubby-cheeked little girls with blonde ringlets, or strong farm hands. I'm neither. If I make myself appear even uglier, and thinner and shorter, I won't be picked at all, and they'll have to send me back!

My plan works. Because the other four boys are picked before me, and now there's only the nose-picking girl and me left at the station. And then even she is taken away. I'm the last one here. Now, I'll just wait for Natalia to come and pick me up and take me back home. Maybe I can ride that train back and forth with her. Maybe I won't have to be a War Child, after all. What would happen if nobody picks me? Surely they can't just leave me here at the station by myself?

Nothing happens for a really long time, so I pull out my sketch pad and start drawing the inside of the station hall. It's quite ornate. People wander in and out of the station, seemingly randomly, because there are no trains coming or going. Our Danish chaperones seem to try to auction me off, but nobody is interested.

Then the door slams open, and a tall, eerily thin woman enters. She seems flustered, as she crosses the vast hall to our chaperones. Her eyes are lifeless and dull. She's dressed well, but has the air of someone who's lost. Maybe she is, and is asking for directions. I lose interest and return to drawing. Suddenly I notice two pairs of shoes pointing at me on the floor in front of me. I look up.

"Paul, this is Mrs. Mortensen, your Danish mother," our chaperone says in her broken Swedish. Her smile is too broad for comfort. "You need to be a big boy, now."

> King Gustav V of Sweden called a meeting of the Swedish Government in response to the controversy caused by the visit of Finland's foreign minister, Väinö Tanner. The King issued a statement confirming Sweden's decision not to help Finland in its struggle against the overwhelmingly superior forces of the Soviet invader. Despite the King's statement, schoolchildren in Linköping decided to publish an appeal for Sweden to help Finland and organize a collection to buy a fighter aircraft for Finland as a gift from the children of Sweden. They raised nearly a quarter million kronor.
>
> Finland's Minister of Social Affairs, K. A. Fagerholm, finally agreed that if the choice stood between accepting the help Sweden offered, mainly in terms of providing homes for evacuated children, and stand alone without help, Finland should swallow her pride and accept what little help was available.
>
> A private umbrella organization, the Finnish Centre for Nordic Aid, was founded to organize the child evacuations. In Sweden, a number of non-profit organizations merged (among them, Save the Children, the Red Cross and the Salvation Army) and founded Centrala Finlandshjälpen, consisting mainly of volunteers.

It was later argued that there was too much good
will and not enough good sense to properly organize the mass of children being evacuated.

Outside the station, Mrs. Mortensen leads me to an open-bed truck, with a man leaning against it. He's smoking. Looking reproachful, his eyes narrow as he scans me from top to bottom, and he says something to Mrs. Mortensen. All I understand is 'best you could do?' Of her reply I can discern something that sounds like 'only one left'. The smoking man shakes his head, blows out a thick plume of smoke and crushes the cigarette butt with the toe of his boot. With both hands deep in his pockets, he turns to me. His eyes narrow even further. What are they going to do to me? I remove my hat, although it's chilly outside in the wind. The man reads my tag, and then his eyes move to my suitcase. Sighing deeply, he shakes his head again. I know what he's thinking. The bag is too small to contain everything a boy my age would need. This'll be expensive for him. I'm grateful.

Mrs. Mortensen picks up my suitcase, tosses it in the bed of the truck, and without a word, they both climb in. She waves for me to follow.

In absolute silence we travel for the rest of the afternoon. The cab is crowded, with the three of us in it, and the man keeps smoking, without opening the window. I try to concentrate on the road we're traveling on, just in case I need to remember it for when I run away, but with all the smoke in the cab it's impossible to see anything through the windows. After endless days inside a blacked-out train carriage, I want to see the sky and some of the landscape, but am unable to do that properly, either.

The road turns to gravel and finally we arrive at the end of a long tree-lined lane. Darkness surrounds the lane, bordered by fields that are enclosed in stone walls, as tall as me. At the end of the lane sits a one-story whitewashed house. The long shadows of dusk cast an eerie darkness over the long drive. A cold grip clasps around my chest. I feel like I'm being taken to a prison.

As we pull up to the house, an older woman comes out of the house, wiping her hands on an apron. She's peeking into the car, and smiling broadly. This one I think I'll like. She looks like a fairy godmother, as she's surrounded by clinging rosebuds on trellises. All thoughts of prisons leave my mind. I'm barely out of the car, before I'm engulfed in her bosom.

"Oh, you poor, poor dear," the older woman says, and hugs me tightly.

Then she continues talking, but I can neither understand her, nor hear her very well, because my ears are smothered by her ample girth. When she finally lets me go, I can see that she's got tears in her eyes. Quickly, she wipes them away with her apron.

"Please call me Mor," she says, and reaches for my tag.

Extending one hand, and putting the other over my tag I introduce myself. She shakes my hand. Hers are the softest hands that've ever touched mine. Yes, I definitely like her. I wonder who she is in relation to Mrs. Mortensen and the smoking man. They're so dull, and she's so sweet. Her hair is as white as snow, and she wears it in an identical knot at the nape of her neck as Mrs. Mortensen's, but whereas Mrs. Mortensen's is so tight that it looks as though it'll pull the skin off her face, Mor's face is framed by a few loose tendrils, making her soft face appear even softer.

I haven't even noticed that she's trying to pull my tag from around my neck, until it slips from my grip. We aren't supposed to ever remove them! Oddly, though, I feel relief with the tag gone. Although it's made of cardboard, it weighs a tonne.

"You won't need this anymore, Paul," Mor says. Or that's what it sounds like. Danish is hard!

She fusses around me for awhile, and then pulls me inside the house, which smells like cooked potatoes and carrots. Instinctively, my stomach growls in response. Over my head Mor is talking to the smoking man, who also calls her Mor, so I'm guessing that he's her son. That's the only thing I understand from their conversation.

Two older boys appear from the back of the house, and are being introduced to me as Anders and Christian, the Mortensens' sons. They are carbon copies of their parents; tall, lanky and with that same glassy, lost expression in their eyes. But they're polite, and with a lot of hand gestures, they show me around the house. Silently, I'm giggling, because this scene strikes me as absurd. If they only spoke slower, I could probably understand most of what they're saying, or at a minimum get the gist of it. And I know that they would understand me, since Swedish is so much easier. Inexplicably I decide to not let them know that I speak Swedish. It's just so much more fun this way!

The culmination is when Anders, the older, probably about seventeen, shows me the water closet, and how to use it, including how to use the soap and hand towel. I feel like grabbing the towel, and hiding my face in it, to hide the roar of laughter bubbling up inside me. Somehow, I manage to keep a straight face. Yes, we do have soap and towels in Finland. Graciously, I just nod to show that I understand. They're making an effort, after all. And then they take me to what I gather is to be my room. Anders points to me, makes snoring sounds, and then points to the bed. I nod in comprehension. I. Snore. There.

The laughter that's bubbling up inside me is about to erupt, when I envision that somewhere else in Denmark Johan, Carl and Little Sister are watching a similar ridiculous pantomime show of their own.

The room is sparsely furnished, with only a bed, a chest of drawers, a desk and chair, a tiny nightstand with a lamp, and a book shelf over the desk. I recognize the names of the authors on the backs of the books, mainly Andersen, Topelius and Lagerlöf, but the titles are unknown to me. Possibly because they're in Danish. A calendar hangs on the wall underneath the shelf, and my jaw drops. It reads March 1940. I *know* it was February when we left! How long were we on that train?

> Along with Sweden, Denmark and Norway, Hungary and Switzerland offered to take evacuated Finnish War Children. The Finnish Government considered the Hungarian school system to be substandard in comparison to Finland's, and the trip to Switzerland was deemed too long and risky. The average trip to Denmark alone lasted twelve days.

BOOK 2

DENMARK

March 1940.

Anders and Christian get up very early each morning, as do their parents, to do their chores, and then they're off to school. After school, they have evening chores. The family eats supper together and then everyone except Mor goes to bed. They very rarely speak to each other, much less to me. Although, once, I heard Mrs. Mortensen ask the boys how their day had been. I think. And after their short, incomprehensible answer, she said something that sounded like 'How nice'. This seems to be her standard answer to everything, and I really don't think she heard a word they said.

They're all hard workers, have no servants and a good-size farm. There are twelve cows, two horses, at least one hundred pigs, a few dozen chickens and probably twenty geese. The geese scare me a little. They're too big for comfort, they make strange noises, and I don't really trust them. The Mortensens also have a dog. She's a beautiful old retriever named Heidi. She doesn't do much but sleep on the hearth in the kitchen. She likes me, though, and gives two slow wags of her tail every time I enter the kitchen. Which is a lot during the first week.

I follow Mor around as if I were tied to her apron strings. She's very gentle and dear, and patiently teaches me what things are called in Danish. By the second day, I've learned to say 'mange tak', which means 'thank you very much'. Which I say a lot. Not because I'm grateful because I'm told to be, but because I'm genuinely grateful. Also, I really like the way Danish feels in my throat. I can't wait to learn more.

Mor tells me I'm to go to school on Monday, and I'm nervous. We go over the numbers in Danish, so if I'm to stand up in class and recite multiplication tables, I'll feel more confident. Up to forty is really easy, but then it gets confusing. Not only do they count in thirds and halves, but it's backwards! For example; seventy-seven in Danish is seven and half of a fourth. I think, but that can't be right. I must not have understood correctly.

Nonetheless, we're having so much fun in the kitchen every day, pointing to everyday household items, such as spoons and forks, saying 'hello' and 'how are you' to invisible people, counting everything in sight, that I soon forget that this is a language lesson. Mor makes it fun. And it's not as difficult as I first thought. Although I still can't understand her when she speaks too fast, and I can't carry on a conversation about spoons and forks, but that's a minor consideration. We bake bread and make dinner. She does the dishes and I dry them. In the evenings, when everyone else has retired, we sit by the fire in the family room, and she reads to me. We're having fun, and I really like her. But - she's not Mother.

On Monday morning Anders and Christian walk me to school. I'm so nervous that my heart nearly jumps through my rib cage. I brought my knife with me, just in case there's a Harri in this school. Not that I'd ever use it, except on a Russian, if ever I were to meet one, but you just never know. If I was an outcast in my own country, how will they treat me here? Mentally I'm ready to run away.

To make matters worse, I'm given a school hat. Not an entire uniform, just a blue hat that sits on the back of my head, with a rim, that neither warms my head nor keeps the sun out. It's useless and ugly. Anders and Christian aren't wearing one, and if I knew the language better I'd question the need for mine.

Anders and Christian go to a different school, but introduce me to the short-cut through the village to my school. I've never been there yet, so I just want to look at everything. It's like a little fairy town. All the buildings are whitewashed with colorful doors and shutters. Many of them have trellises around the doors, ready for the clinging roses to green up. Mother would love it! Some even have thatch roofs. The streets are cobblestone. The two main thoroughfares meet in the center of town, and there's a small town square in front of the city hall and church, flanked by a post office, a barber shop and a bakery.

It's still just barely dawn, but the smells coming out of the bakery are mouthwatering. Although I had a big breakfast of ham, bread with strawberry jam, boiled eggs and porridge, I still have room for whatever smells so good at the baker's. I stop to look in the window. Someone is arranging a huge rack of cinnamon buns on a shelf. They're as big as his hands. He's dressed in all white, and white flour dust is stuck to his arm hairs. He's surprisingly thin, but muscular and fit, probably as a result of heaving heavy dough all day long. If I worked here, I'd have cinnamon buns for breakfast, lunch and supper. And a few times in between as well, and I'd be bigger than a horse.

It's possible that I'm drooling. The baker looks up, sees my forehead pressed to the glass, smiles and waves. I wave back. Then he does something unexpected. He wraps up one of the buns in a paper box, opens the door and hands it to me. I feel my eyes grow to the size of saucers. He smiles, and although I can see his lips move, I can neither understand nor hear a word he says. My mind is clouded by this unexpected act of kindness. Or maybe he's asking me for money. Handing the box back I turn my trouser pockets inside out. He laughs, shakes his head and jabbers on, handing me the box again. My mouth is now so full of saliva that Danish comes naturally to me.

"Mange, mange, mange tak!" I say, as I take off my silly little hat and bow. At least I can be courteous in any language.

The baker turns to go back inside, and I turn to join Anders and Christian. I fully intend to share the delicious cinnamon bun with them. They're gone. Spinning around in every direction, I can't see them anywhere. Didn't they notice I wasn't behind them anymore? Feeling slightly panicked I start running in the direction we were going. Around the corner is a street lined with absolutely identical buildings. I'm lost. I'm lost in a strange country. There's no snow on the ground, so I can't follow tracks or footprints. And even if there were, how would I know which footprints to follow? If I knew the language better, I would ask someone, because there are people on the streets, opening their businesses, starting their work week. I had so eagerly wanted to make a good first impression on my first day in this Danish school, and now I'll be late. I wish Tor were here. He'd help me find my way. Or at the very least, he'd find the way to the nearest forest, and we'd play hooky all day.

And then I see my salvation. A boy about my age, carrying books, and wearing the same silly hat as I am, walking with purpose up the street. His hair is golden blond, almost red, and he's got freckles on his nose and cheeks. He's whistling a tune I'm not familiar with, and when he spots me, he raises his hand and waves. I look around, thinking that he's waving at someone behind me.

The boy catches up with me, and says "You're the new … Finnish boy … coming to our CLASS!" He talks really slowly and loudly, as if were deaf and dumb, not just new to the language.

I nod. "Paul," I say.

"I … AM … JENS!" He's even louder now.

I open the baker's box, and offer him half. After all, the way to true friendship goes through the stomach. I think I've heard a saying like that once.

"MAN … GE … TAK!!" Jens enunciates every syllable.

Maybe he always talks like this, and isn't doing it just for my benefit.

I know the Danish word for 'you're welcome', but am reluctant to use it, because to me it sounds like 'where's the cow?'. So I just nod again. We stand in the street, savoring our treats in an awkward silence.

Jens licks his fingers and says "Good," when he suddenly perks up, grabs me by the wrist, and starts running up the street, dragging me along. He keeps jabbering very fast and excitedly, so I know the slow and loud Danish had indeed been for my benefit. In the distance I can hear a faint bell ringing. Like a small church bell.

Arriving at the school, red-faced and panting, we're greeted by four women. One of them is perfectly round. She's as wide as she's tall. All four women greet each student by name as they rush by, all of them quickly nicking a curtsy or bow as they pass. As Jens and I run up the steps, and come to face the round woman, I notice that she's barely a head taller than me. She crosses her hands in front of her, but her fingers only just touch.

"Good Morning, Jens!" she says. "Good Morning, Paul!"

Instinctively I look down to see if I'm tagged again. I'm not. How does she know my name?

"We've all been looking forward to meeting you, our very own Finnebarn," she says. "Welcome! We're so glad you're here." She speaks slowly, and I understand her, but am unable to form a response.

"Mange tak?" I offer.

A huge smile spreads across her face. Her teeth are enormous, perfectly straight and shiny white. Her eyes get small crinkles around their corners when she smiles, and she looks like a genuinely nice person. She ushers Jens inside, and puts a hand on my shoulder.

"You'll be in my class," she says, and I can see that there are only four classrooms in this school. "My students call me Kjersti. Today, I just want you to sit and listen and learn the language. When you're more comfortable you can start participating. I'm told that you speak Swedish. Do you understand what I'm saying?"

I nod. I like her. I know I'm going to like this school. She leads me to an empty desk in the back corner of her classroom and hands me a note pad and a pencil.

"Make notes of questions," she says.

I must have misunderstood her, because that makes no sense.

In six months, I've gone from a big school, with a strictly conservative and boring teacher, to a small school with a teacher that hits kids, to medium sized school with a teacher who's your friend. I'm reminded of the story of Goldilocks. This one seems just right.

In awe, I watch my fellow classmates engage in conversation with Kjersti as soon as the class starts. From the few words that I do understand, and based on the posters on the walls that she keeps pointing to, I gather that this is a biology class. What's even more amazing is that the students ask her questions, and she answers! This isn't school; it's more like tea time with friends. I can't wait until I've learned more of the language, so that I can engage in the conversation.

Biology is followed by math. Kjersti announces that we're going to do multiplication tables, and inside me I smile smugly. I knew it! Different teacher, different school, different country and language, yet some things stay the same. To my utter astonishment, the entire class erupts in cheers. Either these kids are really strange, or I didn't understand Kjersti correctly. Surely nobody can be happy about math? What's even more astounding is that they start moving desks and chairs to line up against the walls, leaving the center of the classroom bare. I sink deeper into my seat in the corner.

"Can Paul come and play?" Jens asks.

Play? In school? During math? Kjersti cocks her head at me, and her smile welcomes me to join in. The other children have formed a circle in the middle of the floor. Shyly, I take a spot next to Jens.

"Do you know Danish numbers?" Kjersti asks, making it sound like they are people I should be personally acquainted with.

I quietly shake my head, no. She picks up a brown leather ball, the size of an apple, from behind her desk.

"That's all right. Nobody throw to Paul just yet. Listen and learn. Two times seven is…" she tosses the ball to a girl in a yellow plaid dress.

This town is so colorful. I'm so glad to see colors other than brown, blue, black and grey.

"Fourteen!" the girl says. "Six times three is…" she continues and tosses the ball to another girl.

"Eighteen!"

And so the game goes. It looks like fun, and I want to play. I poke Jens in the ribs, and when he looks at me, I turn my thumb towards myself. He nods. He knows what I mean.

"Four and twenty!" Jens catches the ball. "Aaaand… five times five is…" and hands me the ball.

"Five and twenty!" I'm part of the game! There'll be no stopping me now. "Nine times eight is…"

This is a fun game, and you stay in the ring until you get it wrong. Ultimately there'll be just one winner. Or, time runs out. Apparently Jens is really good at this, because everybody keeps throwing the ball to him, at an exhilarating speed. He catches it again.

"Thirty! Someone give me a challenge," he jokes. "Six times nine is…" he hands me the ball.

My mind is racing. Fifty-four. Fifty in Danish is … something half of a third by ten … I look around the circle and eleven excited faces look back. Kjersti keeps nodding and smiling.

"Say it in Swedish, Paul. We'll all learn something," she encourages me.

"Fifty-four," I say. But I want to say it in Danish! "Four and half thirds?"

My pronunciation is horrible even to me, but nobody laughs at me. They all smile and nod. I can hear someone trying out 'fifty-four' in Swedish.

Too soon time has run out, and very quickly and quietly the desks and chairs are moved back to their original spots. Kjersti hands us math problems to solve on paper. She asks me if I want to participate. I can't believe I'm even thinking this, but yes! Absolutely! I want to participate! I want to be part of things! I want to belong, even if involvement includes math! To my utter astonishment I realize that I'm the first one done with my problems. Of course, numbers look the same in any language.

Two more classes follow, involving group discussion, and very quickly I'm lost again, so I start sketching on my notepad. Before my brain registers what my hand is doing, I've drawn our house in Karelia. My house that Father designed, and built himself, the only place I've known to call home and that burned to a pile of ashes. The last day we were all together as a family. I hate this war. I hate what it's done to us. Although today has been a good day, I'd still rather be home, and not having had this experience.

The day ends with Danish class, and I'm given a tattered copy of Hans Christian Andersen's 'The Ugly Duckling'. I lower my head over the text and try to follow along, as someone in the class is reading aloud. Unfortunately, they read far too fast. I'm never asked to read aloud, which is good, because I couldn't even if I tried. I can't see the words in front of me. My eyes are clouding up. Having both read it in Finnish and heard it read to me in Swedish, I'm familiar with the story, but this is the first time I understand the meaning of it. *I'm* the ugly duckling. I've tried so hard to belong, but I never have since we left home.

Kjersti issues homework, dismisses class, and everyone rushes out. I'm gathering my books and pencils, when she comes to me and sits backwards in the chair in front of my desk. She smiles and says something. I recognize that it's a question, but I don't understand the words. There's a 'what' in there somewhere. She waves her arms around the room, and then points them at me.

"What ... do ... you ... think?" she says, very slowly.

She's asking me what I think of the school. Or possibly her teaching method. Or all my crazy classmates. Not being able to communicate is unbelievably frustrating! I want to hug her and tell her she's the best teacher I've ever had! I want to ask if she'll come home with me and marry my Uncle Johannes! I want to tell her she's beautiful and funny and ... Instead, all I can do is nod. Then I hold up a hand and ask her for a moment. I pull out my notepad, and with one arm covering it, so she can't see what I'm doing, I start drawing a rose. I turn the pad around, point to the rose, and then to her.

"This is for me? You're amazing! Thank you!"

Unfortunately, she misunderstood me. I wanted to tell her that she *is* the rose. Now I can't even communicate with pictures anymore. I write the number ten on the notepad, and point to her. If possible, her smile widens even more. She understands. Numbers are indeed a universal language. It's time for me to start paying attention in math class, I think.

Kjersti walks away with my notepad, and starts thumbing through it. She gave it to me only this morning to make notes of questions, and it's already nearly full of drawings and sketches. She looks at them with her back turned to me, so I can't read her face. Then she scribbles something on a small pad of her own. She turns around, hands me back my notepad, folds the note she had scribbled, and hands it to me.

"Give to Mor Mortensen," she says. Slowly.

I'm scared. "What I'm do?" The Danish is terrible, the grammar is wrong, and the pronunciation is off, but she understands me.

"Oh, dear child," she laughs. "I'm not sending you home with a note! Well, actually I am, but not the kind you're thinking of. No, I lead an arts league in town, and I'd like Mor Mortensen to take you to one of our classes soon. Yours is a talent I've rarely seen in a seven year-old."

She keeps talking, but I've stopped understanding. Or listening, to be perfectly honest. An arts class! Wouldn't that be wonderful? I haven't had one since Uncle Johannes. After a while, she cocks her head again.

"What do you say?" she asks.

"I'm quarter of eight," I say, feeling foolish. What I wanted to say was that I'm nearly eight, but couldn't find the words.

"Of course you are," she laughs and ushers me out the door. "See you tomorrow!" she hollers after me, but I'm already gone.

I run down the steps, down the street, trying to remember the shortcut through town. I wave at the baker, who's closing his shop.

"Where's the fire?" he jokingly shouts after me.

Without turning around I reply in Swedish "I'm on my way to becoming a world famous artist, and I've got to tell everyone!"

Spring is springing up all around me. Microscopic green buds are budding, tiny enough that you'll have to really want to see them to actually see them. And I do want to, but not just now. I'm on a mission. I round the corner, already picturing Mother's face when I tell her the news. And then it hits me, as if I'd run into a brick wall. I slow down to a trot, then a jog, then to nothing. The sun is low in the west, the direction I'm headed. I turn around, and stare at the bright red clouds in the east reflecting the setting sun. I stand still, and look at the note in my hand. The biggest news of my life and Mother won't be here to hear it.

On March 6th, 1940, the Soviet Union announced its readiness to open talks with Finland, but would not agree to a ceasefire until the talks were actually underway. The following evening, the Finnish delegation under the leadership of Prime Minister Risto Ryti left for Moscow. The other members of the delegation were political advisor J. K. Paasikivi, Representative Rudolf Walden, and Senator Väinö Voionmaa. The Soviet delegation was comprised of Molotov, Andrei Zhdanov and General Vasilevski. Stalin's absence was symbolic of his contempt for the Finns.

On March 9th, the Finnish Government convened to consider the telegrams sent by the delegation at the peace talks in Moscow. The assembled ministers were shocked by the proposed loss of access to Lake Ladoga and the cession of the district of Salla in Lapland. The Government relied on an assessment of the situation prepared by the commander of the Army of the Isthmus, whose pessimistic evaluation forced Marshal Mannerheim to conclude that there was no alternative but to accept the Soviet Union's peace terms.

Neither the Army nor the civilian population were let in on the details of the peace talks. The fighting continued in spite of the Soviets' promise of a ceasefire during negotiations. Despite heavy losses in manpower, materiel and supplies, the Finns continued to hold the line, and by midnight on March 9th, the entire main defensive line was once again in Finnish hands.

Mannerheim kept urging the Government to consider the offer of assistance by the UK and France.

The child evacuations continued.

Mor is such a darling person. She devotes all her time to teaching me Danish. I feel like a parrot, because Mor has me repeating, repeating, and repeating everything until she feels I get it close to correct. We read everything at hand, from books to old newspapers, and she corrects my pronunciation more than my grammar. And she's so intelligent. She has an answer for everything, regardless of how difficult my question. And - I hate to admit this - but even though I miss my siblings, it's nice to have the undivided attention of an adult. It's almost as if I were an only child, as much time as Mor devotes to me.

Soon I'm much more confident in understanding both spoken and written Danish, but stumble in writing and speaking. She helps me with homework, and for the first time in my life, I've found that math is actually quite fun. It's like Uncle Johannes said; everything in life is math. I think I might want to become a math teacher when I grow up, rather than a world famous artist.

Saturday morning is sunny and beautiful, so Mor and I are sitting on the bench outside the house, letting the warm sun wash over our faces. Heidi, the retriever, is snoozing at our feet. The roses climbing up the trellises are screaming to bud, and with a few more days like today, they probably will.

I'm reading aloud. This time it's a book about pirates, and I think I want to become a pirate when I grow up. The book is really good and exciting, but full of new and difficult words. Mor leans back and closes her eyes. She looks like she may have drifted off to sleep.

"Dee turbulence weathers crushed and fommed again dee hulk of dee shop, making…"

"The turbulent waters crashed and foamed against the hull of the ship," Mor corrects me. "Just because my eyes are closed, doesn't mean that my ears are, Paul. I've heard you read much better than that, so I know you can do it. Read it again. No cheating."

Heidi lifts up her head and sniffs the air. My eyes are already focused on a shape running toward us along the long lane. It's Jens. If Tor had been here, he'd already be halfway down the lane, before we even knew what was going on. In the last week Jens and I have become really good friends. He slowed down his speech, and doesn't yell anymore, and also corrects me without making fun of me. Not that anyone does.

He approaches with a wide grin, takes off his cap and bows quickly for Mor.

"Good day, Mor Mortensen," he says. "Baker Sørensen is making ice. I've got enough money for two. May Paul go with me?"

To buy ice? Whatever for? You go to the nearest frozen lake with two strong fellas and a bucksaw, and haul back as much ice as your sleigh can carry. For free. And then you chip away from that ice all summer long. Why would you go to the baker's and pay for it? And how does one *make* ice anyway?

"He says he's putting in coffee today," Jens continues, smacking his lips. "I've never had it with coffee before, but it sounds delicious!"

Iced coffee? Sounds disgusting to me. But then, Danish red wieners look repellent, yet taste delicious, so who am I to judge? Not to mention the smell of Danish cheeses that turn out to taste nothing like feet. Seems like Danes can make a delicacy out of the strangest ingredients.

"Have you ever had ice, Paul?" Mor asks me, waking me from my reverie.

"To eat? No. To make food not rot. Yes."

Jens roars with laughter, and Mor's eyes twinkle.

"So that'd be no, you haven't had ice. Baker Sørensen churns frozen cream, and flavors it with sugar and berries. And coffee, apparently today. The children love it. I've had it once, with strawberries, and it truly was delicious, but it's too cold. It hurts my teeth. You boys run along, and have fun," she says and leans back, turning her face to the sun again. "Be back in time for supper!"

The ice is the best thing I ever tasted in my life! It only cost ten øre for a fist-sized serving, and I just know that I'll have to find a way to make money, for apparently Baker makes it every Saturday. Jens and I sit on the stone wall bordering the town square, slowly enjoying our treats. Mine is gone dreadfully quickly.

The square is busy. It's market day, and the local farmers have shown up to sell their fare. I see Anders and Christian selling eggs, and wave at them. They nod in acknowledgement, their expressions unchanged.

People pass us, and Jens greets all of them. Many by name. Every now and then someone stops and talks to him, and he introduces me. He doesn't tag me, which I appreciate. He just says 'this is my friend Paul'. It's a small town, and by the time Jens has finished his ice, I think I've met everyone in it.

"Small village? You acquaint every someone?" I ask.

"Naaah, I don't know *every*one. They're just curious about you. Very little happens here except the fair in April, so until then, you're the local attraction," Jens shrugs.

After only a week of parrot-like Danish classes, my Danish is still terrible, but I can discern one thing of interest in what Jens just jabbered.

"What is fair?"

He looks at me as if I had turned green. I'm expecting him to mock and ridicule my ignorance. He doesn't.

"The fair is where they serve food and ice and lemonade and have rides that go round and round, and an enormous Ferris wheel and carousels and you drive cars that you're allowed to crash, and they have these weird people in cages…"

"Who is weird people?"

"You know; women with beards or two people who are joined together or kids born with three eyes or…"

Three eyes. "So I the weird people because I scar?" My heart drops.

I had thought this town was so … quaint… And everyone was so pleasant and happy and colorful and friendly, but it's only because they think I'm a freak. The local attraction. My throat starts to close up.

"Nononono! You're the local attraction, because you're exotic. You know, you've seen a war! Finnebørn have already traveled around the world! Whenever you're ready to tell your story, the entire town will listen. And that scar of yours is barely visible," Jens shrugs again. "What is it, anyway?"

In the absence of my siblings, Jens is my new best friend, so I tell him the real, true story.

"But if anysome asks, I'm said it a birthing mark."

"You want to see a birthmark?" Jens whispers, turns his back to me and lifts up his shirt. The pale, freckled skin of his back surrounds an aubergine-colored bulls-eye, just to the right of his spine. "*This* is a birthmark!"

I make it back well before supper. The kitchen is filled with the delicious smells of baked ham and potatoes. Mor asks me to read the paper aloud for her while she sets the table. My eyes immediately spot a familiar word. Finnebørn. Finnish War Children. It sounds so much cuter and cuddlier in Danish.

"Mor! Here is story with War Children!"

"Read it."

"Hungry and tired, nearly one hundred Finnebørn … something… the train in Copenhagen yesterday morning," I start. "That not true! We eated and sleeped on dee train. We scared and stiff and just want run and go home," I catch my breath. I hadn't meant to offend Mor.

"Keep reading," she says.

"This trainload … something … three-hundred child mark … Three hundred, Mor! … of Finnish children evacuated to Denmark, since dee … What is word, Mor?"

"Unprovoked attack."

"Since dee unprovoked attack by Soviet Russia on Finland. Our cousin to dee east, Sweden, has already offered foster homes to several thou-thous-thousands of children… Thousands, Mor! … dee majority of whom have already lost their Karelian homes, and possibly their fathers fighting at dee front…" I can't keep reading, but I force myself to. "Many more families are in dire need of help, and …something cit… cit-i-zz citizens!… are urged to open their homes to foster a Finnebarn, or … something, can't read that … Finnish War Fund. The aftermath of this war is … pp-pr-pprro…can't read that … nothing short of nasty, and as long as dee Government refuses to offer assistance in dee form of troops, dee least we can do in dee spirit of Nordic … so-li-da…solidarity, is to take in our little brothers in need."

The article goes on, but I can't continue reading. My eyes fall on a picture from inside a train station. Could've been any train station, but I believe it's the same one we came through. The picture shows a line of children, all of them tagged. The article really depresses me. Not only does it make me believe that the war will not end well, that Father may be dead, and that if more children are being sent over, there's no telling when I'll be going back home. If ever.

Mor changes the subject and starts talking about my first arts class on Sunday. I reply to her in simple nods and hums, as I help her finish setting the table. I wonder how my siblings are doing. Did they read that same article? I also wonder if there's any way to find them, to find out where they ended up, so that I can send them a letter. How much news is Mother getting these days? Is she counting the days until we're together again, or has she given up? How many more children can there be left in Finland, if thousands are already in Sweden and Denmark? Has the new baby been sent away too? Did she ever get a proper name?

We sit down for supper. I've lost my appetite, and just stare at my plate. Will I ever go home? Will any of us ever see Mother again?

"Eat up, Paul!" Mor says cheerfully. "There are children starving in Finland."

"No there are not! We all here!" I don't mean to be disrespectful, but the words find their way across my lips before I can stop them.

I rush from the table and run into my room, throwing myself on top of the bed. My sobs shake my entire body, and I'm helpless to stop them. Big boys *do* cry.

I must've cried myself to sleep, for when I wake up, it's dark outside and the house is quiet. The only sound I hear is Mor's rocking chair, quietly creaking against the floorboards. I go to her to apologize for my behavior and must keep swallowing hard to fight back a new onset of tears. This time, they'd be tears of shame. Mor is so sweet and wonderful, and I acted like an ungrateful baby. Silently she picks me up in her arms and just rocks me. Neither of us says anything for a long time.

Finally Mor takes my face in her hand and looks me in the eye. "I understand that you're upset, Paul. Or angry or frightened or sad or homesick. What you need is an outlet. Won't you talk to me?"

She's right. I'm all those things. Angry and sad and frightened *and* homesick. But most of all I'm confused and uncertain, and that upsets and frightens me even more. Although I like this place, it's not home. I love Heidi, but she's not Tor. I love Mor, but she's not Mother. They don't know that I like angel kisses. They don't know that I like spicy mustard on *every*thing. They don't know how special I feel when Mother calls me her 'treasured son'. How could they? Only Mother knows that.

And what frightens me even further is that as soon as the war is over, I'll be going home, and I'll have to say goodbye to all my new friends. But I can't tell Mor any of that. Even if I had the words, I lack the courage.

Holding me close, Mor rocks me to sleep.

After a hundred and four days of continuous heavy fighting, the Finnish troops were suffering from battle fatigue, but Stalin's plans of a quick occupation seemed lost, as the Finns held the line. In a last effort, Stalin sent reinforcements to the Isthmus. The situation in the Bay of Viborg worsened as the Soviet forces kept funneling new troops and equipment into the area in an attempt to extend their bridgehead on the western side of the bay. The Russians had hoped to use this beachhead in enemy territory to get around to the west of Viborg and cut off the Finnish defenders from their vital supply lines, and eventually to occupy this geographically and economically strategic city.

The Finnish and Soviet negotiators met for a second round of talks in the Kremlin. The Finns were in an awkward negotiating position, knowing full well the negative assessment of the situation at the front, and because all communication between them and the Finnish Government had to be conducted through Stockholm, with telegrams often taking several hours to reach their destination. Nonetheless, the Finnish negotiators tried to haggle over the Soviet terms, in an effort to buy time, as the arrival date set by the Allies was getting within reach.

The British troops, scheduled to arrive in Finland on March 12th, 1940, were planning to land at Narvik in Norway, the main port for Swedish iron ore exports, and then to take control of the Malmbanan railway line from Narvik to Luleå in Sweden on the shore of the Gulf of Bothnia. Conveniently, this plan also would allow the Allied forces to occupy the Swedish iron ore mining district, a plan they knew would disrupt a vital source of raw materials for Hitler's war machine.

It's still dark outside, when I wake up to someone hammering on my door. Christian enters, looking flustered and disheveled. He speaks very quickly and excitedly, and all I understand is "…you have to go…".

I shake the last bits of sleep from my head and jump out of bed. The floor is cold under my bare feet.

"Dee Reds are coming?" I ask, thinking that the Russians have invaded Denmark.

Christian keeps jabbering, and tossing my clothes at me. I have to ask him to slow down and repeat three times, before I understand the emergency. As it turns out, one of the cows is calving. There are complications, and I have to go find the veterinarian. While I get dressed, Christian describes the route in great detail. I'm to take the main road, turn right by the old oak that got struck by lightning, go past old Hansen's barn, and if I see the fort I've gone too far. Like that helps. But he keeps pointing due west, so I guess I'll be headed that way.

The idea of a fort intrigues me. Is it occupied or empty? Is it haunted? Does it have a cellar with a prison and chains? And a moat? I make a mental note to myself to ask Jens about it. Maybe we can go and explore it one day.

I wish the Mortensens had a phone. Although, what good would it do if the veterinarian doesn't have one?

Christian goes on to explain that his bicycle is waiting out in the courtyard, and do I know how to ride one? He must think I was born under a rock or something, but I don't want to be rude, so I assure him that I can, and I'm off.

The night air is chilly, making my eyes sting and my hands freeze to the handle bars, but it feels wonderful to be pedaling down the road. I never realized how flat the landscape was. Dawn is slowly rising behind me, and I see a huge old oak by a fork in the road. The oak is split in two, but still alive, and I assume I'm to turn right here. Before I know it, I'm at what seems like the outskirts of another town. People are getting up, going to tend to their chores. Cows are mooing, needing to be milked.

Just before the town gates, I spot a small white sign. 'Drs. Jørgensen og Nielsen, Veterinær'. I cannot believe my luck! Pedaling as fast as I can up the short drive, I realize that I've forgotten the vet's name. Did Christian ever even mention it? I don't think he did. Does it matter? Surely either one can help. There's nothing to birthing a calf; I've seen it done many, many times myself. Once, Renki had to stick his entire arm up the cow's butt, and pull the calf out, because it was turned the wrong way. The cow didn't mind Renki's arm up her butt.

There's a light on inside the house, and a very young-looking man answers my knock. He doesn't look like any doctor I've ever seen. He's wearing black trousers and a plaid shirt, and his hair is disheveled, as if he just got out of bed.

One hand is holding a steaming cup of coffee, and the other pats the head of a dog, the size of a pony.

"Hello, puppy!" I say in Swedish.

The dog is so big, that when it wags its tail it sends a whiplash into the buttocks of the man with the coffee.

Before I know it, the dog's enormous tongue drenches my face, and convulsing in giggles, we're wrestling on the front steps.

"Heel!" the man with the coffee says, and obediently the enormous dog takes his place next to his master. "How may I help you?" he asks me, smiling.

Petting the dog behind his ears, I explain the situation. My grammar is off, and my pronunciation is even worse, but he gets my urgency. Shouting something about the Mortensens over his shoulder, he grabs a black leather bag, and before closing the door behind us, he turns to the dog, who hasn't moved since he was told to heel.

"Back to the hearth," he says, and the dog leaves us without protest.

"What is name?" I say as we walk to his truck and he loads Christian's bicycle in the back.

The vet misunderstands me, thinking I'm talking about the dog.

"Lillen," he says. "Eighteen months old, and as crazy as they come," he laughs quietly.

The dog seems very friendly and well-trained to me. Not crazy at all. Not like Tor anyway.

"Mine dog name Tor," I say. "Much crazy, too. Very like food. Mine bestest friend."

While driving, we talk about all the animals on our farm back home and he asks me if I've ever seen a calf being born. I tell him in as much detail as I can. He asks me to assist him.

It's still dark, although the first rays of dawn are inching across the cloudless sky. Everyone is inside the barn, where a circle of lamps is lit in the stall with the birthing cow. Never having been inside the barn yet, I'm astonished by how neat and orderly it is. Back home, Renki used to keep all his staff in the fear of God to keep the barn immaculate. He'd approve of the Mortensens' barn. No wonder they're always tired, the walls look scrubbed. Recently and a lot.

The barn is very quiet. Christian and Mrs. Mortensen are already milking the other cows, but Anders is sitting on the floor of the stall, with the cow's head in his lap. He's stroking her head and murmuring assuring words to her. As it turns out, this is his cow. There's a fair amount of blood on the floor. The cow is still alive, because I can see her eyes move toward us when we approach. The vet gets all the details from Mr. Mortensen, and they talk quietly for a while. When they break up, everyone becomes all activity. Soap, water and towels are produced, the vet washes up, fresh hay appears, and out of nowhere a bunch of medical tools materialize. I know they're really called instruments, but they remind me more of tools. Like something you'd shoe a horse with. Maybe I brought the wrong doctor.

The vet puts a stethoscope to the cow's belly and listens intently. Mr. Mortensen is holding the cow's legs down. He exchanges a few more technical terms, none of which I understand, with Mr. Mortensen and Anders, and then he sticks his arm inside the cow.

"Be ready with the knife," he tells me, up to his elbow inside the cow.

Is he going to kill the calf? Not with my knife, he isn't. Protectively I clutch my fingers around it. The cow lets out a guttural sound, like someone trying to suppress a belch. I look over at Anders, who's still murmuring to her. He's got worry written all over his face.

The vet is now up to his shoulder inside the cow, whose eye whites are shining inside the dimly lit barn. He reaches deeper, seems to be rummaging around, and turns his head to me.

"The knife! Now!"

I don't want to be part of this, but my body doesn't listen to my brain or heart, and I hunch down, with the knife at the ready. The vet pulls out his arm. In his fist is a long, thick, slimy, spongy, snake-looking thing. The umbilical cord. Of course. I've seen this before. Quickly I slash it, and before we know it, the calf is out. Everyone draws a simultaneous sigh of relief, including the cow. Anders is in such a shock, that he starts laughing, and hugs the cow, who's trying to get to her newborn. The sun has risen and bathes the weak little calf in light.

The vet continues to jabber medicine to Mr. Mortensen and Anders, and they talk over my head. Literally and figuratively. I don't care. I'm just glad the calf and the cow are alright.

After the vet is done washing his hands, and I've cleaned off my knife, he thanks me for my assistance.

"Do you know?" he continues. "There's a Finnebarn in our town. A boy, about your age, I'd say," he says, as if this was a big revelation. There are Finnebørn everywhere but Finland. "Anyway, good job with the knife. Thanks again for your help."

I'm about to tell him that I want to become a veterinarian when I grow up, but Mor interrupts me.

"Paul, you'll be late for school! Quickly, go get washed up and dressed and run along. You can stop at Baker Sørensen's for breakfast. There's no time to cook and eat anything," she says and presses a few coins into my palm.

As I arrive at the baker's, the doors are locked, and I find a note pasted on the door. 'Over at Barber's', it reads. My stomach is starting to growl, and I'm tired, but I don't want to be late for school, so I turn around and look for Jens. Since the second day at school, we've always met in the town square and walked together the rest of the way. But today, I can't see him anywhere. There's a huge group of people milling around the barbershop, all craning their necks, trying to see inside. Wonder what's going on? And then I see Jens elbowing his way through the throng of men. He spots me, and starts running across the square. His huge smile covers half his face.

"You've got to hear this!" he says, and pulls me with him toward the barber's.

We wedge our way between the bodies blocking the entrance.

"What is it?" I whisper.

Jens shushes me. A couple of the adults spot me, and they part way, many of them patting me on the shoulder. Everyone's smiling. The barber has one of the very few radios in town, and right now it's cranked up to full volume. A man's voice comes over a raspy reception. He speaks in broken Finnish.

"Soldiers of the glorious Finnish Army! Peace has been concluded between Finland and Soviet Russia, a harsh peace in which Soviet Russia has been ceded nearly every battlefield on which you have shed your blood on behalf of everything we hold sacred and dear," the voice says.

"What's he saying?" Jens whispers excitedly.

"Peace," I let out in a breath.

The voice continues. "You did not want war; you loved peace, work and progress; but you were forced into a struggle in which you have achieved great deeds, deeds that will shine for centuries in the annals of history."

Then the Danish radio announcer comes on and translates the speech. "That was Marshal Mannerheim, speaking to his troops, after the news of the Moscow Peace Treaty…"

I've stopped listening. Everyone around me, whether I know them or not, is patting me on the back, shaking my hand, hoisting me in the air. Peace! The war is over! I wedge my way out of the barber's, and start running back toward the Mortensens'.

"Where are you going?" Jens shouts after me.

"Home!"

"Come back later! Baker says he'll make ice to celebrate!" Jens shouts even louder.

"I not here later!"

I run as fast as I can. In fact, I'm running so fast that I can taste blood in my mouth. Somewhere, my hat blows off, and I have to return to collect it, and then I'm running again. The war is over! I'm going home! Today! Mother is going to come and pick me up. Father will be there too! The war is over!

A question lurks in the back of my mind and crystallizes with a startling suddenness … Who won? Mannerheim called our troops 'glorious'. As in victorious? He also said 'harsh peace' and 'cede', which I don't understand, but he said 'peace' *three* times, there's no mistake about that! I'm going home!

As I reach the Mortensens', I find Mor at the kitchen table, sipping coffee from a saucer and reading the morning paper. She looks up when I come crashing through the door.

"What in the world, child? Why aren't you in school? Are you ill?"

"War is end!" I'm panting. "Peace."

"I was just reading that myself," Mor says. "Yesterday at noon, the citizens of the independent republic of Finland received the details of the peace treaty…" Mor starts reading.

I give her a quick hug and then rush to my room. I don't have time to read the paper just now, and besides I already know the news, anyway. If only that calf hadn't been born this morning, I would've read the paper at breakfast, and known about it sooner. But I shouldn't blame it on the calf. It wasn't her fault that she chose this day to be born. And besides, that was really exciting. What a day! And it's still just early morning!

I change into my good travel clothes, although they may be a bit too warm, and pack the rest of my clothes into my suitcase. With suitcase in one hand, and my cap in the other, I go back to Mor. I extend my hand.

"Mange tak og farvel," I say.

I know I should be sad to be leaving, but I can't help but smile. I'm so happy to be going home!

A shadow passes over Mor's face. "Where do you think you're going?"

"Home," I say, put my cap on, and exit the house.

The morning sun is quite high already, as I take a seat on the front step. From this spot I have a perfect view of the lane. I'll be able to spot Mother the moment she walks up.

Time passes slowly. The sun is now beating on me, and I have to remove my hat and overcoat, because I'm too hot. The noon sun also beats on the rose buds climbing along the trellises around the front door. Hoping that Mother will be here while it's still daylight, so she can witness the potential beauty of these flowers, that aren't even in bloom yet, I'm mentally willing her to hurry up. She wouldn't want to miss this.

There's no sign of Mother. I wonder if she came by this morning, while I was away. I hope I didn't miss her. Surely she'll come back to get me?

I keep willing her to come. If I don't blink, while counting to one hundred, she's the next one rounding the corner. That doesn't work. If I hold my breath, while counting to one hundred, hers will be the next voice I hear. That doesn't work either. I only get as far as forty, and I get dizzy. I pin my eyes to the end of the lane, for I could swear something is moving. It turns out to be a leaf blowing in the breeze.

Hours pass. No sign of Mother. Every now and then I can see Mor through the corner of my eye. She's checking up on me through the open kitchen window. I hope she doesn't worry about me, or think me impolite.

Maybe we're being picked up in the order we were picked at the station. Which means I'll be last. My back is aching, and I feel the need to move. Walking in circles around the courtyard, I never let my eyes leave the lane. Occasionally a car drives by. Nobody makes the turn.

I start walking up and down the lane. Returning to the house, I walk backwards, never taking my eyes off the main road. There's a plate with a sandwich, an apple and a glass of milk on the bench outside the house when I return to take a seat. Ravenously I bite into the sandwich. Mother will be here by the time I've finished.

She couldn't have forgotten me? The sandwich lodges itself in my throat, when that thought enters my mind. I distinctly remember her saying that as soon as the war is over, we'd be going home. Unfortunately, I also remember her being unable to make that promise when prompted... Pushing that thought out of my head, I won't allow myself to think that. Mother loves me and she's coming to get me. Today. The war is over and I'm going home.

The sun is setting and I'm still sitting outside on the front step. The Mortensens pass me going to the barn, and Mrs. Mortensen asks me what I'm up to.

"War is end. I travel home," I say.

"How nice," she murmurs, and keeps walking.

And then I see her! See them, actually. The shape of a woman, dressed in a heavy overcoat, holding hands with a boy, who nearly comes to her shoulder, approaches along the lane in the long shadows of the setting sun. It's Mother and Johan! How he must've grown. I grab my suitcase, my hat and overcoat and start running toward them. They wave. I wave back. And then they step into the sun.

It's not Mother. What I thought was a tall, thin woman in a heavy overcoat, was in fact, a short heavy woman in a thin overcoat. It's Kjersti and Jens. My heart sinks, and my eyes sting.

"Where were you today?" Kjersti asks. She's short of breath. "We missed you in class. Are you alright?"

"Are you running away?" Jens whispers, eyes gleaming with excitement.

"War is end," I say. "I travel home."

"You *go* home," Kjersti corrects me.

"Don't you like it here?" Jens asks, voice breaking.

"Yes, but…"

How can I explain that I miss my mother? That I want to be held by her again. That I want to be called her treasured son. That all I *really* want is to just hear her voice.

"War is end. I must go home," I insist.

"But you just got here!" Jens argues. "I don't want you to go!"

Kjersti puts an arm around each of our shoulders, and we start walking back toward the Mortensens' house. My feet feel leaden. Heavier with each step.

"They didn't tell me much, when they said we'd get a Finnebarn," Kjersti says. "Just that you'd stay with us until it was safe for you to return."

"But war is end!" I keep arguing. "Is safe!"

We reach the house, and all three of us take a seat on the bench, Kjersti between Jens and me. Somehow Heidi finds her way out, and puts her head in my lap. Absentmindedly I pet her ears, thinking of Tor.

"Come back to school tomorrow, and we'll have a day of Finnish history and current events," Kjersti looks very sincere. "I don't want to discourage you, but just because the war is over, things might not be as good as they were when you left. In fact, they're likely to be worse."

"And Baker will have ice!" Jens chimes in.

"But, Mother say… when war is end …"

"Paul," Kjersti says, and squeezes my hand. "The root of all wisdom is the acknowledgement of fact. Who said that?"

"I know, I know, I know!" Jens hops up and down, waving one arm straight in the air. His other hand is pushing into his armpit, as if thus making his raised arm higher.

Kjersti silences him by raising one hand ever so slightly. He sits back down. I shrug.

"Paasikivi," she answers her own question. "Another orphan just like you. Although, by the grace of God, your parents are still alive. Paul, you must face the facts. You won't be going home today. And while you're here, you might as well make the best of it." She rises off the bench, straightens her skirt, and reaches her hand to Jens. She cups her other hand around my chin. "I'll see you in class tomorrow," she says and they leave.

Jens waves at me. I wave back. With Heidi at my feet, I watch them walk away. Orphaned by living parents. By choice. Theirs.

The Mortensens return from the barn. It must be supper time. They all try to avoid looking at me. Not wanting to see them either, I hide my face in my arms. Curling into a ball, I wish I were invisible. The embarrassment embraces me. My own mother doesn't want me back. Why else isn't she here already? I'm unwanted. Even Mrs. Mortensen wants me to leave. 'How nice' that I'm going home.

It's getting cold and dark, and I'm hungry. It's been a long day, and the smells from the open window are making my stomach growl and my mouth salivate. I put my overcoat and hat back on. Unable to find my gloves, I blow into my hands, and then sit on them. I'm too proud to go back in the house. I'm not wanted back home, and I'm not wanted here. What am I supposed to do?

I can hear the Mortensens moving around inside the house. A voice that I recognize as Mr. Mortensen's says something about 'the boy', and I know they're talking about me. If possible I feel even more unwanted. When the window closes, the tears start. I'm shuddering from both the cold and shame, and curl into Heidi's fur.

The sun has set. The front door opens, and Mor comes out. I quickly dry my tears, and hide my face. She's carrying a plate of food. It smells delicious.

"I thought you might be hungry," she says, and drapes her shawl around my shoulders. "You didn't get very far, did you?"

"I understand not," I can hear how whiny my voice is. "Mine mother say, when war is end I go home. Mannerheim say, paper say, war is end. Where is she? Why come she not? Want she not I go home? Loves she not I?"

Mor pulls me toward her. Urgency sharpens her voice and she starts force feeding me mashed potatoes and gravy.

"I'm certain that your mother wants you home just as firmly as you want to go home. And I'm sure that she loves you very, very much. But she won't come and get you. Not today, not ever."

"No! That not true! I not believe you! Mine mother come, we go home. You see." I start to rise, but Mor pulls me back down.

"Just because she won't come to collect you doesn't mean you won't be going home one day. You and your siblings will travel home the same way you came here, by train, in a group. These things take a while to organize, and from what the paper says, you might not be going home for a while yet."

Grief and desperation grip my heart, and I lean against Mor and let it all out. The tears I had so valiantly tried to disguise come crashing down my cheeks and drip on my collar. I'm crying like a baby, shuddering and gasping.

"Is not true," I hiccup. "I not let be true."

Mor sits quietly and lets me cry. Softly, she rocks me back and forth while her hands are patting and comforting me. Her voice is full of encouragement and love and she whispers endearments into my hair. How can I explain to her that I'm craving for Mother's affections? Mor's terms of endearment, although spoken in earnest, do not measure up to or compensate for a single word of any kind from Mother.

When at long last my tears have dried up, Mor takes my face in her hands, and offers a handkerchief to blow my nose. She smiles and pets my cheek.

"Sometimes I forget that you're only seven, child, you act so mature," she starts. "What do you say? Make yourself comfortable? Come have supper inside?" She leads me back inside the house.

I cast one last look down the now dark lane. Turning back to face Mor, I straighten my shoulders, trying to stand as tall as I can, and say "I'm almost eight!" in perfect Danish.

Foreign Minister Tanner spoke over the Finnish national radio at 12 noon on March 13th, explaining the terms of the peace treaty and the factors leading to its agreement. He praised the stamina and endurance of the Army and the home front in carrying through a struggle in which Finland was left to stand or fall alone. The Foreign Minister also took the opportunity to criticize Finland's Scandinavian neighbors, who hid behind their declared neutrality when turning down all requests for help, and even preventing Finland from getting the help offered by the Allies. Without assistance Finland could no longer continue the unequal struggle, and the Government was left with no alternative but to accept an unacceptable peace.

Finland's casualties in the war were 21,396 dead, 1,434 missing or captured, and 43,557 wounded. (Source: The War Archives.) The estimated number of enemy casualties varies from 200,000 to one million, depending on the source. A Russian general is quoted to have stated: 'We have won only enough ground to bury our dead.' There are no exact numbers available on displaced children.

The last trainload of children being evacuated
to Sweden left Helsinki just hours before the
news of the peace treaty was made official to
the public.
At 3.40 p.m. on Monday, March 13th, 1940, the
Finnish flag was lowered from the flagpole at
Viborg Castle, now Russian territory, for the
last time. The Winter War was over.

April 1940.

Weeks pass, and with Mor's help, I scour every bit of news I can find about the state of affairs back home. There seems to be less by the day, and what little there is, isn't promising. Following Mor's and Kjersti's advice, I make myself comfortable in my new life in Denmark. The village I live in is quite small, and it seems as though I soon know everyone by name. Certainly everyone knows my name. My favorite townsperson is Baker Sørensen, and I spend a lot of time in his shop. He asks me about home and about my adventures evacuating and riding the train to Denmark, and we spend many an afternoon just talking. Danish turns out not to be such a difficult language after all, and I now proudly speak it quite fluently.

Mor tells me about Mrs. Mortensen. Although I thought she was slow, it turns out that when Anders and Christian were younger than me, she was in a freak tractor accident, and is lucky to be alive, much less walking today. The only impairment she has from that unfortunate incident is her ability to speak, and to form her thoughts into words. Out of consideration and respect, everyone talks slowly, or very little to her. She's neither dumb, nor slow, her mouth just doesn't process the information her brain sends it. That's how Mor explained it to me, and I believe her. The roses, which are about to pop, are apparently her project. Mother would be so jealous. I intend to ask Mrs. Mortensen for seeds.

It's Easter Sunday. This is the first time since my arrival at the Mortensens' that I've gone to church, so seeing it from the inside is quite an experience. Being used to our very ornate church back home; this one is the absolute opposite. However, it is a minimalist masterpiece. Or so Kjersti says, and I believe her. It is whitewashed both inside and out, and heavy oak beams, like the inside of a boat, cross the high, vaulted ceiling. Completely absorbed by how that could possibly have been built, I lose track of the sermon. But, it's Easter, so I'm familiar with it. Christ beat death. The only pieces of flamboyance in the church are these incredible mosaic windows. There are three of them. Above the altar, facing north, and at the ends of two wings, facing east and west. Mor says that when the sun hits them just right, and they cast their glow across the whitewashed walls, it's truly like being in the presence of God. Unfortunately, Easter Sunday is cloudy.

After the sermon we gather in the square outside the church. The entire village must be here. Everyone is shaking hands, laughing jovially, patting each other's backs, making plans to visit. Smiling politely, I answer questions directed at me as best I can without seeming impolite. Although my mouth says all the right words, my mind is on Easter lunch. It's taken Mor several days to prepare, and I can't wait to sink my teeth into it. Just thinking about it makes my mouth fill with saliva.

There's a bustle across the street, and I can see someone running up to the Mayor. He leans in to whisper something in his ear, and the look on the Mayor's face is that of shock, fear and puzzlement. They make their way through the crowd, find the barber, and hurry to his shop. The crowd is murmuring. My mind is still on lunch. Wondering how long this socialization will take, I'm tempted to go back into the church, to study the structure of the beams in peace. They fascinate me. Did the trees grow bowed, or did someone bend them? And if they did - how? I'm barely inside the church again, when I hear shouting in the crowd behind me. The Mayor has reappeared, and is trying to get everyone's attention.

The Mayor is incidentally also the postmaster, and therefore knows everyone in the village. He's pathologically shy, of medium height, but built like a barn door. Jens once told me that he has to have his clothes tailor-made in Copenhagen, because he can't fit his shoulders into any regular clothes. Jens further told me that he polishes his bald head with a silk scarf every morning. I didn't think to ask how he would know that. He's obsessively organized, including his appearance, which is always crisp to the point of perfection. With one exception. Well, two, actually. Because he's so shy, enormous red blotches appear on his neck and huge pearls of perspiration bead up on his upper lip whenever he gets flustered. This I know, because he's in my arts class. If I were to venture a guess I'd say he's probably about Father's age. However, because of his bald head and tiny, round spectacles, he appears much older.

As the crowd hushes, and the Mayor faces the entire village, I see the blotches appear and spread like blood on water across his neck. He takes a deep breath and clears his throat.

"I'm afraid I'm the bearer of unfortunate tidings," he starts. He's breathing heavily, and uses his handkerchief to wipe his upper lip. "Germany has invaded Denmark." The crowd gasps. Another wipe of the upper lip. "At this time there's very little news, only that our Government has capitulated."

The crowd explodes in a cacophony. During this time, I've been standing in the doorway to the church, directly behind the Mayor, and I can clearly see the anxiety on everyone's face.

"Will we fight?" someone shouts from the square.

"Our troops put up an effort," the Mayor says, wiping his lip again, "but the opposing force was too overwhelming. Apparently."

"...what about the treaty?..."

"...are we German now?..."

"...will we house German troops?..."

"...what about the Allies?..."

"...will we fight on the German side? ..."

"...who declared war on whom?..."

The questions hit the Mayor like automatic gunfire, and he's doing the best he can to reassure his constituents, with what little information he has. All thoughts of Easter lunch have left me. I only have one question on my mind. Carefully I step up to the Mayor, and tap his elbow. Apparently he hasn't seen me behind him, for he jolts at my touch and gives a slight squeal. The handkerchief flies to his lip again.

"Paul?" he says quizzically.

"Must we to evacuate?" I ask.

I don't care that the grammar is off. Nor does the Mayor. Nor does the entire congregation gathered in the square in front of me. An audible gasp runs through the crowd. Everyone's whispering 'Evacuate' as if hearing the word for the first time. In my mind I'm already packing. The Mayor looks from me to the crowd, and then back to me. I also look over the crowd. My question lingers in the air. Anticipation is on everyone's face. Everyone but one. Mr. Mortensen quietly shakes his head. I know what he's thinking. Children should be seen, not heard. He breaks away from the crowd, walks up the church steps, and grabs my arm. It hurts. The smoke from his ever-present cigarette stings my eyes.

He leans in to the Mayor and whispers "My apologies for the boy. He hasn't been put in place yet," and starts dragging me down the steps.

Baker steps up in front of him and cuts his stride. He puts one strong arm on Mr. Mortensen's and releases his grip of my arm.

"It's a valid question, Mortensen," Baker says. "Paul has experienced this war already more than any of us, and has had to evacuate twice. It's only fair that he knows if another move is in store for him." He turns to the Mayor. "What say you? Will there be a need to evacuate?"

All eyes turn back to the Mayor. The entire square is hushed. It's so quiet that I can hear my own breathing. The handkerchief is tightly pressed to the Mayor's upper lip again, and slowly he lets his hand drop.

Looking defeated, he whispers "I... I don't know..."

Easter Sunday, April 9ᵗʰ, 1940, German forces
crossed the border into Denmark, in direct
violation of a German-Danish non-aggression
treaty signed just the previous year. In a coordinated operation, German ships began disembark-
ing troops at the docks in Copenhagen and three
companies of paratroopers seized airfields.
Although outnumbered and poorly equipped, soldiers in several parts of the country offered
resistance; most notably the Royal Guard in
Copenhagen and units along the Danish-German
border. Coordinated simultaneously with the
border crossing, German planes dropped leaflets
over Copenhagen calling for Danes to accept
the German occupation peacefully, and claiming
that Germany had occupied Denmark in order to
retain its neutrality by protecting it against
an invasion from Great Britain and France.
As a result of the unexpected, undeclared invasion, the Danish Government did not have time
to officially declare war on Germany, and after
just two hours the Danes capitulated.

My bag has been packed for weeks now, as a result of which all my clothes are always rumpled. No evacuation order has yet been given. Nothing has changed. I go to school every day, take art classes on Sundays and help Mor around the house. If the Mayor hadn't told us the country had been invaded by alien forces I'd never have believed him. Life goes on as usual.

Art classes turn out to be more tedious than fun. Being the only child in the class, and the only foreigner at that, doesn't help. They all assume that I'm some prodigy and can whip out a masterpiece with my eyes blindfolded and my hands tied behind my back. So far I've learned two things; my proportion and perspective need serious work, and apparently I spend too much time on details without finishing the 'big picture'. Kjersti says that both apply to the way I see life in general as well. I don't understand what she means by that. But because it doesn't sound much like a compliment, I don't intend to ask.

The days have grown significantly longer and warmer. Although the winter wasn't very cold, and there was hardly ever any snow, when spring hit Denmark, it hit with vengeance. I've never seen so many different hues of green. The ground has thawed, leaving the pastures a thick muck. Yesterday Christian slipped on the muck, dislocating his right elbow. I'm unfamiliar with the circumstances, but last night at supper Mr. Mortensen asked me if I could help Christian with his chores, until his elbow is healed. This thrilled me. Since my arrival I've been begging him to let me help, but he's always refused. When I finally learned enough Danish

I asked him why, and he told me that it would disrupt the system, and thereby make Anders and Christian idle, spoiled and corrupt. Nonetheless, this morning, I'm up and ready before the boys and can't wait to get started. Christian asks me if I want to feed the geese or the pigs. The geese still scare me, so without hesitation I choose the pigs.

"They stink, you know," Christian states the obvious.

I tell him that I was born on a farm and that I'm used to shoveling manure. Christian's response to this is a quick shrug of his shoulders.

Since I didn't bring any work boots of my own, I'm given an old pair of Mr. Mortensen's. Although I'm wearing three pairs of thick socks, the boots flop loosely around my feet, and come up to above my knees. It doesn't matter. It's a pleasant surprise to find out how friendly pigs really are. They're very much like dogs. Especially the little piglets. They're very affectionate and like to be scratched. And their skin is surprisingly soft. Pigs are much more fun than cows, who spend all day just grazing, and give you a hard time if they're not milked the second they're ready. One of the piglets starts rolling around on her back in the muck, like a dog. This makes me laugh, and I go over to give her a belly rub, much like I would with Tor.

"Don't get too attached," Christian's voice startles me.

Turning around, I see him on the other side of the fence, leaning his good arm against a shovel.

"Remember that they're food, not family."

Gasping, I let go of the piglet. "What?!" My heart jerks and misses a beat.

Christian laughs. "Where'd you think ham comes from?" he says, and starts walking away.

Last night's dinner is making its way up my throat, and I look at the little piglet, who's now nudging her snout under my hand, hoping to get scratched again. My boots are stuck in the muck, and I feel light-headed and nauseous. I fly up, my mouth tasting vile, and try to run after Christian. Surely he must be joking. One of my feet slips out of the boot, leaving it stuck in the muck, and I wade through the muck in stocking feet just as I reach the fence and throw up. I can hear Christian laughing as he enters the barn. I hope his elbow is giving him pain!

Hopping on one foot, I retrace my steps and collect the other boot. The piglets surround me again.

"I'm so sorry," I whisper to them. "I ate your ... somebody ... aunt or uncle or cousin. I had no idea."

Unwillingly I start sobbing. I make a silent pact with the piglets that I will never eat ham again, and if at all possible, I'll help them escape, but in the meantime, I'll make their life on the farm as comfortable as possible.

At the breakfast table I start dry heaving at the sight of slices of ham being passed around. I excuse myself, and go to my room to change for school. Although I'd been wearing three layers of socks, the wet muck has seeped through to the skin of my left foot. Quickly brushing it off, I put on clean socks, trousers and shirt, grab my jacket, school hat and books, and run out the door. I force myself to recite anything and everything I know by heart, trying to get the idea of how ham is made out of my mind. The image of the little piglets' faces is burned on my cornea. Thankfully, by the time I reach the town square, those thoughts are gone. Because I left early, I arrive at the square early, so I take a seat at the stone wall, and wait for Jens.

Normally, if ever I'm here before Jens, I'd go into Baker's, but this morning there are angry voices coming from inside, so I decide not to enter. Four heavy looking bicycles are parked in military fashion outside the bakery. The voices are muffled by the closed door, but through the window I can see four shapes moving around, shouting brusquely and then, inexplicably, erupting in laughter. One of the laughing voices is Baker's.

And then four soldiers exit, each holding a cinnamon bun. Even though they seem jovial with each other, their voices sound mean to me. Three of them look identical; young, tall and thin, with long fingers and cropped light hair. The one who's the loudest is tall as well, but has a slightly bulging midsection. His face is absolutely symmetrical, with an impossibly square jaw. Accentuating that image, his chin has a crease, splitting his face in two perfect halves. Last Sunday, Kjersti told me that no face is perfectly symmetrical, and I'd like to invite this soldier to art class to demonstrate that she's wrong.

Subconsciously I may have been staring at him and my heart starts beating rapidly, as he makes eye contact with me. Instinctively I know that these are German soldiers. We are, after all, under occupation. My breath catches in my throat as they approach. Square Jaw starts yelling short, spit-fire words at me that I don't understand. He keeps gesturing with his hand, pointing at me, and then jerking his thumb over his shoulder. Shaking my head and shrugging I try to tell him that I don't understand. He grabs me by my lapel and throws me on the cobblestones. I land hard. Face first.

He sniffs the air behind me. "…Dänische Schwein…" is all I understand.

Yes, I'm a Danish pig farmer. Nothing wrong with that.

I touch my finger to my lower lip. It's bleeding. The other three soldiers are laughing and sit down on the wall. There's plenty of room for a good hundred or so full-grown people, as the wall encloses three-quarters of the square, so I don't see the point of them having to sit exactly where I was sitting. Thoughts of being bullied by Harri flash in my mind, so I brush myself off, and take a seat on the other side of the square. I've barely sat down, before I notice that they're following me, yank me off the wall, and throw me to the ground again. This time I land hands first, and scrape the palms of both of them. Square Jaw keeps spitting out incomprehensible words in German. My pulse is quickening and I can feel the adrenaline flooding through me. By sheer willpower I throw my hands in the air, in a sign of resignation, and try to make my way through them back across the square. Although my instinct is to fight back, my logic tells me I'm out-muscled.

They surround me. Square Jaw grabs my books, and tosses them on the ground. They laugh. Then he spits in my face, and says something between gritted teeth.

"I don't speak German!" I shout in Danish.

Someone pushes me in the back and I go flying forward, straight into the arms of Square Jaw, who pushes me back. They toss me between them like a rag doll. I'm dizzy and nauseous. I feel something hard press against my back, and remember that I still carry my knife.

"I have a knife, and I know how to use it!" I shout.

I've never actually used my knife on a living thing in my life, with the exception of the cow's umbilical cord in March, but they don't need to know that.

As quickly as I can, I reach behind me, grab my knife, and try to steady my legs. I wave the knife at them. They're spinning, and I try to get my eyes to focus. Out of nowhere the flash of a shiny black boot comes at me, and in an explosion of pain, the boot makes contact with my wrist. I hear it snap, and know it's broken from the pain, and the way it hangs. Suddenly my vision is clear as day. I can see my knife flying in the air, and Square Jaw skillfully catching it in his gloved hand. They're all laughing louder now. He wedges the blade between two stones in the wall, and with a quick jerk upward, breaks the blade. My father gave me that knife. The hairs on my neck start to prickle. Anger makes my blood boil, and I charge toward him, pounding my fists into him, kicking and screaming, and fighting the tears that are scorching behind my eyelids. Before I know what's happening, the three thin soldiers hold me back by my arms, and Square Jaw presses the broken blade under my chin. He keeps jabbering in German, spitting with each word, repeating 'Dänische Schwein'. Somewhere while I was being passed around my hat must've fallen off, because he picks it up, turns his back to me, unzips and urinates in it. With a triumphant smile, he turns to face me, and splotches my hat on my head. Hot urine drips down all sides of my head. I struggle to get free, but they hold me in a vise.

All four of them are now doubling over, roaring with laughter. When they finally let me go, my hair is drenched and reeking. One of them kicks me in the back and I go crashing into the stone wall. In a blur of pain and humiliation I watch them get back on their bicycles and pedal away.

Where is everyone? is the first thought that comes into my mind. Usually this time of day the streets are already fairly busy. In a haze I remember that I was here earlier than usual this morning. Something catches the light of the rising sun, and I turn to grab my broken knife. Burying it deep inside my inside pocket I swear I will get revenge. My throat is closing up, and my eyes are welling. But I refuse to cry.

The pain is shooting up and down my arm, and I look at my limp wrist. It's definitely broken. It's already swollen up to twice its normal size. My lip is still trickling with blood, both palms are imbedded with sand and I've managed to scrape both knees. And these are my good pants. I reach for my hat and toss it to the ground. I never did like it, but this isn't the way I had hoped to be rid of it. I'm so glad I hadn't brought my Baden-Powell hat. For if they had peed in it, ... well, I don't know what I would've done.

A familiar whistle comes from around the far side of the square, and I spot Jens looking around for me. He doesn't see me. I'm still crouching against the wall. The pain is so sharp, that I think I will pass out, and now I'm swallowing blood.

"There you are! How was your weekend?" Jens starts, as he sees me. "You'll never guess! Barber told me that the Germans have a camp..." he stops abruptly as he reaches me. "What happened to you?!"

"I met the Germans," I manage, before I pass out.

"... meant to be peaceful..."

    "... Paul...?"

    "... if we resist..."

    "... Paul...?!"

    "... underground..."

    "... Paul...!!"

I open my eyes to the sound of voices, and find that I'm inside the barbershop. As there isn't a public house in this town, and because the barber has nearly the only radio, his shop has become the local hangout, and base for information sharing and general gossip.

I'm surrounded by at least a dozen men, and Jens, holding a wet towel to my head, which feels like it weighs a tonne and is engulfed in a fog. There also isn't a doctor in town, but I know that both Mor and Kjersti's mother are trained and experienced midwives, and that Barber can fix general scrapes and broken bones. In fact, just yesterday, Christian was here, getting his elbow yanked in place and put in a sling.

"Does this hurt?" I recognize Barber's voice, and feel a sharp pain shoot from my fingertip all the way up to my shoulder.

"Aaaow! Yes, that hurts!" I yelp.

And just like that the fog in my brain is lifted.

"Good," he says, and starts plastering my wrist. "No permanent damage."

"Do you want to talk about it?" Jens asks, eyes gleaming with excitement. "How many were they? What do their uniforms look like? What ranks were they? Did they say anything? Were they armed? What did you do to them? "

"I wouldn't give up my seat," I say, and realize only then how pitiful that sounds.

Although I've been brought up to respect my elders, and I understand that this country is occupied, I had acted on instinct and tried to fight. But, on the other hand, the papers say that the Germans are here on peaceful terms, and just like me they're guests in this country. I've done my best to adjust to my new host country, why can't they?

> The occupation of Denmark was initially not an objective for Germany. It was done to expedite a planned invasion of the strategically more significant Norway, as well as a precaution against the expected British blockade.
> The British Government had considered a blockade strategy in an attempt to weaken Germany indirectly. German industry was heavily dependent on iron ore from the North Sweden mining district, much of which was shipped through the northern Norwegian port of Narvik. Britain also wanted control of the Norwegian coastline, as a buffer against a German expansion. Hitler beat Chamberlain to the punch.
> Germany did not plan a military assault on Sweden, as this was deemed unnecessary. By holding Norway, the Danish Straits and most of the shores of the Baltic, the Baltic was thus an inland sea of Germany's. German-occupied territories surrounded Sweden on the north, west and south. The Soviet Union to the east, on friendly terms with Hitler under the terms of the Molotov-Ribbentrop Pact, completed the circle.

It's the last weekend of April and the long-anticipated fair is finally here. Since Christian has his right elbow in a sling and I have my right wrist in a cast, we've both become left-handed, finding that two left hands equal one right hand, and finish our morning chores just as quickly as Anders finishes his. And then we're off to the fair. Mor rides with Mrs. Mortensen in the cab and Anders, Christian, Jens and I sit in the bed of the truck.

It's been raining the entire week; soft, warm spring drizzles, and we've all been praying for sunshine for the fair. And sure enough, our prayers are answered. The day is sunny and cloudless, with a fresh breeze and the promise of a wonderful day.

We're all crisp and cleanly scrubbed. Well, as clean as you can get without a sauna, and are wearing our best Sunday clothes. Since I ruined my good trousers, I'm wearing my new short pants. They were new this winter, and already they're a little snug. But I don't care. I'd wear a dress if I had to, just to be there, the way Jens has been hyping this fair.

The music and loud, excited voices reach us before we even see the fair. It's surprisingly close. I recognize the road I took to go to the vet's, and the fair is set up in a field just on the other side of town. Up on a hill beyond the fields, I can see the ruins of an old fort, and point it out to Jens. We make plans to come play there once school is out. It's close enough for us to run through the forest.

"But only if it's light out," Jens says with a shudder and I assume he's referring to not wanting to take a short-cut through the forest in the dark.

Mrs. Mortensen parks the truck among several others, and we descend from the bed. Mor hands Anders and Christian each a handful of coins, with a reminder that that's all they're getting, and to spend it wisely. They sprint off, before she's even finished her sentence.

"Meet us back here at sundown, or you're walking home!" she shouts after them.

They each raise a hand in acknowledgement. Mor laughs and turns to me, takes my hand and presses a few coins in it.

"What's this for?" I ask, dumbfounded.

"For the fair, of course," Mor replies.

It never occurred to me that it might cost money.

"I didn't do anything to deserve it."

Mor takes my chin in her soft hand, and gives it a gentle squeeze. "Then consider it a gift. Now, who's ready to have some fun?"

"Me, me, me!" Jens shrieks like a little girl, and we head toward the fair.

Finally I understand why I like Jens. He reminds me of my brother, Carl.

The fair is exhilarating. In my wildest dreams, I couldn't have conjured up anything like this. Even Jens' very detailed descriptions were inadequate. Naturally, we start by getting some ice. Then Jens wants to ride a carousel, which I thought looked thrilling when I first saw it, but during the ride I found it dull and boring.

"What's next?" Mor asks us, as we get off the carousel.

"Anders Mortensen wins another one!" a monosyllabic, staccato voice booms behind us. "Step right up! Ladies and gentlemen! Boys and girls! Only five øre will earn you three shots! Three hits will win you! One! Of these! Fine prizes! Step right up!"

The voice piques my curiosity, and holding on to Jens' sleeve we walk toward it. We find Anders hunched over a table, shooting a rifle at a pyramid of wooden blocks. Christian has his good arm full of prizes. A slingshot, a yo-yo, a bow and arrow, all of which frankly they're both too old to play with. We watch as Anders demolishes the pyramid and selects a stuffed toy rabbit as his prize. The small gathering around the shooting gallery applauds him.

"Look, Mor," I say, yanking her sleeve. "Anders is really good!"

Mor beams proudly. "Yes, child," she whispers.

"How did he learn to shoot that good?"

"He learned to shoot *well*," she corrects me, "by going hunting with his father. Christian is also an excellent shot."

"Then why isn't he shooting?"

"You need two hands to hold a rifle, dear."

I feel the urge to try the rifle myself, and mirroring what Anders is doing, I realize that I only need the flexibility to bend a finger in my right hand. Flexing my index finger, I realize that I can.

"Can I try?" I ask Mor.

I give Staccato Voice the money, and he hands me the rifle. Trying to emulate Anders, I lean forward, put the rifle to my shoulder, squeeze one eye shut and pull the trigger. Miss. I try again. I miss again.

"Hold it," Anders says, and puts his hand on the rifle. He adjusts my stance. He presses my head against the stock. "Take a deep breath, aim for the middle one on the bottom row, squeeze, and don't *pull* the trigger, exhale and squeeze."

The pyramid comes tumbling down. "I won!" I turn to Anders. This is the most interaction I've had with him since I arrived. "Thank you!"

Smiling, he gives my shoulder a light squeeze. "Well done."

"Choose your prize! Among anyone! Of the fine prizes on the bottom shelf! Or for an additional two øre! And three more hits! Move up to the next shelf!"

"Get the slingshot! Get the slingshot!" Jens whispers anxiously.

My eyes land on a model airplane on the second shelf. I dish out more money, and take aim. Deep breath, aim, exhale, squeeze, I tell myself.

"Paul!" someone shouts, just as I'm squeezing the trigger.

I shoot a hole in the arm of a stuffed toy bear. Angry and dumbfounded I look around. So does everyone else.

"Tune out the rest of the world," Anders advises me. "Pretend like you're deaf."

Deep breath, aim ...

"Paul!!"

"What?" I turn around, angrily.

This time I managed to shoot the top block. Just the one and I only have one shot left.

"Ignore it and concentrate," Anders says.

Deeply frustrated, and really wanting that model airplane I take my stance again. Just as I'm squeezing, something jolts into me. I look up at the target.

"I hit it! I won! I'd like the model airplane, please," I say, feeling an odd pressure around my waist. The short pants are too snug.

"No win!" Staccato Voice tells me. "Choose your prize! From the bottom shelf!"

"What do you mean 'no win'? Look! I hit it, it's still swaying!"

"And still standing! No win! Step right up..."

"No, wait a minute, sir, you didn't say it had to fall, you just said I had to hit..."

"Pa-ha-ha-uuul..." a small voice whines behind me.

I look down, and what I thought was my pants being snug, is in fact two very small, very familiar arms clasped around me. Looking over my shoulder I see a mass of cherub curls embedded into my back. I swing around.

"Little Sister! What are you doing here?"

"Didn't you hear me? Why didn't you answer me when I called?" she's crying. Huge tears are streaming down her face. "I missed you so much, Paul! Why didn't you see me? Don't you love me anymore?"

I can't believe she's here. The model airplane doesn't matter anymore. I've won a far greater prize than any stupid toy. I'm with my Little Sister, whom I didn't think I'd ever see again. I hug her tightly, and spin her around until she stops crying and starts giggling.

"Put me down! Put me down! I'm dizzy!" she squeals.

I set her down on the ground, and look at her at arm's length. She is glowing. She looks the same. She hasn't grown, because what seems like a life-long separation is in reality only about two months. She's wearing a white dress, and her hair is held in place by a huge white bow on the side of her head. Why do people insist on dressing her in all white? Mother used to do that, too. Don't they know that white washes out all the coloring of her face? My guess is that they want to emphasize the cherubness of her looks. Diminishing that very look are two long streaks of red ice, dried to her chin. I pull out the tail of my shirt, spit on it and start wiping her chin, oblivious to the fact that I have a freshly ironed, clean handkerchief in my pocket.

All the while I'm doing this Little Sister is jabbering. This is the most vocal I've ever heard her, and only now does it dawn on me that we're speaking Danish. In fact, her Danish is more fluent, and more grammatically correct than mine, and I'm older than her. All this time she has been labeled shy, when in fact she was just introduced to the wrong languages. She never mastered Finnish or Swedish, because she was meant to speak Danish all along. I haven't heard a thing she's said. Like an idiot I just stand there beaming at her.

"…and then Carl said that you'd be here for sure, and here you are. But Uncle Oscar said …"

That part I heard. "Carl?" I interrupt her. "You've seen Carl?"

"Yes," she states, very matter-of-factly. She turns, and points to a Ferris wheel behind her.

Squinting into the sun, I try to make my eyes detect a familiar face, when all of a sudden, high above the music and general merriness I hear "Paaaaul! Over heeeere! Looook at meeee!" and I see a figure half standing up in one of the Ferris wheel carts, waving his hands in the air, high above his head, trying to escape being restrained by a bigger figure.

With Little Sister's hand in mine, I start running toward the big wheel. This is the best day ever! I feel indescribably light on my feet, my heart is swelling with joy, and inexplicably I also feel like crying. Happy tears.

Little Sister still keeps jabbering away, as we make our way through the crowds.

"… why are we running? …what's this on your hand? … Uncle Oscar says… Do you have your own room? I do. … They have strawberry iced cream here, you know. … Have you had ice? It's my favorite…"

"Paul!" a stern voice behind us calls out.

We stop and turn and I see Mor huffing and panting and trying to keep up. In her tow I see Jens, Mrs. Mortensen and the affluent-looking couple from the train station, who took Little Sister away from me.

Where are my manners? I'm so overwhelmed with seeing Little Sister and Carl again, that I completely ignored everyone else.

"Mor, Mor! Look! This is my little sister."

Mor catches up with us. She's panting and presses a hand to her chest. "I'm happy for you, child, but don't *ever* run away like that again!"

"But… It's Little Sister!" Doesn't she understand how important this is for me?

"Good day!" Little Sister says.

Before I can finish the introductions, I'm being tackled from behind. Carl has found us, and we wrestle on the ground. We get odd looks from not only the Mortensens but strangers passing us as well. I don't care. At one point even Little Sister joins our rumble on the ground, but is quickly whisked away by her foster mother.

As it turns out, the three of us live only a few kilometers from each other. True to her promise, Natalia had managed to keep us close, we just didn't know it. Our towns form an asymmetric triangle, as the crow flies, with Carl's being the closest one to mine and Little Sister's being the closest one to a big city. Her foster father owns a newspaper in Helsingør. He has his own camera, and has even taught Little Sister how to use it. Before we leave the fair he takes a group shot of the three of us.

Carl's foster parents, on the other hand, run the only public house in the county. They live in an apartment directly above the tavern, and Carl has had a taste of beer already. Strangely, I feel left out of both experiences. But what's even more surprising is that although I'd like to taste beer, the idea of a camera fascinates me more.

It only strikes me today that the Finnebarn that the vet was talking about was, in fact, my little brother Carl. If only I had asked the right questions at the right time, and hadn't been so angry at the war, I'd have known sooner that he was just a forest away from me. Neither of them knows anything about Johan.

Typical of Carl, he's fascinated by my bruised knees, split lip and cast wrist. So, while Little Sister is getting her nose blown by her foster mother, I give him an abbreviated story of what happened.

"Wow!" Carl exhales. "Did they have guns?"

"That's what I said!" Jens pipes in.

Carl and Jens take to each other immediately, like I knew they would.

Looking pensive, Carl adds "It's a little strange. The Germans in my town are all really friendly and nice."

"Of course they're nice to *you*! Your foster parents own the only beer joint!" I snap at my little brother's ignorance.

Mor and Carl's foster parents get along splendidly, and Carl, Jens and I make plans to meet up next weekend. Little Sister's foster parents, on the other hand, seem snobbish to me. They're obviously wealthy, and show no shame in flaunting it. It irks me how the lady constantly fusses around Little Sister, and it takes all the willpower I can muster not to jump up and yell 'She's a tomboy! Let her be!'

They keep telling her it's time to leave, to which she tightens her grip around my hand and says "No! I'm staying with Paul!"

The only time she lets go of my hand is when we stop for another scoop of ice.

"Look at me, Paul!" she suddenly starts twirling in front of me. "Aunt Bodil and Uncle Oscar say that I'll take ballet classes in the fall!" She stumbles, and falls. Picking herself up, she brushes off her knees and starts twirling again. "Can you see me, Paul? Look at me!" The cone of ice in her hand wobbles, and she comes crashing into me. "Did you see me?"

"She's without a shadow of a doubt the clumsiest little girl I've ever met," says Little Sister's foster father. "Was she always this gauche?"

Although he sounds jovial about it, what right does he have to criticize my family? Having already decided that I don't like him, I just shrug. Again, I feel like re-iterating that she's a tomboy, and should be climbing trees and riding bicycles and shooting slingshots rather than taking ballet classes.

As we're finishing our iced cream, the long shadows of dusk arrive and Mrs. Mortensen starts mumbling about evening chores. I tell my siblings goodbye.

"Will you come see me soon, Paul?" Little Sister asks, with a trembling lower lip. The tears aren't far. "Uncle Oscar says…"

"Will you quit calling them Uncle and Aunt!" I hiss at her. "They're not re-lated to us, you know. They're just a temporary placement until we go home again. Why do you call them that anyway?"

Little Sister's lower lip is quivering dangerously by now. "Because they asked me to…"

"You call your foster grandmother 'Mor'," Carl interrupts.

"The entire town calls her that, dummy," I tell him off with gritted teeth. I hadn't realized that until I said it out loud. I turn back to Little Sister. "How do you think Mother will feel when she finds out that you've attached yourself to strangers?"

"I don't know… Paul, I really don't remember her much, and when she wrote, nobody could read her letter to me…" Now she's sobbing.

She climbs up into my lap and I drape my arms around her, trying not to feel the inevitable pang of jealousy that Mother has written Little Sister, but not me. Rocking her gently, she snuggles her head into my neck. I can feel her body relax, and know that she's only moments away from sleep.

"Yeah," Carl says, "nobody could read my letter, either," he huffs, and shrugs his shoulders.

"You *both* received a letter from Mother?!"

"Ummm… yeah…" Carl starts. "You haven't?"

Jealousy, mixed with anger and bitterness starts growing inside me.

As if sensing my emotions, Little Sister lifts her face to mine and says "Don't be sad, Paul. We don't know what she said. Do you think she's angry?"

Continuing to rock her, I do my best to calm her down, even though my own insides are in a riot.

"Of course she isn't angry," I say. "You are her special little angel. Father's little cherub. Everyone's favorite little princess." I angel kiss her just like Mother used to do. A line of soft kisses on her forehead, so soft that they could only be made by angel wings. "And Carl is her little man. Stronger than the earth, faster than lightning and hungrier than a wolf!"

"Yeah!" Carl shouts and raises both fists in the air.

Just thinking about how much Mother used to love us diminishes my jealousy, and the anger and bitterness are overtaken by sadness. I miss her. But I still believe that one day, when it's safe, we'll all be together again. And then, out of the blue, and without a conscious effort on my part, the inevitable question of 'why?' flies into my thoughts again. Why are we here? Why did Mother send us away? Why, if the war is actually over, Finland is no longer at risk, and Denmark is now occupied, are we not back home yet?

Before we leave the fair, I insist on trying my luck at the shooting gallery again. In the end, I win two slingshots, one for me and one for Carl, and a toy doctor's kit for Little Sister. Unfortunately, however, the model airplane had already been won by someone else. Of course, I also lose three rounds, but that's irrelevant.

Flanked by Jens, Mor and Mrs. Mortensen, I walk back toward the truck feeling an odd mixture of happiness and sadness. Mor senses this and puts an arm around me.

"What's wrong, child?" she says. "Now that you know where they are, you can see them any time."

"I know… It's just… Why didn't Mother write *me*? She wrote both Carl and Little Sister, who can't even read, and have nobody to translate for them… and why didn't she write me? Doesn't she love me as much as she loves them?"

Mor stops and turns me to face her. "When was the last time you wrote her?"

I look down at my shoes. "Well… ummm…"

There's a clump of dirt stuck to the toe of my left shoe, and I give it a disproportionate amount of attention.

"Don't you 'well' and 'um' me, young man. Tell me you've written your mother since you've been here."

"Well, actually… um… I haven't." I feel small and ashamed.

"And why is that?"

Humiliation embraces me like a wet fog. "Because I don't have any money." It has never occurred to me before now how well off we'd been in Karelia. Money never mattered until now, when I have none. I make a solemn pledge to myself never to be without it again.

"What do you need money for?" Mor asks.

"Stamps?"

"Are you trying to tell me that you've been separated from your birth mother for nearly three months, and you don't even have the decency to write to let her know that you're alright? That you're alive? To let her know what your new address is? How is she supposed to know where to even find you, if she doesn't know where you are? Shame on you!" This is the most upset I've ever seen Mor. "Promise me this," she continues, "first thing tomorrow morning, after chores and breakfast, you're going to sit down and write a nice, loving letter. Maybe even include a drawing or two. And I'll be more than happy to give you some stamps." We keep walking toward the Mortensens' car.

"You're still not convinced," Mor says. "What's the matter?"

I'm embarrassed by my own ignorance. "I don't know our address," I whisper.

"I do," Mor says, a big smile spreading across her face.

"How?"

"It's on your tag, child," she says triumphantly, and squeezes my chin. "Now, will you promise to write your mother?"

For a brief moment I'd forgotten that I'd once been tagged. This is indeed the best day ever. We reach the truck, and find Anders and Christian sleeping in the bed of the truck, with their waistbands unbuttoned, their cheeks red with strawberry ice and snoring loudly. In my mind I'm drawing that picture already.

"I promise, Mor. Mange tak!" I say, throwing my arms around her. "Mor? Why does everyone call you 'Mor'?"

"Because she's the midwife, of course!" Jens explains.

Mor chuckles. "That's right," she says, and ruffles Jens' hair. "I've brought most of the town's children into the world. Including young Jens, here."

I can feel my eyes bulging. "Really?" This is fascinating.

"Yes, really."

Jens starts ranting, and counting off on his fingers. "And both my parents and the Mayor, and the barber..."

"And Baker Sørensen?" I ask.

"No, not Baker," Mor reflects. "He moved here from South Jutland, I think."

"... and all my cousins, and Kjersti and Anders and Christian ..."

The next day, after morning chores and breakfast, I sit down and start composing a letter to Mother. I've learned a new word. Ambidextrous. It means I'm able to use my right and left hand with equal skill. Mor taught me that word.

Sitting at the kitchen table, chewing on the pencil in my left hand, I feel a mixture of confusion and frustration. After only months away from my Fatherland, my native language is surprisingly difficult to me. And I was never very good at it to begin with. But I keep hearing my old teacher Veera Borikoff's voice saying, 'Finnish is the easiest language in the world. Everything is spelled exactly as it sounds'. I can't imagine what in the world Carl and Little Sister might have written to Mother. Carl had just barely learned to read and write when we left Karelia and has missed months of school since.

By the time Mor starts setting the table for lunch, I've finished the most important letter in my life. Here's what I wrote:

Deer Mother,

How is Tor? Piees tell him I miss him. I think about him evryday! Mor Mortensen has a dog! Her name is Hdi. She is sweet and nise butt old and has ~~arthretes arthtis~~ bad legs. Not like Tor. Eets good like Tor. I saw lil sisstr and Carl yestrday at fare! They are fine. Carl is as tall as me. The Mortensen famely treet me nise. Anders shoots rifel real good! When I can come home? I miss you. and Tor and Father too! I've bin good! Piees can I come home? I'm good in skool, too! Heer is my adres in Dnamark and a drawing I made of Mortensenhouse. That Hdi in windou. Piees rite back. I wanto come home.

Your best son, Paul

May 1940.

The spring has turned from the blooming heat wave of the fair, to icy rain, and back to sunny, clear days, leading all of us, like snakes, to shed our winter skins at the first rays of the sun. Which inevitably has led to half our school being bedridden with bronchitis, including, unfortunately, Jens, whom I haven't seen for the better part of a week.

Carl and I get together every weekend. Jens always plays with us, but since he's sick, it's just Carl and me today. He brought the letter from Mother with him, and anxiously we read it. It's very disappointing. It contains no news about us going home, or how Father is. Rather, it gives a lengthy explanation of how the new baby, whom they apparently have christened Ingrid, after the crown princess of Denmark, is growing. Like we care. With a heavy heart I hand the letter back to Carl. I still haven't received a letter of my own.

When we play in Carl's town, we always go to the old fort. We've discovered that the limestone hills are chalk-like and brittle, so we can easily break off chunks of it. We use it as ammunition, war paint, and to draw on the walls of the fort. But today we're playing Russians and Finns in the beech forest, which lies directly between Carl's town and mine.

I love this forest. It's my favorite place to go. It's almost magical, the way the beech leaves form a canopy overhead. This is a natural forest, so the trunks that fall, are left be, which makes for lots of fortresses and teepees and occasionally even tanks. It's very different from the forests back home. I remember them smelling like pine sap and sand, but this one smells musty and sweet. It's mysterious, like you could imagine a troll or a magic woodland creature to live under every root and behind every boulder, and if you're quiet enough you might just see one. The light is impossible to describe and even harder to capture, especially now, in early summer, when the leaves are at their brightest and the days are long. After a heavy rain, when the ground is steaming and the first rays of sunlight stream like pinpricks through the branches, it's almost as if God were speaking. I often bring my watercolors here, and thought once that I had captured the light just right, but when I saw my painting the next morning in normal daylight, it was all wrong.

I have the worst luck in drawing straws, and have to be Russians again today. Beech nuts are small, and angular, but fly great in a slingshot.

Carl claims they're hand grenades, and shoots them at me three or four at a time, exclaiming "Victory for small, but mighty Finland!"

Danish comes naturally to both of us now. So naturally in fact, that we use it exclusively even when it's just the two of us.

I climb on a rock, and spread my arms out. I'm a fighter plane. "In a last, desperate effort, the Red Army launch their secret weapon; the unbeatable, fire-spewing eagle!" I fly down from the rock and land on top of Carl. I pin him down and cover him in mulch. "Once again, the Reds have proven their superiority in combat. Dear Finland is left wounded and childless." I wave my arms in the air.

Carl is slightly taller than me now and much heavier and stronger, so he keeps punching me in the gut.

"You can't change history. That's not what happened!" He's wriggling, trying to get out from under me.

"Do you surrender, Marshal Mannerheim?"

"Never!" He jerks his knees into my back, and uses that as leverage to wrestle me off him.

"Then prepare yourself for battle!"

We run deeper into the forest. I'm chasing Carl, hurling beechnuts and sticks at him. He ducks behind a fallen trunk and meets my assault.

"Die, Reds, die! Once again, Finnish sisu* has prevailed! Just surrender, because Finland will never give up!"

I halt. "I think we did, Carl," I say, and the meaning of the words only then hit me.

Carl rises from behind the trunk. "What?"

"I think we lost the war."

"But I thought we won?"

"If we won," I ponder, "why are we still here?"

"Because Mother got tired of the four of us and just wants to be with the new baby. She hates us and I hate her."

I plant a fist squarely in his jaw. We wrestle to the ground, and I pin him down again. "Don't you ever say that! You take that back right now! You're stupid, stupid, stupid!" I keep hitting him and the tears are streaming down my face. "Take…," -punch- "…it…" -punch- "…back!…" -punch.

Carl tries to cover his face and curls into a fetal position. I make myself stop hitting him. I remember Father's last words about taking care of each other, and I don't think he'd be proud of how I acted just then. I feel terrible. I sit next to Carl, trying to catch my breath. He's sobbing quietly. He has a split lip, that's starting to bleed. I pull out the handkerchief that Mor always puts in my pocket, but that I've never, ever used before, spit on it and press it against my little brother's lip.

When he finally stops sobbing, he sits up and looks at me. "So, why *are* we still here?" he says, wiping his nose on his sleeve.

"Mother said we'll be going home just as soon as it's safe," I tell him.

"When's that?"

"I don't know."

"Will we go *home* home or another new home?"

I don't have the heart to remind him that *home* home burned down the night we left. "I don't know."

* Author's note: Sisu = steadfastness of purpose, strength of will, perseverance, 'guts'.

"Is Father home?"

"I don't know."

"Is he dead?"

"I don't know."

"You don't know anything! Why should I believe anything you say?"

"Because! This I know: I know that Mother loves us *all* very much and didn't want us to leave in the first place and will do everything she can to get us back. Soon!" I tell him about the conversation I had eavesdropped on, but hadn't understood the meaning of until we were on the train. Was that only this winter? So much has happened since. "You have to believe me, Carl."

"Why?"

"Just because. Now, let's go back."

"But…, is the war really over?"

"Ours is, but the rest of the world's isn't."

"So, are we Russians now?"

"Never!"

Carl puts his thumb and index finger into his mouth, and wiggles at a tooth. It comes out in a bloody mess. I must've loosened it when I hit him. If possible, I feel even worse now. He puts the tooth in his pocket.

"That's been bothering me all day. Thanks!" he says, and I feel a huge surge of relief.

"Are you hungry?"

This is a redundant question, because Carl is always hungry. This is also a genius way to change his focus.

```
Leading up to the Peace Treaty signed on March
13th, 1940 were the realities that forced Sta-
lin to abandon his occupation plans and settle
for a compromise agreement. Because the Finns
successfully held the Mannerheim Line the So-
viet forces were exhausted and Stalin didn't
want his Armies to be bogged down in the Finn-
ish marshes with the spring thaw rapidly ap-
proaching. In addition, the situation was an
international political embarrassment for the
Soviet regime. A final factor accelerating a
move to peace talks was a Russian intelligence
report of the impending involvement of the Al-
lied forces. Stalin's intelligence failed to
report, however, that the Finnish troops were
out of ammunition.
```

> The Moscow Peace Treaty ceded about 10% of Finland's territory and 20% of its industrial capacity to the Soviet Union. The overall results of the war were mixed. Soviet losses on the front were tremendous, the country's international standing suffered, the fighting ability of the Red Army was put into question, and the Soviet forces did not accomplish their primary objective of conquest of Finland, gaining only a few slivers of territory.
>
> Few at the time expected the tiny Finnish nation to survive. But despite the overwhelming odds, Finland reacted with desperate determination, and four months later, after the hardest fighting seen in Europe since the First World War and massive Soviet reinforcements, Finland's lines remained unbroken. Finland retained her sovereignty and gained considerable international goodwill. It was a moral victory for the small Finnish Army, which was outnumbered five to one.
>
> Most War Children were left abroad to ease the situation for their parents, who set out to rebuild their lives. Nearly half a million Karelians, or more than 10% of Finland's population, lost their homes. Those who had not evacuated during the Winter War were given the right to remain within the Soviet Union or emigrate to Finland. Most moved to Finland in spite of being destitute, homeless, and outcasts in their own country.

We're walking toward the Mortensens' house, when Carl suddenly grabs my elbow and pulls me flat on the ground.

"Soldier," he whispers and points.

We crawl on our stomachs toward a small clearing, and I see a German soldier lying on the ground. His gear is strewn about his body, and a bicycle is leaning against a tree trunk. I look around. He's alone.

"Is he dead?" Carl whispers, as we find cover behind a fallen tree trunk.

"No, dummy. Dead people don't snore." Cold chills suddenly run down my spine. I know this soldier. This is the one who bullied me in the town square. "It's him," I say.

"You sure?" he whispers.

I nod. I'm positive. I would recognize him anywhere. That impossibly square jaw that looks as if chiseled from granite, with its split down the center, and that perfectly symmetrical face. It's him. My blood is boiling and I can hear my heart pumping in my ears. I turn to leave.

"Aren't you going to do anything?" Carl hisses, irritated.

"Like what?"

"I don't know… Pee in his hat!"

The thought of revenge is suddenly very appealing.

"What if he wakes up?"

"He's alone. They're not so tough by themselves. Besides, there's just one of him and two of us. We can take him!"

"He's got a gun."

"Okay, so let's not wake him up, but you *have* to do something."

"Maybe I'll deflate his tires."

"Good idea!"

"Why do you suppose he's here? Do you think he's a deserter?" Part of me wants to think that he got discharged for what he did to me.

"Who cares? He's here and he's totally at our mercy!" Carl says, and is already creeping toward Square Jaw.

I grab his ankle. "What are you going to do?"

Carl grins mischievously. "You'll see," he says.

We crawl quietly toward the sleeping soldier. We're Indians attacking a sleeping cowboy. I wish I had my knife. I also wish Tor were here. My eyes spot his ammo belt. Every boy in school has a box of ammunition, because everyone's father hunts, but no one has a live one. I would be the envy of every boy in school if I had one.

I tap Carl on the shoulder and nod toward the ammo. He nods back. He understands.

"Take all of them," he whispers.

"Why? All we need is one each."

"If he wakes up and sees us, he won't have anything to kill us with," Carl argues.

"Don't you think his gun is loaded?"

"Let's empty it!" Carl says excitedly, and reaches for the rifle.

"No!" I hiss.

"Why not?"

"We're not supposed to play with guns, remember?"

"Says who?"

"Says Father. Different place - same rules, remember? Now, be quiet and do your thing!"

I put two bullets in my pocket and continue toward the bike. The valve is on tightly. It takes two hands to turn it, and my left one is still not as strong as my right one used to be. Finally, the valve gives an almost inaudible hiss, and the tire deflates. As I turn to the rear tire, I spot the chain. I've never broken a chain deliberately before, but I know how difficult and dirty fixing one is, so I cave in to temptation and loosen the chain from its spikes. The rear valve is much easier to turn, but makes an odd sound, like pouring water into a bucket. I cover the valve with my hands, but the sound continues. Quickly I turn around to see if Square Jaw has woken up. He's still sleeping, but my brother is holding his canteen between his legs and is relieving himself into it. My heart skips a beat. He's a genius! Why didn't I think of that? Tit for tat!

We hide behind the fallen tree trunk on the opposite side of the clearing, where we have a good view of Square Jaw. He doesn't wake up, and we're getting bored. Carl loads his slingshot and shoots a beech nut at him. It bounces off his belly, but doesn't wake him up. He shoots another one. This one hits his hand, and he sits up with a jerk and grabs his gun. We duck. We hear him grumbling in German. He's yawning, stretching and scratching himself.

Carl starts giggling like a little girl. I quickly cover his mouth with my hand. The soldier takes an inordinate amount of time to straighten up his uniform and tidy himself up. He picks up his canteen. Carl and I hold our breaths. He shakes it to his ear. I'm biting my lip not to laugh out loud. I'm mentally willing him to take a swig. He opens it. My heart is racing. He lifts it to his mouth and takes several long gulps. My insides are in a riot. I want to jump up and point and laugh. The soldier spits and cusses. He sniffs the canteen and cusses again. Bewildered, he looks around.

Carl can't bear to be still any longer. He jumps up, with his arms raised above his head and yells "Victory!"

I grab him by the belt and we start running.

"Halt!" we hear a cry behind us, and then something in German, which I don't understand, but assume not to be polite, by the way it was spoken.

I glance over my shoulder. Square Jaw gets on his bike, but it buckles underneath him, sending him hurling over the handlebar. He's waving his fists and starts running after us. We run so fast that I think my lungs are going to explode and my legs fall off. I know this forest better than anyone else, and I know that if you don't stay on the path you can very easily get lost. So we don't stay on the path.

At long last we reach the edge of the forest and race across the fields toward the Mortensens' farm. We run so fast that we have stitches in our sides. I keep looking over my shoulder. Square Jaw is no longer following us. We lost him!

Red-faced and catching our breath, we enter the house. We're laughing so hard, our sides hurt. Mrs. Mortensen meets us in the vestibule as we're removing our shoes.

"Well, hello, boys," she says in her soft, non-committal kind of way. "And what have the two of you been up to all day?"

"We peed in a Nazi canteen, stole some ammo and broke his bike," I state proudly between peals of laughter.

"How nice," she says as she turns her back to us. "Go wash up. Supper's on the table."

As always, she hasn't registered a word I've said.

> During the last days of the Winter War, Tanner met with Sweden's Prime Minister, Per-Albin Hansson, to discuss the possibility of a Nordic Defense Alliance, to stabilize the situation in the region. After the Moscow Peace Treaty was signed, this plan was published for discussion in both parliaments. However, the Soviet Union declared that an alliance would be in breach of the Moscow Peace Treaty, stalling the plan. Germany's invasion of Denmark and Norway killed the option altogether.

It's the last weekend before school's out and Jens and I have plans to meet in the town square after lunch to buy some ice at Baker's, and then we're spending the night at Carl's house. There's a ball game this afternoon between his town and ours, and we'll meet up there.

Apparently the last week of school consists of verbal tests, to determine whether or not you'll move up to the next grade in the fall. Kjersti says that none of her students has ever failed, and intends not to make this year an exception. Although I want to do well on my tests, I really don't see the point of this. For all I know, and desperately wish, I'll be home by the fall.

Today I have a paying job. I asked Mor if she had a chore I could do for money to buy ice, and after considerable thought, she told me I could help her wash the windows.

"Will you manage, do you think, with your hand in a cast?" she asks.

"I'm am-bi-*dex*-trous!" I pronounce proudly. I like that word.

Washing windows turns out to be a much more tedious job than it sounds. Not only are there about a million of them in the Mortensens' house, but each one is divided into six smaller parts. And they're covered in greenish-yellow grime. Pollen, Mor explains. After a while, however, we have a system figured out. She scrubs with soapy water, and I dry and polish with newspaper. My fingers are rapidly turning black and pruny, but I can taste the iced cream already, and it'll absolutely be worth the sacrifice.

"Come look at this, Paul!" Mor beckons, as she stands outside my window. Covered in dew, and gleaming in the sun, is a huge cobweb. "Nature's own little architect," she says admiringly.

"What's an army tech?"

"Ar-chi-tect," Mor enunciates. "It's somebody who designs buildings and advises on how they're constructed."

This fascinates me. There's a tiny little spider in the center of the web, sitting perfectly still. The web is enormous, covering nearly the entire lower left panel, and is as intricate as lacework.

"Isn't it wonderful how something so little can create something so fabulous?" Mor says admiringly.

"Father wanted to be a farmer before the war," I say pensively. Mor looks at me quizzically. "But he designed and built our house himself. Does that make him an architect?" I think I want to be an architect when I grow up.

We leave my window unwashed, and move on to the next one.

After lunch, I'm sore all over from stretching and bending and pumping and hauling heavy buckets of water, but I have a shiny ten øre coin tightly clasped in my fist, and I'm running down the road toward town. It was hard work, but I've more than earned my reward.

As I get to town Jens is already there, and is finishing his scoop.

"You're late!" he scolds. "It's strawberries today. I know it's your favorite, so you better hurry up, before he runs out."

"Here's my favorite Finn!" Baker greets me as we enter his shop. "I was just about to give up on you."

He reaches into the vat, and scrapes up three enormous scoops, plops them ceremoniously into a waffle cone and hands it over the counter to me.

"I only have ten øre," I whisper, slightly embarrassed.

"A little bonus for you, my friend. That's the last of the batch," he says. "I'd better go make some more before the game. Will the two of you be there to watch?"

My ears have stopped listening, as I salivate over my gigantic pile of iced cream. Strawberries. Back home they don't ripen until midsummer, if we're lucky. Subconsciously I hear Jens talking to Baker Sørensen, as I very precariously try to balance my treat with both hands. Baker disappears into the back of the shop, and soon we can hear him churning more cream. We decide to go and sit outside on the wall. My eyes are focused solely on my treat. I deserve this.

I worked for this. I scrubbed and polished glass until my fingers were wrinkly and black for this. *This* is my hard-earned reward.

Very carefully I start turning away from the counter, and nearly bump into somebody.

"I beg your par…" I start, and look up into the grinning face of Square Jaw.

He's in the shop with his three comrades from before, and they're poking at each other, laughing, pointing and jabbering in German. I'm frozen still. Jens is already outside. Out of nowhere, a hand reaches for my cone, and drops my treasure on the floor. All four of them are sniggering. I feel myself starting to hyperventilate. In disbelief I stare at my treasure, now a mere melting pile of slush on the floor.

Jens comes back in the shop, grabs my arm, and pulls me outside with him. He's talking, but I can't hear him for the blood thundering in my ears.

There are four bicycles parked against the wall in the town square. The town is deserted. Everyone must already be at the game, or on their way there. I eye the bicycles and intend to take revenge once and for all. I want to take the bike and throw it in the ocean. But the ocean is hours from here. And how would I get back? My knife is broken, and lying on my bedside table, so I can't puncture the tires, either. I look around the square for ideas. Ever since the occupation, the Dannebrog has been flying proudly everywhere. By grace of God, it's gone today. Probably taken to the game.

"… even listening to me, Paul? I know you're up to something," Jens' voice startles me from my reverie.

"Revenge," I say, as I study the bikes.

"Are you insane? Do you want your other hand broken, too?"

I miss Carl. He'd get it immediately, and then take it to the next level and beyond.

"Either you help me, or shut up."

On close inspection, one of the bikes' chains has barely visible scratches on it. I know that must've come from Square Jaw fixing it after I broke it. Luckily they're not locked, so I pull the bike out, and start pushing it toward the center of the square. It's surprisingly heavy.

"What are you doing?" Jens hisses.

"Give me a hand, will you?" I hiss back.

One eye constantly on the bakery door, we tie the handlebar to the rope, and start hoisting the bike up the flagpole.

"I think half-mast should send the right message," Jens smiles mischievously. He finally gets it.

Hiding behind the wall on the opposite side of the square, we take a position from where we can see the soldiers exit the bakery but they can't see us.

When they finally enter the square, we can barely contain ourselves. The confusion on their faces, combined with the angry, monosyllabic German shouts is very entertaining. I'm a spider with a web. I'm an architect of evil. Although I may be small, I've shown a soldier not to mess with me.

None of them look up, so they haven't discovered the missing bike yet. More shouting ensues. They start rounding the wall, and I realize that we have nowhere to hide. There are openings in the wall at each corner, and we're crouching by the one between town hall and the church. We can't move backwards, or we'll be clearly visible. Our only option is to sprint through the square, and hope that we can outrun them.

"On my signal," I whisper to Jens, "get ready to run."

"Where?"

"You go that way, I'll go this way," I say, pointing in opposite directions.

As one of the soldiers rounds the corner behind us, we start running. Inexplicably Jens lets out a roar. And before I know it, someone grabs me by the shirt collar. I start swinging my arms and kicking my feet. The soldier with the square jaw crosses over to me, and slaps me, open-fisted, across the face. I'm being suspended in the air by a grip around my neck, and keep kicking wildly. Somewhere I feel I make contact, and the soldier holding me curses loudly. The hand comes slashing in the air toward me again, snapping my head back. Explosions of color flash inside my head. This entire time, Square Jaw is spitting out German words.

"Learn Danish already!" I scream at him.

He raises his hand to strike me again, when I hear an angry German voice behind me. I'm dropped on the cobblestone like a sack of potatoes. As if on springs, all four soldiers form a straight line, stand at attention, swing their right arms out and, in perfect unison, shout something about Hitler.

Scrambling to my feet, I try to make my way out, but my escape is blocked by another soldier, whom I've never seen before. He's wiping soap off his face, so I assume he'd been at the barber's.

He starts talking to Square Jaw. I'm guessing he's an officer, based on how the others salute him, and the insane amount of ribbons on his uniform. Plus, he appears older than the other four, who don't look a day over twenty.

Unexpectedly Jens and Baker appear by my side. Baker starts conversing with the officer in fluent German.

"He's asking what happened," Baker says to me.

"He dropped my ice!" I say, pointing at Square Jaw.

Baker translates. Square Jaw looks angry and is rapidly saying something.

"He says it was an accident," Baker says. "That you bumped into him, and dropped it yourself."

This is ridiculous.

"If Paul did bump into him," Jens hurriedly intervenes, "why is his uniform so crispy clean?"

Good point, Jens!

Again, Baker translates, which is followed by excited arguing and finger pointing from Square Jaw.

"Did you steal his bicycle?" Baker asks me.

Shaking my head, I point up the flagpole. All eyes follow my extended finger. If I hadn't been looking directly at him, I would've missed a glint of amusement flash in the officer's eye. Baker is roaring with laughter. Square Jaw is cursing.

"Genug!" the officer says in exactly the same way Father used to say 'enough' when we kids were bickering.

Square Jaw clamps shut. The officer takes me by one hand, pushing Square Jaw in front of us across the street and into the bakery.

"Baker Sørensen! What's he going to do?" I wail over my shoulder.

I'm scared. I want to fight back, but there are now five Germans and just one of me.

Inside the shop, Baker starts talking to the officer in short, excited terms. He puts both hands on my shoulders and pulls me towards him. The officer points in turn to Square Jaw, the baker and to me. Then Baker leaves Jens and me standing alone, facing five German soldiers, as he disappears around the back of his shop.

"What's going to happen?" Jens whispers from the side of his mouth.

"I don't know," I reply. "Do you suppose Baker Sørensen is one of them?"

"No way! He's too nice."

"He speaks German!" I hiss. I'm seriously scared now.

"He's from the border. They all speak German there," Jens explains.

Baker reappears with a pail and a mop, which he ceremoniously hands to Square Jaw. While he's scrubbing the floor, Baker returns around the counter and starts scooping ice into two colossal cones. Easily four scoops each. He's whistling, and smiling happily while doing that, and hands them across the counter for me and Jens.

"Courtesy of your mopping friend over there," Baker winks at me. "What do you suggest, boys? Five and twenty apiece?"

"Easily a krone each!" Jens chimes in.

In complete awe, we leave the bakery.

> Sweden's and Finland's trade was completely
> controlled by Germany. As a consequence, Ger-
> many put pressure on Sweden to permit transit
> of military goods and troops on leave. Soldiers
> were to travel unarmed and not be part of unit
> movements.
> Finland, on the other hand, agreed to grant
> access to its territory for the Wehrmacht.
> Initially for transit of troops and military
> equipment to and from occupied Norway, in ex-
> change for arms and war materiel, but soon
> also for minor bases along the transit road.
> This agreement was in direct breach of not
> only the Moscow Peace Treaty, but also the
> Molotov-Ribbentrop Pact.

The game turns out to have become an international event. Instead of being played between our two towns, it's now our two towns against the Germans. It's fun to see the people you know this relaxed and in an environment that's different from their daily routine. There's the veterinarian from Carl's town, whose name I still don't know. Carl's foster father is running around the field, big beer belly jiggling like a bowl of pudding. The barber and the priest, both of whom are young, are our star players and our Mayor and the nice German officer act as co-referees.

The nice officer isn't wearing his coat or hat anymore, and his sleeves are rolled up, and when he sees me, he touches two fingers to his brow. I return the salute.

"What are you doing?" Carl hisses next to me. "Are you saluting a German?"

I tell him what happened.

"You had ice?" he huffs, jealously. "And you didn't save any for me?"

"It's frozen cream, Carl," I scoff. "It would've melted by the time we hit the forest."

"Yeah… But still…"

The game is tied and intense. Every time one of the referees blows the whistle, the other consults in the decision. They seem to agree, and there's a sportsmanlike camaraderie about them. They're always too far away for me to distinguish what language they're speaking, but judging from their use of hand gestures, I'm guessing it's sign language.

It's easy to detect who's who, because the Germans are wearing their uniforms, and the Danes are wearing short pants and shirts. Anders is our goalie. With his long limbs, he looks like a frog but has only let in one goal. And that was a completely uncalled-for free kick, hitting the upper right-hand corner. Impossible to block, unless you're three meters tall, which he's not.

Suddenly I can't help but think of Tor and how much he'd have enjoyed this. My heart aches for him. I wonder if he'll even remember me if ever we see each other again. I wish he were here. Subconsciously I drape an arm around both Jens and Carl. Even combined they're not as good a friend as Tor.

"You're thinking about Tor, aren't you?" Carl says.

"How'd you know?"

"Because I was."

I'm startled by a hand on my shoulder. Looking up, I see Mrs. Mortensen standing behind me.

"Look, Mrs. Mortensen!" I say. "Anders is our goalie! He's really good. He's only let in *one* goal, and that was really unfair…"

"Yes," she interrupts me, in her soft, non-committal voice. "Where's Christian?"

I point to a group of men to our right. Without a word, she leaves. I can see her talking to Christian, signal to Anders, and at the next time-out, all three of them walk to the Mortensens' truck and drive off. We're now without a goalie.

"What was that all about?" Carl asks me indignantly.

I shrug. "Evening chores." I feel guilty that I'm not helping out. Christian's arm is still in a sling, after all.

Our team is huddling on the side lines. If we don't find a goalie soon, we'll have to forfeit the game, and that'd be worse than actually losing. The score is one-one right now, with a good fifteen minutes still on the play clock.

Baker Sørensen comes up to us. "Paul, I need a favor," he says. "Could you watch my batch of ice, and sell as much as you can, of course. I've been assigned as the new goalie. You can keep half of what you make." He looks at my cast. "Can you handle it?"

"We'll help!" Carl and Jens pipe in simultaneously and eagerly.

Baker laughs. "I'm sure you will!" He takes off his apron, and hands it to me.

Proudly I take it. I've been assigned a task of responsibility. One not to be taken lightly.

The game resumes. Why Baker Sørensen hadn't been goalie in the first place is beyond me. His hands are enormous. He can wrap the fingers of one hand around the ball, and doesn't miss a single attempt.

Carl tries to sneak a hand into the vat. I slap it away.

"It's for sale. No freebies!"

"You're mean!"

"Hi Carl," a girl in a blue dress and pigtails comes up to us.

Carl takes a step away from her and grunts something unintelligible.

"Are you having fun?" the girl says.

Carl grunts again, and turns his head away. I poke him in the ribs.

"Don't be rude!" I hiss between gritted teeth.

Carl pokes me back.

"Would you like to watch the game with me?" the girl continues. "I'll buy you ice."

Carl is very nearly salivating, but averts his eyes to his shoes, and starts drawing half-moons in the dirt with his toe.

"No thank you. I'm watching it with my brother," he says, without looking at her.

"Oh," the girl sighs. There's an awkward silence. "Are you twins?"

She's not the first to ask us that, and undoubtedly won't be the last. "I'm a year older than him," I tell the girl.

"Eleven months!" Carl corrects me.

"Oh," the girl says again. "May I have two cones, please?"

Scooping ice is much harder than it looks. And, although I was assigned this task, there's no way I can scoop and hold a cone with one hand in a cast, so as much as I hate letting Carl anywhere near the vat, I have no choice but to let him help me. The scoops turn out nowhere near perfectly round, and somehow Carl manages to spill parts of them on his fingers, which he happily licks, when the girl hands me her money. Baker forgot to give me a change purse.

"That's alright," the girl says, when I explain to her that I can't break her coin, and leaves.

"Who was that?" Jens whispers. He can't take his eyes off the girl, and during the short interaction he was uncharacteristically quiet.

Carl shrugs, and continues drawing in the dirt with the toe of his shoe. "Just a girl from school," he says.

"Is she your girlfriend?" I tease him.

"She's very pretty," Jens says, his eyes glued to her.

"She's just a stupid girl, who bugs me all the time," Carl mutters.

"I think she's the prettiest girl I've ever seen," Jens whispers in awe, his eyes still glued to the girl.

I huff. "Little Sister is much prettier."

"Yeah, but... She's your *sister*. She's like a boy in a dress," Jens says. "I think I'll go watch the game with her."

Behind his back, Carl rolls his eyes and his index finger is making circles to his forehead. I agree. Jens has lost it.

"Why would you want to do that?" I ask him.

"Like I said; I think she's the prettiest girl I've ever seen," and he's gone, leaving Carl and me staring at his back.

The evening is warm, the game is exciting, and before I know it, I've sold the entire vat of ice. Baker will be pleased. Carl and I eventually get a system going, where I scoop, he holds the cone, and I accidentally spill ice on his fingers on purpose.

At dusk, the game is still tied and goes to overtime. None of the players are showing signs of fatigue. It seems as though everyone is having a good time. Neither team scores in overtime, so the game goes into free kicks. Our first one is blocked. The first German misses. Our second one is blocked as well, although barely. The second German steps up, throws his right leg back, and incredibly, as if changing his mind mid-kick, kicks the ball with his left foot straight into the net. Germany wins. We demand a re-match.

After the necessary handshakes and butt-pats, Carl's foster father finds us on the sidelines. He tells us that everyone will be gathering in his tavern tonight, and that he needs us to help him.

By the time we locate Jens and find our way to the tavern, it's already nearly full. Everyone is toasting each other, and singing. Loudly and poorly. If the Germans weren't wearing uniforms, I'd never know that there was a war going on. My job is to gather empty glasses from tables, and to bring them back to be washed by Carl and Jens, who cannot stop talking about the girl in pigtails. He tells us that he's in love, and that he intends to write a poem for her tonight, and asks Carl to deliver it for him. He's pumping Carl for information about her, but Carl is uncooperative. He keeps repeating that she's 'just a stupid girl'.

The singing is getting louder with each song. Although the Germans sound like they're having fun, they still sound brusque. It must be the language. While making my rounds around the tables collecting empty glasses I keep a wary eye out for Square Jaw. There are now easily twenty Germans inside the tavern, and just one of me. There's no way I can fight them all. Every now and then, some German hands me a coin and points to his glass. I take it he's asking for a refill, and gladly I accept his money. Between selling ice and waiting tables I will have made enough money today to buy ice for the entire summer. Unless I save it for something more important, of course. Like new watercolors. Or something nice for Mor. Like a new hat, perhaps. She'd like that. One with flowers, I think.

A crash in the corner awakens me from my reverie. A fight has broken out between a soldier and three townspeople. Baker Sørensen tries to step between them and gets a fist in the face. The Danes rush to pull the fighting men apart, whereas the Germans are egging them on. I'm frozen in place. As quickly as the fight started, it stops. All soldiers spring to attention and the room is hushed. The nice officer from earlier has entered. Solemnly he lets his eyes take in the scene, and then very calmly points to the majority of his soldiers, and they leave. The Danes resume drinking as if nothing had happened. The officer takes a seat in the corner with Baker and our Mayor, and I bring them each a fresh beer.

"Take a load off for a while, young Finn," Baker says and pulls out a chair for me. "I was just telling our friend here what an unequaled talent you have, and he doesn't believe that in a seven year-old. Will you prove that I'm not a liar?"

"I'm almost eight," I correct him.

I haven't drawn much since my arm has been in a cast. But I've been challenged, and now I'm nervous. Out of nowhere, a sheet of paper and a pen appear, and the nice officer's eyes bore into me. I point to him, to turn his face in a slight profile, and not look directly at me, and I start drawing. He isn't as handsome as Square Jaw, but he has very nice features. High cheekbones, a tall forehead and a straight nose. Trying not to think too much, I just let the pen fly over the paper. The end result would've been better with my right hand, and if people had left me alone, and weren't constantly peeking over my shoulder. But it's a fair likeness. I hand it to Baker Sørensen, who hands it to the officer. Someone behind him makes a comment, and everyone erupts in laughter. Even the officer smiles.

"They say he's not *that* good-looking," Baker Sørensen interprets.

"Oh, I can make him ugly!" I say enthusiastically, and take back the piece of paper.

On the back side I draw a caricature. They are much easier and infinitely more fun. I hand it directly to the officer, who bends over laughing.

"Much more like it!" Baker says.

The officer tosses me a ten-øre coin, and before I know it, I'm making caricatures of everyone at ten øre apiece. At the end of the night I'm rich. And an established artist!

> In May 1940, Winston Churchill was elected Prime Minister of Great Britain and the British War Cabinet began debating whether to negotiate with Hitler or continue fighting. Germany was advancing to the west, having occupied the Netherlands and Belgium, and was likely to occupy France as well.
> The Soviet leaders continued to involve themselves in Finland's domestic affairs. Germany was eyeing Finland's nickel deposits in the Petsamo area, as well as Finland's proximity to Norway and Russia.

Summer 1940.

School's out, and Kjersti's record is intact. Everyone in our class passed to the next level. My wrist has healed perfectly, and I'm finally cast-free. Free, as in shedding a skin or losing shackles. Mor invented a fun parlor trick that is sure to please everyone. I sit at a table with a pen in each hand, and start a sentence with my left hand and finish it with my right. I don't exactly understand why this is funny to anyone, but now I just do it out of habit.

Yesterday I received a letter from Mother. The Mayor/postmaster actually hand-delivered it himself, something he never does. But, as he said, he knew how anticipated the letter was. And as he was on his way to Carl's foster parents' tavern to enjoy a glass of brew anyway, and the Mortensens' house is on the way, he saw no harm in breaching protocol. Just this once. Eagerly I tore into Mother's letter. It left me feeling cold, angry and sad. Mother is going to have another baby. Why does she keep producing new children, instead of bringing her old ones home? Mor tells me not to be bitter, but I can't help how I feel. Mother went on and on about trivial matters such as my birthday and how quickly new baby Ingrid is growing, but never mentioned anything of substance, such as Tor or whether Father and Uncle Johannes are alive. Although, Mor says that since Mother is pregnant again, Father must've survived the war.

So, today is the morning of my eighth birthday, and the day is promising to be sunny and warm. I'm packing an overnight bag, because Jens, Carl and I are camping at the fort. We're going to revive the cancelled Olympics there. Denmark versus Finland. Jens has been secretive about the story of the fort, but since the days are so long and the nights are light, we've finally managed to get him to agree to spend the night there with us. Just in case, I'm packing an old hurricane lamp that I found in the shed.

A familiar tune catches my attention, and through the open window I can see Jens already walking up the lane whistling, and Heidi leisurely trotting up to greet him. I hurry up and finish packing when I notice that my knife is missing. I'm sure it's been on my night stand ever since the day it got broken, but now I can't find it anywhere. I'd like to bring it with me tonight as protection, just in case the fort actually *is* haunted. The knife is still broken, because unlike broken bones, knives don't heal themselves, but ghosts don't know that.

Now I can hear Jens in the house talking to Mor and Mrs. Mortensen, and I still can't find the knife. I look everywhere, trying to think of the last time I saw it. Just as I'm crawling under the bed there's a knock on my door.

"We're not going to sing to your butt, so would you please crawl out from under there," Jens laughs.

Turning around, I can see Mor carrying a cake, decorated with strawberries, and behind her are all the Mortensens carrying presents.

"How did you know?" I ask astonished.

Naturally I knew it was my birthday, but never mentioned it, because I didn't think the Mortensens should bother acknowledging it. I'm so touched that I'm speechless.

The cake is delicious, made with fresh strawberries. Mr. and Mrs. Mortensen give me a brand-new flashlight, Anders gives me the model airplane that I coveted at the fair, and finally Christian hands me a small object, wrapped in brown paper.

"It's not much," he says shyly, "but I thought it was important to you."

Eagerly I open it. My father's knife falls into my hand. Unsheathing it I can just barely detect a small, hairline crack that has been welded. The knife is sharpened and polished. A lump forms in my throat and my vision gets blurry. This is by far the nicest thing anyone has ever done for me. I was devastated when the knife was broken. And this morning when I thought I'd lost it forever... And I didn't think Christian liked me.

"Not good as new, but still good to use," Christian says.

I don't know what to say. I'd like to hug him, but since I'm eight now, I probably should stop doing that with men. I can't take my eyes off the knife.

"Aren't you going to say anything to Christian?" Mor urges.

Finally, when I look up, my willpower abandons me, and a tear falls down my cheek. Quickly I wipe it off.

"Mange tak, Christian," I say, in a voice that I don't recognize. It sounds old and distant. I wish I still were seven.

```
The 1940 Summer Olympics, originally scheduled
to be held in Tokyo, were cancelled because of
the war. Tokyo was stripped of its host status
for the Games by the IOC in 1937 due to the
outbreak of the second Sino-Chinese War. The
games were then awarded to Helsinki, the origi-
nal runner-up in the bidding process. The games
were eventually suspended indefinitely due to
the war and did not resume until the London
Games of 1948. Helsinki eventually hosted the
Olympic Games in 1952 and Tokyo in 1964.
```

The fort sits on a little limestone hump at the edge of the forest between Carl's town and mine. Most of it is in ruins and centuries of vegetation have covered it. Nonetheless, the tower still stands erect and fascinates me. Although it's square on the outside, it's rounded on the inside. There's a well-worn staircase leading up to the tower, from where on a clear day you could probably see clear across Denmark. I cannot figure out how it's been built. There's not a single chisel mark on any surface, and the rocks are clearly from the limestone on which it stands. Jens and Carl guffaw at my astonishment and say it's nothing compared to the pyramids in Egypt. One day, when the war is over, and I have saved enough money, I intend to go to Egypt and find out how the pyramids were built.

In the meantime, we're competing for national honor. Jens puts in an official protest that it's unfair that there's only one delegate from Denmark and two from Finland, but as Carl and I are in the majority, his protest is overruled. Carl is a natural athlete with the speed of Jesse Owens and the endurance of Paavo Nurmi, two of his heroes. Today, in our Olympics he wins the spitting contest, the running and the slingshot. I win the wrestling and boxing and Jens wins swimming and long-jump. There's no moat, but a little stream trickles through the beech forest, and it's deep enough for us to swim in, and wide enough to pose a challenge jumping across. Our prizes are three pieces of limestone for gold, two for silver and one for bronze. At the end of the day Finland has beaten Denmark two to one. Hardly surprising considering the odds.

It's getting late, and we're all starving. Inside the fort there's a great hall with a fireplace, and we gather sticks to start a fire. The chimney is probably clogged, because heavy smoke starts billowing in just as soon as the fire starts. Luckily there's no roof, so the smoke wafts out, taking all insects with it.

The limestone we chipped from the hill as our prizes works well as chalk, and we decide to decorate the walls with imaginative cave man-like drawings. Carl is working along a wall farthest away from the tower staircase, towards the ruined part of the fort. He stumbles and falls on some vines.

"Fellas?" he says carefully. "You've gotta come see this!"

Something in his voice sounds ominous. He's pointing at a barely visible square of iron, protruding from under the debris on which he fell.

"Get away from there!" Jens snaps. "That's the well of blood!"

"The *what*?!" Carl and I ask fascinated.

Now I'm curious, and stretch my neck to look inside. It's too dark to see anything. Using our knives and hands, Carl and I clear out enough brush to squint an eye through. Shining my new flashlight down the well, I can barely detect a round hollow, easily ten meters deep and about five meters round, dug into the bedrock beneath us. I'm surprised that we've never discovered this before, as often as we've played here. But then again, we usually hang out either in the tower or outside, because Jens is so scared to go inside. I start to clear more debris, when Jens grabs my arm.

"Don't open it! You'll let the evil out!" he says, ashen-faced.

"What? You're just being silly. It's nothing but a deep pit," I argue.

"What's it used for?" Carl asks.

"Nothing anymore, but ..."

"But what? *But what!?!*" Carl is as intrigued as I am.

"Very well," he sighs. His face is oddly morose. "I'll tell you the story, but if you get scared, it's your own fault. And don't go running out and leave me here alone, either!"

Captivated, we all take a seat in front of the fire, squatting down on our sleeping bags Indian-style. The sun is setting, leaving the sky above us an unnerving shimmer of gray and red. Jens reaches for my flashlight and illuminates his face under his chin.

He lowers his voice. "The year was seven hundred and ninety-two, when the Russian Viking Henrik..."

"There are no Vikings in Russia!" Carl blurts out.

"Not anymore," Jens continues, in his narrative voice. "For Bloody Henrik had slain them all..."

"I thought his name was just Henrik," I say.

"Do you want me to tell the story or don't you?" Jens snaps.

"Sorry. Go ahead."

"Bloody Henrik was the second son of the King of all Russia. He killed his father, and tried to kill his brother, too."

"Why?" Carl whispers, mesmerized.

"He wanted to be king," Jens continues. "When his brother found out about his plans, he shunned Bloody Henrik to the oceans. He became the most feared Viking that ever lived. He plundered, killed and stole everything, leaving a bloody trail from Russia to Denmark. When he set foot on Danish soil, he found that the people were unruly but the land was fruitful, so he declared himself Ruler of all Danes. He built this castle. The Danes were a handsome people of pale skin and fair hair, who did not take kindly to being ruled by a brute with dark hair. So Bloody Henrik decided to make himself look like the people he ruled."

"How?" Carl and I whisper in unison.

Jens takes a deep breath. He locks eyes first with me, then with Carl. "He went from village to village and stole all the fair-haired children. Children with hair just like yours!" He shines the flashlight at my hair. "And yours!" He does the same to Carl. "He brought all the fair-haired children to his castle, and when the moon was full, he scalped them!"

Carl and I cringe. "Like an Indian?"

"With a rusty old saw Bloody Henrik cut off the top of the blond children's heads, and made a wig for himself."

"Did they die?" Carl whispers. His eyes are about to bulge out of their sockets.

"Not at first. That's when Bloody Henrik built the well of blood. He tossed the children into the well and they would scream and cry and bleed to death. Sometimes, even now, when the moon is full, as it will be tonight, you can hear their weeping howls." Jens pauses to look at our bleached faces. "One day, a brave boy, called Jens the Magnificent..."

Carl starts sniggering. I poke him in the ribs.

"... the last child ever scalped by Bloody Henrik, took the scalping saw and cut Bloody Henrik's head off! Jens the Magnificent found his own hair, put it back on his head and escaped. Of course, his hair was red with blood by then, and fresh blood dripped onto his nose and cheeks. To this day, whenever you see a Dane with red hair and freckles, you know that he's a descendant of Jens the Magnificent, who slew Bloody Henrik." He turns the flashlight to his face, demonstrating his own freckles and reddish hair.

Carl and I draw a unanimous breath. "Is that true?" Carl whispers.

Jens nods solemnly.

"Then what happened?" I ask.

"Then Bloody Henrik's decapitated body was so angry, that it wanted to go after Jens the Magnificent. But because he couldn't see, his body kept thrashing against the walls, and they came tumbling down. Covering his dead body and severed head."

"So his body is buried somewhere under the ruins?"

"And there are skeletons and skulls in the well?"

"Half skulls," Jens states gravely. "Remember, the top part was cut off. But they're probably all rotted away by now. It's been over a thousand years, after all. And nobody's ever seen Bloody Henrik's body. Or head."

We sit in silence, staring at the fire for a long time. The sun has set, the moon will be rising shortly, and although it is summer and not entirely dark, I have a very uncomfortable feeling. I don't believe in fairy tales or ghosts. And last Christmas, when we asked Mother if Santa would find us at Farfar's house, Farfar told me that there is no Santa Claus. That he was just a ruse that rich parents used on their spoiled, no-good children to get them to behave for a week in December. But there's something about this place that gives me the creeps. It feels as though we're being watched. I hadn't noticed, but during Jens' story Carl kept inching closer to me, and now he's very nearly in my lap. I don't want to be here anymore, but can't show that I'm scared. I am, after all, the oldest one here.

"What was that?" Carl jolts.

I hear it, too. It sounds like footsteps. Now someone is moaning. I reach for my knife. There's definitely something here. Slowly two white shadows appear from the opposite corner. We scream, and huddle together in the corner. The two shapes move toward us, moaning louder now. I can feel my heart thumping against my ribs. Carl is whimpering next to me. I'm scared. The only exit is blocked by the ghostly shadows. Our only escape is to go is up the tower or down the well.

Now one of the ghosts reaches out its arms toward us.

"Give me your haaaiiir," it moans. "I want to be blond like yooouuu..."

We scream again, and press our bodies tighter against the wall. The shadows step into the light of the fire, bending over with crackling laughter. They remove their sheets. It's Anders and Christian.

"You should see your faces!" Anders laughs.

I'm so angry and pumped with adrenaline, I could plunge my knife into him.

"I could've killed you, I hope you know!" I say defiantly.

"Sure," says Christian. "When? Between those girly squeals and passing out from fear?"

"What are you doing here, anyway?"

"Mor sent us to check on you. And we brought dinner," Anders says, and produces a picnic basket. Carl plunges for it. "Good story, Jens," Anders continues. "Since when was Henrik Russian?"

Jens shrugs. "I don't know. I figured it'd have a scarier effect. Paul and Carl hate Russians."

"Jens the Magnificent was a nice touch!" Christian says.

Jens takes a mock bow.

Now I'm even angrier. "So the story isn't true?"

"Of course not! What are you, some baby who believes in ghosts?"

"Well, someone built this castle," I argue. "And you've been scared for months so there must be some story!"

"Oh, the moaning and cries are true," Anders assures me. "I've heard them. But nobody knows the real story."

The others gather around the fireplace, and start feasting on the delicacies in Mor's dinner basket. I'm too upset to eat. Anders and Christian tell stories about how they used to play out here when they were our age, and they both tell a different version of the cries in the night. Christian's version of the castle's history derives from Mr. Mortensen and involves naughty little boys, who were made to spend the night in the well as punishment. Apparently one boy was forgotten, and died. Carl is hanging on every word. Naturally, I too am fascinated, but feign disinterest. Anders heard a different version from Mor. According to him the well used to hold water at one time, and unwed mothers used to drown their newborns in it. The stories vary, but they all include little children. They all agree that the castle was built by a Danish nobleman called Henrik and it was built in the twelfth or thirteenth century. Nobody knows why it fell. Anders stops, mid-sentence.

"Did you hear that?" he whispers.

Cold chills run down my spine. "Quit it, Anders, it's not funny anymore."

I did hear a faint sound in the distance, but I know that Anders and Christian must've asked one of their friends to come and scare us. I'm not going to be fooled twice in one night.

Anders gets up on his feet. He looks pale.

"What is it?" Carl asks.

Christian hushes him. The sound is stronger now, and it sounds as though it's coming from directly below us. There's a distinct echo.

"Paul, I'm scared," Carl whimpers, and reaches for my hand.

I brush him aside. "It's just Anders playing tricks," I tell him, irritated. "Anders, I know you're doing it, so you can stop now!"

"I'm not doing anything. That's the moaning I heard before." The look on his face defies suspicion. He's breathing heavily, and his face looks drained of blood.

Jens and Carl go cowering under their sleeping bags in the corner.

"Let's go home," Christian says.

"Let's go find your ghosts," I say.

"Are you insane?" Anders tries to hold me back.

"Maybe, but at least we'll know once and for all what's making that noise," I say, surprising even myself how grown-up and brave I sound.

Grabbing my flashlight, I notice how violently my hands are trembling. I take a few deep breaths to steel my nerves. It doesn't help. Thinking that I'll stumble into one of Anders or Christian's friends, I hold the light in one hand and my knife in the other, and move toward the sound. It's definitely coming from the well of blood. The high stone walls are bouncing the sound around, creating an echo and raising the volume. I keep telling myself that it's just one of the older boys from town, and the worst that can happen to me is that I'll die of a heart attack if they jump up and scare me. Flat on my stomach on the edge of the hole I shine the light into the well. Then I reach over the edge with my knife. And then I look. At a minimum one half-dozen luminescent eyes stare back at me. The moaning stops. My heart in my throat, I roll over and pull back from the edge.

"There's something down there," I whisper to the others. "And it's *not* human."

Jens and Carl start sprinting toward the exit.

"Wait!" Anders says, and grabs them by their coats. "We have to stick together."

Carl looks like he's about to start hyperventilating. Jens is visibly shaking. Anders and Christian are anxious to leave. I'm immobilized by fear. The weak moaning resumes. As one, we sprint to our feet, and make toward the door. In my haste, I drop my knife. It falls down the well. There's a distinct hissing from below. We stop.

"Did you hear what I heard?" Christian asks Anders.

They take my flashlight, and walk up to the mouth of the well. I follow them, and peek over Anders's shoulder. At the bottom of the well we can see a group of cats. Regular, striped house cats. A litter of kittens is feeding on one of them, whereas another is grooming himself and yet another two seem oblivious to anything. Probably sleeping. We have been scared witless by a colony of felines.

In the morning, we explore the outside of the fort, trying to determine how the cats get in and out of the well. It's far too deep even for cats to climb. At long last we discover a crack in the limestone, barely wider than my fist, but impossible for us to widen or crawl through. So, to retrieve my knife, I'm lowered down the well by rope. By the end of the week, the entire town has heard how we solved the mystery of the moaning fort that has been haunting three generations.

> The infrastructure and economic situation in Finland were dire directly after the Winter War and long into the summer of 1940. Especially damaging was the loss of fertilizer imports. Together with the loss of the best agricultural land in Karelia to Russia, the loss of cattle during the hasty evacuation during and after the Winter War, and unfavorable weather, this resulted in a drastic fall of foodstuff production. Adding to this was the disproportionate budget of 1940, in which the majority was earmarked to the re-building of the military. Some of the provision deficit could be purchased from Sweden and the Soviet Union, although delayed deliveries and outrageous prices were commonly used to exert pressure over Finland. Again, Finland had no alternative but to turn to Germany for aid.

> In June 1940, France fell to Germany, and ru-
> mor had it that Britain would soon negotiate
> peace or face German occupation. Wishing to
> cultivate close and friendly relations with
> the projected victors, Finland stepped up the
> courtship of Germany.
> In July, a German representative queried Ryti
> and Mannerheim whether Finland was ready to
> withstand another assault by the Red Army. The
> common fear was that the Winter War was simply
> a prelude for worse to come. The phrase 'In-
> terim Peace' was coined. Mannerheim estimated
> that Finland could and would defend itself,
> but needed more materiel, and would not attack
> unprovoked.

The summer passes far too quickly. We spend our days playing in the beech forest or the fort, I keep sketching everything I see, and Mor makes sure I read the newspaper daily, so that I understand what's going on in Finland. I never see Square Jaw or his band of bullies anymore. In fact, we rarely see any Germans at all in our town. They do, however, show up for the game every Saturday afternoon. The nice officer is always there, and tips his hat at us when we meet. At the end of the summer, the score is tied between Denmark and Germany. Very diplomatic, according to Baker Sørensen.

Before I know it, the summer is over, and school starts on Monday. Jens and I are enjoying a scoop of Baker Sørensen's iced cream in the town square as we spot the postmaster locking up the door to the post office across the square.

"Afternoon, Mayor!" Jens hollers at him.

Startled, he swings around. A big smile spreads across his face as he sees us.

"Ah, Paul! I have a letter for you. One moment, please," he says and disappears back inside the post office.

A letter! A million mixed emotions are mingling inside me. Mother has finally written again! I've been expecting her to write, because the last letter I wrote included a dozen drawings and watercolors of Mrs. Mortensen's roses. They were gorgeous this summer. Whereas Mother's roses in Karelia were huge, rich in color and very fragrant, Mrs. Mortensen's are rich in variety. The ones climbing up the trellis are especially fascinating, and I told Mother that I will build one for her when I get home.

Ceremoniously the postmaster hands me the letter. The handwriting is a stranger's, and the post mark is illegible but the stamp is Swedish. Has Mother been evacuated, too? Anxiously I tear into the letter. It's not from Mother. It's better.

Hi Paul!

You promised you'd write and you haven't, so I'm writing you instead. I've found an apartment in Stockholm. My new address is on the envelope. Please write!

How do you like living in Denmark? I'm working with child transportations again, and we're now slowly starting to bring children back home. Please be patient. Your foster family will receive all details soon.

Although you must miss your family, and are probably anxious to get back, please know that things are really bad in Finland right now. I'm doing all I can to get you and your siblings on the first train out of Denmark, but you must understand that I can't promise anything. I'm trying to argue with my superiors that children from Denmark should have first priority, because you're occupied by Germany, but the counterargument is that there are Germans in Finland and Sweden, too. Nonetheless, I'll keep fighting for you.

Keep your chin up!

Love,

Natalia.

"What's it say?" Jens asks me excitedly. "Who's it from?"

"I'm going home," I say, barely grasping the words.

"Is this like the time you thought you were going home after the Finnish war ended, or are you really going home this time? Because I don't want you to go."

The words are starting to sink in. "This time, I'm really going home. Come on! Let's go tell Carl!"

Little do I know that 'the first train out of Denmark' doesn't leave for another eight months.

> Although the peace treaty was signed, and the Winter War was officially over, the state of war wasn't revoked in Finland because of the widening world war, the difficult food supply situation, and the battered condition of the military. The continued state of war enabled Marshal Mannerheim to remain commander-in-chief. He was assigned to supervise the reorganization of Finland's Armed Forces and the fortification of the new border. In less than a week after the peace treaty was signed,

the fortification along the 1200 km long border
started, with the main focus on the line between the Gulf of Finland and Lake Saimaa.
During most of 1940, military purchases were
prioritized over civilian needs; military ex-
penditures were 45% of the national budget in
1940. Eventually Mannerheim was able to present a somewhat positive assessment of the state
of the Army.
Late in the fall of 1940 relief to the insecurity of the civilians presented itself in
the form of the arrival of German troops. The
civilian population generally approved of the
presence of German troops. It was seen as a
deterrent for further Soviet threats and a
counterbalance to the Soviet troop transfer
rights, as set forth in the peace treaty. Germans arrived and established quarters, depots,
and bases. Also, road works for improving winter travel and new roads were discussed, and
later financed and built, by Germans. By the
fall of 1940, nearly all of Finland's imports
came from Germany.
Hitler was increasingly interested in the prospect of invading the Soviet Union and in December 1940 signed the directive for operation
Barbarossa.
As the state of affairs in Finland was seemingly stabilizing, the displaced children began returning.

April 1941.

Daily, after receiving Natalia's letter, I go to the post office, hoping for information about going home. Usually I go there once before school and once after.
Nothing appears, and finally, about a month later, I give up. Natalia and I correspond faithfully, and she is the only one who can tell me anything worthwhile,
and keep my spirit positive, although she doesn't have any concrete information.
Mother writes sporadically, and has no news of consequence, including that of me
going home, and whether or not Father and Uncle Johannes are alive.

Then, finally, the day arrives when I get a set date and time on which to
be in Copenhagen. The week leading up to that day is a flurry of activity. All my
good travel clothes are too small, and I have to have new ones made. During my
thirteen months in Denmark I've accrued so many new possessions, that I have
to get a new bag to carry it all. But the worst part is saying good-bye. As much as

I didn't want to be here when I first arrived, I've come to regard this little town as my new home, and everyone in it as my new family. As excited as I am about going home, part of me will stay behind forever.

Kjersti organizes a very nice last day of school, where presents are exchanged, and she brings cake and lemonade. Everyone makes me swear to write to them just as soon as I get home. Kjersti gives me a box of brand new watercolors, with firm instructions to keep working on my art. Like anyone could stop me!

Jens has been acting strange ever since I announced when I'd be leaving. He's quiet and gloomy and keeps to himself. After my last day in school, I see him running down the main street, in the direction of his house. I set out after him, calling his name, but he has a good lead on me, and I'm not able to catch up. He must've heard me, but pretends that he didn't.

As I arrive at his house, I'm greeted by his mother, who looks bewildered. She tells me that Jens took off on his bicycle not two minutes ago, in the direction of the main road. Knowing exactly where he's going, I rush over to Baker's and borrow his bicycle.

Pedaling as fast as I can, I set off toward the old fort. The landscape is flat, and the road is straight, and I can see Jens in the very far distance. Knowing full well that he's beyond earshot I call out after him nonetheless. What's his problem? This is not the kind of farewell I had expected from my best friend.

Reaching the old fort, I climb the tower, and find Jens sitting with his back against the wind, hunched low against the stone wall. He looks a mixture of morose and angry, with one hand aimlessly drawing with chalk on the stone floor he's sitting on.

"What's wrong with you?" I ask, sitting down opposite him.

Pulling the collar of his coat up, to shield from the wind, he simply shrugs.

Trying to coax something out of him I say "I'm sad to be leaving, too..."

"No you're not!" he shouts. "All you've been talking about for the last week is how happy you are about going home, how you can't wait to see your dog again, how coming to Denmark was the stupidest thing that ever happened to you..."

"I never said that!" I interrupt him.

"Yahaa!" Jens insists, and gets all bug-eyed, like he does, when he gets really excited. "I heard you!"

"When?"

"Kjersti asked you what the first thing was that you were going to say to your mother, and you said 'sending children to Denmark is stupid'. I heard you! You can't deny that."

With a heavy heart I move next to him. "That's not what I meant," I say. "I've never told anyone this, because I don't want you to think I'm a mama's boy, but I really miss my mother." I look at Jens, expecting him to make fun of me, but he just looks confused.

"So how is it stupid?"

"Have you ever been separated from your mother?"

"Sure, once, when she was taken to the hospital in Helsingør because she was going to have a baby, but started bleeding, from... you know, where she pees, and she stayed away for several days and didn't come back with a baby at all. I missed her while she was gone."

"Okay, so imagine if nobody told you what was going on. If one day you're just playing with your friends, and the next day you're sitting with strangers on a train, and you don't get to say goodbye to your own mother and you don't know if you'll ever see her again. Imagine if you're sent away from your family and your home, and air-raid sirens are wailing and bombs are falling, and you don't know if anyone survived that. Imagine then if you arrive in a whole other country, you're surrounded by strangers, and you don't speak their language, and they take your brothers and sister away from you. And then nobody will tell you anything! And you don't know where the rest of your family is or if you're ever going home or ever even seeing anyone again. Imagine that, and then ask me again why I think sending children away was stupid!"

Jens sits quietly for a long time, looking lost in thought. Obviously I've hit a nerve.

"So you don't think Denmark is stupid?" he finally says.

"Of course not! I've had so much fun here. And I'll miss everyone like crazy. I like the Mortensens, and you and this whole village. But... I want my mother."

We sit silently for a while, watching the setting sun behind us color the billowing clouds in the east. I can hear Jens next to me draw a deep breath and let it out in a sigh.

"What're you thinking about?" I ask him.

"Nothing... Just how great it's been to have a brother for a year and after tomorrow I'll never see you again."

I spit in my palm and extend it to him. "I swear that we'll be brothers forever."

Jens spits in his palm, and pumps my hand vigorously. "Brothers forever!"

I'm tagged again, standing with my siblings and our Danish families in Copenhagen, clutching our bags, and trying to appear brave, when all I want to do is cry. Saying goodbye is heart-wrenching. Everyone cries, or makes valiant efforts to hold back. That's what I do.

I almost hoped that nobody had come to see me off, because it would've been easier to simply leave, without having to think about whether I'll ever see anyone again. My Danish friends feel closer to me than my older brother, whom I haven't seen in a year, and the insecurity of what to expect at home makes the pull to stay even stronger. Luckily, however, my siblings are traveling with me, and after a year-long separation we're all finally reunited again.

Anders and Christian are the first to actually use the word 'goodbye'. Anders will be joining the Army in a month, and my father has become something of a hero to him. He was so impressed by the Finnish ski troops during the Winter War, that this past winter, when we actually got some snow on the ground he asked me to teach him to ski. Which I did.

"Please give my best regards to your father," Anders tells me. "Um … if he survived. And if not … well … you should be very proud of him."

"Thank you, Anders. I am." I tell him to be safe in the Army and to write home a *lot*.

Mrs. Mortensen looks morose as she presses a tightly folded handkerchief into my palm.

"Roses," she says. "For your mother."

Knowing how difficult it is for her to form a coherent sentence, and having been in the same situation myself not too long ago, all I can do is throw my arms around her waist and hug her tightly.

"How nice," I say, hoping she won't think I'm being sarcastic, but rather trying to relate to her on her own terms.

Jens gives me a chunk of chalk from the fort and says that now I'll have a piece of Denmark with me forever.

All too soon we're told to board the boat for the strait crossing, and Mor presses me to her chest. This is where all my dams collapse, and I start crying too. She doesn't say anything. She doesn't need to. We just stand there, holding each other tight, both of us crying. There are so many things I want to tell her, but there's a huge knot in my throat, and I can't find my voice. I want to thank her for taking me in, and not out of obligation but out of the sheer goodness of her heart. I want to thank her for being patient with me when I was struggling with the language, and for making things so much easier for me. I further want to thank her for being there for me, when I thought my whole world was falling apart. But most of all, I want to tell her that I love her, that I'll miss her and that I'll never, ever forget her. Hugging her tighter, I try to steady my breathing, by taking in a scent memory of her. By hugging her tight, I hope that I can telepathically transmit all my feelings, without having to say them out loud.

Eventually Mor peels me off her, takes my face between her soft hands and looks me deeply in they eyes. My chest is tightening, and the tears are threatening to start again. Mentally I'm willing her not to say anything, for fear that I'll crumple right there in front of everyone. A weak, quivering smile appears on her face; she pecks a kiss on my forehead, and sends me on my way to board the boat.

As the boat pulls away from the dock, we're standing in the stern, waving and crying, until we can no longer see anyone. It's impossible to explain how I feel. It's almost as if I'm being pulled by two equally strong powers into two opposite directions, splitting me into two people. After thirteen months in Denmark, I've rooted. Although I can't wait to see Mother again, I feel empty and lost, and I know I will miss my Danish family and friends forever.

The only one not crying is Johan. In fact, he was the first one at the dock this morning. He was sitting alone in a corner, reading a book, and hasn't shown any emotion of any kind. I haven't dared ask him how this last year has been, but judging by the fact that there was nobody there to see him off, I don't think it was good.

We were all very excited about seeing Johan again. He's grown significantly and his shoulders are disproportionately wide for his body, but he's still quiet and pensive. Carl is now taller than me, and will probably soon be as tall as Johan. Little Sister is still petite, but because her hair has grown so long, her cherub curls have straightened substantially, diminishing her angelic look.

"I don't want to go!" Little Sister keeps crying. "I want Aunt Bodil and Uncle Oscar! Paul, take me back! Ple-he-heease!"

We find a bench on the deck and take a seat. "Don't you want to go home and see Mother?" I ask.

"No! I want Aunt Bodil and Uncle Oscar! Why can't you take me back? I don't want to go! I *don't* want Mother, I want Aunt Bodil! I want Aunt Bodil to be my mother!"

Hearing this breaks my heart even further. There are no words that'll comfort her, and she doesn't stop crying until she exhausts herself and falls asleep.

Once we get on the train, and Carl immediately starts jabbering excitedly about seeing Mother and Father again, and I start talking about Tor, Little Sister perks up.

"Tor, the dog?" she asks. "I want to see Tor!"

The little devil that he can be, Carl can't help himself, and has to take a stab at this opportunity. "I thought you were going back to Aunt Bodil and Uncle Oscar?" he teases her.

If he weren't sitting so far away from me, I'd smack him over the mouth. We've just gotten Little Sister to be positive again and join in our general excited anticipation, and he has to ruin it.

"I want to see Tor," Little Sister states in defiance, the enthusiasm rising on her face. "And Father, too. How big is new baby? Will Tor recognize me? I'm going to play with him first and then new baby and then Tor again... When will we be home?... How much further?..."

The trip home is very different from our trip out. We're sitting in a regular passenger train, the windows are no longer blacked out, and we can actually see the landscape rushing by us. There are a few other War Children on the train with us, and the atmosphere is electric. As subdued, scared and sad as we were on our way down, now we're pumped up with anticipation. We're going home. The only blemish in our otherwise flawless trip home is that Natalia isn't our chaperone. She was meant to be, but had to change shifts with someone, because she's taken ill. I intend to write to her as soon as I get home.

Logically I know that this return trip is faster, because we make fewer stops, keep a steady speed, and don't have to be inspected at the border crossing, but emotionally it seems to take forever. In anticipation of the inspection at the border, I told Aunt Bodil (yes - I call her that now, she's actually quite nice, once you get to know her, and treats Little Sister like the angel that she is) to sew her stuffed toy puppy inside the lining of Little Sister's overcoat. Luckily, that wasn't necessary, and as soon as we're across the border, I tear into the hem of the coat, and retrieve Little Sister's toy.

"Do you suppose we can burn these when we get home?" Carl asks, toying with his tag.

"When *are* we home?" Little Sister is getting annoying. "How much further?"

"Any minute now," I tell her, grab her hand and go to the front of our car. "Let's get there faster! Help me help the train!" I tell her and we start pushing the inside wall of the car.

Carl joins us. We're laughing, as our feet are sliding on the floor, our hands flat against the wall, and very soon it feels as though the train actually *is* moving faster. Eventually even Johan joins us. And before I know it, all the War Children in our car are pushing the wall, laughing and chanting "We're going home, we're going home, we're going home..."

> After the end of the Winter War, approximately one hundred thousand Finns were recruited to strengthen the Army Reserve. Non-commissioned officers who had proven their worth during the

Winter War were asked to stay and train the many new recruits. Finland was aiming to recruit any civilian whose job could be done by someone else, and had, at its peak, nearly sixteen percent of the population in uniform.

In August 1940 the Soviet Union annexed the Baltic countries, and Finland felt the imminent threat to her independence, again feeling surrounded and alone. The Baltics were seized, Germany and the Soviet Union were in a diplomatic state of peace, and Sweden had officially made her neutrality and unwillingness to assist very clear.

In November 1940, President Kyösti Kallio resigned, and was succeeded by Risto Ryti.

The Finnish Army had more than shown the world what it was made of during the Winter War and Hitler wasn't blind to the country's strategic location either. By the end of 1940 Finland and Germany were in talks about strengthening the military and intensifying the number of troops along the border. It wasn't made official, nor was it known by Finnish leaders, that Hitler had plans to use Finland as a thoroughfare to Leningrad, and by spring of 1941 nearly fifty thousand German troops were stationed in Finland. Officially, Finland had only agreed to allow German troops transfers through the country, in exchange for military equipment.

It's pouring down rain. The four of us have our faces pressed against the train window, but all we see are gray streaks of rain blurring the landscape we keep crawling past. The anticipation is overwhelming. Little Sister is nearly hyperventilating. The conductor just passed through our car and announced that our station was next, and our chaperone told us to get dressed and gather our belongings. We've been dressed and had our belongings ready since we crossed the border.

When the train finally comes to a halt, we're standing by the door, fighting to open it. When at long last it does, the rain whips in our faces, and through the sheets of rain we see an empty train station. There's nobody here to pick us up. I feel as gray as the weather, as I scan the entire platform. She's not here. My heart sinks. What had I been thinking? If she didn't come to drop us off when we left for Denmark, why would she be here to pick us up? Maybe these long months of separation have romanticized my memory of her. Was she just some idealized image of my own devising? Maybe she wasn't quite as wonderful as my memory made her to be. Maybe I've imagined her sweet voice, her soft touch and her warm words. Maybe Carl was right; she doesn't love us. After all, if she did love us, why would she send us away?

Another War Child from our train is being carried off by a woman and a uniformed man. All three are crying and huddling close together in the rain. I feel jealous and bitter, and just want to kick something. Hard. And I want to keep kicking it, until it hurts as badly inside as I do. But the only ones on the platform are my siblings, and I'm certain they hurt already.

Just then, the conductor announces that the train is about to leave, and beckons all passengers to board. For a fleeting moment I consider getting back on the train and riding it all the way back to Denmark. The rain is now nearly horizontal, creating a wall between us and the train. When I cast one more longing look at the train behind us, I see a dark figure descending it. She must've boarded the train looking for us, when we were getting off it. My heart skips a beat. The figure plunges through the wall of rain and engulfs us in an enormous group hug. She's here! We're home! And she's every bit as wonderful as I remember.

Unaware if my tears are of joy or relief or fear, I let them stream freely and let the rain wash them away. The rain is soaking through my clothes and every part of me is wet, but I don't care. Feeling Mother's arms around me I'm safe. I no longer know if I'm crying or laughing or both, but we're all talking incoherently in unison. Nobody makes any sense. Only now do I realize that we're still speaking Danish. It's become so natural for us that we don't even think about it anymore. I want to say something to Mother in Finnish but... I can't find the words. Not because I'm taken over by emotion, but because I can't speak Finnish anymore! Johan is happily prattling away, while Mother looks us over, measures our growth, tousles our hair, and keeps hugging and kissing us. How does Johan remember Finnish when the rest of us don't? Little Sister is seemingly shy, and won't let go of my hand. She buries her face in my overcoat and clams up. The three of us are standing like idiots watching our oldest brother engage in a conversation with our Mother, and we cannot even find one word to communicate with her.

When everyone has finally settled down, Mother's gaze crosses mine, and my heart swells with ache. Desperately racking my brain and dying for my tongue to co-operate, I hate that I've forgotten my native language. There are so many things I want to tell her. Where's Father? Why did she send us away? Are we going back home to Karelia soon? But the words won't come to me. I don't belong here. I should feel whole again and safe and happy, but...

"Paul?" she says. "Aren't you going to say anything?"

I clear my throat to gain more time. "Tor ... come he... um, also?" is the best I can do.

"No, my treasure," Mother laughs. "But he's waiting for you at Farfar's house. I drove his car, and thinking about how much you children must've grown, didn't know if there'd be room for all of us and him…"

"You *drive*?!" Johan interrupts her.

"War makes people do the strangest things, son," Mother says. Although her words sound ominous, she still smiles as we gather our now soaking bags and make our way in the rain toward Farfar's car.

"Like sending your children away to Denmark," Johan mutters in Danish under his breath.

I elbow him in the gut. How dare he?

I grab Mother's elbow before getting into the car. Although I can't form a coherent sentence, and am embarrassed by that inability, I need the answer to a question that's been bothering me since we left Karelia.

"Father… is …home?" I ask.

A shadow crosses Mother's face, but she makes a valiant effort to disguise it and smiles bravely. "No, dear. Your father is back in the Army. We'll talk about it over dinner. Who's hungry?"

"Me, me, me!" Carl finds the words nearest to his heart.

The rain has stopped by the time we're driving through Farfar's iron gates. Mother cranes her neck to make eye contact with me through the rear-view mirror.

"How's my little angel?" she asks, referring to Little Sister, who's sitting in my lap, and still has her head buried in my shoulder. "Sleepy?"

"Sleepy," I reply in Finnish, copying what Mother just said. Can't find the words or the courage to utter 'scared', 'shy', 'doesn't know who you are'.

Looking up at me from under her brow, Little Sister whispers in Danish "I don't understand what that lady is saying."

Frightened that Mother may have taken offense, I quickly look into the mirror. All I can see is Mother's smiling face. This breaks my heart even further. This situation is beyond uncomfortable.

Thankfully Tor understands Danish. I've never been so happy to see anyone in my life as I am to see Tor recognize me through Farfar's kitchen window. He pounds his entire bodyweight against the door until it opens, and comes rushing to me. He remembers me! He jumps up on me and we land on the ground, wrestling and giggling like the months in Denmark had never happened. My hair and face are covered in his saliva. He's making sounds I've never heard any dog make before, but the way his tail is wagging, I take those sounds to mean that he's as happy to see me as I am to see him. His tail whips everyone's legs. I'm laughing so hard I can't make him stop. But I don't want him to stop, either. I think I may have missed him the most. It pains me to admit this, but I think I missed him more than even Mother. And at least I can still communicate with him.

Aunt Martta shows up with Ingrid and Gustaf, and we meet our new brother for the first time. They look at us like the strangers we are to them. I feel nothing in common with these babies. In fact, I resent them. And adding insult to injury, Tor seems very taken by Ingrid. I think I hate them. How *dare* this little girl, who was nothing more than a blob whose diapers I changed before I left, befriend *my* dog? This little girl who can barely walk and talk is taking ownership of my dog. I know I hate them now. How come they got to stay and we had to leave? Just as that thought enters my mind, another one takes its place. Mor always told me not to be bitter. 'Bitterness never sows anything but more bitterness,' she says. I can hear her voice stating those exact words, clear as day, as if she were standing here right next to me. Which I wish she were. This is going to be harder than I thought, and I really would've liked Mor to be here to help me. But I know what she would say, if she were here, and could read my mind. 'Don't take your anger out on the innocent.' And she'd be right. They're only little babies, after all. It's not their fault. And Tor has been happy and has had a friend for a year, to make up for me being gone. I vow to make friends with them. Eventually.

It's confusing. I don't know where I belong anymore. Suddenly I miss Denmark more than I'm happy to be here. If I could take Tor with me and move to Denmark, I think I'd be perfectly happy. Every possible emotion is a riot inside me, and I hate that I have no control over how I feel. I'm happy to be back, but… somehow, it just doesn't feel right. Nothing feels right anymore.

Farfar isn't happy to see us at all. I remember not particularly liking him during the short time we spent here after we were evacuated, and that sentiment didn't change while we were in Denmark. As we greet him, all he does is turn to Mother to ask her how much fuel she used to go collect us and does she understand how hard black market gasoline is to come by? Mummo, on the other hand, is sweetness personified. And she understands us. She speaks Swedish to us, we speak Danish to her and she interprets between Mother and us. Understanding Finnish is easy. Finding the words is hard. Using the proper grammar is impossible. Mother and Mummo agree that we should only use Danish among ourselves when nobody else is around or when Mummo is there to interpret.

I hate that I don't know what to do. In Denmark Mor and I had a routine. In Karelia all of us had a routine. I don't remember a routine in Farfar's house. All I remember is that we had to be very quiet when he was around, although I can't remember why. I feel like a visitor in my own grandfather's house, and the feeling bothers me. And all of a sudden, without warning, I feel as sad about being apart from Mor and Jens and everyone as I felt when I was in Denmark being apart from Tor and Mother.

But, on the lighter side of things, the little ones are very well behaved, and on second glance, quite endearing. Gustaf is a very quiet child, who spends most of his time eating and sleeping. His silky wafts of hair show the promise of curling like Mother's and Little Sister's. While Ingrid is the absolute opposite of Little Sister in coloring, their features are nearly identical. Whereas Little Sister is pale and curly blonde, with virtually colorless eyes, new baby Ingrid has sandy blonde straight hair and intense blue eyes. Their dimples are identical, the shapes of their faces are identical and their tempers seem to be identical. However, it's apparent even to me, that whereas Little Sister is petite, Ingrid will grow tall. Her torso and limbs are already long, she eats with the same gusto as Carl and Tor combined, and seems to have the same level of energy as they do. Uncle Johannes would have so much fun drawing the two identically opposite girls.

I still don't know if he made it through the war, and just as I'm trying to figure out how to ask about him in Finnish, Johan snorts at something Carl just said that I wasn't listening to.

Johan has become something of a bitter, condescending and cynical snob. He still speaks Finnish fluently and says loudly "I don't see what the problem is. *I* speak Finnish."

Hardly surprisingly, Farfar agrees with him, and before I know what has happened, we're forbidden to use Danish altogether.

"But what if we have to go back to Denmark? Then we won't know how to speak when we get back there," Carl argues.

Quickly and quietly, with a trembling lower lip, Mother leaves the table after Mummo interprets his question.

"What did I say?" Carl asks anxiously.

Mummo hands him another serving of stew. "This past year hasn't been easy for your mother, dear. And if she can help it, you won't be going away ever again."

> When the displaced children returned to Finland they faced a fresh set of challenges; another uprooting from friends and foster families, the difficulties with language, and the poor economic situation in Finland. Many returned with nightmares, difficulties in concentrating, bitterness, depression and a sense of uncertainty and fear.

> Child psychologists now believe that it is the repression of memories and feelings that is at the heart of trauma suffering. Time does not heal trauma. Many now further agree that one of the most significant war traumas of all, particularly for young children, is the separation from parents, which is often more distressing than the horrors of war itself. Furthermore, to introduce so many changes in the formative years of young children will result in long lasting, possibly permanent, emotional wounds. Although not physically injured by the war, many War Children still feel emotionally scarred by their experiences and consider their sufferings to be disregarded, ignored and belittled.

It must be close to midnight but I can't sleep. No matter how hard I try, I simply cannot catch a dream. A million thoughts keep running through my mind. Tor's head is heavy on my leg. In fact, he hasn't left my side since we arrived. Nor has Little Sister. Although Mother tried to put her to sleep with Ingrid and Gustaf in her room, she blatantly refused, and finally threw such a fit, that the four of us now share two beds in the other spare room.

I'm listening to everyone else's heavy breathing, but even that won't lull me to sleep, so very carefully I get out of bed. Tor follows me. Without making a sound, I open the door, and sneak out. I can hear voices from the kitchen below. Johan and Mummo are talking in Finnish, oddly enough. Quietly I tiptoe down the stairs.

"...they were big, Mummo," Johan is saying. "As big and strong as Renki, and they expected us to work as hard as they did. I was tired and hungry all the time. Once I tried to run away, but got only as far as the end of their fields before I realized that I had nowhere to go. And no money either...They found out that I tried to run away and after that they locked our door at night."

I creep slowly to the kitchen door. Johan is sitting at the kitchen table, holding a mug between both hands. Mummo has both arms around him. Her face is streaked with tears. Through the other door I can see a shape of a person sitting on the floor. I tiptoe around the staircase, through the drawing room and peek through the door to the dining room. Mother is sitting on the floor, leaning against the kitchen doorframe, clutching a handkerchief to her chest. She doesn't see me. Her eyes are swollen from tears and her face is wet. She's eavesdropping on Mummo and Johan's conversation.

Tor is whimpering slightly, and we creep back around the staircase to the opposite kitchen door.

"… just once," Johan is saying. "And I still don't understand why. We were told to go and find a stick, and when we returned, he hit us across our backs with it. And then the next morning we woke up to him hitting us across the bottoms of our feet with the same stick. So, twice really. Usually they punished us by not giving us food."

Poor Johan. I feel so selfish. The worst that Mr. and Mrs. Mortensen ever did to me was to ignore me. Overall, I had it good in Denmark. I find that I have a new-found respect for my brother.

"Did you remember to say your prayers every night?" Mummo asks.

Johan scoffs. "Prayers to whom? What kind of God would let that happen to children? God abandoned me, so I have abandoned him."

"Did you ever tell anyone? Like your teacher, perhaps?" Mummo asks.

"What teacher? We didn't go to school. Once, we were locked in the attic when some ladies came to visit, but they were the only other people that ever came to the farm. The ladies were asking about Finnebørn, but they said there were none there. They lied. They said that they had had two, and they had home-schooled them, but that they had been sent back to Finland after the war was over. They lied again. We never got home-schooled. Pentti never even learned Danish properly."

So that's why Johan still speaks Finnish. He's been with another Finnebarn this whole year! And he probably doesn't even know Danish or remember Swedish anymore, which is why he's speaking Finnish to Mummo. It's confusing keeping all these languages straight. One never knows what to speak to whom.

"The only reason I found out about us being sent back, was when I was cleaning out the fireplace, and there was an unopened half-burnt letter there addressed to me. We didn't know where in Denmark we were or how to get to Copenhagen, or what day it was even, so we finally ran away. Together. We walked day and night, asking for directions, stealing food or going hungry, and when we finally got to Copenhagen Pentti was really sick. But we ran into that nice Karelian girl, Natalia, who was on our train out and she found us a place to sleep. And two days later Natalia was sick, too, but I was on my way back. She made me promise that I would tell someone about this, because otherwise I'll end up angry and bitter."

Mummo tightens her grip around Johan, and starts rocking him. Through sobs, she murmurs something inaudible into his hair.

"I don't hate her," Johan says. His expression is blank, showing no emotion. "She had no choice. She was weak and vulnerable and ignorant of where she was sending us..."

Mummo interrupts him, but I still can't hear what she says.

Johan huffs. "Well, it cannot have been any worse than ..."

"Your Uncle Johannes is missing in action," Mummo interrupts again. "Presumed dead."

BOOK 3

FINLAND

May 1941.

I cannot believe that Uncle Johannes is dead. Missing in action could mean that he's still alive, and I prefer to think that. As long as no body has been found, there's still hope. Mummo says it's been over a year and that he went missing on what is now Russian soil, so the likelihood of ever recovering his body is slim to none. But without a body, there's still hope.

I spent all weekend thinking about him. I thought about him first thing this morning, when I woke up, but my thoughts were abruptly disrupted, when Mother announced at breakfast that we have to go back to school today. There's only four more weeks of the school year left, so we all agree that this is a waste of time, but Mother is adamant. One thing she will not compromise, she says, is her children's education.

Little Sister cries in the window as she watches us walk away. She's started sucking her thumb again, and only speaks to me in a hushed voice when nobody else can hear us. In Danish. Her insecurity breeds an attachment to anything safe and familiar, and I'm now so accustomed to having her attach herself to me, that my hand feels empty without hers in it.

There are no more Karelians in our school, but both Fröken and Harri are still there. He greets us in the school yard by saying "Well, well. Look who's back! Denmark didn't want you either, huh? War Child! War Child! Ugly, smelly War Child!"

We successfully manage to ignore him. It helps that Tor has followed us school, and bares his teeth at Harri.

There are so few children in this school that Johan, Carl and I are now in the same classroom. I miss Kjersti. By the last class of the first day, all three of us have taken turns in getting our fingers slapped and standing in the corner.

Fröken doesn't understand that we don't speak Swedish anymore. She calls us lazy snobs, and keeps screaming "Swedish! Swedish!" her face inches from ours.

Finally Johan snaps, and pushes her away from me. "He doesn't remember Swedish! Leave him alone!" he says.

He's sent to stand in the corner, and the rest of our class is solving equations. I'm done with mine quickly, so I start sketching the view out the window with my left hand. Tor is sitting under a tree in the yard, and he hasn't taken his eyes off the front door since he saw us go in. A ruler being slammed on my desk interrupts me.

"Still the little clown," Fröken says, and pulls out my sketch. She tears it into pieces, and tells me to eat it.

"I'm done!" I tell her in Finnish, and push my equations toward her.

"I said eat the paper!" she hisses at me.

Harri and his cronies are sniggering on the other side of the classroom, as I chew on my sketch. I was actually quite proud of it. The paper forms into a thick paste when it mixes with my saliva, and I can't swallow it without choking.

"That'll teach you never to horse around in my classroom again," Fröken says, and dismisses the class.

We try to get out as quickly as possible, without being assaulted by Harri, which we know is about to happen. He catches up with us halfway back to Farfar's house. He's got his usual four bullies with him, and they're slinging rocks at us. Tor growls and I have to do what I can to keep him from attacking them.

"What's your rush, three-eyes? Running back to mommy now that she's decided to take you back? Hey fellas! Isn't it interesting how nobody's ever seen your father, and yet your mother had a baby? She's nothing but a cheap whore, who sent her kids away so she could do some more whoring!"

"War Child! Whore child!"

Anger explodes inside me, and the four of us attack Harri and his pack head-on. It's one thing to insult me, but how dare he say that about my mother? I hit him straight on the mouth, repeatedly, as though my punches would enable him to not speak those words again.

He was always much bigger than me, and has grown even more in the last year, and I'm no match for him. With one quick kick in the stomach I go flying into the ditch. Tor bites his trouser cuff. Carl tackles him from behind and all three of them fall on top of me. Harri's face is on top of mine, and I bite him on the cheek. He squeals like a girl.

On the road above us, a car approaches, and one of Harri's friends notices it.

"Pssst, Harri," he says. "Your dad."

The car stops and the Mayor steps out, going directly to Harri, and grabbing him by the ear, shoves him in the car.

"Go home!" he says to Harri's friends. "What's going on here?" he asks us, as the others scamper away.

I can see Harri's morose face through the car window. His cheek is starting to swell, and by tomorrow he'll know what it's like to be called three-eyes. I hate him so much right now.

"Nothing Mr. Mayor," I say through clenched teeth.

This isn't over. Harri will get what's coming, but it won't be through his father. I didn't let German soldiers lick me, and I certainly am not going to get licked by this insignificant worm either.

"We were just horsing around."

The Mayor raises his eyebrows at us, and stands quiet for a long while.

"Very well, then," he says finally. "May I offer you boys a ride?"

He must be joking! We wouldn't dream of getting in the same car as Harri.

"No, thank you, sir," Johan says. "Our grandparents live just down the lane here."

"Oh, I know who you are," the Mayor says and smiles. "Your father is an outstanding soldier and a war hero and your mother and grandmother are exemplary citizens. I'm glad to see that you're home safe and sound. Welcome back!"

With that, he gets into his car and they drive off.

> Finland continued its close relationship with Germany, but intended to keep as low a profile about it as possible. Since Marshal Mannerheim spoke German fluently, he often ended up being the negotiator between the two governments. Mannerheim was offered command over the German troops in Finland, around 80,000 men. He declined, wanting it known that he didn't want to tie Finland to the German war objectives.
> Mannerheim kept relations with Nazi Germany's government as formal as possible and successfully opposed their proposals for a treaty of alliance. During the early summer of 1941 Finland had reason to fear on two fronts. German propaganda made claims that the Red Army was preparing to attack. Finland, still in a close relationship with Germany, didn't wish to be considered an enemy of the Red Army, nor an ally of the Axis.
> Hitler's plans for Operation Barbarossa, which had been outlined in utmost secrecy, were building up, and a two-front assault on the Soviet Union was expected in the summer of 1941. Hitler had made his intentions of invading the Soviet Union clear in 'Mein Kampf', based on his belief that the German people needed 'living space', i.e. land and raw materials found

> in the East. It was the stated policy of the
> Nazis to kill, deport, or enslave the Russian
> and other Slavic populations whom they consid-
> ered inferior, and to repopulate the land with
> Germanic peoples.
> Mannerheim advised the Finnish Government not
> to get too heavily involved with Germany.

In the month or so since we left Denmark, Little Sister has gone from being fluent and very verbose in Danish on the train ride back to whispering only to me in
Danish to using monosyllabic sentences to now nearly completely mute.

She has nightmares every night. Since we sleep head-to-toe in the same bed,
she often wakes me up, kicking and sweating and saying things that sound like
'Don't leave me!' and 'Where are you?'. When I wake her up, she's startled and
frightened. Often, she cries. She never wants to talk about her dreams. This worries me. Tor sometimes dreams, but whenever I wake him up, he's just happy
to see me, licks my face, circles around a bit and falls right back to sleep again.
Mummo tells me it's the insecurity and fear of being abandoned that haunt Little
Sister, and that she needs to talk about it. Little Sister refuses.

She stopped talking altogether the day Mother was putting away her clothes,
and found a camera in Little Sister's drawer. I recognized the camera as one of
Uncle Oscar's, and asked Little Sister if she'd been given it, or if she stole it. She
started arguing, saying that Uncle Oscar had given it to her. Mother took it away
from her, and locked it in Mummo's writing desk. Little Sister cried herself to
sleep that night, and hasn't spoken since.

Mother steadfastly refuses to talk about the war or why she sent us away. If
ever anyone brings it up she either leaves the room or changes the subject. We
spend a lot of time talking about Denmark with Mummo, who has become our
confidante. Farfar, on the other hand, is of the old school of thought that 'children
should be neither seen nor heard' so we do our best to avoid him.

Mummo tells us that Mother still believes that Uncle Johannes is alive.
Mother's sister and her family, who also lived in Karelia, did eventually evacuate,
but we don't know where they ended up. Ukki and Muori never evacuated. We
haven't heard from them so we don't know if they're still alive. But everyone
agrees that living in what's now considered Russia is a fate worse than death.

Finnish and Swedish are coming easier to us now, and we can now make ourselves understood. Except Little Sister, of course, who still doesn't speak at
all. Tonight is the night before the last day of school. Evidently in this school,
we have our final test on the actual day of graduation, in front of our families.

Not everyone will be quizzed, but somehow I have a feeling that I will be one of the ones 'randomly' selected.

After scrubbing ourselves in the sauna this evening Mother comes to tuck us in. This is one of the things I missed the most in Denmark. Just a few precious moments, before drifting off to sleep, feeling her warm hand over my crossed fingers as we say the nightly prayer together. After 'Amen', she leans forward and leaves a trace of angel kisses on my forehead. I feel safe and happy. She does this individually with all of us.

"Amen," she says to Little Sister and bends down to kiss her.

"Mother," Little Sister says in a faint whisper. In Finnish.

Everyone gasps. Mother is visibly shaken. Her lower lip starts quivering, and her eyes are welling up. This is the first time Little Sister has spoken to her since we've been back.

"Yes, my angel?" Mother says.

"Mother," Little Sister repeats, smiles faintly and falls asleep.

Mother sighs, and strokes Little Sister's curls. We sit for a long time in silence, watching the two of them. It never occurred to me that this separation might have been as difficult for Mother as it was for us. After all, it was her idea to send us away. Nevertheless, right now I think I'm the happiest I've been in a long time.

Mother eventually gets up, straightens our quilts, and turns the light off. She's about to say good-night and close the door, when she abruptly turns around.

"Should we close the window, boys? Those frogs are awfully loud this evening," she says.

"Frog? What frog? I don't hear a frog," Carl exclaims a bit too hastily.

"It's mating season, Mother," I say quickly. "It's fine. Good-night."

As luck would have it, since our school is so small, we're called up in groups of five, in alphabetical order. Carl is right behind Harri, and has the honors of pulling our prank. He can barely contain himself. We've grown so much that we're all wearing our cousins' hand-me-downs. Harri comments on this when we enter the school, but we ignore him. After a good month of bullying we're going to get Harri today and get him good.

Our group of five consists of Harri, Carl, Johan, me and a little girl from Carl's class, who keeps biting her fingernails. Johan is the first one that the Principal quizzes. Mechanically he recites the Finnish rivers that run into the sea, from north to south. Then it's my turn. I'm asked to recite the seven tables. I'm at 'four times seven is...' when the entire hall starts chuckling. Turning around, I can see Harri squirming. Then he starts screaming like a girl. The hall is laughing now.

"Get it off me! Get it off me!" he screams, arms flailing wildly at the back of his shirt.

No one can contain themselves. We're now laughing so hard, that tears are running down our cheeks.

"Stop laughing!" Harri squeals. "Get it off me!"

The Principal and Fröken come to his aid, but he's thrashing around so much that his elbow hits Fröken in the nose, and one of his knees jackknifes the Principal. The hall is now in stitches. The Mayor steps up.

"Help me, Daddy!" Harri's voice is shrill, like a screaming baby's.

The Mayor yanks Harri's shirt out of his pants, pulls it over his head, and throws it on the floor. Our frog emerges from under the shirt. It looks around for a split second, and then makes a leap toward the benches. The girls are squealing, and start scrambling for the door in a panic.

"Get that frog!" the Mayor bellows.

All the girls are screaming, and all the boys are running to catch the frog. All but one. Harri is left alone in the hall, consoled by the Principal and his father. School is out, and we now have a long, lovely, lazy summer to look forward to.

> Finland mobilized its Army on June 17th, 1941, in anticipation of a German attack on the So- viet Union or a Soviet attack on Finland. How- ever, on June 22nd, when the Germans attacked Russia, Finland declared neutrality, though German planes had refueled at Finnish airbases when they returned from bombing Leningrad and German troops were ready to attack Murmansk through Finland in the Arctic.
> Russia attacked Finland on June 25th, and pres- ident Ryti stated that Finland was at war again. Finland's aims of the war were to get back areas lost in the Winter War and to get a good position to negotiate peace if the Germans couldn't destroy the Soviet Armies. Finland never considered herself as Germany's ally, but as a co-belligerent waging her own war with her own goals.

September 1941.

School's out, because we have to go on a collection drive. Our Army needs our help. The drive started last Sunday after church and will end on Saturday. We're to collect anything and everything we can find made of aluminum, steel, iron, tin, cotton, etc. We have a long list. Mother and Mummo have been asked to go to the post office on Saturday to donate their rings. Mother says she'll give up every other piece of jewelry, except her ring. She says she'll be buried wearing it.

On Saturday, we're to gather in the school yard, and the kid with the biggest contribution will get a gold star. As we left the church, we could see Harri make the rounds in the church yard with his father, the Mayor. We ran to Farfar's house and started our collection drive. It didn't dawn on us until later that Harri was using his father's influence with the church congregation to ask for donations.

Johan, Carl and I have decided to join forces. We've donated old socks, strings from our shoes, old diapers, belt buckles, and old shovel handles we found in the barn. The barn proved to be a gold mine. The first night after supper we asked Farfar what we could have. We'd made an inventory of everything useful in the barn. My thinking was that since this is not a functioning farm, we could have everything.

Here's what Farfar said: "If it can't be used, you may have it." Then he turned up the volume on the radio, and that was the end of that conversation.

His comment leaves plenty of room for interpretation, and if it weren't for Johan's stubborn logic, we'd have stripped the old farm equipment down by now. Or, at the very least, had fun trying. As it stands, though, we've agreed to only take things that we've never seen anyone use.

Carl donates his tin soldiers. Everyone knows what an enormous sacrifice this is. Those soldiers survived the evacuation from Karelia, and the trip to Denmark. And back. I feel selfish and shameful that I will not let go of the most valuable thing I own - the live German bullet. But then again - neither does Carl.

We borrow Farfar's old milk cart, and walk back and forth along the dirt roads, looking for anything useful. We fashion a makeshift harness out of old pieces of rope and some belts that we found, and tie Tor to the cart. He understands his chore surprisingly quickly for a dog that's never been tied to anything, ever. I wish Uncle Johannes and Renki hadn't returned to Karelia. We could use the sleighs and horses. Then we hear that Harri is going door-to-door, so we decide to do that as well. This doesn't go so well. Either we get the door slammed in our faces, or the lady of the house tells us that Harri has already been there.

We come back to Farfar's on the fifth night of the drive, dusty, tired and hungry. As has become her very irritating custom, Ingrid clamps herself to my leg, and I have to drag her with me to be able to walk. Mother and Little Sister are sitting in Farfar's living room. They're knitting! Is Mother going to have another baby? That's the only time she ever knits.

"What are you doing?" I ask.

"We're knitting socks for the soldiers."

I laugh and point at my tomboy little sister. "You look like a girl," I sing-song tease her.

"No!" she yells angrily, and sends her knitting across the floor.

"That's alright, my precious," Mother says, and leans down to collect the thrown knitting. "It's hard for a four year-old."

"I'm four and a *half*!" Little Sister protests.

"Well, let's see you behave like a four and a *half* year-old, then," Mother gently scolds her.

Actually, Little Sister is nearly five, but we've all decided not to remind her that her birthday is just weeks away, since we can't afford to give her presents or have a lavish party like we used to in Karelia.

Gustaf is gurgling in the crib next to the sofa. Bending down to look at him, I see that he's chewing on my model airplane.

"How did he get my plane?" I reach down to take my plane back, but Gustaf's fingers are in a death grip around it.

"Let him have it, son. His teeth are coming in, and that's the only thing that'll soothe him."

"But… it's mine!"

"Son, we're at war. We're lucky to be alive, and have a roof over our heads. Now's not the time to be selfish."

"But, what if he breaks it?"

"If he does, then I'll buy you ten new planes when the war is over."

She doesn't understand how important that plane is to me. It's unbelievably selfish of me to even think this, but I liked it better in Denmark, where, for all intents and purposes I was an only child. Looking at the grave look on Mother's face, I relent, and let Gustaf have my plane. But I give him a look that I hope he takes to mean that he'd better not break it.

I look at Mother's knitting needles. "What are these made of?"

She laughs, and ruffles my hair. "You can't have them, my treasure. Are you hungry?"

"Yes,… But… We're not winning," I hear myself whine. "We just walked past Mayor Holgerson's house, and Harri already has a pile that's so much bigger than ours! And there's three of us and only one of him. Our pile should be three times bigger than his! And Mother - you should have seen his ball of string. It's as big as his head."

"Well, that must be pretty big… Are you still going door-to-door like him?"

"Yes."

"Well, then, of course you're not winning. You can't beat the Mayor's son, especially if he's using his father's status to his advantage, which it sounds like he is. But you can beat him at his own game." Mother leaves the room and returns quickly with a framed letter in her hands and a broad smile on her face. "You're your father's sons. He's a war hero. That's bigger and better right now than the Mayor of anything. Use it to your advantage. Just be sure not to break the frame or lose the letter."

We quickly scan the letter. It's written by Marshal Mannerheim and addressed to Mother. In it he depicts the heroism of our father, how during a certain motti he single-handedly killed twelve Russian soldiers in one day, aided in the capture of a high-ranking Soviet officer and, although being wounded himself and having lost a toe to frostbite, he secured supplies for his unit for weeks. Our Father is a hero.

Carl immediately starts firing at the windows with an imaginary rifle. "Bam! One! You're dead, Red! Bam! Two!" He leaves the room, and we can hear him shooting out of every window on the ground floor.

I look up at Mother. "How badly was he wounded? When did this happen? Did he come home? Was he in a hospital? Why didn't he tell us about this?"

Mother puts up a hand to quiet me. "A bullet grazed his shoulder. Flesh wound only, thank heavens! I received this letter right after you left for Denmark, and no - he never left the front. He kept fighting. He doesn't think it was a big deal. He was just doing his job," she says and her face has an odd mixture of pride and sadness.

All this past week she's looked odd to me, like she's hiding a secret. I asked my brothers about this, and Carl says he hasn't noticed, but then again, that doesn't surprise me at all. Johan says he thinks she might be having another baby. I doubt it. She's too thin. But ever since she and Mummo went to town last Saturday she's looked different. Even Mummo sometimes has a smug smile on her face. Very much like the one I once saw on Carl's face when he found Mummo's cache of sugar, and carved himself a big chunk of it and didn't tell anyone until he got a stomach ache.

"Not a big deal?" I stare at the letter in awe. "It's from Marshal Mannerheim!"

"Bam! Twelve!" Carl rushes back into the room. "Mother? When can I get my own gun?"

Another odd smile crosses Mother's face. "If this war continues much longer, the Army will issue you one, son."

"Good morning, ma'am. My name is Paul, and these are my brothers, Johan and Carl. That's my dog, Tor. He's very friendly. He won't bite, but he might give you kisses," I pause in my rehearsed speech at the first house. Here I had hoped for a smile, but Mother says that not everyone likes dogs. So I continue. "You may not know us, but we're the sons of a decorated war hero, and ask for your assistance in the Suur-Suomi project collection drive."

The lady at the door is about to protest. Her face doesn't look impressed.

"If you don't believe me, perhaps this letter from the Field Marshal will convince you," I continue and show her the framed letter.

She looks at it suspiciously.

"Any rags, aluminum, tin, steel or cotton you might have to spare will be most appreciated and helpful to our soldiers at the front. Including our father. And your...?"

"... husband and two sons," she says, and wipes away a tear. "Won't you come in, boys?"

It worked!

By the end of the day our milk cart is so full, that it takes all three of us and Tor to haul it. This is the most successful day of the entire drive. I wish Mother had thought of this before.

On our way back to Farfar's, we pass by Harri's house, and see the growing pile in his garage. Our spirits sink again.

"Hey losers!" he yells at us as we're passing. "That all you got? You might as well be working for the Russians! Looosers!"

We're walking through Farfar's old wrought iron gates, when Carl suddenly stops.

"Are you thinking what I'm thinking?" he says and taps at the gate.

They're not being used; in fact, they hang off one hinge, and are in dire need of paint.

"I don't know about this, fellas," Johan says. "Shouldn't we ask Farfar if we can have them?"

"We can have anything that can't be used, and don't bother me again," Carl tries to imitate Farfar's grumpiness. "Obviously these haven't been used in years," Carl concludes, already pulling off weeds that are growing in and around the gates.

Johan ponders this for a moment. "How would we even get them off?"

We examine the hinges. "Let's find a crowbar!" I suggest.

We hurry to the barn, find a crowbar and start prying the hinges. The first one comes off fairly easily, but falls on the ground with a heavy thud.

"How are we going to carry it?" Johan asks.

"We're not; all we need to do is lift it on to the milk cart. This'll get us our gold star! Harri is going to looooose!"

The gate is so heavy that we can only lift it tiny little increments at a time, and have to empty the cart to wedge the gate onto it. By the time we get the second one off its hinges and onto the cart, it's deep dusk, we're panting, dirty and sweaty, but we did it! Our pile definitely looks bigger, and most certainly heavier than Harri's. Also, his looks like it's mainly rags, whereas ours actually has iron in it! We hit the jackpot! That gold star is ours, even if we have to divide our pile into three.

> On the home front, civilians were urged to donate all articles which could possibly be useful to the military to a collection being organized by the Civil Guard on behalf of the Defense Forces. Collection drives started early during the Winter War, and were carried on throughout the Continuation War. Scrap metal, iron and aluminum were especially valuable, as were cotton, newspapers and kitchen fat. Metal was needed for war materiel, from guns and ammunition to planes and ships. Some sources of metal ore were blocked by the enemy, so conservation and recycling became imperative. Recovered kitchen fat was used to produce glycerin, a key ingredient in the manufacture of explosives, among other things.
> Gold was used to pay off the debt and purchase new weapons, ammunition and supplies. Despite the war, Finland honored the repayment schedule for her war debts to the USA.
> Girls were taught to knit gloves, scarves and socks for the troops at the front.
> Scrap drives were highly successful in boosting the nation's morale, as civilians, especially children, felt they were contributing to the war effort.
> Suur-Suomi ('Great Finland') was the ideal of not only reclaiming the lands lost in the Winter War, but also claiming all areas populated by Finns or people ethnically related to Finns, including Estonia, Ingria and the Kola Peninsula.

"Straight line, turn around and drop your trousers!" Farfar growls at us.

Tor senses that something is terribly amiss, and standing between me and Farfar, he raises his neck hairs and growls back.

Farfar slaps him across his muzzle. Hard. I gasp. Tor whimpers. He looks confused. He's never been hit before in his life. Farfar raises his hand to slap him again. I grab it.

"Don't you dare strike my dog!" I shout at him.

Farfar pushes me aside. I go flying across the room. Tor starts barking at Farfar using his 'I'm big and tough' bark. Farfar takes him by the scruff and drags him outside, closing the door behind him.

"Ugly mutt," he mutters.

Tor is whining, and pawing at the door. He's anxiously trying to get back in. We stare at Farfar in disbelief. He's taking off his belt. Very slowly, one belt loop at the time. Little Sister starts to sob. The look on Farfar's face doesn't bode well. He's never been especially friendly, but this is even worse.

I step in front of Little Sister. "She didn't do anything! She was sitting here, knitting with Mother!" I yell in Farfar's face.

And where is Mother when we need her? Surely if she were here, she'd not let Farfar do this? Why today, of all days, does she have to accompany Mummo into town?

"You've got to learn, that if one messes up, the entire bunch pays the consequences," Farfar hisses. "Maybe next time you'll care more about your little angel's precious little hide, before you steal from me! Now, turn around and drop your trousers. I'm not going to tell you again!"

Silently I say a prayer of thanks that Mummo and Mother took the little ones with them to town today. We have never, ever been physically punished before, and the thought of this frightens me. One part of me wants to fight, grab the belt, bite his knuckles, and kick his shins. Anything to avoid a lashing, but I can't. I'm frozen in place.

"But, Farfar. You said yourself that we could have anything that wasn't being used…" I attempt a plea to his reasoning.

"Do you want to make it four?" Farfar threatens. It was only going to be three.

Obediently we turn around, form a straight line, bend over and drop our trousers. The first hit stings so badly it brings tears to my eyes. I will not give him the satisfaction of seeing me cry. I brace myself for the next two. I can take it. And then I'll run away. Probably back to Denmark. Just me and Tor.

Little Sister screams, when the belt slashes her bottom. "Farfar, no! I'm sorry! Please don't! Noo-hoo-hooo…! Faaar-faar, please!" She's hysterical. Her voice is so high-pitched it could probably shatter glass.

I take her hand in mine. She squeezes it so hard that her little knuckles turn white. I look over at Johan. He's biting his lower lip. The belt comes slashing down again. The second strike is even worse than the first, because now my skin is sore.

"Stop right there!" a voice booms in the room as the door crashes into the wall.

From between my legs I can see a pair of tattered black boots, but very little else. Tor runs to me, and immediately starts licking my face. The boots quickly cross the room, then there's some shuffling, and the belt drops to the floor. I can see Mother's legs and the hem of her dress in the doorway.

"You got away with this with me, but you'll not leave a single scar on my children! Nobody lays a hand on *my* children."

"If someone had laid a hand on them years ago, they'd know better," Farfar argues. "They're acting like little hooligans, like the children of the no-good son of mine. Maybe I should've belted you more, and you'd had the wits to raise your children right."

My heart skips a beat. I yank up my trousers and quickly turn around.

"Father!"

All four of us scamper around him, throwing ourselves at him. Suddenly the belt to my backside is the last thing on my mind.

We're all talking at the same time, hugging and kissing him, laughing and crying.

"…You're back!…"

"…You won't leave us again?…"

"…We missed you!…"

"…Look, how much I've grown!…"

"…Can I see your scar?…"

"…Where's your gun?…"

"…Did you bring us anything?…"

Agile as a monkey, Little Sister climbs into Father's lap, clamps her arms tightly around his throat and burrows her head in his neck. Her sobs shake her entire body. Father calmly hugs and kisses each of us, and eventually tries to pry us off him. We won't let him go. We haven't seen Father since that night when we left our house in Karelia, and all the fears, anxiety and uncertainty culminate and erupt at this very moment.

Father turns to Farfar. "What prompted this lashing?"

"Your little hooligans stole from me!" he says accusatorily. "And your youngest is the ring-leader."

Father raises his eyebrows, and gently strokes Little Sister's back. "I find both accusations hard to believe."

"Not the *girl*," he says, like 'girl' is a four-letter word. "Him!" he says, pointing to Carl.

"Very well, let me handle this," Father says, still trying to peel us off him.

His efforts are useless. He's back and we intend to do what we can to make him stay, even if we have to glue ourselves to him. We will not be separated again.

"Make sure you do," Farfar says. "I'm ashamed to be related to them. Almost as much as I'm ashamed of you."

I can't believe he said that! His own son is a war hero, what could he possibly have to be ashamed of?

Father looks deflated, as he turns his eyes to us. "Let's go pack, children," he says.

"Where are we going this time?" I ask carefully, not certain I want to know.

"Away from here," he says quietly.

Mother joins us and we go quietly upstairs, leaving Farfar in the middle of the room, with his beltless trousers starting to fall off his waist.

As we're packing our few belongings, Father sits us down on the bed, kneels in front of us, so that we're eye-level, and looks us squarely in the eye.

"So, who wants to tell me what happened? What did you do to make your grandfather accuse you of theft? And use a word such as 'hooligans'?"

We look at each other. I'm sitting between Johan and Carl, and feel an elbow poke me on both sides. Why am I always the spokesperson?

"We won a gold star at school!" I decide to start with good news.

All Father does is nod. He acknowledges the good news, but is expecting me to confess. I sigh. I can't help it.

"Okay, there was this drive for the Suur-Suomi project, and Harri's collection was much bigger than ours…"

"Harri, the Mayor's son? I see," Father says, looking slightly amused. "Very important not to finish second to a politician's son?"

"Exactly! There's no second place in a war! Only winners and losers. Anyway, Harri is a bully and a tyrant and we hate him."

"Hate is a strong emotion, son, be careful how you disperse it."

"We deeply dislike Harri," Johan corrects me.

"Why?"

"He calls me 'three-eyes'!"

"Because of your scar?" Father gently rubs his thumb on my cheek.

I shrug. "Well, that's nothing, really. But he also calls us refugees and Karelians and War Children."

"You're all those things."

"But the way he says it, he makes us sound dirty and poor and just because he didn't have to go to Denmark he makes it sound like we're less privileged.

Like… well, like we're less loved. And then we get into fights and *we* are the ones receiving a note."

"I've spoken to Mayor and Mrs. Holgerson," Mother says, while moving clothes from the drawer to the suitcases. "They're pleasant enough, in that 'I smile so I can count on your vote' kind of way. But they did promise to reason with Harri, which, coming from a politician, is no small threat."

"Next time anyone gives you a hard time for being Karelian, here's what I want you to say: 'I was born in Karelia, but I'm a Finn, just like you'. And walk away. As for him not being a War Child, I can only guess what kinds of strings the Mayor had to pull."

"Doesn't hurt to have friends in high places. Maybe you boys should befriend this Harri," Mother says with a wink.

"Never!" all three of us say simultaneously.

"Alright, back to the scrap drive," Father says.

"Right, so, we saw that the iron gates weren't being used, so we took them for the drive…"

I can tell that Father is trying to suppress a laugh, because his cheek muscles are tensing. Either that or he's so mad that he's grinding his teeth.

"Farfar himself said we could have anything that wasn't being used," Johan cuts in.

Father looks thoughtful. "I seriously doubt that he'd be this upset over those ugly, useless old iron gates," he finally says. "What are you not telling me?"

Tor is sitting at my feet. I start playing with his ears. He senses that I'm upset, licks my hand and lays his head in my lap. Usually this would make me feel better, but not today. Father's only been back a matter of minutes, and already I'm in trouble. I wonder if there's any way I could pin this on someone else.

"Paul?" Father beckons.

Again, Johan pokes me in the side. I poke him back. I really don't want to tell. Father's gaze is burning on me, and I know there's no escape.

"We also took some nails," I say carefully, hoping Father will leave it at that.

"From?"

"The house."

"And?"

"Some towels and socks and boots …"

"But we left one of everything!" Johan interrupts.

"And the pair that he was wearing!" Carl adds.

"And the nails from the house weren't really that big a deal. I mean there are *three* nails holding up each plank, at *both* ends, and two would've been plenty, and we only took nails from the bottom eight rows, because we couldn't reach higher and we couldn't find a ladder and it's not like the house is going to collapse, and really, if you think about it, we're doing this for the country, and…" I have to stop to draw for breath.

Father raises a hand. "Enough. Let's all go downstairs to Farfar. You'll apologize and ask for penance. He might ask you to do chores for him, and you'll do them. Properly and without grumbling."

"Are we still leaving?" I ask.

"Yes, we're going to stay with Aunt Martta, and start looking for another place. That man will not raise any more children."

"Father…?" I hesitate. "Why doesn't he like you?"

Father sighs. "He doesn't like anyone. No one can ever do right by him. He's a miserable, grumpy old man."

"Who gave us shelter and food when we needed it," Mother adds.

"Undoubtedly Mummo's doing. Let's go."

> In September 1941, Britain and the United States demanded that Finland end the war with Russia. President Roosevelt further pledged to defeat Germany, and every nation in alliance with the Axis would be considered a belligerent enemy. British and American delegates met in Moscow to discuss Russia's defense needs in the fighting against Germany and Finland.
>
> With the aid of German troops, the Finnish Army had regained possession of Lahdenpohja and Sortavala on Lake Ladoga. By doing that, Finland had regained the lands lost in the Winter War. Mannerheim rejected German pleas for aerial attacks against Leningrad. He also refused to let his troops contribute to the siege of Leningrad.
>
> By September 8th, the German troops had surrounded Leningrad, cutting off all supply lines. Although Hitler never managed to take the city, the two and a half-year siege that followed was the longest, caused the greatest destruction and the largest loss of life of a major city in modern warfare.

Our penance is to clean up, organize and paint the shed. An utterly unnecessary task. In all the time we've lived here, I've never seen anyone use the shed for anything. Now, we're standing outside, trying to open the old lock. It's pouring down rain. When we finally get the door open, we're hit in the face by the most horrendously foul smell I've ever exposed my nose to.

"Stinky," Little Sister says, and pinches her nose.

It smells like feces combined with dirt, turpentine and mold. Tor starts sniffing the air. Something is moving in the far corner. He stands at point. We can't see a thing, there's no electricity in the shed, and the little lantern Mummo gave us is only casting a faint light a few feet in front of us. Johan raises the lantern. Tor slowly takes a step closer to the corner. His body is very low to the ground. Suddenly he pounces. Little Sister screams. Something comes running straight toward us. Tor follows it. It's a rat. It makes it past us and out of the shed, with Tor close on its heels.

"Tor! Leave it!" I yell behind him.

He keeps running into the woods. A moment later he returns and shakes himself off in the shed. The rat is nowhere to be seen. Tor's record is intact; he has yet to catch a rodent. He goes back to the corner and sniffs around for a while. No more rats come running out.

"This place gives me the creeps," Johan says.

The shed is a mess. There are shelves along all walls but one, which is lined with hooks. Nothing is hanging from these hooks, nothing is lined up on the shelves; everything is strewn around the dirt floor. Water is flooding across it. There's hardly any room for the five of us to stand in, much less turn around without bumping into each other, work or organize anything. Adding to the general mess and small size there's a huge garden swing in the middle of the floor.

Our shoes are getting wet. The roof is leaking as well. This is not so much penance as it is Farfar's way of putting us down. Exerting his power over children. I'm starting to see why Father moved clear across the country to join the Army.

I'm boiling mad at Farfar. I deeply dislike him. No, I hate him. Father has just returned from the war, and will be going back before we know it, and we don't get to spend any time with him, because of stupid Farfar and his stupid shed.

Relenting, I sigh and say "I think the first thing we should do is to dig a moat around this building, to keep the water out."

"And fix the roof," Johan adds.

"I don't want to dig in the rain!" Carl whines.

"Do you think the Army likes to dig foxholes in the rain?" I say. "This is nothing,"

We find two shovels, and a pickaxe, all of which are broken in one way or another. I wish we had known about all this junk during our collection drive, we wouldn't have so much to clean up. There's not a single useful thing in here, except the swing. But, on the other hand, all this stuff can go to the next drive, and we'll win another gold star.

The ground has been softened by the rain, but is very rocky. Every time the shovel hits the ground, it clinks into a fist-size boulder.

"What about me?" Little Sister asks, as Carl is swinging the pickaxe and Johan and I are working the shovels.

"Why don't you start moving these rocks out of our way?" I tell her.

Happily she carries them, one by one, with both hands dragging like an ape, away from our job site.

By the time we've finished the moat it's dark, and Carl is asking about dinner.

"Farfar never said we had to finish tonight, right?" he argues.

He didn't, and we couldn't possibly. This chore will take us every evening after school for several days. Weeks, even.

I go to put the tools back in the shed, when I notice how nicely Little Sister has lined up the boulders along the dirt floor of the shed.

"I made a floor," she says.

The weather goes from late-September downpours to Indian summer in a week. Harvest break began yesterday, but as we don't live on a functioning farm, we have to use the day to work off our penance. It is late Saturday afternoon, and we've just finished painting the shed. Father has been back a week, but because of Farfar's stupid chore, we have barely had any time to spend with him.

The inside of the shed has been organized, as only a logically thinking Johan can, and since there are no spare planks or shingles we decided to tar the entire roof. Nothing can get through it anymore. No bugs, rainwater, or sunlight, for that matter.

Little Sister found a few jugs of turpentine inside the shed, and it's her task to clean our brushes. Happily she splashes the turpentine on the ground, making colored rivers as she does.

When we're done, we step back and admire our handiwork. We're exhausted, but proud.

"We really should do something about that swing," Johan says. "It's a shame not to use it."

We told Father about it the first evening. He told us that he had built it. Designed it, bought all the parts, built the shed around it, as it was to be a surprise for Mummo, and then he had to leave for the Army, and never returned, which he had planned to do, so he never got to tear down the shed and present her with it. He doesn't think she knows it's there. I tried to argue that someone has been using the shed, because of all the broken tools, and shelves and hooks, but he didn't comment and just changed the subject.

"What do you suppose we do?" I ask. "Tear down the shed that we've worked on for a week?"

"Of course not!" Johan scoffs at me. "But couldn't we just pull it out and place it in the garden?"

"Use your head, dummy. That thing won't fit through that door," I argue.

"Hmmm... You're right," he agrees, and uses his hands to measure the door. "But what if we take it apart and put it back together again in the garden?"

Not a bad idea. I don't know if we actually can do that, but it'd be worth the try. Maybe Father can help us.

The sun is setting, and we're hit by a pair of head-lights. Farfar has returned. As if on cue, all five of us, including Tor, duck down. We crawl out of sight. Undoubtedly Farfar has returned and will inspect the progress of our work. Because Father will return to the front soon, we don't want to spend any more time away from him than we have to. We just want to escape Farfar, and be with Father as much as we possibly can. As soon as we hit the road, we start running.

"Boys!" Farfar bellows behind us.

We pretend not to hear, and just keep running. We're proud of the work we put in on the shed. If he has a bone to pick with us, surely it can be done after Father leaves?

Just to be safe, we stay away a little longer than absolutely necessary, and by the time we return to Aunt Martta's it's dark, and past supper time.

"Where have you been?!" an angry, adolescent voice startles us as we tip-toe into Aunt Martta's house.

In the dark house I recognize the voice as belonging to our cousin Ilmari.

"They've been worried about you. Farfar's dead," he says without expression.

My mind is blank. I feel nothing. Then I feel guilt and shame, for not feeling anything.

"Your father went looking for you, and found him, face-down in the yard, next to three empty jugs of moonshine," Ilmari huffs. "Someone had spilled it all out, and he had a heart-attack. Everyone's at the doctor's in town. It got really exciting for a while. Too bad you missed it," he says, turns around, and leaves us gaping.

> Finnish moonshine is traditionally home-made vodka, most commonly made of grain, sugar or potato. The Finns call it 'kotipoltto' (home burnt) and it has the undisguisable smell of turpentine. As rationing became tighter during the war, every available drop of moonshine became worth its weight in gold.

> The war resulted in scarcity; materials that
> were essential to the war, such as gasoline,
> were no longer available for civilians. Luxu-
> ries such as sugar and coffee were in short
> supply and heavily rationed. Rationing contin-
> ued for several years after the war.
> Finland was still a dominantly rural, agrarian
> society during the war, and grains, milk and
> eggs were available, if the farms were running.
> Since the men were at the front, most of the
> operational farms were run by women.

After the funeral, Father helps us tear down the shed and move the swing. The boulders that Little Sister made into a floor are salvaged, and we line them around the new rose garden that Mother and Mummo planted this summer. For someone who's just lost her husband, Mummo looks very peaceful, as she spends the rest of the day slowly swinging in her garden.

We have precious little time with Father. What little time we have we try to make memorable. He plays the violin and listens to our stories about Denmark. But although we nag him to tell us about the war, he refuses. Both Father and Mother assure us that we'll never be sent away again. This idea has never even crossed my mind until they mention it.

Before Father returns to the war, we manage to get Little Sister to explain how the camera works, so Aunt Martta can take our family portrait. It's funny to witness Little Sister, not only knowing how to use this piece of equipment, but also in technical terms explaining its use to an adult. In Danish. Mother wrote to Uncle Oscar enquiring about it, and he told her that it was, indeed, a present for Little Sister.

At the time I have no way of knowing that it'll take eleven years before I can see that photograph, and that it's to be the only one ever of all of us together.

Father goes back to the front the next day, with solemn promises that he will return.

Winter 1941-42.

It's December 6th, and we're invited to an Independence Day[*] party at the May-or's house, after which we're going to have a torch parade through town and then go to church. During dinner the Mayor announces that he's re-joined the Army and that he's going to the front first thing Monday. This is hardly surprising news, as he's one of only a few able-bodied men still around.

---

[*] Author's note: Finland's independence from Russia, 1917.

Harri has been acting strangely all week, and when we're getting dressed for the parade, he pulls me aside.

"I need to talk to you," he says.

Although he's left us pretty much alone lately, I still don't particularly trust him.

"What's wrong?" I ask, prepared for him to pull something.

"Are you being sent to Sweden?" he says, swallowing hard.

"What do you mean?"

"I heard my parents talking. Now, since my father is going to the war, they're talking about maybe sending me away."

I'm confused. I thought only orphans or Karelians were sent away. And if they're talking about sending Harri to Sweden, will we be next? Quickly I excuse myself, and Tor and I run back to Mummo's house.

The house is deserted. Everyone's either in the parade or already in church. I try to look around for any clues. Our suitcases are still in the attic, where they were left after they were unpacked. They're still empty. Our clothes are where they should be, nothing folded into bags. I try to remember if any strangers have been to the house lately, but since I'm always in school or outside playing, I have no way of knowing this.

There's a neat pile of letters on top of Mummo's desk, and I rummage through them. Nothing of consequence. I feel slightly better. But still the uncertainty is nagging me at the back of my mind.

When the others return from church I decide to confront Mother. After she's tucked me in, and we've said our prayers I ask her if we're going to be sent away again. My question startles her.

"Why do you ask, son?"

"Well, Harri is going to be sent to Sweden, and he didn't go the last time, so I was just wondering... you know..."

"Would you like to go to Sweden?" she asks carefully.

"No!" Johan pipes in. "Don't send us away again, please Mother! Not never, ever!"

"I won't, son," she says, and straightens our quilts. "Good-night." Quietly she closes the door behind her.

I must've fallen asleep after Mother left, but I wake up again to the telephone ringing. It's such an oddity to hear it ring, much less to hear it ring in the middle of the night, that naturally I'm curious. I can hear Mother and Mummo's agitated voices, but can't make out what they're saying.

Again, I fall asleep, and wake up to footsteps directly above me. Someone is in the attic, and is trying very hard to be quiet. Tor is already awake, and is pawing at the door, trying to open it.

I creep out of bed, and peek through the door. Mother is climbing down the attic stairs, handing our suitcases to Mummo. I can hear her mumbling what sounds like 'never again', but I can't be sure, because her back is turned to me.

"What are you doing?" I ask.

I must've startled her, because she jerks.

"We're going for a little trip," she says, trying to keep her voice calm.

"All of us?"

She nods. "All but Mummo. Now go back to bed. We're leaving first thing in the morning."

"Where are we going?"

"Aunt Irma's house in Huviniemi. Back to bed."

Huviniemi. I like the sound of that. How can it be anything but fun in a place called Fun Peninsula?

The following morning, we're bundled again into all our clothing, and told to bring just one toy. I insist on bringing Father's violin, but Mother and Mummo agree that it'll be safe here at Mummo's house, and we'll come back when the war is over. I'm worried. If Father is to keep his promise and return safely, it'll be too late and he'll find us gone.

"Are the Reds coming again?" I ask.

"No, dear. Why do you ask?"

"Well, last time ..."

"Why are we moving?" Johan interrupts.

"Why can't Mummo come with us?" Carl inserts his opinion.

"Enough questions," Mother says. Her patience is running out. "Please be quick."

I get to bring my model plane, because it's now considered Gustaf's one toy. I have to leave my watercolors, and do so only after a solemn promise from Mummo, that she'll take good care of them. My knife and flashlight are tools, not toys, so I get to bring them. Ingrid brings Little Sister's toy doctor's kit, because she has no toys of her own. Little Sister very nearly throws a fit, when she's told that she can't bring Uncle Oscar's camera. So, as a compromise I don't bring a toy, but she gets to bring both puppy *and* the camera.

"Don't get attached to material belongings, children," Mummo scolds us. "They're just things. Be grateful for your life, health and each other."

We climb into Farfar's old truck. Gustaf and the girls sit in the cab with Mother, and us boys climb in the back. It's freezing again. I have to remember to ask Mother if next time we move, maybe we could do that in the summer. This time we take very little with us. Just the clothes we're wearing and one bag each, and a bundle of linens. And yet it's very crowded in the back of the truck. Mainly because we have to share it with two cans of gasoline.

Mummo assures us that we'll be back very soon, and to be brave and behave. We promise. Mother starts the truck, and we wave goodbye to Mummo until we can no longer see her. Tor is excited about a road trip, and hangs his head outside the bed of the truck.

The first rays of dawn are just over the horizon, and as we drive past the Mayor's house, I can see Harri in the courtyard. I stand up, gather some snow from the roof of the cab and ball it into a snowball. I raise my hand to throw it, and am about to shout his name, when he turns toward me. The words get stuck in my throat and I drop the snowball. Our eyes meet. He raises his hand, and without any words, we wave goodbye. His face is a reflection of terror. He's tagged.

> In September 1941, Sweden again opened its doors to Finnish War Children. The Finnish Ministry of Internal Affairs formed a central committee to oversee child evacuations, the Child Evacuation Committee. The two main reasons given for evacuating children to Sweden were the return of Karelian mothers, and the lack of food. Priority was given to four categories of children: 1) children of Karelian descent whose parents were returning to Karelia to re-build their homes, 2) orphans, 3) children who had lost their homes in bombings and 4) children of invalids. As the winter of 1941-42 became known as 'the winter of hunger' and rations were limited, many mothers opted to send their children to Sweden, and eligibility was never questioned.
> Fagerholm, again presiding over this decision, insisted that this separation would be brief, six months or less, and that under no circumstances were any children to remain abroad.
> In November 1941, the US Ambassador to Japan warned the United States Secretary of State not to underestimate Japan's war preparations and to take them more seriously than 'no more than saber-rattling'. Churchill vowed to declare war against Japan, should the US become involved.

> Finland again rejected the US suggestions of peace with Russia. The US considered Finland to be fully cooperative with Nazi Germany, but not a threat to American peace. By the end of 1941, most of Karelia was occupied by Finnish troops, and the front kept advancing eastward.
>
> Britain was on the verge of declaring war on Finland. The US continued to urge Britain to withhold a declaration of war, because there was still a chance that Finland might quit the war when she had achieved her main objective: a boundary that would provide a good defense line in case of a future Russian attack.
>
> On December 7th, 1941, Japan attacked Pearl Harbor. The following morning Roosevelt declared war on Japan, and three days later Germany and Italy declared war on the US.

We drive all day, stopping only to use the bathroom and refuel the truck. Always in the middle of nowhere. When we approach what looks like a little town, Mother stops the car, and unbundles a quilt.

"I'm going to cover you up, boys," she says. "Please stay under the quilt, and be very quiet."

"Why?" Johan asks.

Mother doesn't answer. "Just do as I say, and please don't be troublesome," she says, and we drive off again.

We're trying to listen for air raids or sirens or fighter planes, but can't hear a thing apart from our own breathing. It's nice and cozy under the quilt, and we pretend that we're inside the Trojan horse.

At long last we arrive at Aunt Irma's house, and Mother collects us from under the quilt. The house is isolated, surrounded by forests and fields, and it sits on a lake. Aunt Irma is Mother's sister and she has three children that are about our age. Her husband is at the front, and she's running the farm all by herself, with the help of her children and some local women. The farm is enormous. Almost as big as ours in Karelia.

When we arrive at her house in the middle of the night, we're immediately ushered upstairs where we each get our own rooms. Little Sister refuses to sleep by herself, and crawls up in my bed. Ingrid, who's always copying everything Little Sister does, follows suit. I'm too wound up to sleep. Besides, it's too crowded in my bed with two girls and a dog. From somewhere downstairs I can hear Mother's and Aunt Irma's voices. A radio is turned on. Why are we here?

The following morning I'm expecting to get ready to start a new school, when Mother tells me that we're no longer to attend school. She'll teach us from now on, she says, until the war is over. Nobody has any objections to this. Our cousins, however, don't have this choice. Mother pleads with her sister to let her teach them.

"We've been over this," Aunt Irma says. "Nobody around here is talking about War Children. It'll never happen."

"Just make sure that yours don't talk about mine. To anyone."

As it turns out, Mother used to be a teacher before Johan was born. This is news to me. She's actually really good, and her method reminds me somewhat of Kjersti's.

"Since when are you left-handed, son?" she asks me when we're doing math problems on paper.

I hadn't noticed that I had been leaning my head against my right hand, and was writing with my left.

"Since he got his arm broken..." Carl starts.

I kick him in the shins under the table. Mother doesn't need to know. It'd break her heart.

She gasps. "When did you break your arm?" She picks up my right hand, and leaves a trace of angel kisses on it.

I pretend to be nonchalant. "Oh, it was nothing. I fell. Want to see a trick?"

I quickly change the subject, and reach for a clean sheet of paper. Starting a sentence with my left hand I finish it with my right. Mother laughs delightedly. I still don't understand why, but this trick is as sure to please in Finland as it was in Denmark.

After morning lessons, Mother lays down the new rules. We're not to talk to strangers. We're never to leave the grounds. We're only allowed in the barn or the fields, if we're doing chores. If a stranger comes to the house, we're to go hide. If we break any of these rules, 'they' will find out that we're here and 'they' might send us away again.

Little Sister starts crying softly. Mother picks her up, and cuddles her.

"If we're hiding, how will Father find us?" Little Sister says, with a quivering lower lip.

Huviniemi turns out not to be such a fun place after all. But that's mainly because we're so restricted. In all the time I've spent hating school, I now miss it intensely. We're all bored and get into fights and squabbles about nothing. Johan has started saying stuff like 'Behave or Mother will send you away again!' We're not even allowed to read the newspaper or listen to the radio anymore.

For a wealthy woman, Aunt Irma is surprisingly stingy. It seems that every day we have less and less to eat. But that could probably also be because she's very generous to strangers. Daily there are people showing up at the house, either begging for food, or offering to work for food. Mother and Aunt Irma always help them. While the strangers are here, us kids hide in the closet under the stairs. The first time, Little Sister starts crying.

"Are they going to find us and send us away?" she whispers through sobs.

We invent a game. We pretend that we're princes and princesses, and 'they' are evil witches that want to steal us away, and boil us in big kettles and feed us to the rich in Sweden. That'll keep the little ones quiet. I'm also tempted to tell them the story about Bloody Henrik, as Jens told it to me and Carl, but I haven't yet figured out how it's relevant in this situation.

One day, when Mother lets us out of the closet, Johan confronts her, and demands to know why we have to hide and can't go to school. We gather around the kitchen table.

"Did you have fun in Denmark, Johan?" Mother asks.

Johan shakes his head quietly.

"We're hiding only until the war is over," she says. "There's no reason for us to be separated again. I'll get a job, we'll never go hungry, and we'll keep moving if we feel unsafe. This war can't go on forever, and when it's over life will go back to normal. And you'll go back to school."

"You're being awfully selfish," Aunt Irma scolds Mother. "And naïve."

"Am I? Let's see how you feel when yours are taken away from you."

"You think you can feed seven children and a dog through sheer will power?"

Mother gasps. Wide-eyed, she looks from one of us to the other, to see if anyone caught Aunt Irma's gaffe. We sit in an awkward silence for a while.

"Seven?" Johan finally says. "There's going to be *another* baby?" he's getting angrier with each syllable. "When will it end, Mother? Must there always be a baby in the house? Aren't six enough?"

He storms out of the room, muttering under his breath, and we hear a door slam upstairs. The door opens with another slam, and Johan reappears, carrying his suitcase.

"Paul, Carl, Little Sister, you'd better pack your bags, because as soon as that baby is born, we're unwanted again. I'll run away and join the Army before I'll let you send me away again, Mother!"

Aunt Irma slaps Johan across his face. "Don't you ever talk to your mother like that, boy!" she says, waving a finger in his face.

"Irma, don't..." Mother pleads.

"You're a disrespectful, ungrateful little brat, who doesn't understand or appreciate the sacrifices your own mother has had to make for you!"

Johan looks up at her in utter disbelief and hatred. For a moment he looks like he wants to strike back.

"Didn't you hear what she just said? You will never go hungry. You will never be separated again."

"Just words," Johan huffs.

Mother breaks down crying in her hands. I feel so bad. I could slap Johan myself for hurting Mother's feelings. But then I remember him telling how bad he had it in Denmark, that I can't help but feel sorry for him, too. It's confusing.

Johan eventually kneels down by Mother, puts his arms around her and pleads for forgiveness.

Mother kisses his hair and whispers "It's all right, son. We're all scared. I promise that we'll be together forever."

After that, we never questioned any of Mother's decisions again.

In January 1942 Swedish media had become overwhelmingly negative about the progress of the Finnish Army and their ability to ward off the advancing Red Army. This negativity wasn't lost on Finnish media, which feared that the Finnish Government's 'wait-and-see' attitude could come to cost the country dearly, and that Finland might wait too long to make peace.

Mannerheim himself was growing increasingly pessimistic about the position of the German Army and dreaded that the war might end disastrously. Finnish leaders came to realize that the outcome could be fundamentally different from their original objective of reclaiming land lost after the Winter War and securing their eastern border. Mannerheim didn't wish to be used as a pawn in the German war effort, and became even more cautious about joint Finnish-German operations.

Britain started evacuating mothers and children from the major cities as early as 1940. However, as German U-boats circled in the Arctic, the Atlantic and the English Channel, it wasn't safe to leave the country and they were evacuated to the countryside, often Scotland. As the war advanced, fathers were called up to fight, mothers took over their jobs in factories, and the British children were evacuated by themselves.

> Many Finnish mothers, who had been separated
> from their children during the Winter War, be-
> gan questioning the necessity of sending their
> children abroad, instead of the countryside,
> following the British evacuation model. Any
> negative publicity about child evacuations was
> censored, and the state-owned information bu-
> reau founded a separate entity to handle only
> propaganda directed at child evacuations. Some
> of the propaganda was aimed directly at the
> children, enticing them to convince their moth-
> ers to send them to Sweden to 'wait out the war
> in the land of chocolate'.

"What are you doing to my camewa?" Little Sister gasps, as she and I walk in on Johan seemingly taking apart its flash casings.

Although we now speak Finnish exclusively, Little Sister still bends some of her r's like she had a mouthful of hot potatoes. She also freely mixes Finnish with Danish, which nobody blames her for. After all, she hardly spoke any language when we left.

"There's no *my* in a war," Johan answers. "We share everything, remember?"

Little Sister ponders this for a while. "What are you doing to *our* camewa?"

"Nothing. I'm trying to see if I can't make fireworks out of the flash," Johan responds.

He's sitting cross-legged on the floor, with a screwdriver in his hand, and he's working on the flash casings. Once he gets one pried open, he pours the grayish powder onto an old newspaper. We've had our pictures taken before, and I know how blinded you can get from just one little pile of powder. By now Johan is working on his fifth.

"Are you sure about this?" I ask him, feeling slightly nervous.

He nods. "I read all about it. It's called magnesium. That's what they use in fireworks. And bombs," he adds under his breath.

Carl comes crashing in. "What am I missing?" he says, when he sees Johan gather his pile of powder.

"As soon as it's dark, I'll shoot off fireworks on the lake," Johan says nonchalantly. "Want to go with?"

"You know how to make fireworks?" Carl's eyes are full of wonder and admiration.

Johan shrugs. "Nothing to it."

"Uncle Oscar says it's not a toy," Little Sister protests.

Johan hands her the camera. "Take it back then."

She disappears. I know she's going to hide it where she thinks we can't find it.

I ask Johan to show me where he read about magnesium. I have my doubts. Turns out, he was right. What he failed to mention, however, is how flammable magnesium is, and how you can get blinded by looking directly at the flash. We decide then that we'd better have protective gear. We further decide that Mother had better not find out about this, because she's sure to put a stop to our experiment. So, we're French Legionnaire spies, crawling in a palace in Egypt, finding three sacred shields before we blow up the lake, which will flood the palace thus ridding it from evil. I hate that Tor cannot be part of this game, but there's no way I can build a shield for him.

By the time it's dark outside, we each have a board of plywood, with a hole cut for our eyes. We hoped to find tinted glass to cover the hole, but gave up when we found none. Even if we had, we couldn't figure out how to attach it to the board. So instead we covered the hole with paper, thinking it would shield our eyes, but we'd still see the fireworks.

Mother and Aunt Irma are listening to the radio, our cousins are doing their homework and the little ones are already in bed. Very quietly we sneak out of the house. Tor is left behind, and is told to stay quiet. Because it rained the other day, the snow melted, and then re-froze last night, leaving the lake shiny and smooth as a mirror. And just as slippery. The moon is bright, and reflects off the surface of the ice. Johan lays down the pile of magnesium, and we take our positions around it. Since this was his idea, he has the honors of lighting it. I'm glad. I didn't want to do it. I'm still a little nervous about this anyway, but don't want my brothers to think I'm a sissy.

Ceremoniously Johan produces a box of matches. Carl and I hunker behind our shields, eyes peeled on the pile between us. With one hand holding his board in front of him, Johan strikes the match and throws it on the pile. Then everything goes white. I'm completely blinded. Johan is screaming. I can't see a thing, but I smell burnt hair. Johan may be on fire. I don't know if the pile is still burning, or how light it is, but I can hear Mother and Aunt Irma's excited voices coming from the house. Next thing I know I'm being picked up and rushed inside.

Our eyesight returns later that evening. Johan's injuries really aren't that bad, just some scorched hairs and eyebrows, and burns on his forehead. After Mother tends to them she sits us down and gives us the reasoning of our lives. They had seen the wall of fire and light from inside the house, and thought we were under attack from the Russians. Luckily, because of the intense heat, the burning magnesium melted a hole in the ice and extinguished itself. But not before sending out smoke and sparks that flew several meters in the air. We're lucky we didn't burn down everything within a kilometer radius.

This morning, after chores, breakfast and lessons, we're allowed to go skating on the lake. With firm instructions to stay away from the hole our fireworks made, where the ice will assuredly be weak.

The little ones are napping, so we boys race by ourselves to the lake. None of us has ever been skating before, so we're all really excited to have borrowed our cousins' strap-ons.

The day is clear, but cool, and the lake is still smooth. The hole we burnt the other day with our botched fireworks has a thin layer of fresh ice. After hours of falling hard on our backsides, we eventually get the knack of balancing on the ice. We're using brooms for sticks and make snowballs into pucks, and before we know it, we have a hockey game going. It's me and Tor versus Johan and Carl. Tor is my goalie. If it's hard for me to keep my balance, it's even harder for him. At least I can lean on my broom. Soon we're out of pucks, because my goalie keeps chewing them to bits. We head off to shore to make new ones. There are visible cracks in the ice, from it shifting, melting and re-freezing, but it's solid and smooth.

As we're across the lake making more pucks, Tor starts his anxious pant. He does this every time something is happening that he doesn't understand. He stands at point, and I follow his gaze. I can see a small figure moving across the lake, on unsteady legs.

"Wait for me!" a faint voice echoes across the ice.

The figure starts running, and then disappears.

Tor sets off in her direction. We follow him, on wobbling legs, and leaning heavily on our brooms.

"Little Sister!" we keep yelling.

I pray that she just lost her balance, and didn't hit her head or hurt herself in the fall.

Tor has reached the spot where she disappeared. Our fireworks hole. She's nowhere to be seen. Tor is pawing the ice and whimpering. The ice has cracked, and it's wet. Little Sister must've fallen through it.

I turn to Carl. "Go get Mother!" I tell him.

He starts sprinting off.

"Mind the hole!" I grab the tail of his coat and re-direct him around it.

Tor plunges into the icy water. I yell out after him, but he's gone. Johan and I reach in after him, but the only things we can grasp under water are each other's hands. Little Sister and Tor are gone.

The ice cracks under Johan. In a panic, he grabs onto me, and by sheer luck, we tumble back onto the ice, rather than falling in. We let out a simultaneous sigh.

"Better mind the hole," Johan says, somewhat sarcastically.

I lay down flat on my stomach, and dunk my head in the hole. I can't see anything. It's pitch black. When I come up for air, I can hear something. Tor is over by the inlet, where the ice is melted. He's surfaced, and is dragging a piece of cloth behind him. It's Little Sister's coat. Little Sister is attached to the coat. Still flat on our stomachs, Johan and I start slithering like snakes toward Little Sister. She doesn't move.

"Is she dead?" Johan asks.

Just then Mother shows up, pushes us aside, and scoops up Little Sister. She coughs up water, and eventually opens her eyes. Mother bundles her in her own overcoat, and hurries back inside.

"Why didn't you wait for me?" is the first thing Little Sister says, when we're getting warm and dry by the big hearth in Aunt Irma's kitchen.

The look Little Sister gives me is one of hurt, sadness and accusation. She's shuddering uncontrollably. Her teeth are chattering and her lips are purple. She clings to Mother, who has her bundled inside a fur coat, and is rubbing her vigorously.

"New rule, children," Mother says sternly. "Nobody *ever* leaves this house without Tor again."

That night Tor gets a meaty bone all his own, while the rest of us eat pea soup.

In the spring of 1942 the conservative parties in the Finnish Government started voicing their concerns about losing too many children. With children between the ages two and twelve gone the national infrastructure and future generations were at risk. Many Swedish foster parents had already expressed wishes to adopt their chargelings. The total number of children evacuated out of Finland 1939-1945 eventually equaled the number of children born in Finland in 1939. The Child Evacuation Committee had Finnish mothers sign a document prior to sending away their children, that they had no intention of leaving their children permanently in Sweden. Negative press about child evacuations was still strongly censored.

The liberal parties in Finland, however, wanted to tie the country closer to the other Nor-

> dic countries, and the children were used as a
> tool to achieve this goal.
> Many mothers, hearing only the positive, cen-
> sored versions about the evacuations, found
> private channels to send their children away.
> There are no exact numbers of how many left in
> this fashion, or how many returned.
> Fagerholm finally began to realize that the
> evacuations were rapidly getting out of hand
> and began voicing his opposition. He thought it
> a personal 'question of honor to return every
> child to Finland'.

Mother lets us out of the closet after the mailman has left, and her face is omi-
nously drawn. She beckons me into the drawing room, tells me to have a seat, and
closes the door behind us. The look on her face frightens me.

"Who's Natalia?" she asks.

I don't know what to say. She looks angry, like she's trying to control her
feelings, and is near the brink of breaking down.

"Why?" I ask.

Mother produces a letter from her pocket. "Because I received a letter from
her today, trying to convince me to send you to Sweden. Now, how could this
stranger not only know where we are, but that we're still together?"

"I wrote to her…"

"Who else have you written?"

"Father, Mor Mortensen, Jens…"

"Why, for heavens sake?"

"How else would they know where I was?"

"You haven't left the house since we got here. How did you mail these
letters?"

"I put them on the pile with the rest of the outgoing mail. I'm sorry, Mother.
I didn't know I wasn't supposed to."

With a sigh, Mother gets up, strokes my hair, and says "It's alright, my
treasure. Now, please go help your siblings pack."

"Where are we going? Are you sending us away?"

"Well, obviously we're not safe here anymore."

This time, we leave even more hastily, and with even fewer belongings.
Farfar's old truck breaks down, and we can't get it restarted. So, we walk. Long
past midnight we arrive at a small cabin in a forest, where we're greeted by a
surprised-looking older man, whom Mother introduces as Uncle Eino, Farfar's
brother. He takes us to the loft, a space smaller than my room in Karelia, which
we're all to share. My brothers blame me, and give me the silent treatment.

April 1942.

Uncle Eino looks exactly like a younger version of Farfar, but is his absolute opposite in character. He's nice and kind and likes to tell stories. He tells us stories about his youth in the Merchant Marine, how he sailed the seven seas, saw the world, then fought in the Great War. He shows us his anchor tattoo on his arm and I tell him about the barge at Farfar's house. He's very handy, and somehow manages to tow Farfar's truck to his cabin, and fix it. His cabin has no electricity, no water, and the only heat comes from the fireplace or the wood-burning stove. Mother keeps thanking him for taking us in, and Uncle Eino keeps apologizing for not having more to offer than a roof. One night I ask him why he doesn't go to that market where Farfar bought all his stuff.

"What market is that, Paul?" he says, intrigued.

"The black market?" I offer.

Mother and Uncle Eino laugh so hard, that they nearly fall off their chairs.

I like Uncle Eino for many reasons, but the main reason is that he likes Tor. He takes him dove and duck hunting and on long walks in the forest. Tor instantly takes to him. His cabin is in the forest by a small lake and his only neighbor lives on the other side of it. Uncle Eino calls her Hilta-neiti. Apparently she's some old recluse spinster who makes soaps for a living. We only ever see her once a week, when she gets out on her dock to bring in water from the lake. This leads us to believe that she only takes a sauna once a week. Uncle Eino also has a sauna, but it's one of those where the smoke stays inside, and I can't stay in it long enough to get properly clean, before the smoke bothers my eyes.

Uncle Eino is nice, but poor, and has barely enough rations to feed himself, let alone all of us. But he's really smart, and shows us how to pick nettles without getting stung, and makes soup out of them. And dandelion and raspberry leaves. Mother gets a job in a mill, but somehow even with that extra income, we're still always hungry. So, since we now live in such a remote area, and are poor, and it's not considered fair to expect Uncle Eino to provide for us, Mother decides that Johan, Carl and I are big enough and strong enough to offer help on the surrounding farms for food. Uncle Eino will look after the little ones.

Mother gives me a note which I'm to memorize. She also gives me a list of houses that are known to be helpful to evacuees but tells me to avoid Lottas. I don't know what a Lotta is, but the way Mother's nose crinkles when she says it, I'm not about to ask. As I set forth over Vuokatinvaara toward the first house I memorize my greeting out loud.

"Good Morning, may I please speak to the lady of the house? Good Morning Mrs. insert name here. My name is Paul and I'm a Karelian evacuee. Might you have odd jobs needing to be done in exchange for food? Good Afternoon Mrs. insert name here. My name is Paul…"

I repeat the text until I feel I've got the correct politeness, without sounding too needy or starving. Which I am.

The hike across the hill makes me weak. I'm so hungry that by the time I reach the peak, I'm dizzy and trembling. Yesterday Uncle Eino caught a rabbit and made us a delicious stew. Unfortunately there wasn't enough. There never seems to be enough. I'm now so thin, that although my belt is on its tightest hole, my trousers keep falling off. I hate this war.

I stop at a trickling creek and scrub my hands and face. The water is cold. The snow has all but melted and I spot some bright yellow coltsfoots on the opposite bank. I make a mental image of the color and hope to remember it the next time I have access to watercolors. Without warning, my thoughts go to Uncle Johannes. I wish he wasn't missing in action, presumed dead. He would've loved to paint this view. And maybe give me a few pointers as well.

I descend the hill and see a man pushing a milk cart. This is probably the first man older than sixteen and younger than sixty that I've seen since Father was last on furlough. I wonder why he isn't at the front.

"Good Morning, my good sir!" I cry out to him and remove my cap. "Might you be able to help me?"

The man looks at me, snorts and spits. "You's *Karelian*, isn't you?" he says, in a very poor grammar and an odd dialect.

The way he says 'Karelian' makes my skin crawl and my neck hairs prickle. I remember all the fights Johan, Carl and I got into when we still were in school, and if I weren't on a mission for Mother, I'd kick this man in the shins. It's been years since I've been home, and I've been to a whole other country since, but apparently I can't shed my Karelian accent. Part of me thinks I don't want to, now that I've re-learnt the language.

"I was born in Karelia, but I'm a Finn, just like you," I recite the line Father taught me. "So, if it's not too much trouble, would you please point the way to the nearest farm on this list?" I show him the list.

He doesn't look at it. The man looks me up and down, and spits again.

"Couldn't if I wants to. And I don't wants to."

"You can't read, can you? Is that why you're not at the front?" I say, not intending to be impolite or arrogant, but hearing the words as I say them, I realize how they must have come across.

The man reaches for the front of my shirt, and for a moment I think he's going to strike me. He doesn't. He just stares at me for a moment, and then lets me go.

Anne Harper

"If Mrs. Hiltula be on your list, you's on her land. Main house be just up the lane here," he says as he starts unloading his cart into the milk house. "But around here she be known as Myllyniemi's Anna. Myllyniemi being the house." He looks me over one last time. A slow, sly grin spreads across his face. "Free advice from me to you, Finn; keeps your nose out of other people's business and never mention the front."

I walk up the long, birch-lined lane. The buds on the trees are at their utmost spring green, the whites of the trunks shine in the sun and almost sting my eyes. I climb the steps of the main house and knock on the door. As I wait for it to open I admire the façade. It's very unlike any of the other homes in this part of the country, and reminds me of home. It's painted in a rich red with shiny white trim. The house feels warm and inviting. I've grown tired of every shade of gray.

I knock again. Harder this time, and recite my greeting to myself. The door jerks open, and a girl about my height stands there staring at me. She's wearing a black dress, stockings and shoes. The left side of her hair is in a tight braid with a black ribbon. The right side hangs lose in a wavy blonde mess that falls nearly to her waist. My mind is blank. I know I'm supposed to say something, but even if my life depended on me forming a coherent sentence, I couldn't. I'm hypnotized by this girl's eyes. They're magnetic. Maybe it's the faint light of the early morning, or the reflection of her black dress, but her eyes seem like slate. No, scratch that. Like spectralite on a rainy day. No, that's no good either. More like the scales of a perch when the sunlight hits it through water...

"Who are you?" the girl with the eyes says, snapping me back into reality.

This is a good question, and more insightful than she probably realizes. Who am I? I'm only nine years old and I have already been tagged more things than I can recall. And I still don't know who I am. Karelian. Evacuee. Refugee in my home land. Outcast. My Father's son. War Child. Unwanted. Dispensable.

"Well?" she urges.

Like the blubbering idiot I feel I start rambling "Paul from Karelia. Good Morning. Insert Mrs. Name here. Work and food?"

I hear someone laughing loudly behind me. "Hope you mucks shit better than you talks, Finn!" The spitting man passes behind me, pushing his empty milk cart toward the barn. "Mornin, Miss Katja!"

I turn back to the girl with the eyes. "Your name is Katja? You're Russian?!"

A flash of ice burns in her eyes. "Of course not! Why would you say that? You're just a stupid, dirty boy!"

I know I'm not as clean as I could be with warm water and soap, but nobody has ever called me stupid. I've been called every name in the book, but never stupid.

"You're missing a button," she says.

I look down. The spitting man must have pulled it off when he grabbed me. I also have a hole in my sock and a loose thread in my trousers' pocket, which I cannot help but pull, but my clothes are clean, albeit slightly too large, as they are, after all, Johan's hand-me-downs.

I remove my cap and say "May I please speak to the lady of the house?"

Katja takes my hand and pulls me inside the house. I can smell freshly baked bread, and my stomach growls. Long and loud. She pulls me into the kitchen where four women, clad in identical gray wool dresses and gray hats, are busy cooking. They're all wearing black armbands, and, even though my stomach is beckoning me to stay, my head tells me to run. Fast and far. I may just have found the hidden lair of the Germans. The hats are adorned with a blue swastika and roses. I remember the Nazi symbol from Denmark, and I think this may be a women's version of it.

The tallest of the ladies turns to us. I bow. Although I don't think I want to eat here, or work here, I recite my introduction perfectly.

The tall lady laughs. "Around here I'm called Myllyniemi's Anna, not 'Mrs. Insert name here'."

The other ladies laugh as well. A tray of bread is being removed from the oven. The tall lady ushers Katja out of the kitchen with instructions to finish getting dressed, and turns an inspecting eye toward me. I cannot stop staring at her armband. I wonder what they do to evacuees in this house. Maybe they grind them up and make bread. Oddly, my stomach growls again.

"Ever worked on a farm?" Myllyniemi's Anna says, as she slices a thick piece of the hot bread and hands it to me.

All thoughts of ground up children escape my mind, as I devour the bread. I don't think I've ever tasted anything so delicious in my life.

I nod my head so vigorously that I almost get dizzy. I tell her about our hundred head of cattle, our chickens, the fields of potato and rye, the strawberry patch, the apple orchard. I tell her I know how to harness a horse, to plow and cut hay. I feel like I'm bragging, but keep talking to disguise the noises my stomach is making. I finish the piece of bread, thank the lady profusely and lick my fingers. Astoundingly, she cuts me another piece, and asks me where I did all that farm work. As I reach for the second piece of bread, and say 'home' a lump forms in my throat.

We stand silent for a moment. Finally the harsh lines in her face start to soften. She asks if I go to school.

Sadly, I shake my head. "We move too much," I say. "Mother teaches us."

"Your name is awfully Swedish-sounding for a Karelian," she says.

I look up and stand straight and tall. I'm proud of my heritage. That is the one thing nobody can ever take away from me. I may have lost my home, but my birthright is mine forever.

"We're Swedish Finns," I say, perhaps a bit stand-offishly, but I don't care. "Father is from Vasa, and moved to Karelia when he joined the Army."

She asks me if I read and write Swedish. Again I nod so hard, that I think my neck will snap.

"And Danish," I add.

Myllyniemi's Anna looks deep in thought. "Well, Paul of Karelia, I might just have a job for you." She leads me into the dining room. "Let's talk about it over breakfast."

> 'The Lottas' were members of Lotta Svärd, a Finnish women's voluntary paramilitary organization founded in 1918. The name derives from a poem in 'The Tales of Ensign Stål', by Johan Ludvig Runeberg. The poem describes private Svärd, who goes to fight the war of 1808-09, taking his wife - Lotta Svärd - with him. Private Svärd is killed in battle, but Lotta remains steadfast and heroic on the battlefield, caring for wounded soldiers.
>
> During the Continuation War the organization expanded to include over 200,000 volunteers, the largest voluntary organization in the world at the time. During the war the Lottas worked in hospitals, at air-raid warning posts and other supportive tasks in conjunction with the military. Officially, the Lottas were unarmed. They took over the jobs previously occupied by men, and thus freed some 100,000 men for the Army. On the home-front the Lottas worked in factories, on farms and generally assisted in aiding Karelian evacuees, those made homeless, widowed or orphaned by the war, and subsequently, the private evacuations of children.
>
> The organization's emblem consists of a pagan Norse cross and four roses. The Lotta Svärd Foundation still exists to this day, although much of its structure and purpose has changed.
>
> On Mother's Day 1942, Mannerheim awarded the Cross of Liberty to all the mothers of Finland in a non-political effort and a symbolic gesture to reinstate national pride, attempting in his own way to put an end to further child deportations.

Each evening Mother asks us how our day was. Johan and Carl have become day laborers, working one day at a time at different farms. Mother is now noticeably pregnant, and she comes back to Uncle Eino's every night with aches all over her body and a terrible cough. But at least we now have food. Or money to buy food, if anyone has any to sell.

I now know that the women I work for are Lottas. But they seem harmless, and they make really good food. Besides, I still don't know why Mother doesn't like them, so if ever she asks, I fully intend to lie.

I like it at Myllyniemi. My job consists of translating letters. They're boring and they all say the same things; how old some women are, what they do, and how old their children are, if they have any. The letters are all written in Swedish. I'm guessing they're applications to join the organization, but don't care enough to ask. After I've gotten through the original pile of a few dozen, there are only a few every day, so I have the rest of the afternoon off.

Katja and I soon become good friends. She tells me that her father died at the front, and that's why everyone wears that black armband, and that's why nobody is supposed to mention the war to her mother, who's still grieving.

While I was having breakfast that first day, Katja mended the button on my shirt. I was impressed, because she can't be more than seven, but she replied "Every first-grader knows how to sew a button."

The spitting man turns out to be Myllyniemi's Renki, and he's got some breathing problem, so the Army turned him down. He's very nice to Katja and me, eventually, and lets us help in the barn if and when we want to. Nothing is really expected of us.

I like Katja. She's more girly than Little Sister, but I can still talk to her and play with her. Apart from translating letters, Myllyniemi's Anna asks me to help Katja with her homework. She reads and writes almost as well as me, but she struggles with math. I introduce Kjersti's teaching method to her, and math becomes fun even for her. She asks me if I'll marry her one day, and I spit in my palm and extend it to her, promising her I will.

She grimaces, and says that my spit is disgusting.

"But if we're going to be married one day," I insist, "you won't mind my spit. Because we'll be kissing all the time."

Katja thinks about this for a moment, then spits in her palm, and we shake hands. We're now engaged.

One day, as I'm leaving Myllyniemi, Anna comes up to me and asks if I have younger siblings. I tell her I have an older brother, two younger brothers, two younger sisters and a baby due soon. As soon as the words cross my lips, I regret them. I know that we shouldn't tell strangers that we're still here, instead of in

Sweden. But I think I can trust Myllyniemi's Anna. After all, she's going to be my mother-in-law one day.

She doesn't comment on the number of siblings. She just hands me a pile of clothing, and tells me to take what I think we can use. The pile consists of everything from little girls' dresses to heavy overcoats, to fur hats to trousers. So, today, instead of getting paid in food I'm being paid in clothing. Eager to be in the good graces of Mother and my brothers, who now blame me for everything, I gather the entire pile inside the heavy wool overcoat, tie it into a bundle, and start my trek over Vuokatinvaara.

I feel like Santa Claus, and am welcomed as such when we open the bundle at Uncle Eino's cabin. My brothers are talking to me again. Mother, on the other hand, thinks this generosity is far too much for just one family, so she selects a few items of clothing that we may keep and takes the rest to the mill and distributes them there among other Karelian women.

Mother further decides that we must do something for Myllyniemi's Anna as a thank you, but as we now are poor and she's wealthy, the only thing she thinks is worth anything, is my art. So, the next day Katja poses for me, and I draw her portrait for Anna. She's very impressed, and approves our future nuptials. Now all I have to do is to convince Mother.

Summer 1942.

By the summer of 1942, Finland was facing starvation and fearing a heavy Russian counter-offensive. Germany had failed in its Blitzkrieg attempt on the Soviets, and the majority of citizens, and many military leaders and politicians, started doubting the capacity of the German Army and wanted peace. But, as the New York Times wrote on January 11th, 1942 'it is much easier to get into a war than to get out of it'.

The Finnish-German troops were not advancing, and started digging trenches. Since the civilian population faced starvation, the evacuation of children was boosted. The Child Evacuation Committee began moving children from Ingria westward to Finland, and eventually onward to Sweden.

In the summer of 1942, Mannerheim was granted the title of Marshal of Finland. He already had the highest rank in the Finnish military, Field Marshal. As his 75th birthday approached, and his achievements and military genius throughout

his career had made him the greatest soldier
in the history of Finland, a new rank seemed
suitable.
Hitler made a surprise visit to honor Mannerheim's birthday and met in secret with Mannerheim and Ryti. Mannerheim stood firm. He would
not involve his troops in Hitler's plans. Hitler calmly countered with offers of tanks and
troops and even delivered a few moral threats.
Mannerheim's response was to light a cigar,
something he knew Hitler strongly objected to,
as if to say that the conversation was over.

Our newest baby shares a birthday with Marshal Mannerheim, so we name him
Emil. But probably only because both Carl and Gustaf are already taken. Now
there's ten of us.

Emil is a thin, sickly-looking baby. He has the same high brow as Father, but
no hair. Mother goes back to work in the mill a few days after she had him, although Uncle Eino tries to make her rest. I think he's right. She doesn't look well
at all. But as I'm now the primary breadwinner of our family, I try not to worry
about her and concentrate instead on my 'job'.

The summer with Katja is fun. One day we get to take all the cows across
the lake to their summer pasture. I've never seen cows swim before. I didn't think
they could do that. But Renki gets in the rowboat, with us in the back, and he ties
the bull to the boat, and the cows just follow him. Myllyniemi's Anna has allowed
me to bring Tor with me, and he's confused about the cows following the boat.
He does his anxious panting, and less than halfway across the lake, he jumps in,
and tries to herd the cows in the water.

Another day Anna asks me to bring Johan and Carl along for a few days to
help with the plowing and sowing. Carl is beside himself. He so enjoyed farming when we lived in Karelia, and hasn't been on a tractor since. Renki lets him
steer his. Johan, Katja and I, along with some local kids who are too old to be
War Children and too young to be soldiers, walk behind the plow and drop down
seed potatoes. While we do the same with the rye and hay grass, Katja and I make
plans for our future. She has decided she won't mind moving to Karelia with me,
now that she's met my brothers and seen that we're actually quite accomplished
farmers. Because she's an only child, we'll have lots of children of our own. Tor
will move with us, of course. Tor adores her, but doesn't quite like Anna. Probably because she always looks so serious and sad at the same time.

After a week of sowing, there's very little that Renki needs our help with.
There's always lots to do, but he's one of those people who doesn't trust anyone
but himself to get the job done right, so Katja and I spend the summer swimming

or rowing in the lake, picking strawberries, hiking up Vuokatinvaara, where I paint her a landscape with old house-paints on a plywood board, and generally just being lazy.

I'm always paid with a minimum of one loaf of bread, or a bag of vegetables. Once I tried to refuse payment, but Anna wouldn't hear of it.

"Since her father died Katja has been withdrawn. You're the best thing to have happened to her."

That was very nice to hear.

> The international admiration that the Finnish troops had deservedly gained during the Winter War quickly diminished with the official belief that the country had become one of the Axis, although Finland insisted that she was merely a co-belligerent with Germany against a common enemy. By July 1942 the US closed its consulate in Helsinki and asked Finland to cease diplomatic ties by August 1st.
>
> The Finnish Navy was divided into two branches: coastal artillery, and the fleet. A string of fixed coastal artillery forts had been built by the Russians pre-World War I and was now occupied by the Finns. The fleet was small, consisting of merely two coastal defense ships, five submarines and a number of small craft.
>
> The German Navy could only allot a small part of its naval force to the Baltic Sea, as the majority of it was tied up in the war with Great Britain. Germany's main concern in the Baltic Sea was to protect the routes which supplied its war industry with vital iron ore imported from Norway, and transport troops, materiel and food supplies to Finland. Ever since the Soviet Union had annexed the Baltic states, Russian submarines patrolled the Baltic and the Gulf of Finland, attempting to cut off Finland's food and materiel supplies and Germany's iron ore imports. To a large extent, they were successful.

Katja and I also develop a secret code. She agrees with me that I must write to Father at the front, but for fear of being found out, we leave out all the geographic and personal names, and write that we're now living 'near the hill with the cat' and staying with a 'nicer Farfar' and so on. I hope he can crack our code. I use Mummo's as the return address, because the postmaster makes me. Before handing the letter to the postmaster I press it to my head, hoping to telepathically transmit good thoughts to Father, so that he will be safe and know where to find us once the war is over.

We also help the Lottas in their collection drives, something they do a lot. Regrettably I had bragged about how good I was at this, something I wish I hadn't done now. As hard as it was for us to collect much of anything when we lived at Farfar's, it's even harder now when people have very little left to give. Myllyniemi's Anna asks me what we did at Farfar's, so I tell her about the old iron gates and the nails from his house. I leave out the part where we got into trouble.

She looks at me pensively. "That's actually pretty clever, Paul," she says.

The next morning Anna hands me a canvas, some brushes and some old oil paints.

"I have a job for you, Paul," she says.

She's actually smiling, something I haven't seen her do in the months that I've known her. She takes me by the hand and leads me outside onto the courtyard.

"I'm going to tear down that wing," she says, pointing to the west wing of Myllyniemi, the part of the farmhouse that used to be servants' quarters, but now isn't used. "And I'd like something to remember it by. Do you do oils?"

"Not well," I'm being honest. I've only ever done oils in Denmark, and that's now ... how long ago?

"Your best is always good enough," she says, and leaves.

This is an enormous task, and an incredible responsibility. I'm almost tempted to ask Little Sister for her camera, and just take a picture. It'd be much more accurate. But there's a part of me that cannot turn down a challenge. So I lean the canvas against the well, find me a stool, and take a stab at it.

I'm so involved in my painting that I haven't even noticed how long Katja has been sitting next to me, when suddenly she says "Your house looks better than our house."

She startles me. I usually don't like anyone watching me draw, but this canvas is too big to cover up.

"What do you mean?" I ask.

"Your painting. It looks better than the real house."

So, I've failed. But then again, if Anna really wanted something to remember this fine house by, surely she'd like to remember it as it was at its finest, before the war, before losing her husband and before there was no longer anyone around to keep it up.

By the time the sun sets, I'm not done, and hide the painting in the shed, telling Katja not to show it to anyone. I tell Anna that I need at least another day.

"That's fine, Paul," she says. "Just if you could be done by Friday, because that's when I've rounded up people to come for the demolition. If that rambunctious brother of yours is available, tell him to come. I can always use a good helper. He'll be paid, of course."

Trying hard to stifle a laugh, that she'd describe Carl as 'rambunctious' and 'good helper' in the same breath, I just nod.

Thursday evening I present her with my finished painting. It didn't turn out as well as I envisioned it, but Anna's reaction tells me I'm right on the money. Her eyes well up, and she has to take a seat.

After studying it through misty eyes at length, she finally says "It's just as I remember it. In fact, this is better than the plans my husband had drawn up when we had this house built. Thank you, Paul. You have a true talent. You should become an architect."

"I intend to."

She hands me two ten markka bills. I have no idea how much that's worth. I mean, I understand it's twenty markkas, but what will it buy?

Still stunned over Myllyniemi's Anna's reaction to my painting, I hand over the money to Mother when I get back to Uncle Eino's cabin.

She gasps. "Where did you get this?"

I tell her. "Is it a lot?" I ask.

Mother doesn't respond at first. Then, she hides it in her near-empty jewelry box.

"It's enough to start a savings account for you, once the war is over," she says.

Early the next morning Carl and I arrive in Myllyniemi, eager to tear down the west wing. Easily a dozen people are already there, some of them the same kids who helped out with the sowing this spring.

Demolition isn't as much fun as it sounds. Because everything that can be re-used will have to be intact, we have to be very careful. Until we get to the frame of the house. Then Renki hands us each a hammer and tells us to 'go to town'. And we do.

He lets out a sharp whistle. "Everyone else take a break. Smoke 'em if yous got 'em. The brothers Finn will finish the job!" He's joking, of course. "What's yous so angry about?" he spits, turning to Carl and me, as we're pounding away on the studs.

"The Russians!" Carl answers without hesitation.

"Hitler," I counter.

"Father for leaving."

"Uncle Johannes for going missing!"

"Mother for sending us away!"

"The war!"

"The Russians!"

"You already said the Russians," I correct my brother.

"So? I can be mad at them more than once if I want to!"

At the end of the day, the wing is gone, and in its place are neat stacks of bricks, planks, windows and nails. I ask Renki what they're going to do with it all.

"They'll make a nice house for some poor Karelian family," he says. This is the first time I've ever heard him say 'Karelian' without grimacing. "Or's used for barracks on the front. Don't matter. Lorry be here in the morrow."

We're paid in food stamps, and we rush back to Uncle Eino's as fast as we can. We're hot and dirty, and run screaming into the lake by Uncle Eino's sauna. It's just past mid-summer, so the nights are light. The lake is perfectly calm, reflecting the long shadows of the drooping sun. We discover that there's an echo, and keep yelling at it as if we were Indians. Tor and Little Sister join us, although Little Sister stays on the shore. She's still afraid of water. Across the lake, Hiltaneiti comes out to her dock, and waves her fist at us. We're having too much fun in the lake, the water is perfect, so we pretend not to see her. The echo agrees with everything we say.

```
During most of the summer of 1942, Germany con-
centrated its military focus on the Southern
Front, in hopes of capturing Stalingrad. The
Red Army resistance increased. The Germans cut
the rail line into Stalingrad, and the Rus-
sians countered by cutting off the German sup-
ply lines. Wounded soldiers on either side had
little chance of survival.
In August, Hitler again began making plans to
attack Moscow, and turned to Finland for as-
sistance. Mannerheim started hinting that he
was ready to call it quits against Russia, and
cease being an unofficial Axis ally. Feelers in
the Finnish press were followed by an official
Finnish radio broadcast. The main points:
* In return for a post-war guarantee from the
U.S., Finland would consider stopping fight-
ing.
* Finland wanted more information on U.S.
aims for the protection of small democracies
— particularly, protection from future Russian
threats.
```

> * Finland further wished to point out that
> for the past six months the front had been
> practically immobile; in Mannerheim's words,
> the Finns had merely 'assumed a stationary
> guard'.

The night is warm, so we sleep with the window open. Mother and Uncle Eino are sitting outside talking. I can smell the sweet scent of Uncle Eino's pipe, and start lulling to sleep listening to the sound of their voices. The words 'child evacuation committee' jerk me wide awake.

" … she rowed across the lake, which she's never done before, telling me that she's contacted the authorities, and the children will be on the next train to Sweden," Uncle Eino says.

Mother's voice is too low for me to distinguish every word. "We'll move again," she says. "What does she have against my boys?"

"She says they're too loud in the lake, and since I'm now shooting game for a family of ten, she has to go hungry."

"She could use missing a meal or two," Mother says in a voice I don't recognize. "I didn't think we'd need to move again, but I see that I no longer have a choice."

Quietly I wake up Johan and Carl. They look bewildered. Pointing to the open window above the adults, we keep eavesdropping.

"… will the truck handle a trip that long?" Mother asks.

"Sure it will. The truck is as good as new. I fixed it," Uncle Eino responds indignantly. "But I don't think you should be in a rush to move. The war will be over soon. And Hilta-neiti's threats could be just empty words. And even if they're not, it'll take some time for the child evacuation committee to find out about you. And I really don't think they'll take your children away from you by force."

"They did the last time."

We've heard enough. Hilta-neiti has earned what's coming her way. Quietly we crawl down from the loft, and out the back window. Tor is confused, but after I've boosted him onto the ledge, he happily sneaks out into the warm night with us. Never wanting to miss out on anything.

We don't dare take Uncle Eino's rowboat across the lake, for fear of being seen, so we run around the lake. We haven't decided what we'll do, but it'll come to us once we're there. Carl suggests that we put a dead rat in her root cellar, but we don't have anything to catch a rat with. Johan suggests that we make a Molotov cocktail, and blast it in her bedroom. It'll make her deaf and we can be as loud as we want to. Although I like that idea, we also don't have the material to build a bomb of any kind.

When we arrive on her side of the lake, we notice that the door to her sauna is wide open. We peek inside. On the tiers climbing up the walls are row upon row of soap bars. There are easily a hundred of them, if not more.

"Let's throw them in the lake!" Carl says.

"Let's melt them," Johan suggests.

I have a better idea. We each produce our knives and carve the perfect squares into grotesque or obscene shapes. One is always worse than the previous. If she's going to send us to Sweden, we're not going to leave without making a statement.

The next morning we wake up to the echo of Hilta-neiti's screams carrying across the lake. Within minutes she's in her rowboat, and Mother and Uncle Eino get an earful of her accusations.

Mother very calmly and patiently tells her "I can assure you that my boys were in bed. Eino and I sat up until well past midnight, and they were sound asleep when I went to tuck them in. Now, I'm sorry that this has happened to you, but please don't always assume that my boys are at fault."

We never saw Hilta-neiti again.

The next day I'm back in Myllyniemi translating letters, a chore that has become increasingly boring, and monotonous. My mind wanders, and I find myself fascinated by the names of the places where these letters have been written. Like Örnskjöldsvik (Eagle Shield's Bay). Or Abborrberg (Perch Hill). Or Hjärttorp (Heart Croft). There's also a Sala and an Uppsala, but I haven't seen a Downsala yet.

As I'm imagining these magic-sounding places a word in a letter from Riddarholmen (Knight Islet) jumps up at me from the paper and fully catches my attention. The lady writing the letter says she had a Finnish War Child during the Winter War, and would now like to help another. I feel so foolish. This is what the letters have been about. They're applications from Swedish foster families. No wonder Mother didn't want us to associate with Lottas.

Katja is in school, and Tor is snoozing by my feet. Myllyniemi's Anna and the other Lottas are baking bread again. I feel an inexplicable need to run away. Although this has been a very good job, and I'll never find anything that pays so well for so little effort, I can't stay here.

Anna interrupts my thoughts, by leaning over me to check on my progress. "How are you doing there, Paul?"

Although I'm trying to stay calm, I can feel my heart pounding faster and my hands start to shake.

"I know what it is that you do," I say quietly.

"Oh, yeah? And what's that?"

"You send children to Sweden."

"Why yes. That's hardly a secret. Why are you suddenly being so indignant?"

"I have to go," I say, and call Tor. "It's been a pleasure knowing you ... but we have to go."

She tries to stop me. "Is something the matter?"

I'm almost out the door, but decide that I have nothing to lose by making this one final plea. "Please don't send Katja away," I say. "You can send me and my brothers, we've done it before, but please spare Katja."

She studies me curiously for a while. "You don't think she can handle it?" she finally asks.

"She can," I say in earnest. "*You* can't."

With a heavy heart I make what I know will be my last trek over Vuokatinvaara. I've messed up again. Maybe it'd be better for Mother to send me away to Sweden, she'd have less to worry about. I'm a bad boy who is just plain stupid. As I walk toward Uncle Eino's cabin, I prepare the speech I intend to give to Mother. I'll tell her that I hadn't intended to mess up, that I know what I did was wrong, and to beg for her forgiveness, but to be fully prepared if she gets angry enough to send me away.

When I reach Uncle Eino's, I'm greeted by chaos. The adults are in a heated argument. Little Sister and Ingrid are hovering over Emil's make-shift crib, taking his temperature and checking his pulse with Little Sister's toy doctor's tools. Emil is screaming. Johan and Carl aren't back yet.

"What's wrong with him?" I ask Little Sister, who's wiping his forehead with a wet cloth.

"The flu and diarrhea," she states, like a medical professional.

"Uncle Eino says it's a pony-o, and he has to go to the horse spit all," Ingrid offers her opinion.

The adults are still arguing outside. From what I can hear, Mother thinks she can cure Emil with home remedies, whereas Uncle Eino insists that if it's polio, then all of us have to get checked.

By the time Johan and Carl come back that night, we're all packed up in Farfar's old truck. We're going to the hospital.

Mother looks so pale and weak and tired. She's lost a lot of weight since Emil was born, and now that I think of it, I can't remember the last time I saw her eat. We're all always hungry, but that's now become so much of a given, that even Carl has stopped whining about it.

We arrive at the hospital, and Emil is admitted immediately. Mother goes with him, and tells us to stay together and not get into any trouble. In the harsh hospital light, she looks really old, and it alarms me. My beautiful mother is now disturbingly thin, has dark bags under her eyes, and I don't think she remembers how to smile anymore.

Somehow Ingrid managed to smuggle her medical kit into the hospital, and when we're being examined, she offers not only to help, but also to examine the doctor. The doctor lets her. She concurs with his assessment. We're all fine. Emil, on the other hand, has polio, and is quarantined immediately. Through a glass wall we can see his tiny little body inside a tent, which seems to be breathing. The nice doctor who examined us tells us that it's used to make his chest muscles work, and as soon as he can breathe on his own, he'll be able to leave. But for now, not even Mother is allowed in the same room with him.

The doctor pulls Mother aside, and they go into his office. Naturally we're curious, this is about our brother, after all, so Carl, Johan and I press our ears to the door. The doctor turns out not to be so nice. He's trying to convince Mother to send us to Sweden.

"… you'll all risk starvation," we hear him say. "It's only temporary …best for the children, as well as you…"

Mother is too weak to argue. "You're right," she says. "Thank you for your concern."

As soon as she exits the doctor's office, Johan pounces on her. "You promised!" he accuses her. He's angry, but his chin starts trembling.

Without answering him, Mother turns to Uncle Eino. "Please take them back to the cabin. I'll join you as soon as they release my baby," she says and turns her back to us. She leans her frail body against the glass wall that separates us from Emil.

The next morning, I tell Uncle Eino about my stupid mistake with the Lottas, and how I no longer have a job at Myllyniemi. He tells me not to worry about it, but to watch the little ones while he goes to town.

The little ones and I spend the day picking berries and mushrooms and nettles and acorns, just like Uncle Eino showed us this spring. If I can't make a living anymore, at least I can somehow contribute to the meals. Uncle Eino shows me how to trap, skin and cook rabbits and squirrels. We do this for days, probably over a week, I don't know, I've lost count, until one day, Uncle Eino returns with Mother and Emil. They're barely out of the car, when she tells us to pack our bags. We're moving again.

> In late August 1942, Finnish troops cut Soviet supply routes at the front in Salla, Lapland, forcing two Soviet divisions to abandon their fortified positions and heavy equipment. The

Finnish Army advanced behind the retreating
Russians until they had to stop in mid-September,
due to exhaustion and lack of rations. The
German General von Falkenhorst, in charge of
the invasion of Norway and Denmark in 1940 and
later in charge of the German troops fighting in
Lapland, asked twice for reinforcements from
Germany to continue this pursuit immediately
while the Soviet troops were still disorga-
nized. He was refused.

We're now living in a small town just outside Tampere. There's a big sawmill, and Johan, Carl and I all get jobs there. Tampere got badly bombed during the Winter War, and they're trying to rebuild it again. The mill is very busy, and is run by old men, wounded former soldiers and women. Our jobs are anything from sweeping the floors at night to helping to load railway cars. The pay isn't very good; however, we're not starving. Or in Sweden.

Emil seems to have recovered from his hospital visit fairly well, but Mother seems weaker every day. We now live in an abandoned barn on land belonging to an old Merchant Marine friend of Uncle Eino's. Every time we move, it seems like we're moving to something smaller, with fewer belongings. But - we're still together.

Today I'm working at the train station, and spot a line of tagged children being ushered onto a train. My heart immediately jumps into my throat, and although my first instinct is to duck and hide, a tall, slender figure, holding hands with two children, catches my attention. It's Natalia. I can't believe it and start running toward her. She recognizes me immediately. It's not a happy reunion. I'm being scolded.

"Why are you still here?" she says.

I tell her we don't want to go, and she can't make us.

"We'll see about that!" She tells me that she'll only go as far as Sundsvall, Sweden with this particular group, and will come and look me up when she returns.

"Please don't!" I try to plead. "If you do, then we just have to move again, and we're poorer with every move."

She looks at me quietly for a while.

"Paul, do you go to school?" she asks.

"No... I'm working. Mother taught us for a while, but now she's just sick and tired all the time."

"What's wrong with her?"

"I don't know. She doesn't eat. Or smile. Or really talk, either."

"You have to go to Sweden. If you don't go, you'll just add to your Mother's worries. If you go to Sweden, she'll have enough money to feed herself and maybe get some medical assistance. I promise I'll find you a really nice family, that'll take all four of you."

"There's seven of us now," I say.

She laughs. "Well, no wonder your mother is ill."

About a week later, when Johan and I return from work, there's an unknown car outside the barn. I haven't told Mother about running into Natalia, nor have I brought up Sweden again. And last night Carl got really sick with pneumonia, so I haven't really even seen much of her.

Natalia meets us outside. She's carrying Gustaf in one arm, and Ingrid in the other. Little Sister is walking behind her, yawning.

"Hop in, Paul," she says. "Let's go for a little ride."

"Just me?"

She nods, and ushers me, Little Sister, Ingrid and Gustaf into the car. I have a bad feeling about this. As we're driving down the long dirt road, I hear a familiar sound behind the car. Tor is galloping behind us. He's barking and whimpering. I roll down the window, and try to get him to not follow the car. He knows something is going on.

"Ignore him," Natalia says sternly.

"Can't we take him with us on the ride?"

"No, he has to stay here and take care of your mother."

"How far are we going?"

"Sweden."

That's when all the dams break. My throat closes up, and I hang my head out the window, watching my dog trying to catch up behind us, not able to say goodbye to him. I'm crying openly now. Tor's tongue is hanging out the side of his mouth, and he's losing distance. I reach out my hand through the window, and wave goodbye to my dog. I hang my head out the window until I can no longer see him. But a million images of his face flash before my eyes. I close them, trying to savor every memory of him. Leaving Finland again is one thing. Leaving my dog is another altogether.

The little ones are asleep at the train station. Natalia is conversing with what looks like another chaperone. She comes back to us with our tags. Little Sister wakes up with a startle, when Natalia places her tag around her neck.

Her eyes bulge up and she starts screaming "No! No! Noooo!" like a little maverick, who's been able to avoid the branding iron, but now it burns around her neck.

Ingrid and Gustaf are unaware of what's happening, but because Little Sister is crying, they, too, start. I have no words to comfort them. Little Sister starts hammering me with her fists.

"Take me back! I don't want to go!" she's screaming until she loses her voice, and she feels as though she's burning up.

She's still crying when we get on the train and our four identical suitcases appear from the trunk of the unknown car. I hate those suitcases.

BOOK 4

SWEDEN

November 1942.

I hate everything. I hate Mother. I hate her for being a coward and a sneak. I hate that she abandoned me and didn't even have the decency to tell me. I hate Natalia. I hate her for pretending to be my friend. Pretending that she cares, and then taking me away without letting me stop to say goodbye to my dog. I hate this war for making me hate. But mostly I hate myself. I was a stupid, bad boy, and now I've got what I deserve. And I dragged three little siblings with me.

We get off the train in Sundsvall, Sweden, where we're taken to a hospital. We're quarantined until they can determine that we don't carry any diseases. I'm not a doctor, but I can tell that Little Sister is seriously ill. She sounds just like Carl did, and he had pneumonia. I don't know how long we've been here, but we're now separated. Ingrid and Gustaf are in the infant ward and Little Sister is in isolation. She doesn't have pneumonia, she's got whooping cough. I'm not allowed to visit her.

Every few days all the other kids are lined up and foster parents come and pick them up. We're never included in these line-ups. Nobody has told me why.

I don't know who packed my suitcase, but there's nothing but clothes in it. No paper, no pencils. I'm bored. There's no radio and no newspapers, and very little to do but wait. Ingrid loves it here. She has her little doctor's kit with her and follows the real doctors like a puppy. Gustaf brought his (my) model airplane and has become a fighter pilot. Really annoying, and I'm glad we're not in the same ward. Little Sister's ratty old stuffed toy puppy was taken away from her when she was quarantined. I wish I could go see her. She must be scared and lonely. To my knowledge she's never slept alone in her life.

This morning Natalia arrives with another trainload of children. She comes to see me and sits on my bed.

"How are you doing, Paul?" she asks.

I just shrug. I don't want to hate her, but I do. She let me down.

"You're angry, aren't you?" she says.

I don't answer and am mentally willing her to go away and leave me alone. To abandon me like everyone else has, and she will, too. She puts her hands on my shoulders, and forces me to look at her.

"It's not your fault," she says. "You didn't do anything wrong. You're not a bad kid. In fact, you're an exceptional kid."

I still don't answer, and she shakes me lightly.

"Listen to me, Paul," she says. "You can go on hating me for the rest your life all you want. But I want you to understand that I did what I did because I thought it was right. I did it because I care about you. Your mother is very ill, and would've died if you had stayed in Finland. You would've died if you hadn't left. Am I getting through to you? This is only a temporary separation. Before you know it, the war will be over, and you'll be going home again."

"You said that about Denmark, too. And I was left there for over a year!"

She sighs, and lets go of my shoulders. "I know. Probably just wishful thinking on my part. But, you can't go through life angry and bitter. Do I think this is the best thing for children? No. But it's the best thing we can do under the circumstances. Even your mother came to realize that, so why can't you?"

All the anger, resentment and bitterness start boiling over, and my eyes well up. I don't want Natalia to see me crying, and I try to avert my eyes. She pulls me to her and holds me close.

"So, it wasn't my fault?" I say.

"What could you have possibly done to make you think that?"

I tell her about the letters I sent, about the pranks I pulled and my inability to keep my mouth shut, when Mother had made it very clear that we were in hiding. Natalia tries to convince me that I hadn't done anything wrong. I do want to believe her. But if I hadn't been so stupid, we would've stayed in Huviniemi and Mother wouldn't have gotten ill.

"But why didn't she tell me herself?" I ask.

"She wasn't there, Paul," Natalia says. "I took her to the hospital. She was seriously malnourished and was coming down with pneumonia. You must believe that she loves you so much that she would risk her own life in order to keep her family together."

"But why me?" I insist. "Why did I have to go and not Johan or Carl?"

"Carl was sick. He never would've been let on the train. And even though your mother was delirious, she made me swear not to take Johan. I don't know why."

Now I hate Johan for being such a sissy. We sit in silence for a while.

"Now, I have some good news for you," Natalia breaks the silence. She smiles. "Are you ready for this? I hand-picked your new foster family for you. The father is a police officer and the mother is a secretary in a big company. I haven't met him yet, but she's really nice. She works days, he works nights, so there's always going to be someone looking after your siblings when you're in school. And yes - they've agreed to take all four of you. You, Ingrid and Gustaf are leaving today and they'll come and get Little Sister when she's fully recovered. How does that sound to you?"

I think I love her again. "Do they have children?"

"They had two girls…"

"What happened to them?" I interrupt.

"They got married and moved away. They seem really nice. And if I were married, I'd take all four of you."

I ponder this new information for a while. "Are they really old?"

Natalia laughs and ruffles my hair. "You're about to find out. They're here to pick you up."

In October 1942 Russia accused Finland of helping the Germans at Stalingrad and recruiting
'old men and cripples' to help the Germans
storm Leningrad. Hjalmar Procopé denied the
charges, and added that Finland 'wants to cease
fighting as soon as the threat to her existence
has been averted' and her borders and security
are guaranteed. The state-owned Finnish Information Bureau branded Procopé's statement
as 'false and foundationless', as Finland was
not ready for, nor would consider, a separate
peace. Among many Finnish politicians, Paasikivi renounced Procopé's claim and said that
Finland wasn't yet prepared or willing to discuss peace with a hostile aggressor who had
attacked twice in less than two years.
Finland had one of the most difficult diplomatic positions during the war. Internally
her fighting strength was being bled white by
two wars in three years. The economy was disrupted by blockade, the civilian population
was starving and growing more and more dissat-
isfied. In 1942 more Finns died of starvation
or ailments as a result of malnourishment than
from bombs or bullets.
Even the Finnish government was aware of the
increasingly low morale among both the troops
and the civilians. Following the example that
President Roosevelt had set in his 'fire-
side chats', President Ryti gave a speech to
the people at the opening of 'Home Week', a

```
government morale-building campaign. It wasn't
well received.
```

I'm grateful to be alive. I'm grateful to have food. I'm grateful for my health. I'm grateful there's no war in Sweden. I'm grateful that I'm still with two of my siblings. I'm grateful... This has become my new mantra. I keep repeating it to myself so much, that maybe one day I'll believe it.

Lennart and Siv are our Swedish foster parents. And they told us to call them that. No 'Aunt' or 'Uncle' or 'Mr.' or 'Mrs.', just Lennart and Siv. They live in a nice apartment near Stockholm. Ingrid and Gustaf sleep with them, but I have my own room. Although I think it must've been a closet at one point, because it's barely big enough for a cot and a side table. But I'm grateful.

They don't look old, but they act *very* old. Both are always tired, and complaining about achy joints. Which reminds me of Heidi. Which reminds me of Tor. Lennart and Siv don't have a dog. But they're nice. They buy us new clothes, and ask us what we want Santa to bring for Christmas. They don't talk much, but in the evenings, before going to work, Lennart sits in the living room, with Ingrid in his lap, and they tell each other stories. She has a surprisingly vivid imagination.

My first day of school, Lennart takes all of us in his car, and is wearing full uniform. The entire school sees us walk up together. Nobody will bully me in this school. He also tells me not to hide behind my scar, but to use it to my advantage. I ask him what he means by that.

"If anyone asks, make up a story about it," he says. "Tell them it's a war wound. Or tell them you got it in a fistfight, and finish with 'you should see the other fella!' Nobody will ever tease you about your scar again."

Although I've been raised not to lie, this one does sound tempting. And a story like that certainly sounds better than the truth about a sissy mama's boy.

Lennart also gives me a weekly allowance, and takes us to the movies. We eat sweets, and watch the newsreel in a dark theater. This is way better than having to read through the newspapers to find out what's going on with the war. It's so big and so loud, that I almost feel like I'm there.

Lennart is nice in an odd way. It's almost as if he's uncomfortable and is trying too hard. His hair is all grey and he's slightly overweight. He walks with a bit of a limp, because he took a bullet in his hip once, he says. But he has a really nice gun collection, mainly pistols, and says that sometime this spring he'll take me to the station's gun range and teach me how to shoot.

"I can shoot a rifle really well," I tell him.

"Well, then you'll be a natural at pistols," he says.

I can't wait to try.

Siv is short, slim and blonde and always smiling. Her face is horizontally oval, which makes her look plump, although she isn't. Adding to the plumpy look is her exceptionally wide smile. It looks fake to me, but then I remind myself that she's a secretary, and probably has to smile all the time. She speaks proper Swedish, just like a secretary should. And she's a good cook. She always has milk and meat and she bakes her own bread. Often she lets us help her bake and then she helps me with homework. I've missed nearly a year of school, and have lots of catching up to do. But with Siv's help, I'll be caught up in no time.

Natalia lives on the other side of town, and one Sunday she comes to pick me up, and takes me for lunch at her apartment. We go by trolley. It's very exciting. I've never ridden a trolley before.

As we're eating Natalia tells me the bad news. "Little Sister will have to be moved to a hospital in Gåsebeck," she says.

"Where's that?"

"In Skåne. Southern Sweden."

"Why? You told me she was coming to live with us!"

"She's not responding to her treatments. The hospital is getting full, and Gåsebeck is one of the best hospitals in the country. But when she's well again, she'll come to live with you."

"She's going to get well, isn't she? She's not going to die?"

"She's going to get the best care in the world. Now, what can you tell me about her medical history?"

"What does that mean?"

"They need to find out why she isn't responding to her treatments. Anything you can recall about her being sick, or having accidents, or taking medication?"

I have to think about this for a while. I don't know if she was sick or not in Denmark, and since then we've all taken turns with flu's and colds and stomach viruses. As soon as one of us gets sick, another three or four would catch it too.

"She used to get ear infections a lot," I say. "And then her ear started bleeding the night we left Karelia. And I think a doctor gave her something for it, but I don't know what it was. And she gets dizzy a lot. But only when she twirls. And then she fell through the ice and almost died. But Tor saved her!" And that reminds me that Natalia promised she'd visit Mother last time she went to Tampere. "Did you visit Mother?"

Natalia nods, and smiles. "She's doing much better and was asking about you. She's been out of the hospital for a few weeks now. We found a house that they share with another Karelian family, so they have heat and water, and take turns working and looking after the little ones…"

"How's Tor?" I ask. She wasn't getting to the point quickly enough, so I interrupt her.

Natalia turns her head away from me. Then she gets up and starts clearing the table. She doesn't say anything, and I know that she's avoiding my question.

"Something's wrong. What is it? Is it Tor? Is he sick? Has someone been mean to him?"

At long last she sits down again opposite me. She takes my hands in hers. "He ran away," she says.

I have to get back. I have to go back to Finland and find Tor. What if he followed my train like he did the car? What if he got hit by a train or a car or something and is bleeding in the ditch somewhere? Or worse.

I find a map of Lennart's, and discover that it's way too difficult for me to make my way back across water without any money, and it's too far to go all the way around the Gulf of Bothnia. So, one day I skip school and go down to the harbor and ask the first sailor I see if I can work on his ship for a fare across to Finland. He just laughs at me and keeps walking. The next two do the same. The fourth one tells me that the waters between here and Finland are crowded with submarines and mines, and that hardly any ships go between the two countries anymore.

"Why are you in such a hurry to go to Finland in the middle of a war, anyway?" he asks.

"My dog ran away. I have to find him." Even as I say the words, they're choking me. Whenever I used to be this sad or upset, Tor would nudge my hand with his head. I can almost feel his coat under my hand now.

The sailor looks at me for a long while, as if to assess whether I'm serious. Fighting tears, I keep his gaze.

"Dogs are smart people, you know," he finally says. "Don't worry. He'll probably show up in the last place he saw you. Dogs are known to do that. Trust me. He'll be fine."

With a sunken heart I start heading back to Lennart and Siv's apartment. 'Trust me', the man said. Right now I have a hard time trusting anyone. Especially adults.

When I get back to the apartment, I find a note on the hall table that reads 'Paul, you're late. There's an emergency at the station. I had to go. Siv is at the merger meeting until late. Here's two kronor. Go to the movies or something and be quiet! Lennart.'

To my surprise Ingrid and Gustaf are alone in the apartment. Gustaf is sleeping in his crib and Ingrid is sitting on her bed, pressing the toy stethoscope to her thigh.

"What are you doing here all by yourself?" I ask.

"I don't know," she whimpers. "We took a nap. And then I woke up. And it was just us. Will you draw my picture? I'll sit still this time, I promise. We'll send it to Mother. She'll see how much I've grown. Uh-huh?"

'Uh-huh' is Ingrid's new favorite expression. She has started inserting it at the end of her questions, looks up with her intense blue eyes, and usually gets her way.

"Fine," I sigh. "Sit over there."

"Carry me."

"No. You're too big to be carried."

"I can't walk," she says quietly, and starts sucking in her lower lip.

I can see that she's not pretending, just so that I'd relent and carry her.

"What's wrong?" I ask. "What did you do?"

"I didn't do anything," she's sobbing now. "Please don't be mad. Uh-huh?"

"Get off that bed and start walking!"

"I can't!"

I cross the room to her, and try to pull her to her feet. Her legs refuse to bend. I try to pry them down.

"Paul! Stop! You're hurting me!" she screams.

On the bedspread, where she was sitting is a bright red spot. I turn Ingrid around in my arms. The back of her dress is red as well. I lift the dress. Her underwear is crimson. She's bleeding.

"What happened to you?"

Panic is starting to fill me. Somewhere in the back of my mind I'm reminded of a story Jens told me about his mother bleeding from where she pees, and had to go to the hospital.

"What did you do?" I repeat.

"I didn't do anything. I was napping! I'm sorry!" She's crying so loudly now, that she wakes Gustaf.

Suddenly I have to be the oldest, and strongest and wisest. I don't know where the nearest hospital is. I don't know how to get there. And if I don't get there, will Ingrid die or have a baby?

Ingrid straps her arms around my neck, and I try to carry Gustaf in my arms.

"I walk mysseff," he states proudly.

I grab the two kronor that Lennart left for us, and we make our way down the steps. Ingrid keeps repeating that she's sorry. What does she have to be sorry about?

On the street I eventually get us a taxi and ask the driver if he can take us to the nearest hospital for two kronor.

"Two kronor will get you there and back, but that bleeding girl isn't setting foot in my car," he says, slams the door and drives off.

Both of them are crying now. The back of my coat feels hot and sticky. It's a combination of my sweat from the inside and Ingrid's blood from the outside. It smells really bad. Like something rotted.

It's dark and the streets are abandoned. We walk to the corner. Gustaf is holding us back, so I pick him up in my arms. There's usually more traffic around the corner. A car drives by, and I hail to the driver to stop. He waves back at me. Eventually another car approaches, and I get out in the street, to block his path with my body. I've been carrying both my siblings for a while now, and my arms are starting to shake. The second car stops, and the driver rolls down his window. I ask him where the nearest hospital is.

He takes one quick look at the three of us, and says "Hop in. I'll drive you."

Ingrid is admitted to the emergency room. Gustaf and I have to sit and wait. Nobody will talk to us, or tell us what's going on. Finally a lady in a white lab coat approaches us. She introduces herself as Dr. Magnusson, and takes a seat next to me. If I had to guess, I'd put her somewhere between Mother and Mrs. Mortensen in age. She reminds me of that American actress, Katherine somebody, whose movie Lennart and I saw last weekend. She's tall and her face is all angles. Her dark hair is slick around her face, but falls in big, concentric curls on her shoulders. She wears narrow glasses. Although she's not wearing a ring, there's an indentation on her left ring finger. I'd like to think that she's married, but gave up her jewelry for the Finnish war effort. She's too young to be a widow and too pretty to be divorced.

"Your sister will be fine," she says. "You did the right thing by bringing her here."

I let out an audible sigh of relief. Almost as if I had been holding my breath for hours.

"Thank you, Dr. Magnusson," I say.

"I'd like to keep her here for a while. She's suffered serious bruising and tearing, along with the blood loss. Her adductors are badly bruised. Um... that's the muscle in her inner thigh... Which is why she couldn't walk. But she will be able to walk again soon. Do you understand what happened to her?"

"She was going to have a baby?"

Dr. Magnusson lets out a little laugh, and looks at me curiously. "How do you know where babies come from?" she asks.

"I've lived on farms. A lot."

"Well, ahem… Yes. It seems like someone was trying to make a baby with her. And that's bad. Very, very bad. She could've been badly injured, and scarred for life. Would you happen to know who might have hurt her?"

Lennart. I can't believe it. He's a police officer. They're supposed to protect us, not hurt us. But is he going to be in trouble if I rat on him? And if he is, then what's going to happen to us?

"You know something, don't you?" Dr. Magnusson urges.

Quickly she looks around, and then whisks us away to her office. She closes the door behind us, and kneels down by me. The look in her eyes demands attention.

"Look," she says. "You cannot be loyal to the monster who did this to your sister. If you know who did it, you have to tell me. Neither you nor Ingrid will be in trouble. I promise."

Here's another stranger, yet another adult who asks me to trust her. There's something about her that makes me want to trust her, and eventually I do.

"Lennart," I say. "Our foster father."

"You're Finnish War Children?" she says, surprised.

I nod. Dr. Magnusson's eyes darken, and a muscle twitches in her jaw.

"I'd like to examine you and your brother as well, and then you'll spend the night here. Tomorrow I'll get your belongings, and find you another foster home. You'll not spend another night with a pervert like that."

It's much later than I had hoped when I finally wake up. It's already morning, and I can hear traffic through the window and people talking outside the door. I had hoped to sneak out in the middle of the night, and then sneak back in again, but for some reason I must've been more tired than I anticipated, and slept right through the night. Quickly I check on Gustaf and Ingrid, who are both sound asleep.

Sneaking out of a hospital by yourself is much more difficult than sneaking out of Uncle Eino's cabin with a dog. There are people everywhere, and it's brightly lit. The window doesn't open, so that's not an option. Opening the door a crack, I can see nurses loitering around the reception area diagonally across the hall. At the end of the hallway is a janitor with a pushcart heading my way.

My plan is to sneak out, and if anyone stops me, to simply ask for the bathroom. But then I spot an even better opportunity. From my left, a young couple turns the corner, and walks down the hallway toward the elevators. The lady is carrying a newborn, bundled in blankets. The couple is beaming, with really stupid grins plastered on their faces. Part of me can't help but think how their expressions will look after their seventh child. When they pass the door, I join them. I plaster a matching stupid grin on my face, and anyone who sees us will just think that I'm a proud new brother.

It works! I'm out of the hospital. It's still dark outside, but I'm sure I can remember the way back to the apartment. Unfortunately the only way I know how to get to Natalia's, is to take the trolley at the stop outside Lennart and Siv's apartment. Siv should still be in bed and Lennart should just be on his way home. But as dark as it is, I think I can still hide in the shadows, should he see me. Which he has no reason to. He doesn't know where we spent last night.

The trolley stop is deserted, and stands between two streetlamps, so it's dark. Which is good. I look up at the apartment, and there's a light on. Siv must be up and getting ready for work. Mentally I'm willing the trolley to come. I'm crunching Lennart's two kronor in my fist, and have every intention to spend it all. The trolley is approaching just around the corner, when I see him walking up the street toward the apartment. Anger starts boiling inside me. How dare he do what he did to a little girl? What gives him the right to hurt a helpless vulnerable child? Just because he's a police officer, doesn't make it alright to wound anyone, much less my baby sister.

The trolley stops at the lights, and although part of me wants to rush to it, another wants to square things with Lennart. I spot his limp, and like Tor chasing a rabbit I sprint across the street, and plow my head into his injured hip. I want to hurt him as badly as he hurt Ingrid. He must've seen me coming, because he half-turns, and my head-butt lands in his groin. He keels over with a noise that sounds like a kettle whistling. I throw his two crumpled bills on the ground. I'm not sorry, and rush back across the street to catch the trolley.

Throwing the money away was stupid and impulsive and now I'm broke. The trolley driver won't let me get on. So I follow it on foot. It doesn't go very fast, and makes many stops, so it's never out of my sight. I don't know Natalia's address, but I could describe her building in a blizzard. Silently I pray that she's there. I have no way of knowing whether she will be or not. Luckily she is, and opens the door in her robe, holding a chipped coffee cup in one hand.

"Paul?! What in the world? Are you alright?" The questions keep hitting me like sniper fire, as she pulls me inside her apartment.

She sits me down at her kitchen table, and offers me coffee and toast. Not until now had I noticed how cold it was, and the coffee cup feels nice under my fingers. Natalia spreads strawberry jam on a piece of bread, slices some cheese and hands me the sandwich. It's delicious, and I finish it in four bites.

"You liked that, huh?" she says.

Resisting the temptation to lick my fingers I say, "Thank you, yes. Strawberries are my favorite food."

She reaches for a spoon, plops it into the jar and hands it to me. "Go crazy," she says.

I haven't had strawberries in ages, and I finish the jar in silent reverie. When I lick the spoon Natalia asks me why I'm here.

I tell her what happened with Lennart and Ingrid.

"They're going to look for another family, but I'd rather go home or stay with you," I say in earnest.

"We've been over this, Paul. They won't let an unmarried woman have War Children. Especially not one who works and is gone for long periods of time."

"Then we'll work with you on the trains. And you don't even have to pay us. Or you can send us back home. But I don't want another family. Last time you said you hand-picked them. You said that they were nice. What he did wasn't nice. Please send us back home! You can do it. I know you can."

"I wish it were that easy," she says and starts clearing the table. "You're probably better off at the hospital until I can find you another family..."

"Don't I get any say in this?" I interrupt her. "Ever? Nobody ever bothers to ask me what *I* want. I didn't want to go to Denmark. I didn't want to come here. Doesn't my opinion count? Huh? Because I'm just a kid? I thought you were my friend!" I'm so upset, that I run out.

She catches me at the door. "Paul, wait! I *am* your friend. And I *do* value your opinion. And if I for a second thought you'd be better off in Finland, I'd take you there myself. I'll find you someone good. Please let me make it up to you."

She leads me back to the kitchen table, and we sit in silence for a while, each staring into our coffee cups.

"I know who I want," I finally say.

"Really? Who's that?"

"There's this lady, whose application letter I read. She ended up in the re-grets pile. She's the director of an art gallery and her husband is an engineer. They live in a villa."

"Are you making this up? Where did you find this letter?" She looks at me suspiciously.

I tell her about my 'job' with the Lottas in Myllyniemi.

"Well, if she went through the Lottas, then there must be a reason for her being turned down by the Child Evacuation Committee," she says thoughtfully. "What else do you remember about her?"

Biting my lip, I try to picture the letter. Now I wish I had paid more attention. All I remember is the lovely handwriting and her magical address.

"They're both in their fifties..." I say.

"Not a factor..."

"...and they don't have any children..."

"Shouldn't matter..."

"...and the husband travels a lot for work."

"Yes, that's a strike against them. Another one is that she works as well."

"But they sound like really good people..." I try to argue my case. "They really want to help! And she's the *director* of an *art* gallery!"

"That's the decisive factor, isn't it?" Natalia smiles at me. "The art part?"

I nod so hard that I think my neck will snap.

Natalia sighs. "Alright, I'll see what I can do. But I make no promises, so don't go getting your hopes up. And I need more to go on. If you could think of their names or their address, that'd be really helpful."

"They live on Wild Berry Lane and their names are Mr. and Mrs. Paul's new foster parents."

By January 1943, the German troops on the Eastern Front were out of ammunition, starving and unable to organize another offensive. Hitler demanded that they 'do the honorable thing' and fight to the last man. By February, they had lost the battle of Stalingrad, and Russia went on the offensive. The tide of the war seemed to be turning and the defeat at Stalingrad was the first indicator that Germany might actually lose the war.

Mannerheim ordered the preparation of rear defensive positions across the Isthmus. He feared that Germany's loss would be catastrophic to his troops, if the German siege of Leningrad failed. The Red Army would surely come crushing through Finland. He no longer believed that the Allies made a distinction between Germany and its co-belligerents, and urged that Finland come to a separate peace, without having to sacrifice everything.

The Finnish troops were showing signs of exhaustion. Many perished from starvation or malnutrition.

Spring 1943.

Natalia keeps her word. She locates my new foster family, the von Schoenfeldts, Hugo and Birgitta, who happily welcome me to their home in Malmö. Although nobody has confirmed it, I think their German-sounding name is the reason for their original rejection. Unfortunately, however, they only take me. Their house is enormous, and they would've gladly taken all four of us, but by the time we locate them, Ingrid has attached herself to Dr. Magnusson, Little Sister is well again and now living with a family in Halmstad, and Gustaf is elated to be with an Air Force officer's family in Uppsala. Not only are we separated, but we're spread out all over the country.

The von Schoenfeldts are nice. If I didn't know that they were married to each other, I'd think they were related. Their coloring and features are nearly identical. They're both tall and very thin. They both have dark hair, and even though Hugo applies vast amounts of Brylcreem to his every morning, by lunch time, the curls have sprung out and he looks like a girl. They both have hooked noses, although hers is more prominent, because she uses reading glasses, and keeps fidgeting with them, thereby drawing attention to her nose.

There's always music and company in the von Schoenfeldts' house. They introduce me as 'our boy Paul', which at first makes me cringe, because I look nothing like them, and could never pass for their kin, but now I've come to enjoy hearing it. It's the 'our' part that warms me the most. I feel like I belong. And like they want me to belong. As for music, I haven't heard any since we practiced 'Den Blomstertid' at our school in Österbotten for our graduation. Due to an unfortunate frog-related incident we never got to sing it.

I have my own room on the second floor. And my own bathroom. I think the von Schoenfeldts must be quite well off, although they don't make a big display of it. Not like Uncle Oscar and Aunt Bodil in Denmark. When they first took me to my new room, I thought that I had to share it with someone. The room is filled with toys. There's a train set, model airplanes, tin soldiers, a telescope and bows and arrows. The wall paper has a cowboys and Indians motif. When I asked whose room it was they told me that they had decorated it in anticipation of my arrival. I thought they were joking, until I saw the rest of the house. It's beautiful. It's old, and although I haven't counted all the rooms yet, I'm sure that it's as big as ours in Karelia. If not bigger. The rooms certainly are more spacious. They have high ceilings and huge windows. Theirs is the last house at the end of the lane, and just a lawn and a path away is a nice wooded area. I can't call it a forest, because it certainly isn't like any that I've ever seen.

The house is decorated like a museum. There's beautiful old furniture everywhere and, naturally, lots of wonderful art. I use every bit of scrap paper I can find to try to sketch everything, when Birgitta notices me. Not only do we go and buy me proper art supplies, but she also finds me an art instructor. I'm back to taking art classes.

As much as I enjoy painting and drawing, I'm more fascinated by Hugo's work. He owns his own engineering firm, and they design and build bridges. Among other things. He has a study in the house, and often he lets me watch him design at his enormous drafting table. It's so clever. It tilts, so that you can stand up straight while working at it. It's like a table that's also an easel. He says that one day this summer, after school's out, I may go with him on a job site. I can hardly wait!

We spend hours at a time at the table, where he shows me the blueprints of projects that he's working on. He calls them skeletons.

"Like the bones under your skin, holding your body together," he says.

I'm reminded of a day, ages ago, back in Karelia, sketching our old house with my Uncle Johannes. I wonder if they ever found him.

Hugo shows me how they make models out of sticks, before they even start building the bridge. It's fascinating, and I think I want to be an engineer when I grow up. I tell him as much.

He laughs. "If blueprints and stick models are what made you change your mind from architecture to engineering, I'm sorry to burst your bubble. There's a lot of the same in both. And, if you do become an architect in Finland after the war, you'll never be unemployed."

"What do you mean?"

"Re-building Finland will take decades," he says. "But that's just my assessment as an engineer."

The thought scares me a little.

One day after my art class, Birgitta asks me if I'd let her host my first show in her gallery.

"Something small," she says, "with only a few invited guests, possibly an art critic for the local paper. You'd only need to display a half dozen or so paintings…" She's obviously rehearsed a speech to try to convince me.

"I'll do it!" I interrupt her enthusiastically. I wish Uncle Johannes were here.

We have a date set for my show, and I select four landscapes and two sketches to display. Both of my sketches are drawn from memory. One is our house in Karelia, and the other is the old fort in Denmark.

The show doesn't start off well. All the people are snooty-looking snobs who seem more interested in the free wine and cheese than my art. Until one pompous-looking man asks Birgitta when he'd get to meet the artist.

She pushes me forward. "This is him!"

The crowd hushes. The pompous man looks me up and down, and turns back to Birgitta. "You're joking," he says. "How old are you, son?"

"Ten," I say.

The pompous man leaves us without another word. He makes a slow circle around the room, stopping by each painting. He tilts his head this way and that, moves closer and steps back. He spends the most time by my sketches. When he's done, he gathers his hat and overcoat, shakes Birgitta's hand and says "Thank you for inviting me" and leaves.

Nobody ever told me that he's the art critic until Birgitta shows me the paper the next day. Here's what it says. I've edited the boring parts.

```
The Arts in Finland Have Suffered a Severe Blow.

I was fortunate enough to have been invited
to [Birgitta's Gallery] to review the works
of [me]. Upon entering I thought I was pre-
sented with the creations of someone mentally
retarded. Until I was told that these were the
works of a ten year-old Finnish War Child. The
child has unquestionable - albeit raw - tal-
ent. The misery of war that this child has al-
ready experienced shines through in his art.
The melancholy use of grays and blues didn't
escape the attention of this seasoned critic.
[…] I was told that the child has an interest
in architecture, as his attention to detail and
chosen subjects so clearly demonstrate. [...] I
say 'Bravo!'. Keep taking lessons, or stick
with architecture.
```

"Is this good or bad?" I ask Birgitta after I've read it.

"It's terrific!" she beams. "Don't you think so?"

"Why does he tell me to stick with architecture?"

"Because no one ever gets a full blown positive review from him. He seems to always have to write something negative, even when he's critiquing an established artist."

"So, why does he say that the arts in Finland have suffered a blow?"

"Because you no longer live there," she says, and cuts out the article for me.

We go out and buy three more copies of the newspaper, and send the review to Mother, and to Kjersti and Mor.

By the end of the week, every piece is sold and I'm commissioned for two more landscapes and a portrait. I send the money to Mother. Not wanting to repeat my mistake from Denmark, I write to her every week. I have yet to hear back from her, and I'm starting to get worried. She must know that I know about Tor running away, because I ask if he's returned in every letter I write. Her lack of response makes me fear that something bad must have happened and she just doesn't want to tell me.

The first letter I receive at my new address on Wild Berry Lane is from Mor Mortensen. She tells me that both Anders and Christian have volunteered in the Finnish Army and are now fighting in Lapland. I pray for their safety. I haven't prayed in a long time, and feel a bit guilty, but I hope God hasn't forgotten me. I also hope that Anders and Christian haven't forgotten me, so I quickly write them a letter, thanking them for their help and reminding them to keep safe.

Katja writes often. Although her news is inconsequential, at least she's still in Finland.

Surprisingly, the one who writes me the most is Dr. Magnusson, Ingrid's foster mother. Natalia and I managed to convince her not to burden Mother with what happened to Ingrid, so she keeps me up-to-date instead. Which I appreciate. One day, when we're all home again, and Mother is feeling better, I may tell her. But now's not the time. Ingrid is doing well, Dr. Magnusson writes. She has no recollection of what happened, and is seeing a social worker. They say that she may be repressing the memory, and that it may surface one day, but then again it may not. She seems happy and is developing normally for her age. That's the best news I've had in a long time. Since my art show review, anyway.

Remembering how desperate I was for news from home, I make it a point to write to my siblings a lot. Hugo and Birgitta give me pocket money for doing nothing at all, and most of it I spend on stationery and stamps. With Natalia's help I find Gustaf and Little Sister's addresses. Gustaf's foster parents write to tell me that he's fine and that he's been in the cockpit of a fighter plane that's being sent to Finland. Although I'm happy for him, I'm also a bit jealous. If it hadn't been for my model airplane, that Anders won and gave me, and Gustaf stole, he would never have been interested in planes in the first place. They send me a photograph of him, and my heart aches. He looks just like a miniature male version of Little Sister. They haven't cut his hair, so his blond curls form a halo around his head. He looks like a little doll in his sailor suit. The von Schoenfeldts had a similar portrait taken of me. Like in every other photograph lately, I look terrified. Probably because I'm expecting the photographer to catch on fire.

My heart nearly explodes one day when I receive this letter from Little Sister.

hi paul! i'm in skool now. i have a bisikle.

its blue! my best frend is ahry. we ride our bisikls otgethr i play peano!

do you mis me? bye! litl sistr xoxxx00xx000xxx

I laugh when I've finished reading her letter and then I read it again. So very like Little Sister to only think of herself. Her first, and only, word until she was about three years old was 'me'. And I'm glad she's got a new friend. But for the life of me I cannot imagine her having enough patience to take piano lessons. The von Schoenfeldts have a grand piano, and Birgitta plays beautifully. She offered to give me lessons, but after a few attempts we both decided that I'm definitely tone deaf.

Of course I miss her. And now I understand why letters to the front are so important. If Father receives just one letter like this one from his little angel, that'll surely give him the strength to keep fighting. That is the reason he's fighting, after all, isn't it? The safety and well being of future generations.

And then, at long last I receive a letter from Mother.

My most treasured son,

Thank you for the lovely birthday card! What a pleasure it was to receive it. It is clear to me that your talent is evolving, and that you're given the support and encouragement to continue your art lessons. I'm thrilled to see the results of both. Your uncle Johannes, may he rest in peace, would've been proud. Your talent has greatly surpassed even his.

May he rest in peace? So Mother must've come to terms with him being dead? No more 'presumed dead', just dead. I almost don't want to continue reading, and only skim the parts where she talks about how well everyone is doing. Johan and Carl are back in school and Emil is healthy. Then she thanks me for the money I sent her, and tells me that I'll have a nice sum in a savings account after the war, when I come home. She doesn't understand that I sent the money for her, but if she's going to be too proud to accept my help, I won't send her more.

We all miss you terribly, but we know that you're well; you're behaving and representing our family and our country with honor and pride.

Your father came home on leave and we had a family portrait taken. That's why it's taken me so long to write, I wanted to send you a copy.

What portrait? I shake the envelope, and a small black-and-white photograph falls to the floor. Father is handsome in his uniform, and Mother is smiling into the camera. They're flanked by Johan and Carl, and little Emil is sitting on Father's lap. Anger starts boiling through my veins, and tears are prickling behind my eyelids. How dare she? How dare she not only have this picture taken, but then send it to me, as if she were telling me how well things are, and I'm not part of it? And how dare she call this a 'family portrait' when half her family isn't in it? I only hope that she had the decency not to send it to anyone else. I'm so angry, that I almost tear the picture to pieces. But I don't. I sit and stare at it for a long time. Father isn't wounded. And he was still alive when this picture was taken. And Mother seems to have gained some weight. I wouldn't be surprised if she were going to have another baby again soon.

Unfortunately I have to be the bearer of sad tidings, my treasure, and I count on you to be brave when you read on. Son - Tor has died.

That's it. I can no longer hold back the tears. I feel like vomiting. Through a blur I force myself to read on. Although I don't want to, I must find out what happened.

Please don't be alarmed, no one did anything to harm him, his heart simply gave out. After you left, he took to disappearing for hours, but always returned for supper. Then one day when he didn't return, we all went looking for him. Carl stayed out all night looking for him, and then we had to send out a search party for him, as well. We looked for days, to no avail, and were all saddened and quite desperate. Then, weeks later, Uncle Eino contacted us. Tor had shown up at his cabin. He lay down on the porch and never moved from that spot. He wouldn't eat, he wouldn't drink, and he wouldn't go inside. He just lay there, watching the road. A few days passed, and then he died of a broken heart. That's how much he missed you, son. Uncle Eino buried him by the lake. With you away, he was the only living tie I had to you. His death has left a void in my soul and an empty hollowness in my heart. Our family is incomplete without him. He was the world's greatest dog and the best, most affectionate, most loyal friend you could wish for. We are all truly blessed to have had him pass through our lives.

Please stay strong, my treasure, and know that our thoughts, hearts and prayers are with you and that we ache in anticipation for the day that we're all together again. May it be here soon.

God bless,

Mother

I tear up the letter, envelope and photograph, as if by doing so, I could reverse the bad news. I no longer have any reason to want to return home.

In my anger I write a hateful letter back to Mother. I tell her to never, ever (and I underline the word 'ever' three times) write me again, unless it's to tell me that the war is over and we're going home. Then I accuse her of letting my dog die. Further I demand an explanation to why she sent us away the second time, when she promised she wouldn't. I rush to the post office and mail my angry letter.

The following morning I wake up full of remorse. I'm at the post office before it opens, and ask to have my letter back. It's already been sent.

Back at Wild Berry Lane I find the pieces of the photograph and Mother's letter, and with Birgitta's help we glue them back together. There's one piece, right above Mother and Father's heads, which we cannot find.

"That's where you, Little Sister, Ingrid and Gustaf will be," Birgitta says.

Probably not after Mother reads my letter.

> Public consensus wanted Marshal Mannerheim to run for president in 1943. At the very last moment he declined and President Ryti was sworn in to a second term. In his inauguration speech he declared that Finland longed for peace, but couldn't see any signs of the end of the war. He also added that Finland wouldn't be so heavily involved in the current conflict had it not been attacked in 1939.
> Reflecting the Finnish people's melancholy attitude toward their war with Russia was a comment by a Finnish soldier: 'The Russians have killed our men, the Swedes have taken our children and the Germans have taken [...] our country.' (Times, March 8th, 1943)
> President Ryti wasn't unaware of the low morale of his citizens. He was also aware that nearly all of Finland's food imports came from Germany and that Germany still had about 100,000 troops in his country.
> An estimated twelve hundred Danish and eight thousand Swedish volunteers fought in the Continuation War. Sweden also sent twenty-five warplanes.

June 1943.

It's my fault that Tor is dead. If I hadn't been so ill-behaved and stupid, I'd never have been sent away. If I hadn't been sent away, Tor would still be alive. If someone had been mean to him or run over him with a car, I could find them and beat them up until they feel as bad as I do. Now, all I can do is beat myself up.

Every day I feel more and more angry with myself. More angry than sad at first. But then, when I try to sketch Tor, the sadness overwhelms me. I can see him so clearly sitting in the school yard waiting patiently for the bell to ring. I can feel his wet nose on my cheek, when he was waking me up in the mornings. I can hear the funny noises he made when he was rolling in the grass, with an itch he couldn't reach. His body heat keeping us warm in the sleigh when we escaped the Reds, and on many a cold night since. And although I really don't want to remember Karelia, I'm drawn to the image of him pounding up our hill, soaking wet and shaking himself dry over Little Sister and me in the strawberry patch. And the image of him pulling Little Sister out from under the ice. When my world ended, Tor never left my side. He raced through the snow to catch up with my sleigh. He was always there for me. And then I just took off and left him without even stopping to say goodbye. I bet he wondered what he'd done wrong for me to abandon him.

I can no longer see my sketch for the tears. When I'm all out of tears, the sketch comes to focus. I have captured Tor's image but I'll never capture his spirit.

> Dreams of 'Great Finland' had died, and in June 1943 J.K. Paasikivi was again summoned to represent Finland in peace negotiations with Russia. The U.S. and Sweden acted as intermediaries. Finland insisted on the pre-Winter War borders, whereas Russia held to the demands of the borders as drawn up in the 1940 Moscow Peace Treaty. The fighting continued. The Russian Army had advanced westward to the Svir river, but the Finns held them back.
> Germany put further pressure on Finland by threatening to block food imports if Finland continued negotiations.

The school year ends, and I barely make the grade. Since Mother's letter I have stopped caring about anything. What does anything matter anymore? Hugo and Birgitta try to cheer me up, by telling me that we're going on a trip this summer. Hugo is working on a project up north, and Birgitta has arranged for us to drive through Halmstad, pick up Little Sister and then drive on to see Ingrid and

Gustaf. I feel somewhat better. I just hope that Mother didn't tell them about Tor. I certainly don't intend to bring it up.

Little Sister's foster family is nice. They have a thirteen year-old son, Göran, who's a quiet bookish type. Like all other men in her life, Little Sister has him wrapped around her little finger, and talks him into letting me borrow his bicycle.

The 'ahry' that Little Sister wrote about turns out to be Holgerson's Harri from back when we lived in Österbotten. They don't live close, but they go to the same school. Harri recognized Little Sister in school, and took her under his wing.

He's changed. The bully that he used to be has metamorphosed into a fine friend, and Little Sister's new hero.

We're riding our bicycles on a hill near Little Sister's house, when he stops abruptly.

"Behold, the mouth of the race course," he says dramatically.

As soon as we arrived at Little Sister's house, she's been talking about her and Harri becoming race car drivers when they grow up, and they've been practicing on their bicycles. Naturally I'm curious, and I want to have a crack at it myself. Little Sister's bicycle turns out to be adult-size, and she rides it with her leg through the frame rather than over it. I can barely reach the pedals riding over the frame myself. Only if I stand up can I reach them properly.

The race course is a dirt path. It's hilly and curvy and abandoned. There's a thick forest on either side.

"You ride here?" I ask Little Sister incredulously.

Even for me the first hill seems a bit too steep. Adding to that, there's a sharp blind curve at the bottom.

Both of them nod and smile.

"And she wins a lot!" Harri adds. "But that's probably because she can't really reach the brakes properly. She just goes flying around that curve! You should see her! She's fearless."

Well, if my Little Sister can do it, then so can I. The path is only wide enough for two bicycles at a time, so Harri convinces Little Sister to let him and me try first. Unbelievably she doesn't even pout, or try to talk him out of it. Smiling, she accepts his decision.

Mounting the bicycle, I take a few deep breaths. Then I let go. If the hill looked steep while we were sitting on top, it's even steeper when we're riding down it. Harri and I are neck and neck.

"Mind the bump!" he yells, and jerks up his handlebar. His tires fly in the air, and he lands ahead of me.

We're going too fast for comfort, but I don't yet dare to apply the brakes. Harri is ahead of me now and skids around the curve. He comes to a halt, and turns around to look at me.

"What did you think?"

I'd like to play nonchalant, but it was just too exciting. "Let's do it again!" I say.

"That's just the first hill!" Harri says. "There's more ahead."

"I want to try flying over that hump!" I say. "How'd you do that thing with your handlebar?"

"Oh, it's nothing," Harri says as we turn our bicycles around and start walking back up the hill. "I'll show you."

I still cannot believe Little Sister can do it, and challenge her to show me. Like a flash, she's over the hump and around the curve, giggling the whole time. Rosy-cheeked and huffing, she pushes her bicycle back up the hill. The shy little girl I once knew is gone and is replaced by a daredevil.

"Let's race!" she says.

"Sure, but it's not a fair race," I say. "I'm going to win, because I'm older! I'm always better than you, because I'm older than you!"

Little Sister pouts for a moment, and I can see the wheels virtually turning in her head, working on a stinging come-back.

"Yeah?" she finally says. "But you'll die before me, because you're older!" She gets back on her bike and we race down the hill. She wins.

After hours of riding on the 'race course' we're dirty, exhausted and scuffed, but for the first time in months I haven't thought about Tor.

The next morning we say goodbye to Harri. He looks sad and remorseful.

"I'm sorry I was mean to you," he says unexpectedly.

"When?" Surely he can't be talking about something that happened two years ago?

"You know,… back home." He goes on telling me how he was picked on when he first arrived in Sweden. How he used to get in fights every day, and how his class mates used to call him names. "Just like I did with you. Now I know how it feels. It's not fun."

I don't know how to respond to that. He looks so serious and hurt at the same time.

"No, it isn't fun. But it's alright," I finally say. "Don't worry about it. We're friends now."

But Harri won't let it go. "I was so cruel and insensitive. Guess I got what was coming to me." He pauses, and the look in his eyes makes him appear much older. "My father was killed, you know," he continues.

"I'm so sorry, Harri," I say. "I didn't know. When? How?"

"This winter. Took some shrapnel in the face," Harri is trying to sound strong, but his quivering voice deceives him. "Mother says I'll be going home soon. But I think I'd rather stay here."

I've been gone eight months, and have only heard from my mother once. If she wrote and told me I was going home, I'd count the days. Harri is being a selfish brat. And I tell him as much.

"I can't believe you're being so selfish, Harri Holgerson! If your mother wants you home - you go home. Don't argue! She needs you!"

"But your little sister needs me here."

Now I feel foolish. Not only have I failed as a son and as a friend and but now also as a brother.

"If you'll let me, I'll look out for her. I'll stay here, and then, when the war is over, we'll go home together. I'll be like another big brother to her," he says in a solemn promise.

We spit-shake on it, tell each other goodbye, and swear to write.

Hugo traveled north ahead of us, so Little Sister and I are riding alone with Birgitta. We pass the time singing and telling stories. Every story of Little Sister's involves a dog. Usually the name is Tor, and Birgitta and I exchange looks in the rearview mirror. It's obvious Little Sister doesn't know what happened to Tor, and I don't intend to tell her.

We arrive in Stockholm and visit Ingrid. She has grown significantly, and starts happily prattling away, as if we only saw each other yesterday. Dr. Magnusson quietly tells me that Lennart had to resign and was beaten to an inch of his life by 'unknown assailants'. Although nobody will confirm it, she suspects that this was done by his former colleagues.

She says "The police doesn't look kindly on child molesters tarnishing the badge."

I feel that justice has been served.

As it turns out, Uppsala and Stockholm aren't that far from each other, and Ingrid and Gustaf have met on a few occasions. When Gustaf shows up at Ingrid's house, he looks at me as if I were a stranger. Then he looks at Little Sister playing with Ingrid. He doesn't recognize us, and it's breaking my heart. If he doesn't recognize me, how will he react when he sees Mother again? Or Father, whom he's only ever met once?!

I lean toward him, determined to make some sort of connection. All our foster parents are watching, and this moment embarrasses me.

"It's me, Paul," I say. "You brother. Don't you remember? We took the train together. And we stayed in a hospital. And you took my plane…"

A glimmer of recognition glints in his eye, and he takes my hand, and starts walking me to nowhere in particular.

"Paul," he says. "Come. I need you."

Since we're in Stockholm, I beg Birgitta to let me go and visit Natalia. She insists on going with me, and this time we have Natalia's address, so I don't have to go by Lennart and Siv's apartment again.

There's no answer to our knock at the door, and we know we should've let her know that we were coming. But just as we're about to turn around and start down the stairs, there's a weak voice from inside the apartment.

"Who's there?"

"It's me! Paul!" I shout excitedly.

"Who?" the voice says.

I'm flabbergasted. Surely Natalia remembers me? We've been writing to each other faithfully for months.

"Paul from Finland," I say. "Come on, Natalia. Open the door. This isn't funny!"

The door opens a hair, and an old woman looks out at us.

"Oh, I beg your pardon," Birgitta says. "We must have the wrong apartment."

"You're looking for Natalia?" the old woman says. "She moved." Her gaze stops on me. "Yes, yes, you're Paul. How silly of me. Of course I know who you are. Just last week I received your letter to her. I haven't had a chance to forward it yet. Please come in," she says and opens the door wider.

We step into an apartment that smells of cabbage and ammonia. When Natalia lived here the place was sparsely decorated with only the bare essentials. And those were often broken or chipped. Now, every square centimeter of the apartment is crammed with odd pieces of furniture. As if someone had tried to move a five-room house into a one-room apartment. There's an odd high pitched sound coming from the kitchen, and I'm guessing the old lady must be making tea.

"Hush, puppy," she says. Her voice is soft and kind, and in some ways she reminds me of Mummo. "Now where did I put that letter…?" she keeps rummaging around the cramped apartment.

"Why did she move?" I ask, disappointed that Natalia hadn't told me herself.

"Someone tried to hurt her," the old lady says. "So she had to go into hiding."

"Who?"

"She didn't say. Someone who was in trouble because of her, I think she said."

Lennart. There's no doubt in my mind. I have to find her to find out if she's alright. I wonder if this happened before or after he got beat up himself. Natalia knows a lot of people. Maybe it wasn't the police at all who beat him up. Maybe it was someone working for Natalia.

"Ah, here it is," the old lady hands me my last letter to Natalia along with her forwarding address.

It's the old address that I used in Denmark. The one where they stored letters for her until she found this apartment. Just as I'm about to tell the old lady that, the sound from the kitchen continues, and draws me to it like a magnet. There's no door to the kitchen, and just inside the doorway is a huge cardboard box, the bottom of which is covered with newspapers and an old towel. I have found the source of the ammonia smell. There's a little white puppy in the box, and he has just used it as a toilet. The puppy starts whining, and wags his stubby tail when he sees me. He tries to climb up the side of the box, but can't, and falls right on his behind. I can't help but laugh, and I pick him up. He's hardly the size of both my hands put together, and squirms uncontrollably, as I try to hold him. He's an adorable little rascal.

"He likes you," the old lady's voice startles me.

"Oh... I'm sorry...um... I-I-I didn't..." I stammer, and set the puppy back in the box.

The pathetic little whimpering starts again. The old lady walks over to the box, picks up the puppy, and hands him to me.

"It's alright. Kids and dogs, can't go wrong, I always say."

Eventually the puppy either exhausts himself, or takes a liking to me, because he settles down. I don't want to like him. I feel guilty for liking him so soon after Tor died.

The old lady and Birgitta have been talking, but I haven't heard a thing they've said.

"Paul?" Birgitta says. "Would you like to keep him?"

"Who? The puppy? I-I-I can't." I try to set him back in the box, but the whining is heart-breaking, so I keep holding him.

"Why not?" both ladies ask in unison.

"What will happen to him when I leave?" I state the obvious.

"You take him with you."

"What will happen to me when he dies?"

Birgitta comes over to me. She puts one hand on my shoulder, while the other is stroking the puppy. "Paul, you cannot go through life not attaching yourself to someone you care about, just because you're afraid of getting hurt. Everyone dies eventually. It's what you have with them while they're alive that counts. And

I know what you're thinking. This puppy will never replace Tor. No puppy ever will. But you have so much love in your heart. Loving another dog won't push Tor's memory aside. And don't you think this puppy deserves to have a happy life?"

"He'd be better off here," I say.

The puppy looks me straight in the eye, as if accusing me. He has unbelievably long, white eyelashes. His eyes are brown, just like Tor's, and he presses his cold nose to my cheek.

"I've been trying find a new home for him," the old lady says. "But so far I haven't found anyone who can take him. I found him under the stairs last week. He was all alone. Abandoned. His mother had probably weaned him, and left him to fend for himself. I'm too old to take care of a puppy. I can barely make it up the stairs once a day, and he needs more exercise than I'll ever be able to give him."

The old lady needn't have made that speech. When she said the word 'abandoned' I immediately felt a connection with him. He's orphaned by living parents, just like me. I look at Birgitta for confirmation. She smiles and nods her head. As if reading our minds, the puppy nuzzles up to my chin, and sighs. Sweet puppy breath on my skin. Only Tor and I ever had that kind of telepathic communication. Although I know it's silly to even think it, I like to believe that Tor has returned to me.

> British and American troops had forced the Germans out of North Africa and were turning their focus on Italy. By July 1943 Sicily was invaded by the Allies. Hitler pulled the majority of his SS corps out of Russia and into Italy, convinced that his elite corps could beat the Allies in time for the anticipated winter offensive on the Eastern Front.
> Marshal Mannerheim began Finland's disengagement by taking out a battalion from the SS, then asking his German counterpart to release his Finnish troops. He was refused. Mannerheim then wanted to build a new defensive line behind the Germans, should they pull back their troops, to defend against any Soviet advance. Finland was holding the line, but a Russian offensive was just a matter of time. Hitler told Mannerheim that Finland would be under Bolshevik rule if she left her German protection. In reality the Germans needed Finnish forces to meet the advancing Soviets around Leningrad, and Mannerheim was fully aware of that.

```
Mannerheim's position was a difficult one. Al-
though not a politician, he was a brilliant
strategist, but tried to keep his opinions to
himself, unless directly asked, or in his dip-
lomatic form of suggestions based on the state
of the military.
The Finnish and Russian peace negotiators had
come to a standstill. Neither would budge on
their demands. The only consoling bit of news
was that Stalin - now coached by Roosevelt and
Churchill - no longer had any intentions of
invading Finland.
By September 1943 Hitler was convinced that
Finland would leave the war and seek a separate
peace. As an action against this he set forth a
plan where German forces would seize islands in
the Gulf of Finland. Tensions between Finland
and Germany were getting much more animated and
heated as the Finns now agreed that reaching a
separate peace with the Soviets was the only
sensible solution.
```

Little Sister names the new puppy 'Cotton', because "When he curls up to sleep, he looks just like a wad of cotton. And he's just as soft," she says.

December 1943.

Malmö is really close to Denmark, so instead of a Christmas present, I ask the von Schoenfeldts if they would take me to Denmark to visit all my old friends. They're thrilled. We spend hours each day planning our trip. Letters fly across the strait and soon it seems like everyone in my old town knows that I'm coming to visit. We're all looking forward to a reunion.

Every evening, sketchbook in hand, I tell Hugo and Birgitta stories about my year in Denmark. I draw pictures of the quaint little town, and all the people in it. I tell them about Mor and how kind and helpful she was to me. And Jens and Kjersti. And Baker Sørensen, and his strawberry ice. They laugh when I tell them I didn't know that iced cream was a treat; that I thought it was just ice. They hear the story about Bloody Henrik and the fort, although when I tell it to them the house is fully lit, and it doesn't have the same scary effect as it did when Jens told it to Carl and me at the actual fort. But Hugo and Birgitta act scared, nonetheless. I leave out the part about the German soldiers, because I don't want to worry them. They already know that I'm ambidextrous. There's no need for them to know how I got that way.

We plan to leave right after my last day of school. There's no big to-do in this school. We simply receive our report cards, and enjoy no school for ten days. I can't get to the von Schoenfeldts' fast enough. Our bags are packed. Hugo is leaving work early. And then we'll be on our way.

As soon as I come through the door I know something is wrong. Cotton isn't at the door greeting me. I look all over for him, and finally find him in Birgitta's lap, licking her tears.

"What's wrong?" I ask, as I take a seat next to her at the kitchen table.

She's got the hiccups. Just like Little Sister when she's been crying a lot.

For the longest time she doesn't say anything, just keeps crying. I've never seen her this upset, and now I'm even more worried.

"What's wrong?" I repeat.

Eventually she calms down. "I need you to be a big boy, Paul," she says through sobs.

Why do adults always start bad news by saying you need to be a big boy? They always say that right before they pull the rug out from under you. It's never 'you need to be a big boy, because I bought you a brand-new bicycle and then we're having strawberry ice cream for supper'. It's always bad news. Now I'm scared. The first time I was asked to be a big boy, the Red Army was on our tails, and we left Karelia in the middle of the night. Although I don't know what she's about to say, her demeanor and choice of words suggest something is terribly amiss. Like the country is invaded. Or the war is over and I'm sent away again. Or…

"Little Sister's foster mother, Mrs. Almquist, rang," Birgitta says. "I'm sorry…" she breaks down in hysterical sobs again. "She's dead."

For a moment I think Mrs. Almquist has died, but then I realize that dead people can't make phone calls. My pulse quickens, and my breathing becomes more troubled. Birgitta continues, like telling me every detail somehow makes it easier.

"Sled… She took it down a deserted hill… There was a hump and a curve in the road. She couldn't control it. … Hit a tree… Her neck snapped. … Dead…" She starts crying again.

It hasn't hit me yet. "Where was Harri?" I say. "He swore he'd look after her. He *spit* swore!"

"He was with her."

"And?"

Quietly Birgitta shakes her head. "His skull cracked. Göran was with them. He's fine. He called for help. … But it was too late."

I stare at her for a long time. And then words start to register. A cold chill runs through my body. In my head I repeat every word she said in hopes that I didn't hear her correctly.

I know the road. They were trying out a sled on the race course. An image of her sweet face flashes in my mind. Our little angel has become an angel.

Before I know what I'm doing, I'm running. I don't know where or why, but suddenly it feels like I'm suffocating inside the house. Birgitta calls out after me, but I can't respond. My throat is swelling up, and I feel like vomiting. It's so cold, that my mouth is burning as I keep running, but I have to get away from the news. Birgitta's words keep echoing inside my head. 'Her neck snapped'. 'She's dead'. Dead. Dead. Dead.

I keep running faster. Each step I take pounds the word 'dead' in my ears. The cold air makes my eyes water, and I let my tears flow freely. My chest starts to convulse, and when I reach the edge of the forest, I lean against a tree and vomit. I can hardly breathe, and collapse on the ground, shaking uncontrollably. It feels like a cold hand is squeezing my heart. My fists are pounding the ground, and I'm crying. Crying like a little baby. It wasn't supposed to be her! *I* was supposed to die first! She said so herself. I'm older, so I'll die first. How's Father going to take this? She was his little angel. His little reason to keep fighting. And what reason do I have to live now? Uncle Johannes is dead. Tor is dead. And now Little Sister…

A soft whimpering distracts my thoughts. Cotton has caught up with me, and places a paw on my arm, as I'm lying face-down in the snow. He nudges my face with his nose. He's cold. I pick him up, and bundle him inside my overcoat. He's my reason for living.

> A separate peace with Finland was discussed at the summit meeting of the three major powers in Tehran in December 1943. Roosevelt spoke in favor of Finland, and so did Churchill, even though Britain had declared war on Finland. Stalin admitted that 'a people that had fought so valiantly for its independence deserves consideration'. He presented his terms for peace: restoration of the borders of the 1940 treaty; annexing Petsamo to the Soviet Union; a fifty per cent restitution; the expulsion of Germans from Finland; and demobilization of the Army. Roosevelt and Churchill didn't comment. Their main goal was for Finland to remain an independent and democratic country.
> The Finns feared that Marshal Mannerheim would be tried for war crimes, as part of the peace

treaty. The Soviet leaders were well aware that
there would be no stable solution with Finland
unless it was backed by Mannerheim, and assured
the Finnish peace negotiators that he would not
be tried.

Finland suffered because Germany didn't supply
arms in the manner to which it had agreed. In
December 1943, Stalin began planning for large
scale bombing raids on Finland, with Helsinki
being the main target. By the end of 1943,
nearly forty thousand Finnish soldiers had
been killed or wounded since the Continuation
War began in June 1941.

Instead of going to a happy reunion in Denmark, I'm going to my Little Sister's
funeral for Christmas. The sadness that engulfed me has been replaced by a feeling of hollow emptiness. It feels like a light has been extinguished, and I have
no hope of ever lighting it again. Secretly I wish that this war will go on forever, or that Mother has a bunch of babies and forgets about me. There's no way
I can return to Finland and explain to my parents why I let their little angel
go to heaven.

Looking around the chapel, I feel like I don't belong here. It's all wrong.
Except for Hugo and Birgitta, and Little Sister's foster family, I know nobody
here. Göran tells me that Harri's mother came to claim his body to be buried
in Finland. Little Sister will be laid at rest in a strange country, surrounded by
strangers.

I have vowed not to cry. I'm done crying. Birgitta says it's alright to express
your feelings, and that boys do cry. But I won't. I'm strong, as I shake people's
hands, and nod politely when they murmur words of comfort. Void of all feelings,
I listen to an unknown priest talk about a little girl he never knew. Along with
everyone else, I sing a hymn that I've never heard before, and doubt that Little
Sister had, either.

And then they bring in the casket. A small, white box, carried by four men
dressed in black. They place the casket center-front in the chapel, and the priest
asks if I want to say a few words, as the only representative of our family.

Thinking that I can distance myself from my feelings, I step up to Little
Sister's white casket. The priest opens the lid, and I see my darling little sister's
angelic face and blonde curls inside the box, and I can no longer hold back the
tears. She looks so real. Like she's just napping. She looks like she did when I last
saw her. I want to step up and shake her and wake her up. I want to scream to God
to take me instead. My tears are blurring my vision, and I can't breathe. It feels

like the walls are caving in, and I think about how uncomfortable Little Sister is going to be in that little box for the rest of eternity.

The chapel has grown quiet, and all faces are on me, expecting me to say something. Valiantly I put both hands on Little Sister's crossed fingers. I recite the prayer that we used to say every night with Mother. I only know it in Finnish, but I don't think it matters much.

"Good night, Little Sister," I say, as I let go of her hand. Then I notice that something is terribly wrong. "Where's puppy?!" I turn to the Almquists.

There's an audible gasp in the chapel. The priest tries to usher me back to my seat. I tear off his grip.

"Where's puppy? She's never slept alone, not once in her life. She'll be scared without puppy! Where's her puppy?"

I'm getting hysterical, and all the anger I've felt about the injustice of her death comes pouring out. Hugo and Birgitta are at my side, trying to pull me back.

"Please don't make a scene," Birgitta whispers. "I'm sure the Almquists have him."

I can hear Mr. Almquist behind me, turning to his wife. "What's he on about?" he asks.

"That little black toy, that she always carries with her," Mrs. Almquist responds.

"She must have her puppy!" I may be louder than is appropriate behavior inside a chapel. "I will not let you bury her alone! Don't you understand? She needs puppy!" I'm convulsing as I run out of the chapel.

There's a push-hearse sitting just outside the door, and I throw myself on it.

Why? I ask God. Why her? Why did you have to take her and not me? She never did anyone any harm. She was loved by everyone, and was sweet and kind. It wasn't her time to die. Why couldn't you take Hitler or Stalin instead?

Someone taps me gently on my shoulder. It's Göran.

"I understand," he says solemnly. "Let's go."

"Where?"

"To get the puppy."

"Won't they bury her while we're gone?"

He thinks for a minute. Then he bends down, and deflates one of the tires of the push-hearse. I may have underestimated him. He's not so much a bookworm as he is a natural-born prankster.

"They'll have a slight delay," he grins. "Let's hurry."

"Don't you think they can take her to the grave without this? I mean, she's so little that I could carry her myself."

"They can't. It's too icy. If they slipped and dropped her..."

I put up a hand to silence him. I don't want to hear it, much less picture that awful image.

"Let's run!" I say.

Little Sister's room at the Almquist's is exactly like it was when I last visited. They haven't touched a thing. We look for puppy everywhere. In the pockets of her coats, in her schoolbag, under the bed, in the closet. It's nowhere to be found.

"Are you sure it's here?" I ask Göran.

"Positive," he says. "She had brushed his hair just before ... you know ... that night..."

Then it hits me. If puppy isn't with Little Sister, there's only one place where he'll be. Gently I pull back the bedcover. There, safely tucked in under a blanket, head resting between two pillows, is Little Sister's beloved stuffed toy.

Returning to the chapel, the priest is just finishing his blessing of the casket, and is about to close the lid, when I slip puppy under Little Sister's arm.

"Sleep well, Little Sister," I whisper and put my hand on her cheek for the last time. "Don't be scared. Tor will be with you."

Both Birgitta and Mrs. Almquist are of the opinion that the best way to re-cover from grief is to talk about it and analyze it. And they do that a lot. Mrs. Almquist blames herself. I blame her too. But mainly because it lessens the feeling of guilt that I've placed on myself. They have Göran re-tell the story of how the accident happened so often, that I feel like I was there myself.

Apparently they had been sledding all day, and were getting really good at it, when Little Sister suggested that they lie on their stomachs. Göran says she was the only one who could steer the sled around the curve, and the boys took turns going down the hill with her. The last run, however, the sled hit the hump in an odd way, sending it spiraling. Little Sister was giggling and screaming with delight.

And then everything got quiet. Too quiet. Göran raced down the hill. He found both lifeless bodies at the trunk of a tree.

"She was uncommonly clumsy, wasn't she?" Birgitta says after a while.

"I always thought there was something off with her equilibrium," Göran adds.

Equilibrium. I know that word. Where have I heard it before? My mind goes back to a bombed hospital room, where an unknown doctor tells Mother that

Little Sister's equilibrium may be affected. I didn't understand the word then. I do now.

Mrs. Almquist is sobbing softly. "She was so beautiful. So sweet and kind and helpful. So full of life…"

"It was an accident," I speak for the first time since the funeral. "Please don't blame yourself." I walk over to her, and drape my arms around her.

I've just about had enough of this nonsense, so I ask Göran to help me sort through Little Sister's belongings. Cotton follows us. He's had enough crying, too.

"What do you suppose your mother will want to keep?" he says.

"I honestly don't know," I say. There's more than one truth in that statement; I don't feel like I know Mother anymore. "What did she say when you told her?"

Göran gasps. "We haven't. I thought you did."

"Why would I do that? You told Harri's mother."

"She speaks Swedish. And she has a telephone."

"Couldn't you have written her? She's got a million people to translate. Plus, she does understand Swedish, even if she doesn't speak it. She'll definitely understand 'your daughter is dead'."

"So what you're saying, is that your mother still doesn't know?"

"So it would seem. And I don't want to be the one to tell her, either!"

"Me neither!"

We decide to leave that to the adults, and start packing Little Sister's belongings into four piles; charity, home, the Almquists, me. The pile marked 'home' is the smallest one. I can only think of taking a photograph, an unfinished letter to Mother, Little Sister's camera and a ribbon that she used to wear in her hair, and still has a crease in it from the bow. Subconsciously I press the ribbon to my nose. It smells like Little Sister. I never realized that she had a scent. Quickly I wrap it tightly in an envelope, hoping to seal in some of the scent for Mother. Cotton sniffs it too, then whimpers and paws at it quietly and lies down on top of Little Sister's pile of clothing. He misses her too.

As we're almost finished, I spot a small cigar box on the top shelf in the closet. I've never seen it before.

"Is this yours?" I ask Göran.

He shakes his head.

"How could she even have reached up there?" The shelf is too high for me to reach without climbing on a chair.

"She's very agile for a girl," Göran says smugly.

"For an *un*commonly clumsy girl," I add, and we laugh.

Maybe Birgitta is right. It does help to talk.

"This isn't her handwriting," I say. Someone has written 'VERY EXTRA TOP SECRET HALS' in red crayon across the lid. "What's Hals*?"

"That's a silly thing they did," Göran says, smiling at the memory. "Harri would come visit and shout 'Hals!' from the door, exposing his throat. She'd respond the same way. They'd say the same when he left. It means both 'hello' and 'goodbye', I think."

"Why hals? That makes no sense."

"Well, you know how some people say 'hugs and kisses' without actually hugging and kissing? Same thing."

"That's weird," I say, eyeing the box. "And it's even weirder for my little sister to have a secret stash."

"Everyone has a secret stash," Göran says. "Don't you?"

"No," I say, feeling like I'm missing out on something.

What could I have to keep secret? Since we came back from Denmark we had to share everything. My most prized possession, Father's knife, is always with me. The live German bullet is at Mummo's. My Baden-Powell hat is at Uncle Eino's. I keep my money in a piggy bank. And since I've been living with the von Schoenfeldts' I've been an only child, so I don't really have to hide anything from anyone.

The box contains various odd pieces of paper, with random letters and numbers on them. There's also a torn corner of a sketch that I recognize. It's the little girl I drew with her stocking sausaged at her ankle at a train station when we left for Denmark. How did Little Sister end up with it? I'm fairly certain I gave it to Natalia. There's a map of Finland and Sweden, with various x's marked seemingly randomly across Finland, and a dotted line around the Gulf of Bothnia from Sundsvall to Vasa.

And finally we find two tightly wrapped bundles of paper. One is marked 'L' or possibly 'V', the other 'HW' or 'MH'. They're definitely in Little Sister's handwriting, but it's impossible to tell which side is up. The bundles contain money. Lots of it. The inside of the paper bundles are marked .50+.50=1.00+.25=1.25 and so on. The last line reads 25.75.

"Where did all this money come from?" I ask Göran anxiously.

Silently I pray that it's not stolen. It feels like I'm invading Little Sister's privacy. She obviously had a secret life that I knew nothing about, and went to great lengths to conceal it.

"She got pocket money," Göran shrugs. "And money for doing extra chores. And getting good grades. Just like me. I guess she never spent any of hers." He's

---

* Author's note: Hals = 'Throat' in Swedish.

playing with the cigar box. "That's strange," he says. "This is a fake bottom." He pries the bottom open, and out falls an envelope.

'TO BE OPENED BY LITTLE SISTER ONLY IN THE CASE OF THAT SOMETHING BAD HAPPENS TO HARRI HOLGERSON!' it reads. It's the same handwriting as on the lid.

"We shouldn't," I say looking at Göran, hoping he'll contradict me.

"I think we should," he says. "Something bad *did* happen to him. We have his full permission."

The envelope contains the floor plan of a house. In the corner of an un-marked room someone has written 'five up and seven in'.

"Does this mean anything to you?" I say. Göran looks as puzzled as I feel. "You must know what they were up to. You played with them. She lived with you. You were around them all the time."

"Not all the time. In fact, I rarely played with them. They were into things that I didn't care for. Like the race course…"

"But surely you must've noticed if they were planning to do something …" I cannot even finish the sentence. Do what? Just because I've found some unlikely objects in my dead sister's possession doesn't mean that she was going to blow up a bank or anything.

"They were secretive, and kept to themselves. And they spoke Finnish."

"That makes no sense. Harri is a Swedish-Finn and Little Sister doesn't speak Finnish very well."

"Didn't," Göran corrects me.

"What? Oh, right… Didn't."

"No, I mean, she might not have spoken Finnish in Finland, but she did with Harri. I'm sure of it. Or else they just made up their own language. No offense, but Finnish sounds like gibberish to me."

I can't help but laugh. "True!" I say and show him the floor plan. "Do you know this building?"

He shakes his head. " 'Tell your brothers that I'm sorry', " he reads the back of the drawing. "What does that mean?"

The memory makes me shiver. "I can't believe he couldn't let it go."

"Let what go?"

"Harri used to be a bully. He'd call me three-eyes, and pick fights with me and my brothers all the time."

"Harri?" Göran says. "He was the kindest kid I've ever met! And very fond of Little Sister."

"War changes people," I say.

We continue trying to make sense of the contents of the box.

"What about all these numbers and letters?" Göran asks. We study the scrap pieces of paper. "The only thing that makes sense to me is 1943, which is now, and 706, which is July sixth. Did something happen on July sixth?"

"It could just as easily be June seventh. Besides, we don't know that these are dates," I say. "Because if they are what does 2021 mean? That's really far in the future. I think this is just Little Sister practicing her writing."

"Why would she save it, though?"

"Good point. Do you suppose we might find anything over at Harri's?"

"Natalia," Göran says unexpectedly.

"What?"

"Look!" He's getting excited. "The letters on this piece of paper spell Natalia. Do you know a Natalia?"

"I do. So does Little Sister. And probably Harri, too. Do you think these numbers correspond with the letters?"

"Like a date?" he suggests.

"Not enough digits. An address, perhaps?"

"Not enough letters," Göran says.

"A phone number!" we shout simultaneously, and run to the phone, Cotton close at our heels.

After a few futile attempts, we give up. There's no key to know in which order to unscramble them, and since I don't know where she moved, I'm not much help.

We give up and head to Harri's foster family's house.

We're greeted by his foster father. "I'm sorry boys," he says. "We gave everything to Mrs. Holgerson when she came to pick up his body."

"Do you remember seeing a box like this?" Göran says, and shows him Little Sister's cigar box.

He shakes his head. We're at a dead end. Then something dawns on me.

"Is this your house?" I ask, and show him the floor plan.

He studies it, and smiles. "A very rough sketch, but if pressed, I'd have to say yes. Why?"

"Would you mind if we had a quick look in Harri's room? Please? We won't break anything."

He lets us in, and I go straight to the corner marked on the map. 'Five up and seven in' could mean a number of things, but I start by going five paces up along the wall, and seven in, and I land on an empty book case. Göran goes the opposite direction, and hits a window. The floor is solid, with no trap doors or loose planks. As is the ceiling. We're on a wild goose chase.

"Find what you're looking for, boys?" Harri's foster father comes to the door.

I feel deflated. Maybe I'm reading too much into the seemingly random 'treasures' of a seven year-old. If it hadn't been for the 'very extra top secret'-part, I'd probably not even have been curious. Making one last sweep around the room, I'm ready to call it quits. Then my gaze lands on the bookcase.

"Does this move?" I ask.

"Not easily," Harri's foster father answers. "Why?"

"He may have hidden something behind it," Göran answers.

It takes both of us to move it, and sure enough; there's Harri's cigar box! We thank Harri's foster father profusely, tell him that we'll send the box to Finland, and rush out of the house.

Harri's box contains another map. Finland is marked 'Mata Harri' and Sweden is marked 'Victory'. The same dotted line is drawn between Sundsvall and Vasa.

"Look!" Göran is beside himself with excitement. "MH on the money. Mata Harri. And V for Victory!"

"Yeah, but… what does that even mean?"

We're back at Göran's house, comparing the contents of the two boxes. Inside the fake bottom of Harri's box is another bundle of money marked 'Paul'. Somehow, I was to be involved. In what, though? There's also a train timetable in Harri's box, with a few departure times circled in red crayon.

"19:43 departing from Sundsvall to Vasa!" Göran reads, his excitement growing.

"So?"

"So… I don't know…"

Birgitta tells me we're leaving for the hotel in ten minutes, and suggests that I walk Cotton. Göran says he'll try to unscramble Natalia's phone number while I'm outside.

"Try a Sundsvall exchange," I suggest.

When Cotton and I return, Göran is on the phone, waving me over. He puts a hand over the receiver.

"Natalia," he whispers. "Doesn't believe me. Says because she doesn't know who I am, she's reluctant to share any information with me. You convince her." He hands me the phone.

"Hi, Natalia, it's Paul. We found some odd things among Little Sister's belongings, and thought maybe you could help us out."

"What were you doing going through your sister's things?" she starts by scolding me.

"She's dead."

There's a silence on the line.

"So your friend told me. I'm so sorry, Paul. Truly I am," Natalia says. "Do you have the password?" she asks in a fake serious tone.

What password? I have no idea what she's talking about.

"Victory?" I suggest.

"Wrong."

"Mata Harri?"

"Wrong again. One more guess, and then I'll hang up."

"Hals?"

"Very good! Now, how can I help you?"

"By telling me what's going on!"

"Hals wanted to go home together and I was to help arrange it. But they swore me to secrecy, because they didn't want to upset their parents at home or their foster parents here. You were supposed to go with them. If, on the other hand, any one of you was sent home before the others, the other two were supposed to come and get that person. Hals was prepared to put this plan into action, because Mrs. Holgerson was threatening to bring Harri back home by force, if she had to. And although both wanted to go home, they were aware that it's not safe yet, and wanted to stay together. And close to you."

"That's it?" I'm thinking that this is an enormous let-down. "Say - why do you call them Hals?"

"Harri And Little Sister. H.A.L.S."

"So, *are* we going home soon?" I ask, even though I really don't want to know. The prospect of returning home is even more frightening now that Mother doesn't know that Little Sister is dead.

"When it's safe, Paul," Natalia says, and we both know that those words mean nothing.

Summer 1945.

> The peace negotiations were fruitless, and Stalin decided to force Finland to surrender. The air campaign in February 1944 included three major air attacks on Helsinki involving a total of over six thousand bombing sorties. However, Finnish anti-aircraft defenses managed to repel the raids; it is estimated that only a small fraction of the bombs hit their planned targets. Due to radio intelligence and effective anti-air raid preparations, the num-

ber of casualties was small in proportion to the effort.

The Allies stormed the beaches at Normandy on June 6th, 1944, and three days later Stalin launched a massive offensive on Karelia. Over three thousand tanks crossed the Finnish defense line and Viborg fell on June 20th. Although the Finnish Army had been successful in using the Molotov cocktail, that wasn't nearly enough to stop the Russian tanks. Finland lacked modern anti-tank weaponry, and Germany was willing to supply them. At a cost. In exchange for a guarantee that Finland wouldn't again seek a separate peace. The Ryti-Ribbentrop letter of agreement of June 26th, 1944, signified the closest to an alliance that Finland and Nazi Germany ever came during World War II. According to the agreement - in the form of personal letter from President Ryti to Adolf Hitler - Ryti undertook not to conclude peace in the Continuation War with the Soviet Union unless in agreement with Nazi Germany. The letter was expressed as Ryti's personal undertaking, deliberately avoiding the form of a binding treaty between the governments of Finland and Germany, which would have required involvement of the Finnish Parliament.

The Finnish Army was able to hold back the Russian advance at the 1940 border. Although the Finnish troops were exhausted and battle-weary, they once again held the line. Unable to press forward, Stalin transferred the majority of his troops for the 'race to Berlin'. The battle along the Finnish border became a peripheral operation in the larger scheme of his intentions.

President Ryti resigned on July 31st, 1944 and was succeeded as President by Marshal Mannerheim through extraordinary appointment by the Parliament. The Ryti-Ribbentrop agreement became obsolete. Mannerheim informed the Germans that he did not consider himself or Finland bound by Ryti's concession, leading his country into a separate peace. The Moscow armistice was signed on September 19th. Finland had to make many concessions:

* The Soviet Union regained the borders as drawn in 1940, with the addition of the Petsamo area.

> * The Porkkala Peninsula was leased to the USSR as a naval base for fifty years and transit rights were granted (this was later abandoned early in 1956).
> * Finland's Army was to be demobilized with haste.
> * Finland was required to expel all German troops from its territory within 14 days.
> Thus began the third war that Finland fought in five years: the Lapland War.
> According to the Moscow armistice, Finland was under obligation not only to demobilize, but to fight the Germans out of the country. The Finns and Germans had agreed on a friendly troop withdrawal, which Russia viewed as a breach of the armistice, thus forcing Finland to intensify hostilities.
> The majority of the population of Lapland was evacuated to Sweden or Southern Finland, as the retreating Germans, who were pushed toward the Norwegian border, burned everything in their path. The city of Rovaniemi was entirely scorched. All important bridges were demolished, main roads were mined and telephone lines were cut. The last German troops were expelled from the country after seven months of fighting by a diminished Army consisting mainly of fresh recruits.
> By the end of World War II over 80,000 Finnish soldiers were killed or wounded, 3,000 civilians had lost their lives, nearly 100,000 citizens were homeless and over 70,000 children were abroad.

The news about the war being over meets me with every emotion imaginable. Fear of the unknown, uncertain future. Happiness that Finland is at peace and not part of the Soviet Union. Anxiety that I may be sent away again. Relief that Father survived. Sadness that I'll have to leave Hugo and Birgitta. Pride that Finnish sisu prevailed. Jealousy, anger and bitterness that my siblings got to stay and I had to leave.

Over the past few months I've started leaving out letters to nobody in particular, in places where I know Hugo or Birgitta will see them. The letters express my wish to be adopted. Of all the emotions raging inside me, insecurity is the one that I cannot suppress. And ridiculous as it may sound, I want to stay in Sweden with Little Sister.

Since the news of the peace broke, I've spent many afternoons in detention. Concentration has become impossible. More often than not, I find myself staring at my teacher, but not hearing a word she says. I dread the day that I come home from school to find a letter from the Child Evacuation Committee, telling me that it's time to return to Finland. The mere thought makes me ill at ease, and gives me nightmares. So I don't go home. Even after school's out for the summer. The nights are light, and I stay out late with my paints, and make futile attempts at putting color on canvas.

This evening, when I finally return home and open the front door, Cotton immediately jumps in my lap. My chest tightens. I can sense that something is wrong. Hugo and Birgitta meet me in the parlor. Birgitta is wringing her hands. Hugo is pacing. They beckon me to sit.

"We received a letter from Finland today," Hugo starts.

My heart skips a beat. This is the news I don't want to hear, but brace myself for it.

"We've been corresponding with your mother over the past few months, and she's finally conceded."

"But the decision is ultimately yours," Birgitta says. "We would be honored if you'd consider becoming a permanent part of our lives. We have the papers, ready to be signed. All we need is your decision."

Hugo crosses the room, and puts a hand on my shoulder. "Son, we understand if you'd rather go back to Finland, and the decision is yours. As for Birgitta and me, we'd love to make you a legal member of our family." He pauses and looks me deep in the eye.

I'm so happy I have no words. When he said 'back to Finland' all I could picture was a burning sky. But when he said 'our family' I pictured myself with Cotton, Hugo and Birgitta.

"Maybe you should take some time to think about whether you want to become Paul von Schoenfeldt," Hugo continues when I don't answer.

There's a knot in my throat, and I keep swallowing hard. I don't need time to think about a decision that fate has already made for me. At last, one that's actually in my favor.

EPILOGUE

June 1952.

Unlike the rest of the Eastern Front countries
that had been occupied by Germany during the
war, a Soviet occupation of Finland never occurred, and Finland retained sovereignty. Neither did Communists rise to power as they did
in the Eastern Bloc countries. A policy called
the Paasikivi-Kekkonen Line formed the basis
of Finnish foreign policy towards the Soviet
Union, aimed at Finland's survival as an independent, democratic society sharing a border
with Communist Russia.

In 1948, Finland and the Soviet Union signed
the 'YYA-Sopimus' (a Treaty of Friendship, Co-
operation and Mutual Assistance). Under this
treaty, Finland was obligated, siding with the
Soviet Union, to resist armed attacks by 'Germany or its allies' against Finland or against
the Soviet Union through Finland. At the same
time, the agreement recognized Finland's de-
sire to remain outside great power conflicts.

Carl Gustaf Emil Mannerheim died in 1951 at the
age of 83. He was buried in Hietaniemi Cemetery
in Helsinki with military honors. His birthday
is still celebrated as a national holiday in
Finland.

In 1952, Finland made the final payment of her
war debt, US $570 million.

Why am I here? I don't know these people. The anxiety of the reunion makes
me light-headed and nauseous. What if they don't want to see me? After all, the
invitation didn't come directly from them.

It's the eve of my parents' anniversary and I'm nervous. It's closing in on a
decade since we last saw each other. The bitterness and anger have vanished, and
yet I fear that seeing them again will bring it all back. I don't want to be here.
I don't feel like I belong. Johan and Carl sent the invitation. Birgitta and Hugo
made me come. Thankfully they decided to go with me.

During one of my many trips to Denmark, Kjersti gave me a box of my old art that she had saved over the years. Among them I found a drawing of our house in Karelia. She had written 'Paul's first day of school, 1940' on the back. Looking at it now, I can easily spot several dozen mistakes, but I remember how proud I was at the time. I had it framed and wrapped and will present it to my biological parents at their anniversary party.

Never having been to my parents' new house in Toijala, I don't know where we're going. The dirt road that we're on would've been dusty had it not been for the rain this morning. A light, warm summer rain, that cleared the air and gave way to a lovely sunny day. There aren't many days like this in Finland. The season is too short. But the few days that turn nice are savored.

Cotton is curled in my lap, and absentmindedly I stroke his back. He's getting old, but still does silly puppy-like things, like fetch and chase his tail.

Something outside the car strikes me as familiar. This dirt road looks like any number of roads we've been on since we drove off the ferry this morning. But still I have an eerie feeling that I've been here before. When we pull up at my parents' house I understand why. Father built the new house on the land where we hid in a small abandoned barn. Last time I was here. The dirt road is the same one we took with Natalia, with Tor running behind us. A cold chill runs through my spine, and I pull Cotton closer to me. I don't want to be here.

If I thought I was uncomfortable, it's nothing compared to my siblings. Gustaf and Ingrid, now eleven and twelve respectively, don't recognize Mother and Father, and don't speak Finnish. They treat Mother and Father with the polite respectfulness that you do with strangers. They both stick close to me. My Finnish is terrible. By some foresight Birgitta hired a tutor for me as soon as we decided to come, and slowly my native language returns to me. But it's still a struggle. Father, Johan and Carl effortlessly switch back and forth between Finnish and Swedish and interpret for us. There are two new brothers, whom I've never met. They know about me, of course, and act suspiciously toward me. As if I were the prodigal son. Which is so far from the truth, the mere idea is ridiculous. They view me as if I were the lucky one, as do I them.

It's as if we're divided into three categories of children: those who were sent to Sweden and were adopted there, those who went to Denmark and returned, and those who were never sent away. I have nothing in common with the third category. My life is a kaleidoscope - no matter how I turn the tube, I can never again view the original image.

Johan, Carl and I fall into our old routine seamlessly. We've corresponded over the years, and Carl and I attended Mor Mortensen's funeral together earlier this summer. Although we're separated by culture, distance and language, we have an unbreakable and silent bond. We share memories and experiences that need no words to be understood. It's taken me ages to get them to accept that I don't hold them staying and me going against them anymore. Although initially I did.

Father and I take a tour of his house together, during which we carefully avoid talking about anything but the house. He designed and built it himself. It's big enough to house all of us, and when we realize that we'll never live together as a family again, we quickly change the subject. Father is now a well renowned carpenter, and suggests that once I get my degree in architecture, we go into business together. Johan and Carl already work for him. I promise I'll think about it, although I know what my answer will be. I want to design commercial, not residential.

I hadn't realized that this house was a bigger copy of our house in Karelia, until we enter the drawing room. Father's violin hangs on the wall, just like at home and at Farfar's. Regrettably, he tells me, he no longer plays it.

And then my eyes land something that makes my heart swell with ache. On the sunniest wall of the brightest room they have erected what can only be described as a memorial for Little Sister. The ribbon I sent Mother is there, along with framed portraits of Little Sister. The picture we took of all of us together is centered between a vase full of Mother's roses and a lit white candle. We pass it in revered silence. The permanent, inevitable separation of death has marked all of us. There are no words to describe what a treasure my little sister was, how much I hoped to watch her grow into the person she had the capacity of becoming, and how much I miss her. Every day. Out of all of Mother's losses - wealth, children, home, country, parents, and siblings - she will never recover from the death of her daughter.

I've successfully avoided Mother, until she finds me admiring her roses. They are again the envy of the community. Mrs. Mortensen's seeds have taken root, and are blooming beautifully. I make a mental note to tell her next time I see her. Someone has built Mother a trellis around the verandah, and it pains me that I wasn't here to do it myself, like I promised I would.

We stand in awkward silence looking at the roses, when Cotton sprints by. His tongue is hanging out one side of his mouth and his body is streamlined. Seconds later Carl passes us, chasing Cotton. He's now the tallest of us all. Taller even than Father, and built like a soldier.

"You know, Carl has tickets to the Olympics," Mother says proudly.

"I'm surprised he isn't in them," I snap.

"Sarcasm?" Mother scolds me. "Do your Swedish parents approve of that? Not a very attractive trait."

I raise my eyebrows at her, thinking that the long-overdue confrontation might finally have come, and I just hope that I can keep my calm.

"As unattractive as scolding your biological son who you let grow up and be raised by strangers?" I say.

Mother looks at me stunned for a long while. Her eyes are welling up, and she keeps swallowing hard.

"Sit down, Paul," she finally says, and pulls me next to her on the garden swing. "You're bitter, and I can understand that. There's nothing I can ever say to make the hurt go away, but hear me out, please, ...m-my son... I did what I thought was the right thing to do. At the time. Under the circumstances." Her voice breaks, and she takes a deep breath to steady it. "Not a day goes by when I don't think about how I could've done things differently."

My pulse is getting rapid, and I feel my adrenaline rush. This cannot end well. I don't want to hear it.

"I'm not having this conversation with you," I say, and start getting up.

Mother grabs my arm. The look of hurt in her eyes makes my heart ache. Silently I sit down again, trying hard not to look her straight in the eye, for fear of losing control myself. Just the touch of her hand on my arm makes my eyes water. I love her so much, but I'm angry at her. The little boy inside me wants to throw himself around her neck and cry 'Why did you abandon me?!'

Neither of us speaks for a long time. We're both trying hard not to touch or even look at each other, and yet wanting nothing more than to clear this uncomfortable current between us. We're like the opposite poles of a magnet.

"Why me?" I finally ask. "Why not Johan and Carl?"

She doesn't answer immediately, but from the corner of my eye I can see her fidgeting with a handkerchief.

At length, she answers. "You have a talent," she says. "I knew it had to be cultivated, and at the time I couldn't possibly have been able to offer you any of the things you so rightly deserved. I was struggling just to keep us all alive..."

"Producing more babies certainly didn't make that any easier!" I regret the words as soon as they're out of my mouth. I wish the earth would swallow me whole. If possible, I've hurt my mother even more, and the scared little boy inside me is kicking me in the guts.

"Has it really been that bad?" Mother asks. "Hugo and Birgitta are nice, and very fond of you, and seem to treat you well. Had I not thought that, I'd never have agreed to let them adopt you. Have you not been happy with them? Don't they give you everything you could possibly want?"

She's looking at me. I can feel her gaze on me, but I don't dare look at her.

"They're not you," I say quietly. It needs to be said, but I'm not sure Mother needs to hear it. "I have everything... except you..."

Mother breaks through the negative current. She drapes her arms around me and we sit there quietly trying to fight back tears. Then, as if I were seven years old again, she leaves a trace of angel kisses on my forehead.

"You'll always be my treasured son," she says. "No war, no move, no adoption can change that. You're my son and I don't want you to hurt any more."

"Nor I you."

The following morning I drop Birgitta and Hugo off at the ferry to Sweden, and drive north alone. There are two more things on which I must achieve closure, and I must do that by myself. The first one is Tor. I don't much believe in visiting graves, but more than doing just that, I need to speak to Uncle Eino, and hear him tell me about Tor's last days.

Uncle Eino hasn't changed at all. He's a bit shorter than I remember, but that's about it. We sit on his porch watching Cotton romp in the lake, and he tells me all the stories nobody ever bothered to tell me as a child. It's easier to hear this from a person who wasn't directly involved. He tells me about how desperately Mother tried to keep us together. What a hero she is to him. How broken-hearted she was about Tor, and how she blames herself for Little Sister's death. He's not making excuses for her, he's just trying to get me to understand, and not feel angry or bitter.

"One day, my boy," he says, "you'll hold your first-born in your arms, and you'll understand how torn apart your Mother was by the decisions she was forced to make. Only a parent can ever fully comprehend that type of agony. Let's hope you'll never be put in that position."

Early the next morning Cotton and I say farewell to Uncle Eino, and head across Vuokatinvaara. So many emotions from my childhood come rushing back to me. The fear of discovery and being sent away. The fear of disappointing Mother. Hunger. Cold. The inability to understand what was going on. And the powerlessness to do anything about it once I did. Suddenly I feel like the vulnerable child I once was, again.

As if through mental telepathy Cotton finds my favorite spot on the hill. The spot has burned itself on my cornea. This is where Katja and I used to come and pick berries. Even though the sun is still below the horizon, I can see the outlines of Myllyniemi below me, and try to muster up the courage to visit Katja. This is the second thing on which I need closure. Katja and I have been corresponding sporadically over the years, so I know she wasn't sent away to Sweden. For my own peace of mind, I must know that it was better for her to stay home. I feel guilty for not having told her I was coming. Will she even recognize me? How will she react to seeing me again?

"Paul?" a female voice behind me says.

I turn around and face the most incredible eyes. A color I have attempted, and failed, to replicate numerous times.

"Katja," I say, for lack of anything more intelligent.

"Why didn't you tell me you were coming?" she asks.

"I wasn't sure you'd want to see me," I say, and only then do I realize how odd it is to find her here. "What are you doing here?"

"I don't know," she laughs and shrugs. "I woke up this morning and just felt like going for a hike."

Silently she loops her arm around mine, and we sit down on the ground. The sun is rising in the east, coloring the sky every imaginable hue of red, and we sit in silence watching it. Mesmerized. Katja leans her head on my shoulder, and eventually Cotton lies down by our feet. The silence between us is relaxed. Although I have a million questions, they can wait. Right now, I'm perfectly comfortable, and feel like I could stay like this forever.

Katja eventually breaks the silence. "Your scar didn't heal," she says.

"Some scars never do," I say, feeling the dark cloud of anger and bitterness build up again.

"What was it like?" she asks.

"What was what like?"

"Being a War Child. What was it like?"

"Present tense, Katja. What *is* it like? If I live to be a hundred and four, I will always be a War Child."

"Won't you share it with me?" she asks earnestly.

I look into her eyes, and know that I will spend the rest of my life trying to capture their color on canvas. I feel the ever-present urge to belong stronger than ever. And without a shadow of a doubt I know that in her I've found the answer to the nagging feeling of emptiness that has bothered me since that freezing morning so many years ago, when we left Karelia.

I take her hand, kiss it, and say "How are the strawberries this year?"